Messiah of the Slums

I0659623

I am going to light a fire in Paradise, and pour water on Hell, so that veils completely disappear...

Rabia of Basra

A love story
by
Charlotte Pickering

Messiah of the Slums

DEDICATION

This book is dedicated to the victims of gang culture.

FOREWORD

I am an addict of novels, and indeed chaired the Booker Prize committee. I am a Member of Parliament for an inner-city constituency, whose residents are brave and resilient, but who suffer from deprivation and unemployment. Many of my constituents are of Pakistani heritage, so a character in a novel who is known locally as The Paki Witch has my attention (even though it emerges that she derives from Afghanistan). I am a sucker for crime fiction, so a novel with brutal crime at its centre has me turning the pages ardently. So Charlotte Pickering's novel gripped me from the start.

It is a sign of huge talent that, in one book, an author can mingle the rough, the heart-rending, the humane and the mystical and meld them all together into a smoothly-running novel. Pickering has achieved this, notably. I of course shall not spoil narrative surprises by revealing plot-twists, of which there are many. What I can say is that this novel teems with characters - intriguing, lovable, pitiful, repugnant – whose fate I was desperate to discover. I was charmed, gripped, saddened, vitalised, disgusted? and surprised, and never disappointed. It takes great skill to entwine all of these factors in a way that repels and charms, simultaneously.

The setting is a Merseyside council estate, and in the latter part of the last century local authorities erected such estates in a worthy attempt to fulfil housing need, without taking into account the human impact of cramming families and individuals into a gaunt tower-blocks that too often, while providing all the amenities that had not been available to tenants who previously had festered in slums, nevertheless could be grim and unwelcoming – even when the lifts were working. When I became an MP, several such blocks had been erected in my constituency. At first, slum-dwellers almost fought to become tenants: until they got there, when many fought to get out. They were known locally as forts, and several subsequently were demolished, at huge human cost and huge financial cost to the council tax-payer.

So Charlotte Pickering has provided thrills, heart-warming plot developments and grim accounts of gangland and, thereby, social commentary that tells us more about what life in Britain has been like for too many while those in charge pass by on the other side. A novel with all these achievements that also entertains is a rare achievement; but then, Charlotte Pickering is a rare writer. Don't stay up too late in your eagerness to find out what comes next.

*-**Gerald Kaufman**, Member of Parliament and former chair of the Booker Prize Committee.*

PROLOGUE

Nobody knew at the time how the Shriveton Community Centre bonfire started that Halloween night. Emergency services were too late at the scene, and the victim was ashes when their foam and fuss finally ended the flames. The story of the young Asian woman burned at the stake in a Liverpool estate resounded in the news, stopping people in their tracks, like a call from a minaret. A macabre stench of petrol and grease and smoke floated above the chaos of the gathering crowds as reporters generated copy:

GIRL DEAD IN HALLOWEEN FIRE
Exclusive by Ethan Greenberg

Police and fire services have sealed off the entire Shriveton Shopping Parade area as a scene of crime.
The victim of tonight's fatal fire has been named as Jessenia Rabia al-Rahoud, from the the Shriveton area of Liverpool.
Ms al-Rahoud lived in the Skylark Tower block close to where she die d. Very little is known yet about the victim. Originally from Afghanistan, she was flown to the UK for surgery following a grievous assault
by a gang of Taliban militia two years ago. An unidentified British soldier had heroically interrupted them on the Hindu Kush mountainside, and they fled.
Police are investigating the possibility of an honour killing.

In the days following the fire, community leaders, desperate to preserve harmonious relations between ethnic groups in the city, were quick to point out that Ms al-Rahoud had lived alone, in the predominantly white Shriveton estate, and had had no contact or dispute with the wider Muslim community in Liverpool. Notwithstanding her black *hijab* and *abaya*, she did not appear to be a practising Muslim, although a pocket-sized Koran in her own language was found in her flat. No living relatives could be traced in either Afghanistan or the UK.

As the days went by, more information about the Asian woman emerged. For instance, she had always been known by locals as the Paki Witch or, by those very close to her, as Jessie Rout. Hearsay had it that, among other miracles, she had made a blind man see, healed a prostitute's third degree burns and destroyed the Incubo, the untouchable drug baron who had run Shriveton for years. But nobody would come forward to be interviewed about these events, despite huge incentives offered by the press.

Civil and religious authorities, anxious to avoid upsetting each other, settled on a celebration of life ceremony for Jessie Rout at the Shriveton Community Centre. Ascetic and obscure, her little life appeared to have been spent doing good works. The Liverpool Mosque representative who spoke at the service likened her to Rabia, her Muslim saint namesake. The Roman Catholic Bishop of Liverpool called her a modern day Theresa of Lisieux. The Leader of the City Council praised her indefatigable community spirit.

It wasn't long before the Shriveton bonfire site became a shrine. Some of Jessie Rout's most devoted followers – including Bob Reilly, whose vision she had miraculously restored, and the boy who had loved her, Jamal Bannigan – constructed a small grotto out of scrap and stones and cement. It had the appearance of a life-sized nativity set.

Pictures of the victim, cut from the newspapers and sealed in poly-pockets, were affixed to all walls of the little cave. An altar stood against the back wall. On it was a Perspex box displaying her hijab a compass-embedded prayer mat, her Dari Koran and small wooden *rihal*[1], and her passport picture in which her face still bore

---

1

Prayer stool

the wounds inflicted in Afghanistan. Statues of the Sacred Heart and Virgin Mary stood like freeze framed actors on either side of the display box. At their feet were strewn miracle-medals, rosary beads, images of the crescent moon and star, crucifixes, Muslim prayer beads, a laughing Buddha miniature; and tea lights, which never seemed to go out.

People of all religions and none came to the shrine. They left photos and poems and prayers concerning sick or dead or missing loved ones. Eventually, the council turned it into a proper building. And in the years that followed, many more miracles were ascribed to Jessie Rout, the Paki Witch, nineteen-year-old Messiah of the Slums.

CHAPTER ONE

July 26th 201-

Shriveton Park Woods, Shriveton Estate, near Liverpool

Chloe had just finished with a rough and disgusting client in the bushes behind the kids' playground. Usually it was bedsits and backs of cars. But being straight out of the nick, he didn't have a car or a room. He'd needed a hand job, and had offered her fifty if she could oblige, there and then. Of course she'd said yes.

But he'd left her, half-dressed and crouching facedown among the dry, orange carpet of fallen leylandii foliage, like a crippled animal in the forest. She was dizzy from a knock to the head as he'd slammed her to the ground. He'd gone without paying, too.

She couldn't summon the will to get up and dressed. A black hole of desolation – impenetrable and consuming – was claiming all that was precious and pure in her life. It corrupted or threw off course anything even remotely within orbit of her. Friends and family of the drug addict must flee or die if they are themselves to survive. Chloe knew that: she was all at once consuming and consumed.

She wasn't making enough money from the men to support the habit, which cost £100 a day just to achieve anything resembling equilibrium.

Social services were hounding her about the baby – it wouldn't be long before they took him from her. She'd left Joel by himself in his cot to meet with this jailbird, and had already been away for an hour, and now her arm and insides were hurting so much she couldn't get up from the floor. *And* she needed to get up to the Zone on the way back.

In the shadows to her right, now, she thought she saw a female figure standing in the clearing, and wondered if it was the result of concussion, for there had been no sound of footsteps on the dry litter of leaves all around. Propping herself up on an elbow, Chloe twisted round, painfully. Then she saw.

It was almost ten o'clock, a warm July dusk. The bushes and surrounding tree-crowns cast further shadows, but the black-swathed Paki Witch had a weird luminosity to her, such that her form seemed to cast light, not shadow. She was both diamond and soot – elemental, brilliant, soft and deep. The kindly, intelligent expression of her hijab-framed face had a hypnotic quality. Heavy-lidded, superbly defined by black brows and lashes, her dark eyes made good all that was reflected in them. The Asian woman's immaculate beauty transcended all that was temporal and physical; and inspired in her humble observer profound awe.

To Chloe, at that moment, the Paki Witch lit up the whole world.

Chloe had seen her around the estate before this encounter. Many people knew the Paki Witch by sight, the only Muslim in the whole of Shriveton, who supposedly lived in the Skylark tower block. Chloe didn't even know the Paki Witch's proper name (she couldn't have been christened the Paki Witch, after all). Seeing her up close in the Shriveton Park bushes was rather like seeing a celebrity in person – you'd always known about them, but never imagined or particularly desired that they manifested in the three dimensions of your own reality.

"This isn't you," said the Paki Witch.

Her voice sounded to Chloe as true and clear as an angel's would. The Paki Witch smiled as she picked up the bits of clothing lying around. Chloe sat up, embarrassed, trying to cover her partial nakedness with leaves.

While Chloe dressed, the Paki Witch scooped up some of the foliage and earth from the ground, and ran it through her fingers; her downcast eyes stayed on its dry, particulate mass showering dustily back to earth.

"I can't get off the drugs," announced Chloe, fully dressed again and watching the sifting motion of the Paki Witch's long, pink padded hands in the dirt.

The Paki Witch smiled at her, and stood up, and said, "A new shoot will grow for you."

As she moved, the green canopy of surrounding shrubs and trees seemed to lose dusk's gloom. It was almost dark, and yet Chloe was sure she could see beads of water in the creamy petal folds and matt leaves of a nettle plant at her feet. Beside her, she noticed the slow lemon blush of an unfolding evening primrose.

"Take my hand," said the Paki Witch.

When Chloe took her hand, all the soreness and bleeding went.

As if in a dream, Chloe went home to the baby. She didn't score on the way, but instead comforted, fed and changed her infant son, without thinking of herself at all; and felt such love for his helpless little person.

August 16th 201-

Incubo Land

The Shriveton estate, on the outskirts of Liverpool, was where kingpin Incubo plied a sizeable portion of his narcotics trade. Most of the drug trading occurred on the Shopping Parade, which was linked by a pedestrian flyover to two tower rises, Skylark and Tallis, as well as the lower lying remainder of the estate.

Shriveton was essentially a housing association and council-owned conurbation, plus schools and a church, all spanning three square miles. Densely populated, homogenously poor and remote from the city centre, it had long provided the most propitious conditions for a brisk drugs business serving the city and environs. People there like Chloe Tudor guaranteed good daily business, and had helped the Incubo amass a considerable fortune.

It was a sunny August afternoon, one month after Chloe Tudor's encounter with the Paki Witch in Shriveton Park woodland. As on all days – even Christmas Day – a cell of twelve were working one of three, eight-hour daily shifts, vending drugs.

Their patch was known as the Zone and was located at the upper-lying Shopping Parade, with its pedestrianised surroundings which law enforcement vehicles could not instantly penetrate. The Zone employed a minimum of eight guards, plus a supplementary team of young teens on bikes, for the external boundary.

Foot soldier wages were low, but their status high. Working for the Incubo was the low-achieving Shriveton boy's sole chance of gaining glory. Each Shriveton Zone worker was a foundation stone in a gigantic pyramid of manpower and money, at the apex of which sat the Incubo himself. He ruled a global narcotics empire spanning all continents except Antarctica, and was a name without a face. Through his goodness, his Zones could offer narcotics to tens of thousands of people every day of the year.

Shriveton Zone transactions took place by the ruck of bins behind the Parade, which could only be accessed from the alleyway between the disused library and the Community Centre. This was staffed today by Sammy and Billy, who admitted the punters one by one.

One of the perks of Sammy's and Billy's role was frisking the young girls, especially the fresh addicts whose femininity had not yet been ravaged by addiction. Of course, time-wasting gropes cost money (fewer throughputs to the trading heart of the cell), and were discouraged.

If clean, the customer would be directed to yet another two soldiers in the shop area. One would take the money. The other would pass over a vial. It was extra for a sharp.

On this particular August afternoon, the Zone shop was manned by Tez and Zollo.

"Surprised to see you 'ere at the front line, Zoll," said Tez, with irony. Zollo spent very little time in the Zone. His job was simply to relay information between the most senior man on the ground, Zone Chief Tez, and higher up the command chain. "Why you 'ere?"

"Inky likes to do his spot checks," growled Zollo, demonstrating his importance by fiddling with the stock.

The Incubo's industry was founded on the very simple premise that people do drugs because drugs are *good*. The drug addict is possessed, a thrall, claimed absolutely by the hit that surpasses even the best of orgasms. Any subsequent effort of body, mind or spirit to break from thraldom is brutally suppressed by withdrawal symptoms. The only way out then is the exorcism of rehab. How much easier to come back *just one more time* to the Zone.

"The beak's good," sniffed Zollo, slapping his nostrils free of the powder which, as a senior officer in the Incubo army, he could help himself to. A gossamer of white dust matted the greasy sheen of his spectacle lenses.

"Best in the land," said Tez, picking up the spent vial from the floor by Zollo's dirty workman's boot.

Zone gear was sold in vials bearing Union Jack colours – blue for heroin, red for crack and white for cocaine, each branded with the Incubo's trademark *I*. The transaction completed, addicts would scuttle off downwards into the housing estate. Some couldn't wait, and would devour their transubstantiating narcotic sacraments under the flyover, in an area known locally as the Wasteland.

Slumped against one of the concrete flyover posts, their unseeing eyes fixed on the dragon underbelly of the walkway above, and buttocks planted on the banks of grey-brown puddles of floating litter and hypodermics, they might be in paradise for as long as half an hour.

"Respect, Tez and Zoll. One Bobby, cheers," said first customer of the shift, Guantanamo, who carefully decanted two fistfuls of shrapnel on to the table.

Guantanamo lived in a makeshift shack of milk-crates, bin liners, old fencing and cardboard on the Wasteland beneath the walkway. He was named after his unchanging orange and filthy shell-suit.

Tez counted the cash, his eyes dipping to the repulsive pus-filled injection craters on Guantanamo's moon-crust forearms. Nobody anywhere could understand why Guantanamo hadn't died ages ago.

"Twenny exactly," nodded Tez.

Zollo slid a blue vial over the table, and asked, "Sharp?"

"No." Guantanamo never bought a sharp – he reused old ones, hence the appalling state of his arms.

Clutching his vial to his heart, Guantanamo scuttled away like an animated lobster: down the alleyway, past Sammy and Billy; out through the unnoticing, pram-wheeling mums, children and pensioners on the sunny Shopping Parade terrace outside; and on to his Wasteland home.

A Sharp Exit

In the dell of the Shriveton estate, next to the church of the same name, and visible from the vantage point of the Zone, was St Theresa's secondary school. Although most of its alumni went on to legitimate occupations, this institution also provided a substantial number of the Shriveton Zone's client-base and staff.

Today was exam results day. Kids, glad to be with everyone again, sat on benches and walls in the school grounds, poring and pointing and pouting over results sheets. Teachers – all in jeans and somehow, now the exam rite of passage was through, more human – and Father O'Connor, the chair of governors, fluttered about offering advice. Apparently one boy, Jamal Bannigan, had passed every single one of his subjects.

Chloe Tudor had come up to school with the pram. She'd

relapsed just days after her encounter with the Paki Witch in Shriveton Park. This meant that she was lost forever, and she knew it. Even the Paki Witch could not save her.

Calling in for her exam results on the way to the Zone would delay gratification, and make the hit better when she got it. Unfortunately this was the only positive of her detour. Her visit to school confirmed that she'd failed everything. This was entirely unsurprising; Chloe had stopped attending school for much of her pregnancy, and only sporadically after the birth of Joel, now almost six months old.

She crumpled up her results slip and buried it in her pocket next to her kitten-shaped crack pipe.

"Chloe, come and sit with us," called Ellen from the heart of a gaggle of kindly girls sitting together on one of the playground benches. Ellen used to be Chloe's best friend.

Overhead in the distance, child foot soldiers on bikes arrived at the Shopping Parade for the beginning of the next shift.

"We've missed you!" persevered Ellen.

Chloe was waiting for the 2pm Zone shift. They were a nicer crew. She was hoping Billy Stokes wouldn't be on. He had horrible long nails and always searched inside her pants.

She was going to wean herself off it... Get to rehab in another town... After this hit, though.

Chloe mumbled an embarrassed greeting in reply, as her fingers squeezed the crack pipe in her pocket. Crack was so amazing. But it didn't last – only a few minutes. And then the terrible depression afterwards. There were other side effects, but it was the blackest *feelings*, like acid on the soul, that destroyed her absolutely.

From the beginning, drugs had wildly distorted her mind. It had been only a matter of weeks since starting on crack that she'd become hopelessly dependent. Sometimes she would watch, an impotent spectator, as her own arm flesh stretched over the sharp-angled limbs of arachnids and insects – like filo pastry over a toast rack. She'd heard that these hallucinations were a psychotic side-effect of crack withdrawal. But they felt and looked so real. *Were* insects able to live under your skin?

Luckily, Ellen's step-dad Frankie had always lusted after Chloe. He had his own taxi, and terrible bad breath. He'd paid her fifty the first time – so eager. After that it went down to twenty five, but he'd wanted it every day. Then he'd got anxious about the whole thing and broke it off. But by then she'd got some other men – friends and friends-of-friends of his. They would pay as much as fifty for a still-fresh sixteen year old.

She needed fifty quid to buy an adequate hit of crack. But she needed a hit twice a day – more, ideally. Worrying about getting the money for the gear was exhausting.

It wasn't long before she'd started on heroin because the crack had turned bandit on her. Also, she couldn't keep up with crack financially. Heroin was a better option – longer lasting, longer between hits, less of a depressant. And cheaper: fewer men per hit. It was an easy equation. The heroin made her weary and acutely constipated, and the last thing she wanted was to have sex, but there was no other way.

Somewhere in the far recess of her personality was a horror of *being* an injecting junkie. Chloe Tudor, bag head. Nobody starts off wanting that – they start off with the kitten-shaped crack pipe, don't they?

Don't they?

Luckily, Zone pimp Spider had told her recently that he could help her operate more safely. He'd have to take a cut, but she'd still clear thirty per man. Also, he got his girls cheaper, purer gear. She'd probably only have to work three nights and she'd be in clover, especially if her mum minded Joel. Spider owned several classy massage parlours in the city centre. Better clients for her. Spider screened them. Professionals. Treated a girl better. She'd mention it when she next bumped into him.

Chloe Tudor, prostitute. Nobody starts off wanting that – they start off accidentally sleeping with the kingpin when they're fourteen years old, don't they?

Don't they?

The kingpin had called her his American Beauty, because of her age and blonde big-hair, and heavily manicured teen look. He'd taken her on a holiday to Amsterdam in the best hotel, where you have dressing gowns in the bathroom and people to carry your luggage. She had tried brand new things like caviar and oysters, and that sensory sugar, cocaine, and her hatred of him had built with every passing moment. The pathetic record producer front he had erected for her was especially despicable: it was obvious he was a gangster.

Once crack had taken a real hold of her, their association had ended, with him impressing in no uncertain terms that their affair must remain a secret. The penalties for porosity in gangland were unthinkable – he'd shown her a few photos of what his employee Tez had done to snitches.

"Haven't seen you for ages, Chloe," Ellen said, with a nervous, schoolgirl smile.

Few of the St Theresa's girls could conceal completely their shock on beholding Chloe, who had disappeared from their milieu many months ago. Once a curvaceous and immaculately groomed beauty with her heart set on going into hairdressing, she was now unkempt of head and wasted of limb. A multiplicity of tattoos gave her flesh the appearance of a snake-pit floor.

"How's little Joel?" hazarded Ellen. A cooing chorus of enquiry and compliments rose as the girls crowded round the pram to see Chloe's small, sleepy baby with curds of sick in his cheek and neck folds, and dirty bib. He was smelly and needed changing, but quiet in the soft, pastel haven under the pram hood.

"'E's great," said Chloe. She'd espied a red leather purse peeping out of Ellen's tote bag on the empty bench beside them. Ellen had a job in Poundland and always had money. A distraction was needed.

With a brisk, "You can 'old him if you like!" Chloe snatched the infant from his pram and thrust him into Ellen's inexperienced arms.

"Oooh, 'ang on, Chlo, I don't think I've quite got him!"

Ellen and her friends grappled and cooed for some moments, before Chloe took him back.

"Gotta, take 'im for 'is check up," she lied, tucking a now-squealing Joel back into his padded grotto.

Her eyes kept flicking up to the Zone in the distance. On the Shopping Parade terrace above she could see that the change of shift had been accomplished. Long-nailed Stokes would have gone. A sharp exit was required so she could score and ensure that the insects didn't start scampering beneath the filo pastry again.

"We're always your friends, Chloe," Ellen called after her.

On her way up to the Shopping Parade, on the walkway over the Wasteland, Chloe crossed paths with the Paki Witch, who smiled at her. For a tiny moment, Chloe felt a succouring surge of peace, like a waft of lavender and strawberries from a walled English garden. Joel stopped crying. An awful awareness of the divine bore down, weighing every movement, as if each step towards the Zone was defying heaven's gravity of goodness.

But the enormity of her own failure at relapsing meant that Chloe couldn't face the Paki Witch. It was easier, although very difficult, for Chloe to look away while hurrying by.

Stepping on to the flagged terrace of the Parade, Chloe looked back, forlornly, expecting to see the retreating willowy black figure of her potential saviour. But the Paki Witch was not in sight. That was strange: the Paki Witch could only be out of sight if she'd run at full speed in the direction of Skylark flats. Even Chloe, who'd just achieved an unclassified in Religious Studies, knew that Muslim women never run – they weren't even allowed to do PE.

Chloe believed in the Paki Witch. In fact, seeing her just now made her want to sob. If only she'd thought to touch her robe as they passed just now, so that some of her power would have transmitted, like it had when they'd first met a few weeks previously in Shriveton Park, after that horrible experience with the jailbird. Later the same week she'd smoked weed with Troy. For some reason, the old cravings returned and Chloe had started up on the heroin just a couple of days later.

Although the relapse had been absolute, not one hour had gone by without Chloe thinking about what the Paki Witch had said that time in Shriveton Park. *A new shoot will grow for you.* She hadn't added a conditional: *if you want it/if you're lucky/if you get religion or rehab.* All she'd said was *a new shoot will grow for you.*

Life since that encounter in the Shriveton Park woodland had been very much a defiance of this prophecy, however.

If *only* she had touched the Paki Witch's robe just now.

Chloe crossed the paved terrace to the Shopping Parade barrier, which overlooked the Wasteland and wider estate. Down below she could just make out Ellen and friends in the schoolyard in the shadow of the Tallis and Skylark blocks. How far away they were, those school girls, with their idle chat about boys and clothes and college courses.

Ellen's red purse was in the tray of the pram, under Joel's changing bag. Chloe crouched down to investigate its contents. A twenty pound note and some shrapnel: enough for weed to bring her down later. The black hole of self back. It deflected the light beam of remorse for nicking her best friend's hard earned money; it devoured her scrap of faith that the Paki Witch would redeem her.

She was going to score one more time.

Troy Bannigan, one of the outer foot soldiers, reluctantly agreed to look after Joel while she went in.

"Just leave it alone now, girl," he said. He tapped his temple: "It's gettin' to yer."

Beautiful Troy – with his mad blast of hair sprouting from a red

Hendrix bandana, like a ghetto crown – was one of the few kind ones. There was very little kindness or friendship in the bowels of hell. But Troy had always shown her compassion. In another life, a parallel universe, she and Troy might have dated – they were in the same league of outstanding attractiveness. She'd talked to him about her life on several occasions. Troy knew her better than anyone else. His sadness at her decline was genuine.

It was impossible to explain why some fell faster and further than others. She knew kids who'd given crack one or two goes, and who sporadically partied on coke. They led almost-ordinary lives which didn't involve daily trips to the Incubo's Zone. Why drugs had taken such a hold of her was one of life's mysteries. She must be bad inside. This was her punishment.

Troy put his arm around her shoulders. "Get into rehab, Chlo," he said. "You'd get free rehab, cos of the baby."

"Am goin' soon," she mumbled. "But I gotta come down first."

"Billy's workin' overtime," he mumbled. "Don't that make you think about goin' in?"

But Chloe went forward, amongst the oblivious other shoppers. She was sweating and her teeth were chattering slightly. Her teeth were looking poor these days. She'd been the first among her friends to try a home-tooth-whitening kit a couple of years ago. Now she rarely even brushed them – or her hair for that matter. She was nodded through by the next tier of guards, and then admitted into the dark alley between the Community Centre and empty library.

Billy Stokes, a large, uncouth twenty-something, with tattoos and a shaven head, grinned when he saw her, and muttered something to co-worker, Sammy. It was obvious that Billy wanted to do the frisking. Even though he saw Chloe as a shabby little tart these days, his sharp ended fingers were still itching to feel her up for free. Sammy discreetly turned away and started rolling a cigarette.

The alleyway was very secure – only a metre wide, bordered by two tall buildings. Inner foot soldiers were on one end. The seller and cashier (Tez and Zollo, today) were at the other, out of sight in front of the bins, with a patrol of armed motorcyclists and foot soldiers. Beyond these, by the string of unused garages to the rear of the Parade, was a barricade of car auction rejects which stayed put week in, week out.

It was inconceivable that anybody could enter the alleyway without being seen and causing a considerable fuss. Yet now, just as Billy had pushed his shambling, six-stone, sixteen-year-old punter against the wall, and was groping up her short skirt, a faceless spectre appeared from nowhere. The rude red of the bins at the end of the alley cut a black template of the interloper's small, female figure, which was advancing in the gloom.

"It's *her*!" squealed Sammy, dropping his partially constructed cigarette. "The Paki fuckin' Witch!"

Although few would admit it, the sight of the Paki Witch *anywhere* unnerved the average foot soldier, let alone her sudden manifestation in this tightly guarded, narrow alleyway.

"How the fuck she get 'ere, Sammy, lad?" yelped Billy, unnerved, but less so than his colleague, who was spluttering fearfully.

"I don't fuckin' know!" Sammy fumbled frantically for his handgun, shouting to the intruder: "'Ave you just come up from the back there, by the bins, love?"

Questions danced like sub-machine gun rounds in their minds. They couldn't see her face. Was it the Paki Witch or someone disguised, from a rival gang? Was she armed? Should they call to the shop floor boys at the bins, or might that provoke her? Was she an assassin? Should they run out, to the inner foot soldiers at the front of the Community Centre? But that would leave Zollo and Tez exposed with all the cash and gear.

Before Billy could reach his gun, the woman in black had taken Chloe's arm and moved her swiftly out through the alleyway; within moments they were in the midst of pensioners and mums with prams and special constables on the Shopping Parade terrace.

It had taken the unarmed Paki Witch less than two minutes to spring Chloe Tudor forever from Hell.

Meanwhile, panic erupted in the alleyway, into which Tez and Zollo had run. Nobody could possibly get into the alleyway without passing the other cell members. Zollo and Tez were spooked to the core – Zollo was especially shaky as he protested, adamant, that they hadn't let her in the back way.

Yet, she *must* have come into the alley from the trading zone – there was no other route which could have brought her there.

Paranoia set into the cell almost immediately. There were huge sums of money at stake. The Shriveton Zone was netting around a million a month. People from all over the city and surrounding counties came there to score. An understanding with the local police Superintendent Meyers ensured that the police stayed out of Zone affairs.

Mistakes of this kind could not be made. One of them must have let the Paki Witch – or whoever was impersonating her – in.

11

It was noted privately that Troy was always friendly with Chloe.

All efforts to find the Paki Witch, Chloe and the baby yielded nothing. The word *rescue* seeped into the rumour machine. Tez closed the whole Zone for almost forty-eight hours afterwards, as a precaution. Much revenue was lost, and confidence badly shaken. End users were forced to trek to Manchester to score. Worse still, the following week in Southampton, the Serious Organised Crime Agency (SOCA) made a huge heroin haul, believed to be an Incubo consignment which had been abandoned as a result of panic along the supply chain.

The Incubo relayed his fury to the Shriveton cell. Huge losses had been sustained.

Someone must pay.

CHAPTER TWO

1st October 201-

Seaforth Docks, Liverpool

With great satisfaction, Zollo breathed in the oil and salt of the dockland air. To his right, the lights of the Irish Sea traffic glistened beneath a cookie-dough moon drizzled with inky clouds. Ahead, hulking and dockside, was his long awaited container ship, a giant floating cuckoo's nest carrying Incubo seed.

Tonight's consignment of earthenware crockery, in which were embedded five kilograms of cocaine, would plug a nasty hole. It represented the only fresh stock since the disappointment of Southampton weeks ago, when fear following the Paki Witch's supposed infiltration of the Zone had gone viral.

Seaforth was always watertight, provided privileges weren't abused. Enough money had changed hands to ensure that security would not be making an appearance for the next hour. Zone Chief Tez and foot soldier Troy were already in the warehouse into which the earthenware crockery crates had been disbursed. Their whispers, cigarette smoke and sounds were flooding the vast vault of space around them as they unloaded one of the crates.

"You got?" called Zollo, making his footsteps suddenly thunderous in the emptiness. He'd crept in silently and unannounced, watching as Troy, unobserved by Tez, slipped one of the white lozenges of booty up his sleeve, which now he plunged into his jacket pocket.

"Yeah, we got," said Tez, not flinching from his industrious repacking of the straw and bubble wrapped pottery of the carton.

Tez was unperturbed by Zollo's entrance. In contrast, his companion, Troy, was inordinately nervous, and now pulled his shaking hand back out of his pocket. With frenzied intensity, he joined Tez in the repacking of the cargo.

"Four kees," said Tez. "That what you expectin'?"

Zollo gave a wry smile, as his eyes flicked once more on to Troy's jacket pocket.

"That'll do," he replied.

Shriveton's Poor

At the core of the Incubo's gangland philosophy was the belief that the poor will always be with us. The 21st century Shriveton poor – the Incubo's primary source of income – were for the main part descended from nineteenth century Irish immigrants. Their Potato Famine refugee forbears had been crammed into slums near the Liverpool docks where, a century and a half later, the Incubo's consignments of heroin and cocaine would enter the UK.

The end of the inner city slums came after World War Two, when bombs had corroded the Liverpool landscape like acid on tooth enamel. The poor were decanted from the city centre tenements into new council estates, like Shriveton, on the remote outskirts of the city. It was the dawn of a new era. No more arguing with neighbours over the shared kitchen or smelly toilet at the end of the corridor. Each family had its own toilet and kitchen.

Moreover, the tendency to aggregate along religious lines – which the fellowship of shared wartime anguish had already begun to dissolve – finally subsided. Protestant and Catholic families lived in the same street, attending different schools, but playing with, dating and even marrying each other. The new, post-war era meant that denominational differences became the province of historical interest only.

Life improved for most of this displaced population. The exceptions were the so-called half-caste kids, like Lilly Bannigan, whose mothers had been successfully prevailed upon by battle-bound American airmen passing through, via the Burtonwood air base. The half-caste kids were regarded by some, even themselves, as lesser. Despite the countering kindliness of enlightened people in their midst, these black/white kids felt they were on the outside.

Although Lilly Bannigan's grandsons, Troy and Jamal, were born after Martin Luther King, Malcolm X and Nelson Mandela had radically altered western racial perceptions, they enjoyed even smaller prospects than their recent ancestors, not least because their mother had killed herself while on remand for heroin possession. Aged seven and nine, the boys went to live with their grandmother in her Tallis Tower high rise Shriveton home. It was a familiar family history in Shriveton: the parent generation taken out by drugs.

The Incubo's narcotics had turned Shriveton, which had seemed so promising at the beginning, into a slum. Unlike their Irish ancestors, these slum dwellers were literate and had running water. But a profound inequality of power kept those at the bottom – like Chloe Tudor, and the Bannigan family – in an inescapable state of wretchedness.

More than three decades on from the Toxteth riots of 1981, and one from the 9/11 bombings of the World Trade Centre in New York, religion and race issues were not the problem in Shriveton.

The problem in Shriveton was the Incubo.

Creating and then preying upon the poor in spirit had amassed him an incredible fortune, not just in Shriveton, but worldwide. His empire ranged from South American coca growers, the cannabis plains of Northern Pakistan, and the opium fields of Afghanistan; to distribution, via ports, processing plants and export front companies, in the Americas, North Africa and Europe; and, finally, on to foot soldier dealers on UK street corners.

Locally, the Incubo's organisation was not to be confused with teen gangs such as the Shriveton Sons, known simply as *the Sons*, who deployed their tiny armoury of weapons and brain cells defending a plethora of imaginary local boundaries. In recent years, the Sons earned their right to continued existence by serving the Incubo whenever required. Little acts of violence (threatening or maiming defaulters), setting up distractions for the police to cover a shipment, and even murder, were the sorts of duties required of them.

A further insurance against interruption of trade was taken out by the Incubo with the police. Bribery and blackmail of key officers, the provision of crucial information on rivals' criminal activities, and huge donations to police interests, maintained the Shriveton status quo.

The rescue of Chloe Tudor changed everything. It infected the Shriveton poor with the idea that the Paki Witch could save them from the Incubo. Some of them came to love the Paki Witch more than any one or thing in this world.

Jamal Bannigan was one.

Crime and Punishment in Incubo Land

Sixteen-year-old Jamal Bannigan's life changed beyond recognition when his brother, Troy, was killed in an alleged dispute about territory with the Sons. Troy Bannigan, friend of Zone escapee Chloe Tudor, worked as a foot soldier at the base of the Incubo's huge corporate pyramid. Like all foot soldiers, Troy risked his life and liberty for a pittance selling dope – just for the chance to be a contender.

While still at school himself, Troy had minded a smoking gun for Zone chief Tez. The only living soul Troy had told about the gun was his brother, and even Jamal hadn't known where it was hidden in their Tallis Tower flat. When all the nasty business had died down, Troy returned the gun to its rightful owner, who shortly afterwards had rewarded him with a job at the Zone.

Older than his only sibling, Jamal, by two years, Troy could be loud and rash. Shifts as a lookout at the Zone, and selling ten quid wraps and bits of E on the Shriveton street corners had turned Troy into a kingpin, in his own imagination. Shortly before he was shot dead in Shriveton Park, Troy had returned home, late from some sort of special task at Seaforth Docks with Tez, and had confided in Jamal:

"Am on the inside fuckin' track, know what I mean, Jammy? I'm gonna strike out on my own. Settin' meself up, kid. Got some fuckin' mad leads, kid."

Jamal felt a horrible knot in his stomach, like he used to feel whenever he and Troy were taken into care. He advanced the obvious objections. Branching out on one's own in the Inky's heartland was insane. And anyway, where would Troy get the capital to set himself up?

"Seaforth consignment tonight sorted all that. Just gotta sort cutting agents, now. Lidocaine, probably, cos I gotta source. Mad, innit?" was the elliptical response.

After a pause, he added a dark rider: "Anything happens to me, Jam, make sure you get me phone."

Again, Jamal mumbled in despair about the gangland imperative of *not* going against the Incubo. But, of course, Troy knew best and ignored him.

"You're looking at a kingpin, 'ere," he boasted. "Tez looks at me. I see him. Always looking at me, he is. He singles me out, gives me little bits o' jobs. But he's not promoted me, kid. I realised he thinks I'm a threat to him. That's why he pleading with me to get out of it."

"What, Tez told you to leave being a foot soldier?"

"Yeah. Been on at me loads this past week. He knows I got what it takes to challenge him. That's what's behind it all. Though obviously he don't say nothing. Mad, innit? But I've 'ad enough of being at the fuckin' bottom."

In that same week, the Shriveton rumour machine erupted with the news that Troy had slept with Leanne, the alpha girlfriend of Gaz Skelton, head of the Sons. It was a drunken conquest which fired a gun into enemy territory. Jamal had been so astonished by his brother's stupidity in sleeping with the girl that he couldn't think of anything to say. Consequently it was not a topic they ever discussed.

6th October 201-

Shriveton Park

Three nights after the supposed tryst with Leanne, the Bannigan brothers went to nearby Shriveton Park. Their Nan was on a drinking binge, and consequently their home was trashed and stank of vomit and urine. Troy had bought them each chips for tea, which they ate sitting on the Shriveton Park swings. It was a cold and clear evening, almost two months after the disappearance of Chloe Tudor. Some innocuous kids were huddled around a little bonfire nearby, smoking and drinking cider.

"The Paki Witch done Chloe a big favour," reflected Troy as he rolled a single-skin, after-dinner spliff. Conversation had turned to the subject of the Paki Witch whose status, for steadily increasing numbers of local people, had changed from oddball to saviour since Chloe's rescue. "Chloe's better off out of it, innit, Jammy?"

"D'you think the Paki Witch is real?" ventured Jamal. "I've never seen 'er."

Troy gave a manly snigger.

"It's all just talk," he said. "People like Chloe believe in 'er. I mean, the fuckin' woman exists. I seen 'er meself lead Chloe out of the alleyway, that day at the Zone, innit. She was linking Chloe's arm, like. Chloe was kind of in a daze, though I suppose that coulda been the gear, like."

"What she look like, the Paki Witch?"

"It's 'ard to say. She looks small from far away. But up close, she seemed massive to me, proper massive."

"So you seen her close up?"

"Yeah, cos I minded the pram while Chloe went into the Zone, innit. The Paki Witch and Chloe come over to get Joel off me on their way out."

"So – well, anything else about how she looks?"

"Well, not much. She's a Paki, obviously. The eyes are big, fuckin' really dark. Like someone on acid, innit. You don't see nothin' else when you come up close to her – only her eyes. It's like she sees everything, but she's somewhere else all the time. When you look at her eyes, you kind of want to go to wherever she really is. Mad."

After some moments' thought, Troy added, "I suppose nobody *doesn't* believe in the Paki Witch, if you know what I mean."

"No. What do you mean?"

"Well, now and then, like, some kids skit her, call her suicide bomber, and stuff like that. But nobody would never take her out, know what I mean?"

"The Paki Witch is untouchable, then?"

"Yeah, she's untouchable."

"What, even Inky couldn't take her out?" asked Jamal, wide-eyed with amazement.

"Don't think so, man. Don't think no one round here would touch her, know what I mean? Inky couldn't contract out the hit. He'd have to come and do it his fuckin' self."

"So the Paki Witch is more powerful than the Incubo."

Troy shrugged, "In a funny way, maybe."

Plumes of exhaled smoke pushed from Troy's perfect lips into the icy night, as he turned the discussion back to his chief fantasy: that his new enterprise meant that he was *on the inside track*, and that greatness would soon ensue. They sat, shivering on the swings, as Troy word-painted their fabulous future. It was only a matter of time before he made enough to get them all out of Shriveton forever. His cocaine-cutting factory would spring them, as he had the business skills to make it happen.

"The thing is, Jammy," – Troy sucked long and hard to wrest the remaining millimeters of cannabis from his little spliff – "to never use the fuckin' gear yerself."

Even just sitting with Troy in the dark park eating chips could colour life in for his younger brother – especially when he did his impressions of celebrities or school teachers. Troy was tall with a lollipop Afro, and a martial arts physique still lingering from the days before drug dealing took him out of the gym and into the clubs and streets. Gypsy-handsome, with bed-beckoning, sleepy eyes and a smiling, sensuous mouth, he had the look of their idol, Jimi Hendrix, about him.

Troy was the centre of his little brother's universe. He'd been mother, father and best friend to Jamal for the whole of his sixteen-year life.

When his killer materialised out of nowhere on a motorbike that night, Troy was singing the hymn *I Watch the Sunrise* in the voice of Jamal's chair of school governors and parish priest, Father Kevin O'Connor.

"You only cross the Sons one time, Bannie!" a pubescent male voice sounded above the growling bike engine.

Troy stopped singing and turned round, seeing the sawn-off shotgun in the hand of the rider only as it fired.

The gun's muzzle lit up as obscene shots tore the night, like a light sabre plunging through a Rembrandt canvas. A roar of pain issued from Troy as he fell to the ground.

Ammunition sulphur spiked the motor fumes hanging in the wake of the retreating bike. Ferrous blood tumbled on to the playground floor. This was not like the virtual games, with the interfacing glass screen, and characters with digital blood. There was no restarting a level. This killing was real and invasive of all the senses.

The cider-drinking bonfire kids had disappeared. Their little stove threw orange light on the kiddy sponge-floor of the crime scene. Blood oozed from Troy's head as if it were a toppled chocolate fountain, and showed shiny and viscous in the small light of the stove-flame.

Jamal was screaming in his man-boy voice for help until he stopped dead as he remembered: he must get Troy's phone. He snatched it from Troy's still-warm jeans pocket then sat on the ground, clasping his knees, head down, rocking to and fro. In the chapel created by his intersecting arms, chest and lap, his muttered repetitions of the *Hail Mary* sounded loud as God through the approaching sirens. Now men were running towards him, their chunky uniformed bodies like liquorice-allsorts figures against the rotating blue light of the police cars.

Sawn-off shotguns don't fire bullets, Jamal realised that night. A cluster bomb of pellets explodes at the end of the truncated barrel. The injuries are particulate and widespread.

The two shots took off Troy's handsome face and front-lying hair. He died instantly. Nanny Lilly couldn't have an open casket for his funeral because no undertaker in the world could have made good what the nightrider had done. The word on the street was that Gary Skelton, who disappeared from Shriveton immediately afterwards, had done it. But nobody came forward, and so the police couldn't progress the case.

Nobody was ever charged with the killing.

7th October 201-

Matherfield Park, Liverpool

"Tez!"

Tez turned round sharply, his face draining of colour when he saw who it was. The Staffordshire bull terrier at his side stiffened and gave a little growl. Slack jawed, and horrified, Tez stood speechless. A sheath of leaflets plus magazine slid out from the *Sunday Mail* crooked under his arm, and slumped to the floor.

It was early Sunday morning. Lights from sandstone-quaint Matherfield General Stores cast bright oblongs through the obstinate shadows of evergreens lining the cobbled main street of the village. From across the village green, where a timber bus shelter vaunted a tasteful *Best Kept Village* sign, the church bell chimed eight.

Matherfield Park was for wealthy people, and retro red telephone boxes, and village fêtes peddling homemade, housewifely cakes. Even the chippy was posh. No polystyrene trays, wrappers, broken bottles, cans or syringes littered the pavements. Hedge-lined roads – complete with signs warning careful motorists of equine traffic – meandered to and from the village timber-framed pub and charming terrace of pretty shops, which included the General Stores. The closest Jamal had ever come to Matherfield Park, in all of his sixteen years, was the electrical goods Troy had stolen from one of the houses there.

"Sorry, man," mumbled Jamal, embarrassed and a bit baffled by the palpable terror he had elicited in Zone Chief Tez. "Just wanted a word, like."

Realisation washed over Tez's features, like water on a parched river bed, salving the crackling tension: it wasn't Troy, it was his *brother*. Tez stooped to pick up his newspaper droppings. Then, after what seemed forever, managed a gruff, "What about?"

"Our Troy."

Closing his eyes – it almost looked as if he were trying not to cry! –Tez shook his head a few times, and said, "I'm sorry, Jammy. I 'eard 'bout it."

Then he lit a cigarette, his every facial muscle contorting in intense concentration, while his unsteady hands cupped the Zippo flame as if it were a precious jewel. He exhaled a massive plume of smoke in the cold morning air:

"Fuckin' proper shame, lad. Gutted for you."

"I know who done it," declared Jamal. His huge, innocent brown eyes stared expectantly at Tez.

In the unreal hours that had passed since the shooting in Shriveton Park, a million negative thoughts had whirred and tumbled and melted to nothing like Rizla papers in a rainstorm. Only two persisted: Gaz had been the killer on that bike; Gaz must pay. These ideas had spurred Jamal to make the trip to Matherfield Park to find Tez, his best hope of redress.

The freezing moisture of the early morning had beaded on his puff of black hair, and conspired with the Noddy-like flush of high emotion and the exertion of the journey here, to give him the appearance of a macabre puppet suddenly dropped into Tez's Matherfield Park set. Fearful and agitated, Tez looked at him:

"Leave it, Jammy."

"Leave it?" Jamal was incredulous. "The cunt can't just fuckin' gun down our Troy."

"Listen, Jammy, Gaz is a soft twat, an' the bizzies have probably picked him up already."

"The bizzies haven't goddim!"

"You don't know that"-

"I fuckin' do! The bizzies told me they ain't arrested no one."

"Let it go, Jammy."

"I thought you'd want to find him! Troy was one of your soldiers."

"Shh, shh. Keep it down, lad."

"You're the fuckin' boss round 'ere, though! You of all fuckin' people shou-"

Tez grabbed him, and shoved him against the sandstone wall of the Matherfield General Store. The dog started yelping, and Tez called her off, just milliseconds before she took a chunk out of Jamal's leg.

Achingly huge sobs found the resonant frequency of all the sorrow inside Jamal, as he pleaded: "Look, I need him to answer for our Troy!"

Tez downgraded his grip on Jamal's arms to a supportive clasp, and suggested, "Let's sit down and have a smoke. And a talk, like."

He tied up the dog, then guided his unwelcome guest towards the timber bus shelter across the road. There were no CCTVs on the boundary wall of the village green, and Tez was always mindful of the fact that a low profile was essential.

Jamal felt dizzy and strange as he sat down. The horror of Troy's murder had made an amorphous sludge of most of the hours that followed it, and he would never be able to recall much of it. Yet his Sunday morning exchange with Shriveton kingpin Tez never faded from his memory, although he would never understand why.

"I never been 'ere," Jamal said. "To Matherfield, like."

"It's nice," mumbled Tez, lighting a cigarette. "The people are easy to like. They're all so fuckin' rich."

On seeing Tez on the bench, a passing, middle-class jogger redoubled his pace, and zoomed into the General Stores. He emerged in a few moments, carrying a Sunday Observer, still avoiding eye contact.

"That cunt's my next door neighbour," grouched Tez. "Smoke?"

Nobody wants to live next door to a man like Tez. The merest glimpse of his thinning dark hair (always asymmetrical, because his wife cut it for him), the barbed wire of wrinkles outlining his emotionless eyes, and the lean, pale lips which never seemed to break into a smile over his stained teeth, would invariably send fellow Matherfield Park residents scampering off in the opposite direction. The dirt of his criminal lifestyle sullied and diminished him, and was ingrained in the money which had bought him in. Although only twenty five, he already looked middle-aged, and resembled a vulture with his hunched shoulders, hooked nose and beady, dark eyes which never even took time to blink, so wary was he of the Damoclean calamity which could erupt at any moment.

By contrast, Tez's Matherfield Park neighbours were mainly professionals: lawyers, doctors, accountants, with a little roughage provided by the occasional self-made businessman. Shriveton's Superintendent Meyers lived just around the corner from the village green bench where they sat.

Jamal stared at Tez's proffered cigarette packet, with its contents like loose teeth, as if someone had just punched it. At that moment, Jamal couldn't remember whether or not he smoked. So he shook his head and said, "You're me only 'ope, Tez. I know the bizzies won't do nothin'. Troy was all I got, Tez."

Awkward, Tez tried and failed to think of something to say, and instead patted the soaking material of Jamal's scruffy jacket.

"I need you to find that twat Gaz," Jamal said, still crying. "I gotta find him. I'm gonna tell the bizzies it's 'im. I haven't yet. They don't know. Nobody knows, 'cept me. I was there."

"Never tell the beaks nothing, kid. You know the rules, kid."

"I never said nothin' last night. But I heard his voice. It was definitely Gaz on the bike. No one else seen it. No one come forward, like."

Emotion overcame him again.

"Sorry, man, sorry," sobbed Jamal. He wiped his nose and face on his sleeve, like a little boy.

"No, it's –" began Tez, looking around with great trepidation.

"You gotta help me, Tez."

"OK. But I can't move, Jammy. Not straight away. The fuckin' bizzies will be all over me."

"But you own the bizzies."

"Careful, now Jam. Careful. Talk like that is unwise, kid. Just leave the whole fuckin' thing for now."

"I want him, Tez. It's all I want. That. I want *that*. There's nothin' left for me anywhere. I have to even for Troy."

"Look, I'll sort all the funeral. It'll be a big splash. And then –"

"And then, what?"

"And then, we'll – we'll 'ave a look."

"When?"

"I don't know. Soon."

As if he were sleepwalking and the dream screen in his head had changed to a completely different reel, Jamal stood up, and mumbled,

"I gotta even for our Troy."

Boots and heart heavy, head bowed to the ground, like a shell-shocked trench soldier, Jamal wandered off in the direction of No Man's Land he called home.

25th October 201-

Shriveton

Burial, Gangland Style

Zone Chief Tez organised and paid for foot soldier Troy Bannigan's funeral on the Incubo's behalf. It was more lavish than any funeral St Theresa's had ever seen, and it featured, at the special request of the deceased's Nan, two horse-drawn hearses, one for the body and one for the vast array of floral tributes. The kids collected dung from the roads afterwards and posted it through the paedo Moskowski's letterbox on Tallis Row. The rest was launched at the police, who managed nonetheless to maintain a very low-key, watchful presence.

Flower-wrought letters – *LFC, grandson, brother,* and *Bannie* – leaned against the brassy coffin, like drunken showgirls. Residents stood in silent respect on the roadside as the cortège made its way to St Theresa's. Recollections of the deceased's drug-dealing and dole-screwing final incarnation were tactfully suppressed for the day, not least by parish priest Father O'Connor, whose funereal address recalled first Troy's triumphs as centre forward for the lower school team, then his role as Joseph in the primary school nativity play, and went on with:

"He was a popular and well-liked lad..."

The murder of his beloved older brother had transformed Jamal. He had stopped going to school altogether, and become, overnight, as reclusive and melancholic as Troy had been gregarious.

Dry-eyed and stiff as stone beside his grandmother on the front pew, a polyphony of thoughts about his present and future played in his mind. Each was shaped by a singular, base theme, which reverberated around his universe:

Someone must pay.

CHAPTER THREE

Monday October 25th 201-

Claridge's Hotel, Mayfair, London

Kachya

"The Clicquot, please, love," he told the waitress, sniffing. He'd just snorted a huge line of cocaine in the Claridge's gents. This would be a long day, and he'd needed the boost. "La Grande Dame Rose 1998. A glass."

Today he was Paul Wilkins: self-made-moneyed in a slightly tanned, moderately bejewelled way. He'd opted for a white wide-boy London accent, kept in check *most* of the time. Muted extroversion was the keynote of this auburn haired character. The beginnings of silver tapered from his temples. Since turning forty, two years ago, he included the grey, whatever colour he went, to appear natural.

Small changes of this kind were very effective when you operated under a number of different identities. Without the theatrical effects, he was a nondescript individual – slim, greying, balding fair hair, pale-eyed and of medium height. For Paul Wilkins he'd opted for some well-placed midriff padding.

His phone buzzed in his pocket. News from Liverpool: the Shriveton funeral was passing without incident. Good news. The Liverpool Zone *must* stabilise. Closing the call, without speaking a word, he picked up the wine list again.

London's Claridge's provided the perfect meeting place for today's business, which was the conclusion of a lucrative deal, vastly skewed in Paul Wilkins' favour. His guest, known simply as Ashok, the representative of Bangladeshi billionaire Amin Chowdhury, would intuit in the selection of this flash location an intense desire in his host to appear established and confident, despite humble beginnings. One must allow one's opponents to feel they have the power.

"I'm so sorry, sir, we don't do the Grand Dame by the glass," she replied. She was probably Russian (he found it hard to distinguish between Slavonic accents, and avoided using them himself). Her hotel uniform was slightly too big for her small boned frame.

Disguise was his business. Dying the hair accelerated the thinning, which was why, for some characters, he used wigs or hats. Care must be taken to ensure brows were appropriate to the hair colour, too. Contact lenses, spectacles and even prosthetic teeth could utterly alter a face.

So far he had avoided plastic surgery beyond the rhinoplasty, undergone over twenty years ago, before starting his course at RADA. The training there had prepared him perfectly for acting work which, despite his restructured nose, had only ever been for nondescript, short contracts. Bitterness would have set in, in a lesser being; but not in the creator of Paul Wilkins and fellow avatars.

For Paul Wilkins, he had opted for dark brown contacts, some heavy plastic framed Armani spectacles, and upper jaw prosthesis to make him look slightly bucktoothed. If he ended up screwing the waitress later, he'd probably have to slip out the teeth, and lose the padding. Unless he did her from behind, which was his preferred option with casual close encounters so they didn't get a close look at him. Such trysts, which amounted to little more than collaborative masturbation, he usually resisted because of the exposure involved. The cocaine and the thrill of closing the Bangladesh deal made him horny, though. He deserved to cut himself a bit of sexual slack today.

His handkerchiefed sneeze now disguised both the simultaneous sniff and gulp needed to clear residual nasal powder.

"Well a bottle, then."

"Very good, sir. I bring you now."

"If you could keep those tables free."

He indicated the adjacent tables with a sweep of his arm, with a bulging gold Cartier watch, the sight of which elicited a thrilled, orgasmic gasp from the waitress.

"We don't want to be disturbed."

"Of course, sir."

"My guest will be arriving shortly."

The waitress returned with the champagne. Trim of figure, tidy of appearance, and obliging and deferential in a way peculiar to Eastern European servants, he had liked her immediately, not least because her long, green eyes, crooked teeth and flaxen hair reminded him of Chloe Tudor.

Chloe: the sort of mistake that middle-aged, rich and powerful men occasionally don't get away with. He took a swig of champagne, and nodded approvingly, holding out his glass for more.

"Good," he said, through a belch of premium grape fumes, the punishment of luxury administered by his recently acquired ulcer.

The bizarre rescue of Chloe, which had sent shockwaves reverberating throughout the Incubo empire, was quite literally a running sore, not merely in Paul Wilkins' guts, but in his life. Shriveton, *the* major UK distribution centre, had been compromised.

"Can I get you anything else, sir?" asked the waitress. She was so school-girlishly pretty. Yum.

He took her hand, small and soft and white as a snowdrop beneath his own orange-skinned, big-nailed and golden haired paw, and said, "Later, you can."

His dark eyes surveyed her whole body, appreciatively. The girl blushed and gushed, and moved away, saying, "Ooh, I not sure, but OK."

He pushed a fifty pound note into the warm, kiddy flesh of her cupped palm.

"Sir, I should not take this, but –"

"Of course you should, and you will," he chuckled. "What is your name?"

"Kachya, sir."

"And where are you from Kachya?"

"I from Ukraine –"

"Well, Kachya. I will call you when I need you."

With a shy, "Yes, sir, I am at your service all the time!" she retreated, nursing her hand which he had clutched so tightly. He watched her go, noting with approval her attempt to appear unruffled and dignified. His type: a pretty, proud, young and unspoiled menial.

He took a large consolatory slug of champagne. That was

exactly how he had seen Chloe Tudor, in the beginning. When he'd first encountered her in one of his Liverpool One night clubs, she'd been obscuring her youth and vulnerability with towering heels and false eyelashes like black plastic combs glued above her cat–green eyes. A master of disguise himself, he'd seen straight through hers immediately and recognised her to be the schoolgirl she was.

He'd been Guy Turner then, not Paul Wilkins. Guy Turner was an executive producer with Sherman Records. Guy Turner came from the land of *yes*: wealth, status, power.

Chloe Tudor came from the land of *no* – no money, no qualifications or life experience, no job, no cigarettes, no home life and no chance of escape. By being a fourteen-year-old schoolgirl in a city-centre night club, she was spooling more *nos* for herself, and he'd known he could move in with impunity.

Impresario Guy Turner plied her with cheap champagne and cigarettes (she'd loved the multicoloured Sobranie) and told her anecdotes about various pop stars on his books. She was an unusually alluring member of the slums on which he and his other avatars depended. From the moment he set eyes on her, he knew he must have her, whatever the risk.

Music biz supremo Guy Turner had given Chloe a brush with true greatness, namely himself. Much as he had tried not to, and unique as it was in his entire experience, he had fallen for her in a way which baffled, frustrated and scared him. He could not explain his feelings for her at all. They seemed to come from outside him, and persisted long after their association was over.

"You *are* the slum you come from!" he'd snarled at her in an apoplexy of frustration towards the end of their short relationship. "Is that all you want for yourself?"

The only certainty in Chloe's mind was that she hadn't wanted any more of Guy Turner (he'd never figured out why, and even thinking about it now upset him). Wealthy and admirable in every way, Guy Turner was too good for her anyway. All that could be done with the head-veal like Chloe's was to spice it up with tabloid tits, celebrity gossip, four-chord hit records, or false promises of a lottery win.

"Can't you understand? I am providing you with an alternative, Chloe."

While she'd looked on, blank and uncomprehending as usual, he'd hated himself for his involuntary articulacy. It was so *entirely* wasted on the nubile numbskull he adored and despised in equal measure.

By her sixteenth year of life, she said *yes* to hard drugs and other men, one of whom gave her a baby. With great reluctance, Guy Turner had ended their short association, by which time Chloe had a five hundred a week habit, and was getting restive. She'd had to go. Her Paki Witch rescuer had thought so, too.

And there was the rub which had ulcerated his stomach and his serenity: the Paki Witch. To this day, neither she nor her rescuer had ever been apprehended.

He'd *never* make another mistake like Chloe.

Belching again, and sighing out the winey fumes, Paul Wilkins watched Ukrainian Kachya's cute little butt as she hastened away from him. Little Kachya would provide a charming conclusion to the business in hand.

The much anticipated Ashok now arrived.

"I apologise for my lateness," he said, shaking Paul's hand and sitting down rather awkwardly in the low-slung armchair opposite. A flush of obscure aftershave swelled from his immaculately dressed person. "My client called me with some instructions."

He was nervous, but hiding it well, unlike Kachya who presented herself at the table again.

"Oh, no worries, Ashok," beamed Wilkins. "It's given Kachya and me a little chance to chinwag. Now what will you have to drink? I have this excellent Grande Dame champagne."

"Oh, no alcohol for me. I will have mineral water."

"Yes, sir," said Kachya. "We have Pellegrino or Perrier or –"

"Oh, any will do," grumbled Ashok, without looking at her. "Water is water."

"Will you have something to eat?" enquired his host.

"Oh, no. I haven't time. I have a flight to make. Thank you."

Kachya withdrew.

"My client can confirm that the licences have been accepted," said Ashok, in a muted voice.

False exporting companies had been set up in Bangladesh, using the tax certificates of the perfectly legitimate Bengal Spice and Condiments (BSC) of which Ashok's employer, Amin Chowdhury, was a senior executive. With a global workforce of 5,000 and various government awards for innovative business practice and good international trading relations, BSC was part of the Bangladeshi establishment. Chowdhury appeared on national TV regularly, and was a key figure in the hinterland of Bangladeshi political life. BSC's outstanding export performance made it a flagship of South Asian commerce.

"So straightforward?" said Paul. "I thought it would take

longer."

"It's easy to falsify VAT certificates in Bangladesh. Most officials are corrupt."

"Good news." Paul lifted his glass as for a toast, as Kachya arrived to deliver Ashok's drink. "Thank you, Kachya."

"Do you know her?" asked Ashok, irritated.

"No, but I expect to." He took a swig, adding, "Relax, Ashok. We have a deal now. Everything is organised here. The Incubo is satisfied."

Ashok hesitated, then passed over the papers in his hand with, "My client would like the money transferred into these accounts."

Paul looked through the documents and nodded. "All fine."

"Before we close proceedings, though, there a couple of points."

"Fire away, Ashok."

"My client is concerned about rumours regarding distribution in the UK. You indicated that the Liverpool area was instrumental to the latter stage of operations, and we have learned that there has been some difficulty there."

Wilkins felt a punitive sting in his guts, as he replied, "Liverpool is completely stable. The port remains porous to our interests. The distribution outlets there and in surrounding areas are secure."

"But my client heard there was some problem in the main outlet there recently which halted trading for a short time."

Wilkins covered his hesitation with a leisurely sip of champagne. "A perceived risk meant that as a precaution the Shriveton Zone was closed briefly."

"My client heard that the area – Zone as you call it – was penetrated by a law enforcement agent, a woman. A Muslim woman."

"It was a momentary lapse in security, which was sorted at the time, Ashok."

"But the closure of the Liverpool outlet meant that a consignment had to be abandoned in Southampton. Our trading partners in Karachi were not pleased, Mr Wilkins. We need assurances."

"Look, we had one incident in the Liverpool outlet – unique in the decades of trading in the same Shriveton Zone. A woman –" recollections of the disastrous intervention of the Paki Witch prompted a renewed and nasty rawness in his digestive tract – "*accidentally* wandered into the heart of the action, so to speak. We had to act safe, Ashok, and suspend operations. She wasn't from the police or SOCA, but we couldn't take that chance. It's a shame about Southampton, I agree."

"Very well. There is one final point. I must inform you that there is an amendment to the sum involved. Another million. Sterling."

Wilkins paused. The fury he felt was completely concealed. Ashok appeared nervous but resolved.

"This was not the deal, Ashok."

"Unfortunately, my client has incurred many extra costs in progressing the situation to this level."

With a grunt Wilkins stood up, and stretched, arching his back, so that he had the appearance of a squirrel stretching for an elusive nut. A keener observer than Ashok might have noticed, through the taut material of his stripy shirt, straps keeping the padding around his midriff.

"No deal," he huffed. Slinging his jacket over his shoulder, he called, "Kachya!" as he moved away a few paces from the table.

Ashok shuffled with great agitation. Kachya arrived.

"Can I help you sir?" she asked, not flinching as Wilkins placed his arm around her waist cupping her bony buttock with his open palm as he announced, "The bill, please, Kachya."

"Yes sir, I go get." She scampered away, blushing.

"You will need to discuss with your superior before you dismiss this deal, surely, Mr Wilkins?" hissed Ashok.

"There is nothing to discuss. The price has been set. The Incubo will not pay a penny more."

Kachya returned with the bill. Wilkins handed her four fifty pound notes. Like so many of the bank notes in UK circulation, it would be dusty with cocaine. He had no idea whether these notes came from one of his UK Zones, or from his plethora of legitimate businesses. But Kachya wouldn't be worrying about its origins. She'd decided to turn a blind eye to her own scruples and physical indifference to him.

The blind eye of others could be almost invariably depended on in most matters, he found. It had made him a multi-millionaire.

Ashok was talking quietly in Bengali into his mobile phone.

"I bring your change, sir," said Kachya.

"Keep the change. But do verify the bank notes, by all means. When does your shift end, Kachya, so we can get together? I suddenly find myself at a loose end."

She was flustered and embarrassed. He knew why. She would be feeling oddly treacherous that this generous customer knew she must verify the bank notes with her superior. Also, in order to get more of these same bank notes out of him, she must give him her shift end time in the hearing of the Asian man who would be a witness to her moral frailty.

"Two o'clock I finish, sir. In few minutes."

"Good." His finger stroked the little booklet of fifties in his still-open wallet while Kachya tried, and failed, not to look, agog. "I'll meet you in the lobby. Leave your maid uniform on."

"Yes, sir. Thank you very much, sir."

"Please wait a moment, Mr Wilkins," said Ashok, ending his phone call.

When the waitress had gone again, he added. "My client has taken on board the reassurances you have given me just now. Please, to finish your champagne, and resume discussion."

Smug, Wilkins sat down again, and watched Ashok pour him more champagne. The Bangladesh route would revolutionise heroin trade in the UK, and make the Incubo one of the wealthiest men on the planet. By extrapolating the sweep of the lucrative Golden Crescent – Iran, Afghanistan, Pakistan – exits of raw crop were increased, spreading risk of detection, and opening up competition in the exporting sectors, thus lowering on-costs, and increasing profit. This deal with Chowdhury's people meant that cargo could be doubled – to 10kg or even more – per trip. BSC was thoroughly insulated from the daughter companies carrying the freight. It was watertight.

The Incubo liked to stick with heroin. Over the decades he had formed astonishingly successful links with indigenous producers, including the Taliban in Afghanistan, whom he supplied with M16 rifles. (The M16s were highly prized currency because they meant that US-supplied ammunition could be bought from the Afghani government on the black market.)

Heroin was his bread and butter. In his long experience as an importer of drugs and arms, the Mexican cartels (and the Columbians who superseded them) were greedier for complete dominance of trade. Their personnel were often erratic, even downright crazy, and on occasion too disorganised to negotiate extremely complex deals.

He sniffed again, then blew his nose.

"Sorry. Terrible hay fever."

Ashok looked on, a ghost of knowing in his wry, "Hay fever in October?" observation.

Wilkins shrugged through another spluttering sneeze.

"So we have a deal?" asked Ashok.

"Yes. I'm glad you've rethought."

"Excellent. My client is reassured by my telephone conversation just now. If you could organise the advance payment now?"

It crossed Wilkins' mind to screw Chowdhury down by half a million, but it was too much effort. Plus, he'd be having the waitress shortly, and uncertainty about the deal might compromise his sexual performance, cocaine notwithstanding!

"Sure, Ashok." Wilkins opened his phone. No further word from Tez, which meant the Shriveton funeral was passing off without incident. "I'll confirm with Bern now, and organise the transfer."

He dialled Switzerland. His portfolio of legitimate eatery pubs, sports clubs and catering wholesalers would be funding this particular deal with the subsidiaries of BSC, via a small fictitious UK importing company, Sea Land Foodstuffs, cooked up for this very purpose. Packages of heroin would be buried in cargoes of cooking oils, exotic spices, granite and toiletry products for Sea Land Foodstuffs at Edgware Road. Sea Land Foodstuffs had no website, landline or forwarding address. Indeed the company mobile number registered on the shipping documents was a tourist number purchased by Paul Wilkins at Carphone Warehouse last week. Almost all agents involved in the complex transaction were invented.

His terse, "Roger, SLF, authorise transfer," completed the transaction. Minutes later, Ashok took another call, to which he answered a series of *yeses* and then stood up, and offered his hand.

"We have a deal, Mr Wilkins."

They shook hands, and Ashok departed. Wilkins went into the art deco splendour of the lobby, where, leaning against one of the extravagant pillars, he made a phone call.

"Here for another half hour, wrapping things up," he told the men outside who had his back. After this he would be driven to Heathrow, where Paul Wilkins would disappear in the gents, and re-emerge as Callum Bowes-West, bound on an internal flight to Manchester. "I'll call you to bring the car when I'm finished."

His foot tapped the black and white glossy flooring as he talked. It was the only and very small outward indication of the triumph he felt as champagne and cocaine conspired with sheer relief at getting this vital deal through. Plus, he was about to enjoy the delicious Kachya.

Sinking on to a nearby luxurious lobby Chesterfield sofa, he sat watching the people buzzing around. He was always on the lookout for new types to copy.

Soon Kachya arrived, a nervous ingénue, still wearing her maid outfit.

"I booked a room," he told her.

"I am so happy, sir," she piped, obediently, as he ushered her into the lift.

Lawdens Lane, Shriveton

Love is Blind

"Morwenna Griffiths, from Social Services. The Deputy Head from St Theresa's Primary School suggested I call. I'm sorry I'm late, Mr Reilly."

Morwenna, a stocky, sensible middle-aged woman, held out her big warm hand to him.

She was indeed late – by more than hour – having been stationary on Boundary Lane, the artery to the Shriveton estate, behind a very slow moving cortège. The streets were full of mourners. Apparently (her line manager had informed her by phone) the local schools and shops had closed for the funeral today of Troy Bannigan shot dead in a gangland dispute.

"I forgot there was the funeral today," she continued, waving her hand a little.

"Is it still all going on?" the old man asked in a loud voice. His eyes did not register the movement of her hand.

Morwenna perceived the tell-tale milky opacity to Reilly's eyes. It was obvious that he couldn't see anything through the cataract barricade. He thought he was looking at her, when in fact his unseeing eyes were fixing on the parade of shops overhead. People were leaning over the wall of the shopping parade terrace to look down at St Theresa's Church, the hub of today's ceremonial action, in the heart of the lower-lying remainder of the estate.

"Yes, such a shame." Morwenna dropped her unshaken hand, sad. The school was right – the old man really was blind. "Did you know the young man being buried?"

"No. Gangster, he was. I keep myself to myself. What d'you want?"

"I need to see how things are going with you and the children, Mr Reilly. I did send a letter, saying I was coming today?"

"Oh, er, yes. Letter."

The Reilly case was very familiar to her. This poor old man was desperate to keep the illusion of functionality going. His phobia of all things medical meant he refused to sort out his eyesight. Blind now, he could not care for his two grandchildren, nine-year-old

Tom and seven-year-old Maisie, whose neglected state had been flagged up by the school months ago. Maisie and Tom had been residing with him for most of their life: Mum was a long-term drug addict who'd left Liverpool six years ago and never been seen or heard of since. Their father was in prison.

"Maisie and Tom are off school with this funeral thing," he said, defensively. "They gone up the Parade to watch. I can see 'em from the front door."

"Can I come in, please, Mr Reilly?"

He thought about shutting the door on her, she knew.

"I did write to you, telling you I was com-"

"OK."

Gingerly, Morwenna navigated the pile of free newspapers and unopened letters, plus kid's scooter and pile of shoes in the hallway. The carpets were sticky, and the air thick with stale sweat and fried food. At the end of the hallway she caught a glimpse of a spectacularly messy kitchen.

"You want a brew?" he asked.

"No thanks!" Steam flew from her mouth as she spoke. Inside was as cold as outside.

He shuffled into the front room, which was tidier and warmer than she would have expected. An ironing board, pitched at child height, was up in the corner, and the TV was given over to a first generation PlayStation and cluster of games. Radio Merseyside was fizzing at very low volume from a large stereo player, from which a defunct cassette drawer dangled. Everywhere was sealed in a film of dusty grease.

He crossed to the window overlooking a muddy postage stamp of front garden. In the middle, a broken bike was planted like an abandoned battlefield wagon.

"So how are things, Mr Reilly?" Morwenna parked her ample self on the sofa and took out her laptop.

"They're OK," he said, hesitantly, pulling at the curtain. He was checking that the curtains were open, she knew.

"Mr Reilly, the school have sent me because they are worried about Maisie and Tom." She accompanied her utterance with a Morse code of typing. Getting the paperwork done as you went along was the key to success in her line of work.

"Look, we're OK." His voice was quieter, and breaking up with the beginnings of tears. He sat down, a sunken-chested silhouette against the light trying to penetrate dirty net curtains.

"Mr Reilly, it's been very tough for you, I know. Looking after two small children is not easy. And now you seem to be losing your sight –"

"I can see OK. With the lights on, especially. The kids are OK."

"The school feel that Maisie and Tom are not being cared for properly, that their basic needs are not being met, Mr Reilly."

"That's not true!" he shouted, bringing his fist down impulsively. It missed the chair arm and connected with his own thigh.

After some more typing, Morwenna asked, "Can I have a look around the house, Mr Reilly?"

He hesitated, and stammered, "Look, you could be anyone. How do I know who you are?"

"Well – apart from the letter which I *did* send – I have my identifying credentials right here."

She lifted off the badge dangling conspicuously from her thickset neck. His eyes didn't connect with the movement, so she went up to him, and passed him the badge. It stayed in his broken-nailed arthritic hand as he shook his head.

"You can't see it can you, Mr Reilly?" she said.

He shook his head, tearful now. "Look around if you want. I can't do nothin' except trust you."

The children had been known to Social Services for most of their lives. Stability had been achieved once residency with their grandparents in Lawdens Lane was finally established five years ago. The death of their grandmother had been a wobble last year. But key workers had pronounced the situation to be just about satisfactory until Mr Reilly's eyesight deteriorated to blindness which meant that now the Reilly children were a textbook case of non-malicious neglect.

Their heads were alive with lice which never went away, their clothes dirty and not changed from one week to the next, and their shoes so ill-fitting that the parish priest had provided new pairs out of church funds the previous week. Academically they had plummeted.

Morwenna's tour of their chaotic and filthy home confirmed all reports.

"Well I've had a look round, Mr Reilly," she said, returning to the front room and sitting down. Bob Reilly was exactly where she'd left him, impotent as the lenses in his eyes.

"Call me Bob. Don't like all the formalness."

"Sorry, Bob," said Morwenna. Her fingers were doing a furious QWERTY dance as she documented her findings. "Now from a child protection point of view, we have to look at the needs of Maisie and Tom."

There was a delay in which he chewed his lip and opened his mouth several times as if to speak, only to falter and fall back into a state of silence.

"Look," he eventually spluttered out, "they are 'appy. They been through so much. And so have I."

"I know. I know you have, Bob, I know you have."

"Don't take them off me."

"Well, these days, that's not how it works. As you know, Bob. Our role, my role, is to stabilise the situation..."

Morwenna gave the usual spiel about the impermanence and hypothetical nature of all arrangements and scenarios which might or might not ensue, subject to what was decided by people further up the line than she herself was. Another visit would be arranged, very soon, and whatever procedures decided on would be put in place properly, with due reference to everyone involved.

Concluding with an assurance that the needs of everyone would be taken into consideration, Morwenna clamped shut her laptop and announced, "I'll see myself out, Bob."

"Don't take Tom and Maisie away," he pleaded, stumbling behind her as she went. He tripped over a pile of shoes by the front door and fell against her.

"Oops!" said Morwenna.

Her nose wrinkled with the strong and unpleasant odour of personal dereliction – sweat, sour breath, and poor toilet hygiene – that wafted into their shared air from him. She opened the door in a hurry and gulped fresh outdoors. Compared to the squalor of the Reilly home, the Shriveton streets seemed less ghastly than usual.

Faint ribbons of tobacco smoke fluttered down from the funeral spectators still lining the nearby Shopping Parade wall. Shriveton was entirely still. No cars were moving. Everyone was either inside staying out of the way, or watching the gangster funeral. Only the seagulls, and one small Islamic-clad female figure crossing the walkway from the tower blocks, were moving. Morwenna had noticed the same solitary Muslim woman walking when she'd turned off the ring road into the estate on her way to the Reilly home.

"You're not going to take them away are you?" Bob said again. The morning sun made jewels of tears in the milky opacity of his eyes.

"It's not up to me," she said. She gave his hand a kindly squeeze. "Bob, we're trying to help you, too, remember."

He curled his hand around hers, desperate, helpless. "I'm not a bad man, love."

"I know that Bob."

"I've tried me best."

"I know that, Bob. We all do. The team will work with you, remember."

"Everything gone against us. This friggin' place." He shook his head. Big tears fell into the grey slalom of his stubble. "Gone to the devil 'imself it 'as. The whole estate. What chance 'ave people like us got, eh, girl? The only thing we got's the Paki Witch. And that's the friggin' truth."

The old man disappeared behind his peeling front door.

Morwenna frowned, quizzical. One of her more hopeless clients, Chloe Tudor, had once mentioned a character called the Paki Witch. Chloe had believed the Paki Witch had magical powers. Who knows, perhaps that lone Muslim woman she'd seen before *was* this Paki Witch?

What a backward, hopeless place Shriveton was. Fifteen years on in the job, and Morwenna's career had taken her here. No wonder she was depressed!

At least her car wasn't on bricks. She slung her laptop case on to the passenger seat, next to a box of tissues, and got in. As was her habit on these sorts of visits, she used a tissue to open the glove compartment and to extract the gel hand cleaner she kept there.

However, beyond applying its contents liberally to her hands, Morwenna did nothing. Something intangible, outside herself, was claiming her attention – not a sound, not a sight but pure prescience. Nobody was around, and there didn't appear to be anything physically different to the surroundings. Her phone fizzed with the usual calls and texts, which she ignored, unflinching. The laptop sat folded shut in its bag, her paperwork incomplete. Subdued utterly and inexplicably by the moment, and feeling intensely alive despite her torpor, Morwenna Griffiths waited.

CHAPTER FOUR

Monday 22nd October 201-

St Theresa's Church, Shriveton

"He was a popular and well-liked lad..."

Father O'Connor's hypnotic Southern Irish burr, powered by a PA system borrowed from a local DJ, reached every corner of his big hangar of a church. Usually as empty as an atom, even the balcony was full for Troy Bannigan's funeral, such that there was hardly room for the organist there. Viscous solemnity had retarded everything to a standstill as Shriveton watched and listened. Jamal could not help but interpret the grim collective respect as an injunction to him personally to take restorative action.

He was heartbroken: his brother had been zapped like an abattoir cow in the middle of a public park, and nobody arrested. Sorrow was rotting him from within. Troy *must* be answered for. Shriveton Son Gary Skelton had fled the area, and, in any case, the police had no evidence to bring charges against him or anyone. But he must be found. It was Gaz's voice he'd heard that night in Shriveton Park: *You only cross the Sons one time, Bannie!*

In his mind, Jamal had shot, stabbed, and run over Gaz (driving forwards and then backwards over the body); he'd drowned him in the Mersey, whacked him on the head with a baseball bat and poisoned him. None of these imaginings brought any consolation, but they ran in his head anyway, spurred by a tinnitus call of duty.

The church was scrambling Jamal's dark neurosis with pleasant

39

old memories of him and Troy being wine-slugging altar boys there, and of school nativity plays and birthday parties. The last time he'd been here was for his Mum's funeral, but somehow he could always just block that out.

The priest's plodding oratory style was something he and Troy had always gleefully lampooned. Straights like Father O'Connor talked so much, but always from the sidelines. *Straights* were what he and Troy labelled the social pillars they spent their whole life dodging: school teachers with their *levels* and *targets* and *appropriate behaviour*; social workers with their *service user needs* and *intervention criteria;* and the bizzies, who were just intrinsically hateful. Your life bumped up against them, as surely as the fat-lady curves of dinghies, with their class A consignments bound for the Shriveton Zone, bobbed against those Costa del Sol quays Troy had dreamed about being promoted to.

In half an hour, Anfield Crematorium would turn eighteen year old Troy's dreams to smoke, and his body to ashes for distribution on the neighbouring football ground. Gangster paradise.

Every pair of eyes focused on today's ceremony was surely looking to him to exact revenge. Yet there was nobody he could share his sheer terror and fury and impotence with. The only person he felt remotely warm towards was Tez, but not yet quite enough to confide in him. In the days since Troy's passing (Jamal could not say *death*), Zone chief Tez had behaved like some sort of kind uncle. He'd paid for everything funereal, albeit on the Incubo's account. Jamal longed to broach the subject of revenge again with him as soon as the time seemed right.

"Sorrow has touched this family already," continued Father O'Connor.

The October sun streaming through the Station XIV of the Cross window above him caught the shiny dome of his head. He was slightly flushed, and seemed very angry. Jamal didn't know why the priest should be angry. After all, Troy wasn't family to him.

"Troy and his brother Jamal lost their mother to..." Father O'Connor's little gulp swallowed Mum's heroin addiction and suicide. "... ongoing health complications when Troy was nine years old. But former St Theresa's altar server Troy was always laughing and cracking a joke, *and* he had a sense of humour. Our thoughts and prayers go to their guardian and loving Nan, Lilly..."

Lilly, very much worse for drink, began sobbing volubly, which attracted various pitying looks and tuts from fellow mourners. Jamal was still surprised she'd actually left the couch, where she

40

had lain, blubbering and boozing since Troy's murder. From the couch she had received all visitors (consecutively) – Incubo envoy Tez, detectives, priest, social workers and hashish-bearing old pal Hughie McHugh, known as Macca, never Hugh.

"... and to long-time family friend Hugh, who is here today supporting the family."

A singularity in a charity shop black suit, purple shirt and red windsock hat partially containing his dirty dreadlocks, Hughie McHugh had been at primary school with Lilly. They'd had a sporadic friendship-cum-sexual link for decades. Periodically Macca would travel from his town centre bedsit, knowing that (through Troy) she always had plenty of pot to hand.

"Our thoughts and prayers go out to Jamal, Troy's younger brother, who cradled him in the last moment of his life."

Jamal had been frightened in the empty park, beside his dying brother. He'd sobbed in the arms of a stocky, kind-voiced bizzie, while scene-of-crime experts and paramedics buzzed around Troy's body. Her perfumed body smell had cancelled the stench of his brother's blood. He'd clung to her like a suckling baby monkey, wishing she could swoop him up and out of the jungle forever. It embarrassed and baffled him now to think about it.

The WPC had poured him sweet tea from a flask in the police van, and told him: *It's ok to cry, Jamal.*

This was a lie, he knew – but what do you expect from bizzies?

Macca placed his big arm around Jamal's unwelcoming shoulders. A flush of oniony sweat, and too little patchouli, issued from the consoling armpit.

"I would like to make a plea on behalf of Troy's family for peace and harmony," pleaded Father O'Connor. Genuine feeling raised even higher the priest's feminine-sounding voice – to the point that he sounded like a tearful girl.

Not for the first time, Jamal wondered why Father O'Connor kept persevering with his crappy Shriveton flock. Only the old ladies and primary school kids listened to him. The older kids despised him for his sundry crimes, which included being bald, Irish and gay. Everyone else ignored him as absolutely as they would a visiting politician or professor of quantum physics.

"Drugs and gangs have *decimated* our community," the priest went on. "They are a scourge on our young people, especially the boys, who end up getting attracted *and* drawn to the wrong crowd. It's up to us, the adults, the grown-ups, to set a good example to our young people. We can oppose the evil in our midst."

Plunging nicotine levels were causing Lilly to ferret around in her handbag for her ciggies. The quarter-bottle of vodka in there clinked against her house keys.

"We, as a community, must believe that Troy's death can be the tragic signpost to a new, better way for Shriveton..."

Can signposts be tragic, mused Jamal? Weariness was building within him in inverse proportion to the declining nicotine levels in his self-centred grandmother. In addition to which, the armpit and breath odours from pew neighbour Macca were growing unbearable. Indeed, Jamal was minded to rip Macca's consoling arm off and batter him around the head with it.

"... away from violence and reprisals. We must focus on a new dawn, on forgiveness, not revenge. And now let us sing our final hymn, one of Troy's favourites I believe, *I Watch the Sunrise.* "

After the service, Jamal, Sammy, Macca and a guy from the Co-op carried Troy's coffin to the flower-laden horse-drawn carriage outside. Billy Stokes had wanted to, but Jamal refused. Troy had never liked him for some reason. Of course, they'd asked Tez to be the fourth pall bearer, but he'd pleaded organisational duties as an excuse. So the Co-op guy did it.

Indeed, apart from Lilly, Jamal was the only blood family representative at his brother's funeral. Somewhere in the world they had a father, who had stayed away on this day as he had on most days. Like their mother, Jamal and Troy had only seen their father on a few occasions. Jamal had a very vague recollection of a tall, dark-skinned (darker than his own or his mother's) man called Clive, in a grey suit. He spoke with a different accent, Jamal remembered, and was always agitated and in a rush. The sight of his father, resigned and stationary in the dock of Chester Crown Court, all those years ago, had been memorably strange because it was so unlike Clive to be still. Clive's Rolex watch, slung elegantly beneath the bump of his ulna bone, had caught the lights of the court buildings, and made five-year-old Jamal feel very proud.

Mum had dragged Jamal, his pushchair – which he'd outgrown but which was necessary on long trips – and Troy along to the trial. Clive's defence team had wanted to create a mitigating family backdrop to the doomed accused. Despite the charade, which had entailed several very early morning treks by public transport for them, Dad had gone down for supplying class A, attempted murder, GBH and ABH, anyway. Moreover, his well-documented previous form had not helped his corner.

Residual memories of Moss Side gangster Clive included visiting Risley Jail with Mum and Troy. Clive had looked like an unfamiliar plumber in his prison uniform. A meticulous frisking by female prison guards established that Mum and offspring had brought no dope with them – whereupon it became clear that Mum and this dead-eyed bloke across the table had nothing to discuss.

Unlike himself and his brother, with their extravagant black names and almost white mother, Jamal's dad was proper black. In the parentless years that would soon follow, Jamal would wish so much that his mates could have seen his dad at the time of his trial, before he got sent down – strong, Rolexed, good-looking, with all the allure of a different city, big money and connections.

The very concept of Clive filled him with a paradoxical blend of guilt and anger. Clive, the hard man of Moss Side, would have lost no time in avenging Troy. But the same Clive had abandoned them completely, and wasn't even present at his own son's funeral – not that Jamal had stooped to attempt contact, or knew where to begin to find his father. Jamal liked to think Clive was dead. It was easier, just as it was easier to never think of his mother at all.

Now Macca's red hat was bobbing, like a poppy on an oil slick, as Troy Bannigan's coffin pushed through the sea of mourners outside the church and was placed in the horse-drawn hearse. The people patted and hugged Jamal, offering condolences and eulogistic observations about Troy, whom violent death had transformed into a hero of Homeric proportions. One young lad in the crowd, his hoody pulled low over his face, clung to Jamal like a baby monkey for almost a minute, then pressed a card into his hand and melted into the crowd. Emotion was running high in everyone except the quiet and peripheral police presence, it seemed. Even Tez had been tearful.

The slow procession to Anfield began. Staring out at the silent wall of onlookers flanking the streets, Jamal sat with Lilly and Macca in the cream leather comfort of the car, behind the second horse-drawn hearse carrying the floral tributes.

Turning on to Boundary Lane, the whole of the estate came into view. Jamal noticed a slight, dark-robed female the distance. She was walking along the Wasteland under the flyover in the direction of the Shopping Parade, trailed by two little kids. Her progress was intermittent; for every so often she stopped and reached out her hand to one of the subhuman forms huddled against the supporting pillars of the Tallis and Skylark walkways: these were addicts waiting for the Zone to reopen so they could score. When the black-robed figure stopped, her little kid followers stopped, too, maintaining the distance between them. She paused by a shed-like structure, beside one of the flyover pillars, the home of vagrant, orange-suited junkie, Guantanamo.

"Is that the Paki Witch?" said Jamal, pointing. He could see clearly in the distance a dark, veiled woman standing in front of the notorious madman, Guantanamo.

Lilly, limp with drink and desolation, was swigging from her vodka bottle and lamenting with Macca that she had not been able to have a smoke before getting into the car.

Macca turned to look out of the window, and gave a disinterested, "Can't see nothing lad. Haven't got me fuckin' specs," before reabsorbing himself into Lilly's nicotine niggles.

Jamal had never seen her in his life, but he felt sure it *was* the Paki Witch, and he found the sight of her oddly reassuring and significant. His eyes fell on the *jammy,* in big loopy writing, on the unopened card the clingy lad in the crowd had passed him just now. Sympathy cards had made a sorting office of his Nan's flat, and he was about to stuff this one into his pocket, when for no particular reason, he changed his mind, and opened it and read:

jammy
the packi wich will set you free like she done me all you
got 2 do is ask her
i no this. luv chloe
x-x-x RIP bannie luv of my life x-x-x

For the first time since the night of the murder, his tears fell.

Shriveton Shopping Parade

The Blind Man Miracle

Shriveton was eerily still as all attention centred on Troy's funeral. While the majority of local people were not in attendance, any disapproval of the gangland scene was prudently suppressed. Nobody was anxious to share Troy Bannigan's fate. It was presumed that he had betrayed his drug overlords in some way, and had paid the usual price. The local schools and shops had shut for the funeral. Even the nearby Zone had respectfully closed for a couple of hours. Shriveton was on hold, a captive audience, obediently paying homage to one of its fallen.

Shop workers and locals leaned against the perimeter wall of the shopping parade, smoking and not saying much as they looked down into the estate. Hordes of mourners, like a cluster of black ants, clustered around the hive of St Theresa's beyond the tower blocks, in the dell of the estate.

Unremarked by the onlookers, the Paki Witch now entered the freeze-frame of the shopping parade, trailed by a boy and a girl in scruffy, outdated LFC shirts. They were whispering urgently to each other, until the boy spoke:

"'Scuse me, but are you the Paki Witch?"

The woman stopped and, her back to them, waited. They approached and, facing her, the boy spoke again: "Are you the Paki Witch? We've been followin' you since Tallis."

"We told our grandad we was comin' 'ere to the Parade to watch the funeral," said the girl.

"But we come to find you.-"

"Yeah, we been followin' you all through the Wastie," said the girl, referring to the Wasteland beneath Skylark and Tallis Walkways. "Didn't you see us?"

"Shuddup, Maise," snapped the boy. He spoke in a business-like tone. "First of all we need to know if you are definitely the Paki Witch."

"Who do you say I am?" replied the woman, turning round tilting her head and smiling.

The girl, eyeing the Paki Witch with great curiosity, ventured, "Someone from the 'arry Potter films?"

"I think you *are* the Paki Witch," said the boy, interrupting. He was looking at her intensely, beseeching and a little fearful. "So we was wondering if you could cure our grandad."

"We got ten quid for you if you can," piped the girl, producing a note from her pocket.

"Now let me think about this," said the Paki Witch, wryly, sitting on the window ledge of the betting shop and indicating they join her there, which they did. From the other side of the square, some of the funeral spectators turned to look at them. One or two waved shyly at the Paki Witch, who smiled at them.

"Why do Pakis wear veils?" asked the girl, staring at the black folds of fabric, like luscious petals, that framed the Paki Witch's face. "You're like a princess," she exclaimed in wonder.

"Everyone wears a veil of some sort," replied the Paki Witch. "Except, perhaps, little children, like you. So, what are your names?"

"I'm Tom, and she's Maisie."

"Well, Tom and Maisie, tell me about your grandad."

"He's blind," said Tom. "Well, he's gone blind. Cat'racts. Hey, I thought you'd talk like a Paki."

"Yeah, you talk like us!" said his sister, still mesmerised by the kindly, dark-robed, brown-skinned stranger who struck her as considerably more exotic than anything in her (principally televisual) experience. "Do you live in a palace, and have servants and things?"

"Well, I'm just a visitor here," answered the Paki Witch, "so I don't have any of those things. Tell me about your grandad."

"He's gone blind," said Tom. "He tries to hide it from the social workers and the school."

"Yeah, but they know," added Maisie. "We dunno how they know he's blind, though, 'cos we never told them. And we're worried in case we have to go back into care. He won't see the doctor about his eyes, will 'e, Tom?"

"No. 'E's terrified of doctors and 'ospickles. Says they all twats 'cos they killed our Nan. She 'ad Alzheimer's and the 'ospickle left her in a corridor til she died."

"Our Mum can't look after us 'cos she's a smack-'ead," volunteered the girl, adding the rueful afterthought, "I didn't like being in foster care. And our dad's in the nick."

"'Cos the bizzies stitched 'im up!" Outrage, the kind that aggrieved elders and peers can easily stoke into a mind-warping conflagration, glimmered briefly in the boy's eyes.

In the distance below, Troy Bannigan's coffin passed like a lozenge through the crowds of mourners outside St Theresa's, and was loaded into the horse-drawn hearse, tiny as a toy. The mourners swarmed around as the slow procession to Anfield Crematorium began. People watching from the Shopping Parade perimeter wall started talking again, and some put out their cigarettes and walked back to work in the shops.

"Take me to your grandad, then, Tom and Maisie," said the Paki Witch, who was regarding with compassion the scene below as she spoke.

The girl gave a whoop of glee, and the boy tried to achieve manly control of his own delight by saying, "Do you want the tenner now or after?"

"Oh, I'm very rich already. You keep it. Let's go, Tom and Maisie."

Sensing that something interesting was afoot, and having nothing else to do in any case, some of the Parade spectators – two single mums with prams and an old man wheeling a Raleigh Shopper bike – who had overheard this exchange, followed. Along the way, several school kids, eager not to return to their lessons, joined the procession, as did a few black-clad mourners who could not be bothered making the trek to the Anfield Crematorium. Quite a procession soon gathered – mainly school-shy children, although subsequent mythological retellings would have it as a primarily adult crowd of many hundreds – led by the Paki Witch.

"I haven't even told 'er where me grandad lives," whispered Tom to Liu, an enquiring schoolmate who lived above the Chinese take-away on the Parade. "But she knows the way. I dunno 'ow, though, 'cos we never 'ad nothing to do with 'er before today."

"She's a witch, all right," breathed Liu. "I can't believe she's Chinese."

"She's not Chinese, bellend!"

"She is. She talks Mandarin. She cured me Nan's kidney stones – remember I told ya?"

"Oh yeah. But you never said she was Chinese."

"You never asked. But she is."

"Bellend."

"Does your grandad know she's coming?"

"Don't be soft."

As they followed, the crowd muttered and whispered to each other, and particularly to Tom and Maisie, about the Paki Witch. Everyone had got the idea that she was going to work some sort of major miracle. But none dared talk to her directly, notwithstanding the kindly smiles she gave them as, every so often, she glanced behind her.

Maisie and Tom's shabby house in Lawdens Lane was a few blocks from St Theresa's church and high school. The Paki Witch followed Tom and Maisie down the weedy pathway leading to the front door, leaving the cluster of curious observers peering from the threshold of Bob's peeling and rickety wooden fence.

Tom hammered on the door, and shouted *Grandad*! several times through the letterbox. A bumping and slow advance could be heard from within as Bob Reilly made his way to front door. At the same time, a stocky, middle-aged lady emerged from the parked car on the kerbside, and joined the crowd.

Hair unkempt and grey stubble sprouting from the age-loose skin on his face, Grandad started grumbling at Tom and Maisie. He reached for them in the space around him, and it was only when he could place his outstretched, grasping hands on their heads that he knew where they were. Everyone present could tell he was completely blind. He was entirely oblivious to the illustrious guest directly before him and the silent crowd just meters ahead.

A social worker had just called, he complained, and they

weren't helping the situation by coming home after the funeral instead of getting back to school.

"Grandad, we've bought someone to see you," cut in Tom. "She's 'ere now."

The old man became panicky. "Who is it?"

"Don't be afraid," said the Paki Witch. She touched his hand. The anticipatory drawing of breath from the crowd was audible, but *still* Bob did not register their presence.

"Are you from social services?" said Bob Reilly, still fearful, but somehow consoled by his visitor's touch and voice. "Tom, is it someone from the social?"

"No, Grandad," the boy answered. "It's the miracle woman. *The Paki Witch!*"

Bob winced. "Don't call her *Paki* for Christ's sake. I mean –"

"Let her in Grandad. She's gonna make you see again."

Bob Reilly stumbled back into the house, followed by the Paki Witch and the two children. Maisie neglected to shut the door, and the crowd saw him bump against the wall, shaking his head, and muttering tearfully to his visitor, with his head turned in the opposite direction to where she stood, on the threshold.

"Let me help you," said the Paki Witch.

Taking his hand again, she guided him into the front room where Radio Merseyside was murmuring in the greasy gloom. Some of the more brazen crowd members crept along the hallway, and stretched their necks over each other and into the small aperture of living-room door.

Back to the dirty, net-curtained window, the Paki Witch's small figure, swathed from head to toe in black, was visible to those watching from the fence outside. She stood before the old, blind man. Anxious hope and a sense of awe had rendered Tom and Maisie speechless, although there were some murmurs from the invaders by the living-room door as now the Paki Witch wet both thumbs with her own spittle.

"Who's 'ere?" Bob cried out, alarmed and cringing. "What's 'appening?"

Reaching up, the Paki Witch cupped his face in her small brown hands. Then, careful as a curator handling a priceless treasure, she drew her pink-padded thumbs across Bob Reilly's eyelids, and stood back.

He opened his eyes, and uttered a strange high-pitched cry of astonishment. He was facing the window.

"Can you see anything?" she asked.

"Only outlines, like moving sponges," he replied, as he looked around him.

She sucked her thumbs again and repeated the process, then stepped back.

He opened his eyes a second time and shrieked, "I can see! I can see plainly. Oh, God, I can see! Is this a dream?"

His whole person became impossibly animated and young as he took in everything around. Some of the people in the hallway scampered back to those still waiting outside, and in manic tones reported what they had just witnessed.

Maisie and Tom rushed up to embrace him. He took them in his arms and babbled incoherently with joy, as Maisie shouted, "No it's not a dream, Grandad. I told you the Paki Witch is real."

"I must see 'er."

He twisted away from them to find his healer, but she was not among the small crowd which had leaked from the hallway into the living room. So he pushed his way through the onlookers and ran into the hall, calling out for her – *Lady, lady, come back!* Running through the front door, he called out to the crowd assembled at his front gate, "Where did the woman go? I can see, I can see. Can you 'ear me? The Paki Witch has given me my sight!"

Like snails in rain, yet more neighbours protruded from doorways all around. Instantly, they were contaminated by his joy and came over to join the astonished crowd at his gate.

"The Paki Witch never come out the front," shouted Liu from his perch on social worker Mo's car bonnet. "She must be in the 'ouse."

She couldn't have gone out of the back, because there was no key to the backdoor, which had remained locked for well over a year now. So Bob and the kids began a thorough search of the whole house. To no avail. The Paki Witch had gone.

That afternoon, *Liverpool Star* cub reporter, Ethan Greenberg, arrived to find Bob Reilly engaged in a furious and purging clean-up of his house. Several kids, straight out of school, were circling on bikes in the road outside Bob's house, waiting to see if the Paki Witch would return. The remainder of the crowd had shifted from Lawdens Lane to the adjacent Shopping Parade. There was a buzz of elation in the air.

"She 'ealed me," proclaimed the old man. "The Paki Witch restored my sight! When I finish 'ere, I'm goin' up the Parade to tell everyone 'bout it."

"What does she look like?" enquired Ethan.

"I never 'ad a long look at 'er. She's Indian. Muslim clothes. You know, like their women dress. Black. Veils round the 'ead. That sort of thing. Never seen 'er face properly but 'er touch is like, like an angel. She cured me totally with 'er 'ands."

"Who do you think she is, this miracle worker?" asked the Ethan, a smile on his downy lips – the old man's joy was simply infectious.

Among other bric-a-brac, the frantic tidy-up had unearthed a blue-eyed, pale-skinned Sacred Heart statue which Bob Reilly now planted in prime position on the sill of his living room window. On the floor, in an organised mound of other rubbish, was a bolus of filthy net curtains.

"She's the One," he answered.

"But isn't that at odds with your beliefs?" ventured Ethan, wry eyes on the Caucasian Christ on the ledge. "I mean she's not Catholic, or even Christian?"

Bob Reilly shrugged and patted his statue, "Neither was 'e."

CHAPTER FIVE

Monday 22nd October 201-

Shriveton

The Wake

After Troy's remains had been scattered on the hallowed Anfield turf, the funeral party adjourned to St Theresa's club. A free bar and lavish spread awaited them, provided by Tez, whom everyone eulogised while taking their fill.

Spurred by these hymns of praise, Jamal decided to ask Tez for *a private word*. Despite being a very busy man, Tez had taken time out of his Zone Chief schedule to ensure that Troy's aftermath was, in his own words, *done proper*. It was time to ask once again for retribution, Jamal felt, and the opportunity presented itself when the Zone Chief separated from the mourners to go for a smoke outside in the litter-strewn club car park.

"Tez, can I 'ave a private word, like?" Jamal asked tentatively.

With a terse nod Tez acquiesced, and shooed Billy Stokes away. Eager for his genius to be recognised, Billy Stokes had been following Tez around like a lapdog ever since Troy had died. Gangland deaths always resulted in personnel shuffles, and Billy fancied his chances of a promotion.

"Tez, 'e gotta answer for our Troy," said Jamal, returning the departing Billy's hostile stare.

"Who's gotta answer?" Tez's hard, beady eyes fixed him.

Jamal's insides liquefied. His fist squeezed tightly around Chloe's card in the deep recess of his suit trouser pocket. Their faces were close as lovers, and suddenly Tez's scary reputation, rather than his liberality with funeral expenses, asserted itself in Jamal's imagination. Prematurely aged, pallid and hollow of cheek, Tez's every lineament seemed etched by corruption. Dark hair – greasy and thinning – hung over his shrewd, small eyes which had seen horrors Jamal could not even conceive. The mind behind those eyes was machete sharp, and driven by a titanium will which had never bowed or buckled in the years he'd been sergeant-major to his army of thugs and criminals. Obedient minions kept Tez and his wife Jewel safe in their Matherfield Park home, as they all made their Incubo general a fortune.

"Gaz," said Jamal, hoping his nervousness wasn't transmitting.

Beside Tez, he was a portrait of unspoiled male youth. A still-persisting innocence was air brushing to perfection his amiable full mouth, big brown eyes, frothy micro curls, and smooth, freckly brown skin.

Tez made himself step away. Leaning against the wall of the social club, his gaze switched to the Parade and Wasteland walkway in the near-distance. An unfocused glaze overtook his expression as his attention was devoured by a vortex of inner turmoil.

"Tomorrow takes care of itself, Jammy."

"He needs takin' out, Tez."

"Inky makes the laws 'ere, Jammy. Remember that. Don't never make no laws yourself."

"But our Troy needs answerin' for."

"And you're not the one to do it."

"I know I'm a bit new on the block, like. But who'll do it if I don't, Tez? I mean, I was thinkin' –"

"Leave it, Jammy. You not cut out for Zone life, kid."

"But I gotta –"

"Stay clean, Jammy."

"Yeah, but –"

"Stay out. It's better on the outside. You come inside," Tez's face buckled around his cigarette as he inhaled, and his eyes remained resolutely fixed on the Parade and flyover, "and you'll never get out again. And then all them simple things are outta reach forever."

The heaviest sadness weighed Tez now, and a huge, smoky sigh issued from the bottom of his being.

But Jamal was too caught up in himself to spot and learn from what was being said: "Tez, you been so great 'bout the funeral and stuff, but I was just –"

Tez cut through him, eyes still staring ahead, talking to himself more than Jamal: "People on the outside are kings, Jammy. You see a fella and his mate tryin' to fix a car, workin' together 'cos it'll mean not goin' the garage... Or having a pre-match bevy down the boozer... Or 'ikin' in the 'ills on an 'ot day, and findin' a lake and just jumpin' in. All them fellas are free as kings.

"But when you one of Inky's slaves, kid, all them simple things are like," – he shook his head –"I dunno, like afternoon tea in fuckin' Claridge's for one of them bag-heads shootin' up by the Wasteland pillars over there.

"Once you come into Incubo Land, all the good things are outta reach, kid. Forever."

"I know, but our Tr–"

Jamal started violently as Tez, with an unexpected surge of energy, stepped forward and hugged him. It was a harsh, violent embrace, which lasted just a few seconds before Tez pulled away. Embarrassed, Tez threw himself back against the wall again, staring at the floor where his smoking cigarette had fallen, and said, "Listen to me, Jammy. All them dreams you can live now. *All* them things!"

There was a wobble of passion and pleading in his voice, although he spoke quietly. His face was weirdly twisted as if he were mastering supreme emotion.

"The best favour I can do you, kid, is to tell you this: you *are* one of the kings. Go to college. Or get a fuckin' straight job. You done good in school. Don't never come in with the Incubo. Tomorrow will take care of itself, Jammy."

Billy returned, his dull mind comprehending the obvious disturbance in Tez as he nervously communicated, "Better come in, Chief. Fuckin' story 'bout the Paki fuckin' Witch startin' up in 'ere."

Tez walked back into the club. Instantly, his demeanour had reverted to the cold purposefulness of gangland overlord. Jamal followed him inside, and rejoined his Nan and Macca at their table.

He couldn't grasp the significance at all of Tez's words to him in the car park. Indeed within moments of sitting down he felt angry and disappointed. Tez had given him nothing. He was still at the starting line, and until the gun went off in the temple of Gaz Skelton, he would stay there while the universe laughed at his cowardice.

Word was going around St Theresa's Club about a supposed miracle wrought by the Paki Witch a few hours earlier. Apparently she'd restored the sight of Bobby Reilly, an old man from Lawdens Lane behind the Parade. It had pulled quite a crowd, so people were saying, and the press had called to report on the newly-sighted man.

Tez was markedly uncomfortable: the Paki Witch story had gathered viral momentum and nobody in the St Theresa's club seemed to be talking of anything else. Indeed, had it not been for the free hospitality, most of those present would have left to investigate for themselves. Tez engaged in furious texting and a furtive phone call before exiting peremptorily with Billy. The additional grand he put behind the bar on his way out prompted more hymns of praise, sung by delighted guests who (as was the case all days) had nowhere else to go, and nothing else to do except consume the crumbs from the Incubo table.

Claridges, Mayfair

Sting

Room service, for room three two four! and a brisk knock disturbed them.

Wilkins sat bolt upright in the gloom and reached to his briefcase beside the bed. His hand on the cool metal of his Type 64 inside, he responded in an even tone, "We haven't ordered room service."

The sugary light spilling from the half-closed en-suite door powdered Kachya's slender, partially clothed body as she scrambled for her clothes.

"Room service, sir!" came the same insistent, Asian-sounding voice from the hotel corridor.

"Don't let them know I am here. I lose my job!" Kachya bundled herself into the bathroom, accidentally dragging the bed sheet, like a wedding train, as she went.

Suddenly, the lock apparatus clicked, releasing the door. With a fumbling prestidigitation, Wilkins concealed the transfer of gun from briefcase to his dressing-gown pocket, and sprang from the hotel bed just as a young Asian man, wearing hotel uniform and carrying a clipboard, entered. An identically-attired plump Caucasian colleague hung back in the corridor, slumped against the wall. His fat hand was on a trolley, swathed in a white cloth, on which sat oysters and champagne. With his free hand, he was texting on his phone.

Wilkins felt his bowels liquefy as his eyes fell on the trolley. It felt like a set-up, and he half-expected a fire-armed assassin to spring from the sheathed trolley bearing those goodies, Al Capone-style. He glanced back to the crumpled bed for his own phone, but couldn't see it. There hadn't been time to notify his men outside. But at least he had the gun. Self-reproach almost equalled his fear – how could he have allowed himself to get into this? It was complacency and champagne-fuelled folly. He'd had men in his service killed for far less.

"This is outrageous," growled Wilkins, squaring up to his intruder.

"I am so very sorry to disturb you, sir," said the Indian attendant, looking very pained by the duty he was performing. He tapped his clipboard. "Most unfortunately, there has been a problem with your credit card in the restaurant."

"I paid cash, you dick'ead. Cash!" he retorted, so furious and afraid that he was forgetting to stay in character. His native Merseyside accent was seeping in.

"That's not the information I have been, erm, receiving, sir," said the attendant. He folded back some papers on his clipboard very carefully. "The account record here has credit card decline on it. If you care to look at my paperwork, sir"

"Listen, I couldn't give a toss about your records. I paid cash in the restaurant."

"Well this is very hard to explain, sir. It really is. I know this is very embarrassing. For me especially, I can assure you so very much, sir."

"Look, there has been a mistake. And I haven't ordered room service." With a forward step, so that they were almost toe to toe, Wilkins attempted to usher him out.

"If you could just give me your name, sir, that would be so very helpful." The Indian remained rooted to the spot. "I am offering so very many apologies for this difficulty, which will be most swiftly resolved with your cooperation, sir."

"Dalglish."

"Ah. Dalglish. How are you spelling that?"

Exasperated, Wilkins spelled the name for his inquisitor, who squinted at various sheets of paper, elaborately checking and rechecking by flicking through the documents in his arms. Every so often he tutted and clicked, shaking his head, and mumbled, "Oh, dear me, sir, oh dear me! It is all so very confusing, sir."

His plump colleague in the corridor, an uncouth and

uninterested fellow with a moustache, shuffled and chuckled at some aspect of the text conversation he had been engaging in. The chuckle transmogrified into an explosive and moist cough all over the fine fare on the trolley beside him.

"I am so sorry about this, Mr Dalglish," said the Indian, looking genuinely distressed as he finally stopped shuffling through the papers on his clipboard. "I am realising that I have made a mistake. A most terrible error."

"I know you have!"

"Indeed, the declined card belongs to another customer in another room, who has ordered this." He indicated the trolley with a wave, which prompted a watery smile from his colleague. "I am so very hugely apologetic for this."

"Look, just go," said Wilkins.

"I will be going, Mr Dalglish. Please accept my most profound apologies."

"I accept them. Now goodbye."

"If I could just explain how this very confusing situation has been arising, Mr Dalglish."

"I'm not interested. Go now." Wilkins' every fight and flight instinct was firing, but there were too many variables, not least of which was the obscuring white cloth on the trolley, for him to risk aggressive escape.

The Asian hotel attendant was still wittering, "Please let me make amends for this gross inconvenience, Mr Dalglish. How about some compensation for you, Mr Dalglish, in the form of this most exquisite champagne and six fresh oysters?"

As the plump fellow in the corridor gave another spluttering cough over these very items, there was a bustle from behind as Kachya, terrified and fully clothed except for her shoes in her hand, suddenly shot from the bathroom, and flew past them and disappeared around the next corridor corner.

The Asian man gave a knowing and discreet smile and withdrew in a stream of ungrammatical apologetics. Undisguised mirth rippled the retreating, bulky frame of his Caucasian colleague who followed, wheeling the trolley. Wilkins slammed the door, threw on the light, and ran to his stuff. It must have fallen on to the floor as Kachya accidentally dragged the sheet when she escaped to the bathroom. Everything was there – wallet, phone (the cover was slightly askew as a result on falling on to the tiled floor), and briefcase with a change of clothes. The Ukrainian tart, whom he had *not* managed to screw, hadn't even thought to grab some notes from his wallet on her way out.

He had only himself to blame for this farce, which could have been so much worse. He had taken a chance; been lazy in thinking he could round things off with the waitress. In doing so he had utterly exposed himself.

It was time to get out of London and go home.

Another encoded text – indicating that all was well, and the Shriveton Zone up and running again after the respectful closure for the funeral – came through from Tez.

It was particularly important that Shriveton regain stability. It was a crucial distribution point in itself, and would play a key role in the additional trade secured today with Chowdhury. The extra funds funnelling through the newly-established trading artery between the Golden Crescent and Bangladesh would prop up the Incubo's legitimate businesses, which had been almost decimated by the US sub-prime debacle.

SHRIVETON MAN CLAIMS MIRACLE RESTORED HIS SIGHT

Exclusive by Ethan Greenberg

Police and community leaders in the Shriveton area of the city remained on alert throughout the day following a resident's claim that he had been miraculously cured of blindness by a local woman.

This supposed miracle took place in the front room of Bob Reilly's (68) council home in Lawdens Lane, a few streets away from St Theresa's Church, where the funeral service was taking place of Troy Bannigan (18), the Shriveton man shot in an alleged dispute between rival gangs. Schools and shops in the area remained closed for the morning.

The identity and location of the miracle worker remains uncertain, although she is believed to be a young Muslim woman from Shriveton's Skylark Towers. Some believe that she is responsible for a number of similar miracles in the Shriveton area.

A 48-year-old Knowsley Council worker, who did not wish to be identified, witnessed the alleged healing. She claims that she visited Reilly that morning and found him to be totally blind.

"I saw the healing with my own eyes," she said.

"The woman came into Bob Reilly's house and touched his eyes once, then twice with her thumbs. And he could see again

perfectly."

A small crowd gathered at the Shriveton Shopping Parade this afternoon, including Bob Reilly, who was talking openly about his experience, repeatedly describing his healer as The One. Several individuals present, who refused to be identified, expressed their hope to the Star that the young miracle worker can redeem the estate, which many residents believe is run by drug barons. Some of those in today's crowd were calling her the Shriveton Messiah.

"We operate a zero tolerance of drugs in this area," said Superintendent Simon Meyers of Merseyside Police, whose officers dispersed the crowd peaceably later in the afternoon.

Shriveton

Slum Platinum

Jamal left the St Theresa's club when, at around teatime, his Nan began demanding weepily of the priest, who was trying to leave for his next service, *Why didn't God save my two picaninnies?* At the same time, Macca's spliff in the gents was arousing consternation among church-goers who'd dropped in on their way to evening Mass to pay their respects to the dead youth.

The walk home through Shriveton confirmed for Jamal that the place, which for a couple of hours had enjoyed a magical solidarity in the face of gangland sorrow, had returned to business as usual. Tez must have somehow restored normality in the wake of the blind-man miracle, because there were no gossiping huddles on street corners, as was the case when anything major happened such as a shooting or an arrest-generating/public-appeasement police swoop. The Parade was open and boy foot soldiers on bikes were policing the perimeter of the Zone. For a terrible moment Jamal envied the satiated addicts slumped against Wasteland pillars. Unlike the other passengers on life's seas, sunk by leaden resentments and regrets, or surfing on some crazy tidal wave of anticipation, the addicts floated on the surface, in a dream of Now provided by the Incubo to whom they had handed everything over.

Jamal wished he could hand over the task of avenging his brother. Tez's refusal to get involved still smarted faintly, but Jamal was only too aware that his own spirit and instinct remained numb and unresponsive, like leper-limbs. He must do something, even if it amounted to no more than having another look at Troy's phone. It felt like the answers lay there. For example, Jamal thought he could glean a fence contact, and a Lidocaine supplier called Oz. Everything else in there was an incomprehensible mishmash of calculations and inscrutable text shorthand. Jamal had never doubted that Troy had been researching how to set himself up in the bash trade. Nor had he doubted that, as was typical for Troy, these plans had never become reality.

Perhaps, Jamal's reasoning went now, if he could resurrect some of Troy's contacts, he could make enough money to get a gun, or an assassin, to sort out Gaz. If he could borrow from one of the local loan sharks, and get even a half kee of cocaine, maybe, and one of Lido, he could make enough to sort everything out. He'd follow in Troy's footsteps, but only for, say, a month. And then he would get out.

He'd already planned his exit. He'd go abroad somewhere, start again.

Only a month ago, Jamal Bannigan, the only boy in St Theresa's in years to pass all exams when he was sixteen, had been on a completely different path. Now it felt like the closest he would get to university was scoring a kee of Lidocaine from Oz, the crooked campus technician – if he was lucky. Otherwise he'd probably become an Incubo foot soldier, and hope that one day, under the umbrella of Incubo protection, he summoned the balls to kill Gaz.

Everything had been up in the air ever since the shooting. His Nan hadn't stopped drinking. The police and social services had been in and out of their tiny Tallis flat. Tez and the priest had been frequent visitors, and gangster pals, girlfriends of Troy and old school friends, and even teachers, had called round. A confetti of sympathy cards covered every surface.

He'd kept reading Chloe's card at the Crematorium and wake, and then plunging it deep enough in his pocket to guarantee it would not fall out. It was important to think pragmatically – of revenge! – if he was ever going to activate those leper-limbs of spirit and instinct, but somehow he kept coming back to her card.

He was reading it as he returned from the parish club wake and stepped into his Tallis Tower home which stank because they'd run out of Dettol. At some point during her post-shooting alcoholic bender, Lilly had pissed the sofa. Jamal had learned over the years that Dettol was the only thing that got rid of the smell of puke or piss. Flash, bleach and the rest didn't cut it. Only Dettol.

The flat being uniquely empty, he began an earnest search for Dettol, starting in the bathroom. If there was none to be had, he resolved to go and buy some on the Parade. Once he'd cleaned up the flat, he might take another look at Troy's phone.

Crouching down to peer into the rickety cupboard under the wash basin where cleaning fluids lived, he lost his balance, and fell bodily into the bath panel. Brittle clattering reverberated around the silent, tiled space. The panel sprang forward to reveal, below the fibrous bath belly, a pale caramel, fresh chip in one of the age-darkened floor boards. It was only because he'd fallen in so strange a position, lateral to the outside wall, that he'd noticed it at all.

In that moment, he just knew. Gripped by an urgent hope, he swung on to his hands and knees, knocking his head against the bath rim in his haste. He coaxed his big finger tips into the groove, and carefully levered up the wall-edge floor board. Then, stretching his whole upper body to reach far along the outside wall, his fingers crept through the labyrinth of under floor piping, to the furthest corner of the room.

It was so obvious. He could hardly believe he'd not thought of it before: Troy's hiding place for the smoking gun he minded briefly for someone a few years ago, just before he started work at the Zone. Jamal had known about the smoking gun at the time, but never found it. Troy had boasted the hiding place was almost impossible to access, even if you knew where to look.

But now the warm flesh of Jamal's foraging palm was met by the cool, cling-wrapped curves of two cuboids: ingots of slum platinum his brother had banked for him in the cramped, smelly, untidy vault they called home. He could almost hear Troy announce, laughing, *Mad, innit?*

Also present was all the hardware required to get those two slabs of narcotics up from the floor boards and into the blood supply of whoever wanted to buy it: scales, plastic sachets, blades, spoons and a roll of white labels embossed with the Incubo *I*.

A near-delirious excitement gripped Jamal at the thought that both bags were Incubo cocaine. But although a taste test conducted while he was still prostrate on the bathroom floor confirmed that the powder in each packet numbed the tongue, only one of the packets bore the Incubo embossed italicised *I* on its white label. The other must be the Lidocaine Troy had mentioned, and which was referenced as Lido Oz on his phone, with a number and hotmail address. The previously incomprehensible notepad jottings on Troy's phone, which he'd glanced at only vaguely, now fell into place: they related to the acquisition of all the equipment required for a bash factory. Troy hadn't been planning it; he'd already set up.

Something akin to a prayer of gratitude formed in Jamal's mind. At the time, the knowing disgust of the police at the state of his Tallis Tower home had stung very much, but now he rejoiced in it. It was he – and not the bizzies during one of their for-the-sake-of-appearances visits immediately after Troy's murder – who had found Troy's stash.

The fact was, nobody, including the bizzies, wanted painstaking investigations in Incubo Land, where the law of the streets prevailed. Every potential witness, including Jamal (taking Tez's sage advice, *Don't tell the beaks nothing at all, kid*) had been mute. They were right – and this haul under the bath proved it.

Jamal sprang into action. He unscrewed the bathroom mirror and lay it flat on the top of his chest of drawers in his bedroom. Angling a chair under the handle of the door to prevent intrusion, he began cutting half of the cocaine with two thirds Lidocaine. The arithmetic streamed in his mind like Rosary prayers: he would resist the temptation to bag it all. Keeping half a kee aside meant that if he could get another kee of Lido from the Oz source, he was looking at an additional take home of £20k minimum for himself. If he couldn't get Lido he'd take a chance with some other reagent. Something would turn up. His luck was changing.

As he worked, he became so immersed in the process that he forgot about everything – the stench in the living room, the need to strike down Troy's assassins, or his own future. The cutting and bagging up became an end in itself. It came naturally to him – although he had never even seen it done before – as if drugs had always been, after all, his destiny. This was the easy part, he knew. Selling it would be harder, but he'd find a buyer soon enough because, sold as Incubo cocaine, these 1500 one-gram wraps would have a potential street value of £60k and could be distributed in less than two hours.

And so it was that Jamal Bannigan set up a cocaine-cutting business in his Nan's Tallis Tower flat, with a potential million pound per annum turnover. There was a brief wobble at approximately bag 900, when it occurred to him to wonder how it was that Troy had acquired a kilo of cocaine while scraping by on Incubo foot soldier wages. Perhaps he still owed money for it, and that was why he had been killed? However, this neurosis was soon allayed: nobody had ever come around searching for any gear. Troy had no doubt stolen the cocaine, and got away with it. He'd mentioned a Seaforth consignment on the night of his murder.

All was well.

CHAPTER SIX

Monday 22nd October 201-

4pm Shriveton

The Robber and the Open Door

The door to the Skylark flat had been ajar, and, there being nobody else around, the robber went in, propelled by the abject desperation of his circumstances as much as the criminality endemic to his nature. An iPod, a kettle even – or just some food – would be enough. Not that he had any expectations of a Skylark flat. Everyone in Shriveton was poor. But he'd nothing left, and *that* door was open.

So in he came, thinking not much, except that tonight he'd sleep rough, unless by some miracle the Sally Army gave him a bed. Only the Sally Army gave him the time of day. His prison-tattooed knuckles and battered features marked him out to the world, and himself, as no good. He'd been born to and raised by robbers. There was no changing now.

In the first few hours of freedom from his last stretch, having nowhere to stay and nobody to see hadn't mattered. Like any man straight out of the nick, all he'd wanted was sex. He'd got that from some blonde teenaged bag-head in the Shrivie woods. Without paying, of course. (Well, he was a thief, wasn't he?)

Two months on from prison's certainty and release-day's stolen orgasm with the prostitute, the winter was starting to bite his rough-living, old-lag bones.

This Skylark flat was empty, and the big, early-evening sky, showing through its curtainless windows, stole his eyes, like a barmaid's tits blooming over the counter. There was no furniture, just a mat with some sort of compass on it. (Must be one of those play mats kids have for their toy cars.) And a little wooden shelf, which was for some reason on the floor. There was a book on it. He couldn't read – never had been able to, it wasn't as if he'd gone rusty or anything. But it didn't look like the alphabet they'd tried to teach him during his prison stretches. (Must be a foreign language.)

His hopes were falling as he went into the kitchen. He went through every cupboard, every drawer. Nothing. Not even a knife and fork.

"Fuckin' trust my luck," he cursed, and was turning to leave when a high voice sounded.

"What? You're going empty-handed?"

He froze where he stood, in the entrance to the kitchen, and beheld a small woman, dressed entirely in black, sitting cross-legged on the play mat in the front room.

Normally, when interrupted during an intrusion, he would run, or fight and then run (having emptied their pockets as they lay bleeding on the floor). But now he was incapable of movement, for he was riveted by her hijab-framed face.

"You're going away empty-handed?" she repeated, and smiled at him.

She – she must be the Paki Witch people here often talked about. He'd never seen or thought about this Paki Witch. Until now, when she was before him, in the flesh.

"Well, there's nothin' in 'ere except you, love," he stammered after a very long silence.

"And?" she stood up. Her figure was fairy-like, and her manner fey. She was smoothing down her black robe which clung to her small waist and alluringly full hips.

"Well, like I said, there's nothin' 'ere."

He could hardly believe that he was standing still, engaging with her. But his whole being was fixed by her.

"There's nothing here except me?" She smiled at him again, and his stomach flipped. Tears formed in his eyes.

"Yeah."

"Well, you can't go away empty-handed. After all, you *are* a robber. It's against your code of practice. You must take what's here."

"But, I – I'm terrible dirty," he declared, pathetic, ashamed.

With light footsteps, she dodged past him and into the kitchen, where she ran the tap, saying, as she left him alone there, "Wash here. Then you'll be able to take what you came for."

Embarrassed, he washed his hands and his face, splashing innumerable palmfuls of cleansing water over his eyes, which couldn't stop crying. She'd left a towel on the draining board for him.

After a long time, he returned to the living-room, still clutching the towel. She was sitting on the mat again.

He knelt before her and pushed the towel towards her on the floor. Then, after much reflection, he confessed:

"I am a wicked man. I've stole things because I wanted them. I've stole things because I needed them. And I've stole things that I didn't want or need, just because I *could* steal them. And now I'm sorry for all the bad I done."

She nodded and said, "You know, repentance is a gift."

"A gift?"

"A gift. And in making the gift, the giver has already taken you closer to heart than this." Her perfect brown finger traced the undulations of his tattooed knuckles.

He snatched his hand away – more for her sake, than his own, for he did not wish to sully her with his nature. Holding the hand she had touched fast to his face, he spluttered through an ocean of regret, "I never done a good thing in my life, though. How did I deserve to be – to be with *you*?"

"The door was always open, my friend. At last you came through it."

She stood up, then, and so did he.

"See?" she said, holding the door open for him. "You do not leave empty-handed. You take me with you."

"In my heart," he blubbered through his waterfall of tears.

With his tattooed knuckles, he struck his chest. And, with an awkward, lop-sided bow, he left, a changed man.

7pm Marporley Hall, Cheshire.

Paul Wilkins had changed outfits, phones, cabs and cars several times to eliminate any chance of being followed during the homeward journey. An internal flight to Manchester returned him by 7pm to his Cheshire residence, in time for supper. By the time he stepped on to the gravel driveway of Marporley Hall, he was multi-millionaire property developer, hotelier (owner of the Bowes-West group of hotels in major cities, including London, Chicago, Amsterdam, Istanbul and Mexico City) and philanthropist, Callum Bowes-West.

Although Marporley was set in a small plot – previous cash-strapped owners had sold off all but two acres of the rolling Cheshire Plain land – it retained its landed-gentry grandeur. Oil paintings, parquet, taxidermy, knightly weaponry, stained glass and brass, plus a sweeping, Wilton-plush staircase which dominated the entrance hall, set the tone for the rest of the twelve-bedroomed country seat. He'd picked it up for a song during the 1990s recession.

"Leader of the Health Authority and his party are due for dinner in less than an hour, sir," announced his housekeeper, Mrs Ingham, who was flustered and a little reproving as she took his coat and bags. "Had we forgotten? Cook's prepared gin and oysters especially!"

"No, Mrs Ingham, of course I had not forgotten!"

He was so tired that even climbing the plum and gold carpeted stairs was wearisome. On days like this, the dead weight of his bondage to evil was almost unbearable. It was only by forcing himself to think of the considerable pay-offs of his existence that it was possible to keep going. The greatest of these pay-offs was being esteemed member of the British establishment, Callum Bowes-West.

"You look worn out, sir," bustled Mrs Ingham, with frowning concern. She regarded her employer as some sort of saint, and pandered to his every need, down to warming his socks with the iron in the morning for his precious feet. "You need to think of yourself for a change."

"One must fight the good fight," he mumbled. "I'm off for a bath. Make sure the gin is chilled for our guests, dear Mrs Ingham!"

Late 1980s London

Identity Switch

Callum Bowes-West was born, aged twenty four, in 1991. Before that he had been Jude Atkinson.

Several post-qualification years of bricklaying, burger-building and radio commercial voiceover jobs (which sometimes only paid if he pursued them litigiously through Equity), had caused Merseyside-born, RADA trained and aspiring actor Jude Atkinson to change direction. Meagre finances and no lucky breaks meant that Jude had spent the late Eighties *not* rubbing against the padded shoulders of his yuppie contemporaries who were making fortunes in the City of London, where he lived. This annoyed Jude, who knew he was destined for greatness, even if the casting agents didn't see it.

A ruthless self-assessment yielded two singular assets. The first was his superlative intelligence, functions of which were articulacy and adaptability. The second was his conspicuous ability as an actor: he could mimic to perfection, and portray character and mood with convincing and unerring subtlety.

Like many of his RADA peers who did *not* happen to be blood-related to a mainstay of the industry, Jude did various low-skilled jobs, his last one being clerical temping work for Asian Foods and Spices (AFS), an import company on Edgware Road, London. It was here, in 1990, that the perfect way to deploy his two singular assets (intelligence and acting prowess) occurred to him. It was here also that he met fellow temp and artiste Callum West.

Rochdale lad Callum West was trying and failing to make it as a singer in the metropolis. Callum had nothing but music – no parents, no family, just a squat in Bow where he lived alone. A spurious dream, fuelled by the emptiness of his childhood years, had driven him far away from his Lancashire roots.

Similar in origin, age, build and artistic bent, both Callum and Jude were also quiet, unassuming and unmemorable physically. Consequently, neither made a strong enough impression individually to really embed their respective identities in the minds of those around them, most of whom were also temp staff. They were referred to as the *Blood Brothers* – the North-of-England Willy Russell show was huge in the West End at the time – or *twinnies* in the office, and were generally confused with each other.

However, the similarities were surface only. Ever watchful and opportunistic – unlike Callum West, who was becoming rather fond of cocaine and the new drug, Ecstasy, breaking into the scene – it was obvious to Jude that some of the business going on in AFS, and indeed in neighbouring businesses in the same office block, was not legitimate. Moreover, he observed that Callum and all the other AFS workers were so preoccupied with their own microcosmic concerns that they were completely oblivious to the criminal trading activity operating subliminally in their midst.

Ubo Inc. was conceived when Jude Atkinson realised that whole subsections of AFS's nominal ledger were, in fact, an elaborate accounting front for the narcotics trade. While AFS accounts personnel worried about hairstyles, bitchy friends or cheating guys, they would be administrating front companies for narcotics import and export.

Jude realised he could make a fortune based on his premise that the self-absorption of the average person is tantamount to a moral slumber, into which iniquity may easily steal and sow its seed. He reasoned that violence and poverty, those favoured bedfellows of the narcotics industry, ravage whole continents because most people are asleep most of the time.

The important thing was to keep them asleep. He resolved to spend his life doing just that. Working carefully and hard, it was not long before Jude had inveigled himself into the consortium of drug smugglers operating in tandem with, and out of, AFS legitimate enterprises. This same consortium had established links with the Golden Crescent of Iran, Afghanistan and Pakistan.

A little bribery and manipulation of the drug traders and their contacts paid huge dividends for Jude. Soon, very small consignments of his own were being transported along with those of the Edgware Road consortium. His confidence and knowledge of the business grew enough for him to branch out on his own.

His company, Ubo Inc., existed on letterhead only, and would last for little more than a year, by which time the Incubo was well and truly spawned. A supporting array of various temporary identities was created to manage the monies and liaise with the suppliers and transport personnel. In no time, a two kilogram consignment of heroin found its way to Southampton from Pakistan, via Turkey, in a consignment of floor tiles for Ubo Inc.

By the autumn of 1990, the Incubo's enterprise was well and truly born. Unsuspecting container ships in sleepy, chaotic regions could be impregnated with a cuckoo cargo of drugs or arms. They were sailing anyway. An extra kilo or two on their load would be undetected. It was a simple idea, and not, of course, in any way original. But it was amassing Jude Atkinson a fortune similar to the Hollywood stars. And he liked it.

Perhaps his cleverest idea during this period was to establish a stable, legitimate persona which would enable him to enjoy his wealth properly in the decades that followed. Stepping into someone else's shoes was the ideal way of achieving this. Obviously, the owner of those shoes would need to disappear. The trouble with missing persons is that they may return. The same cannot be said of dead people.

Jude's increasing prosperity meant that he could supply drugs to Callum, whom he had been very carefully befriending. As solitary, northern-born, struggling artists, they had so much in common.

"Hey, we really are blood brothers we are, aren't we?" said Callum, on the first evening Jude ever visited him in his Bow squat. It was September 1990, and Jude had just given him a few hundred quid to help him out of a hole with a Brixton coke dealer.

"You're the posh one our mother gave away," added Callum, who had auditioned unsuccessfully for *Blood Brothers* in the West End when he'd first come down to London.

Merseyside born Jude – always so generous and solicitous when they worked alongside each other in the office – did indeed behave like a loving brother. This was all the more commendable given that Jude had recently lost his temping job with AFS. The firm had given up on him, after a string of sick notes excusing him on the basis of acute depression about his own artistic failure.

"Wish our mother had given me away!" replied Jude, assailed briefly by an unwelcome recollection of his mother, whom booze had rendered eternally pathetic and inadequate.

"At least you have one," replied Callum. "I never."

Smiling carefully, Jude made his singular announcement. "Hey, Pete Waterman told me he's holding some auditions at the Brixton Academy in a couple of months. They want a new Rick Astley."

"What, you know Pete Waterman?" Callum looked as if he were about to collapse with grateful incredulity.

"Yeah, I know Pete."

"My God, that's... that's amazing."

"I can mention you to him when I see him next."

"Could you?"

"Yeah, will do. You know, I can get some really pure coke and other shit for you for nothing, Cal. Save you bothering with these Brixton cunts, mate."

He dug into his pocket and produced a little wrap of knock-out cocaine (so pure you could be chewing coca in a Columbian field!). He went on, "Some guys who run security in Stringfellows and all those clubs owe me big time. Try a bit of this Charlie, mate."

Callum was wide eyed with wonder – *how* had he managed to find such a great friend? How lucky was he?

Within a few months of this visit, Callum was sacked from his job and succumbed to heroin, which Jude provided him for nothing. Jude, whose magical Pete Waterman contact was waiting just over the horizon to welcome Callum to fame and fortune, kept up the hope and trust in his *twinnie* by being his only and unlimited heroin supplier.

Thanks to an identity switch, the outside world would see *Callum* and *not* Jude come good in the end. It was true that Callum's music career never took off, but he nonetheless got himself up and running again, and would go on to become a multi-millionaire hotelier, property developer and philanthropist. Of course, he didn't keep in touch with any of his peers on the AFS team, but they occasionally caught news of his charitable activities on TV and in the press.

It was the actor waiting in the wings, Jude Atkinson, whose fortunes suddenly declined. Apparently, he'd got into heroin after losing his job at the office, whereupon he disappeared. He died three months later, in early 1991, a miserable and lonely death in a squat in Bow, which he managed to burn down, along with himself.

Aged twenty four, Callum West had killed himself and someone else in the same moment. The new identity was going places and would require a double-barrelled surname. Since he'd simultaneously died and been born in the Bow flat of his too-trusting *twinnie*, he opted for *Callum Bowes-West*.

22nd October 201-

Marporley Hall, Cheshire.

How far he had come since being born, aged twenty-four, in 1991! Bathed, coiffed and immaculately dressed for dinner, multi-millionaire property developer, hotelier and philanthropist Mr Callum Bowes-West trotted down the Wilton carpeted staircase to greet tonight's dignitaries of the North West of England public and private sector. Another huge line of cocaine had numbed his nasal passages and tonsils. Delicious. And utterly necessary – he was exhausted.

On the table, along with the oysters, Veuve Cliquot and prime Happy Beef Cheshire Roast, was the matter of the substantial Bowes-West donation to the Liverpool Central Infirmary rebuild project. Modest, forward-thinking, and the embodiment of community spirit, Mr Bowes-West deflected the universal gratitude for his gargantuan contribution to the public good with a shrug.

"My adolescence was spent in Rochdale kids' homes, and the streets of London," he said, sorrow touching his features, which caused some of those present to shake their heads in pity. "If the new hospital means less suffering in the world, then that is reward enough for me."

What a wonderful man Callum Bowes-West was! Despite his inauspicious start as a Rochdale orphan and failed singer, he had devoted himself and much of his fortune to good works such as the LCI Rebuild project, which they were all desperate to get under way for the sake of their respective careers.

As the present company of local councils' financiers, local health authority senior management, banks and large and small businesses expressed their profound gratitude, the phone in his pocket vibrated with an incoming text. It was Tez, requesting phone contact.

Excusing himself from the table, Bowes-West locked himself in the cloakroom on the lower floor and took the call. As usual, Tez thought he was calling go-between Zollo. Direct contact with any of the Zone staff had been kept to a minimum until very recently. But following the springing of Chloe Tudor, Bowes-West had felt it prudent to keep a closer eye on proceedings there.

Tez's communication was not encouraging. Although it had reopened after the Bannigan cortège left for the Anfield Crematorium, the Zone had been forced to close again temporarily because of extraordinary events unfolding in Shriveton. Apparently a blind old man there was claiming that the Paki Witch had restored his sight.

For some hours since his alleged *cure*, the old man had been engaged on some maniacal house-cleaning enterprise. Once that was completed, he had taken himself up to the Shopping Parade, followed by a crowd of local people. The crowd had swollen to fill not only the Parade front itself, but the Skylark and Tallis walkway. The people sang songs, and listened to speakers among them, one of whom was the notorious Shriveton burglar, Jimmy Benton, who arrived later on, proclaiming the Paki Witch's divinity on the grounds that she had cured his criminality.

Tez and his men, with the help of the Incubo's tame Merseyside Police Superintendent Simon Meyers, had managed to return Shriveton to normal such that Zone trading had resumed by early evening.

"You have to find her," said Bowes-West/Zollo.

She was nowhere to be found, objected Tez. Although belief in her was widespread, the majority of people in the area had not actually met the Paki Witch. Apparently she lived in Skylark Towers, where Jimmy Benton alleged he had met her that very afternoon. But nobody – not even the other residents of the block – knew which flat.

Nobody present would have guessed his inner turmoil as Bowes-West rejoined his illustrious guests at the dining table. They were establishing exactly who was paying what towards Liverpool Central Infirmary rebuild. He pledged £15m with a diffident, "Someone must pay."

Tallis Towers

By the time his Nan staggered in with Macca, just after eleven, Jamal had bagged and cleared everything up, and made pseudonymous Messenger contact with Lidocaine-supplier Oz.

"Where's the mirror gone, Jammy?" croaked Lilly after a visit to the bathroom.

"Broke," mumbled Jamal.

"How?"

"Punched it."

"Oh. That's bad luck breaking a mirror. Innit Macca?" Lilly crouched over her handbag, fumbling and swaying with intoxication. "Oh, fuckin' 'ell, got no cigs. Run the Parade and get us some, Jammy."

"I got your ciggies here, Lil," said Macca, looking heavenwards as he caught Jamal's eyes as if to say, *She's completely paralytic.* "You just bought forty at the Parade, girl."

"Did I?"

"Yeah. Your 'and cut, is it, Jam?" asked Macca, faintly intrigued by Jamal's furtiveness. His consoling arm, issuing a flush of armpit onions, reached around Jamal.

"No." Jamal moved away.

"Giz a fag, Macc." Lilly started crying (again), as she swayed precariously.

"It's been a fuckin' tough day, Jammy," belched Macca, passing to Lilly one of the packets of cheap cigarettes he pulled from his pockets. "What you done with the broken glass, Jam? Cos she's so fuckin' out of it, man, she's gonna fall into it if you left it lying around."

"Outside bin."

"Oh, I dunno what to do with me fuckin' self," announced Lilly, intensely moved by a sudden awareness of her own pain. She cast to the floor the unopened packet of cigarettes and collapsed in sobs on to the sofa, pleading: "What am I going to do with my fuckin' self? Jammy? Tell me?"

But her grandson was tired of her drunken effusions and could only shuffle away. He despised her without reservation, and felt no sympathy, only resentment, towards her at that moment.

"Have a look at Corrie, love," suggested Macca, flicking on the TV. "Take your mind off it. You can't do nothin' else. Jammy's 'ad a tough day, an' all. Now where's that weed you said you 'ad in, girl? 'Cos otherwise, I 'ave to get off, see."

Without waiting for a response, Macca embarked on a purposeful search of the usual places – mantelpiece ornaments, sideboard drawers, her makeup and hand bags and coat pockets.

With outstretched multi-ringed hand, Lilly reached towards her grandson, wailing, "Jammy, me two picaninnies is dead!"

Jamal remained at the living room door, his eyes avoiding her desperate pathos.

"Your Mummy and Troy is dead, son," she repeated.

Her cirrhotic body was shaking with wretched sobs, and a slurry of tears and makeup occupied the lines around her dark eyes, making a hideous ghoul of her.

"Any idea where you put your weed, Lil, love?" called Macca from behind the sofa. "Can't fuckin' find it nowhere."

It looked dangerously like Macca wanted to widen his search, which was the last thing Jamal wanted, given the fifteen hundred bags of bash he had just created and stored in his bedroom cupboards. (All the hardware was back under the bath.)

"Try the cushions, Macc," he said. "She's been 'idin' it there lately."

"Dead before they was twenny-five years old, Jam!" she croaked. "Troy was only eighteen. A boy."

Her voice ululated as Macca yanked the cushion from under her head, which fell with a bump against the grubby sofa arm. Eyes closing, her little sorry form, swathed in mourning clothes, melted into the angles of the sofa.

"Nice one, Jam!" declared Macca plucking a bolus of cannabis resin from inside the faux-suede cushion.

Discarding the dismantled cushion on the floor, he cupped his hands around the treasure, and breathed in gratefully its oily aroma. Then he hitched up the flaccid Lilly's knees to make room for himself on the sofa beside her, and, with the dexterity of a master craftsman, started building a huge spliff.

"You'll feel better when you get your fuckin' chops round this, girl," he told her. He hadn't noticed that she had found a reprieve from life's whips and chains in the short-lived oblivion of the sleeping alcoholic.

"She's crashed out," said Jamal.

"Fuckin' 'ell, yeah." Macca didn't even look at her. "Long day for her, nigger. Long fuckin' day. Fuckin' long day. Giz a brew, lad. Fuckin' parched."

"Could do with getting her to bed, like," mumbled Jamal, staying put in the doorway. Behind him, across the hallway, the door to his bedroom was ajar.

Macca's fingers continued working even as his head twisted, Exorcist-like, to look at Jamal.

"I'll just roll this, nigger. Eh, Jam, there's a strong smell of piss in 'ere, by the way."

"I know. We've run out of Dettol. Meant to get some, but I keep forgettin'."

There was a pause as Macca, squinting, espied in the background the bathroom mirror – conspicuously whole and glinting in the light of Jamal's bedroom – atop the chest of drawers. Their eyes met for a micro-second, during which Macca's fingers were still as he said, slowly, "Remember, you can count on Macca, lickle brother."

"Nice one." Jamal remained at the door, and chewed his lip, then repeated, "Listen, Macc, it's been a long day, and I need to get me Nan sorted out."

"Sure, Jammy, sure."

He stood up, spliff in his smiling lips, and stretched. His long-limbed, tall person seemed to fill the whole living-room like a huge Mardi Gras festival figure.

While he called a taxi, Jamal took the opportunity to close the bedroom door on the betraying mirror.

"Take the weed, mate," said Jamal, returning.

"You sure?" said Macca, stuffing the cannabis bolus immediately in his coat pocket.

"Yeah. Tez will get her some more."

"He's a fuckin' saint, that Tez," said Macca. He picked up the unopened cigarette packet from the floor and stuffed that, too, in his pocket "Put another grand behind the fuckin' St Terry's bar on his way out."

"Mad, innit."

"A fuckin' saint he is."

Soon, the taxi text prompted an oniony embrace on the threshold, during which Macca pledged brotherhood, dependability, trustworthiness, street-wisdom, contacts and service. With a final, *He's a fuckin' saint that Tez*, he departed down the stairs.

Switching off the living-room light, Jamal went to the window and waited to see Macca emerge below. Everywhere was quiet and still. In the distance, a solitary addict in an orange tracksuit shuffled discreetly along the Tallis flyover in the direction of the Zone, which would be still open although the rest of the Parade was in darkness. The rattle of a waiting black taxi in the centre of the otherwise empty forecourt was the only sound. The driver's elbow was propped against the open window as, undisturbed, he enjoyed a quiet cigarette, which he held out of the window.

With a wave, Macca greeted the waiting driver and carefully tapped out the hot end of his spliff on the ground. Like a huge, colourful and ineptly operated puppet, he bounded over and ducked into the carriage.

As the cab pulled away, revealed in the space it had occupied was a slim, black-veiled figure, with her face upturned and pale in the moonlight, and looking up directly at Jamal's window. She was standing alone, still as a church statue, in the expanse of unoccupied forecourt. There was no way the driver and Macca couldn't have seen her, and yet their behaviour just now indicated they had not.

A croaking, semi-conscious plea from his Nan on the sofa broke the moment, drawing him from the window.

"The Paki Witch 'ealed a blind man. I shoulda asked for her help wi–"

She exploded into a dreadful, bronchitic episode which transmogrified her whole person into a boiling, spewing, noisy cauldron of phlegm. This happened periodically when her smoking and drinking levels had exceeded their usual excess. Jamal propped her up on the cushions and sat with her until it stopped, holding a bowl under her face to catch any sick and sputum – the usual procedure. When she stopped, he got her into the bathroom and then put her to bed, bolstering her again into upright position with heaped pillows.

Afterwards, he went back to the window again. But the Paki Witch had gone. Without knowing he did it, his hand closed once more around Chloe's card.

CHAPTER SEVEN

Tuesday 26th October 201-

Shriveton Park

It was 7.45am, and still dark, and the just-risen sun was bleaching a vitiligo sky. Jamal was sitting smoking on the Shriveton Park swings, a few metres from where his brother had been killed. A barricade of floral tributes – an indecent splash of summer in the cold October scene – marked the spot.

Local frustration had not been vented by the pomp and ceremony of Troy's funeral, nor soothed by the undercurrent of whispers about the Paki Witch healing Bob Reilly and converting Jimmy Benton. Tez and some of his men had with ease dispersed the small crowd of women, kids and old people at the Shopping Parade yesterday afternoon. In the evening, local kids, restless and high after the funeral, had congregated at the swings, subliminally craving resolution. Now Jamal's downcast eyes saw, without seeing, their teen spirit's spent carcass – a morning glory of vodka bottles, Rizla packets and even a syringe – on the spongy, orange playground floor.

The sense that something significant was afoot had infected Shriveton, but as yet Jamal was oblivious to everything except his own pain and singular purpose.

Despite continuous coffee and cigarettes, every so often his eyes had slid shut during the night hours, and he'd seen *her* face looking up at him from the Skylark car park. *Her:* Chloe's saviour, stealing into his thoughts to tell him:

No.

But he'd carried on bagging up bash, and eventually, at 6.45am, via Facebook, Messenger, texts, then payphone contact, he'd met with Krevvo, one of Troy's peripheral acquaintances with links to the Manchester gangs. Krevvo was eager enough for gangland glory to take all 1500 bags in order to impress his Wythenshawe associates. He would take the rest as well, once Jamal had got the kee of Lidocaine from Oz, which was set up for two days' time.

Nineteen grand in cash and a Heckler and Koch MP5 submachine-gun, complete with silencer, plus ammo, lay in the rucksack at Jamal's feet on the playground floor. By next week he would have as much again. Then he'd be in a better position to *do* something.

The MP5 was necessary. In case word got out that he had set up in business, the first thing he needed was the means to defend himself from the inquisitive advances of competitors and underworld taxmen. The second thing to do was to execute whoever had grassed him, as he'd made very clear when he transacted with Krevvo.

For a few moments, the purchase of the MP5 had silenced the vengeful demons within himself. But by the time he'd sealed the deal with Krevvo and walked to the swings, a host of satanic mental implants were contaminating his resolve. He was, after all, only sixteen and scarcely out of boyhood, and too young to be murdering people, even if they had it coming. He'd only just started smoking cigarettes. He couldn't drive or vote or buy a drink in a pub. Not that he drank, anyway: his Nan's revolting excesses had always deterred him there. He didn't even smoke pot, or do other drugs – for no particular reason.

He'd never even gone out with a girl. Whereas Troy had all the wit and charm to draw in girls, Jamal was terribly inhibited and preferred being on the computer or reading. Like everyone, he'd always fancied Chloe Tudor, of course, at school (before she became a bag-head, obviously). Even without her addiction, though, Chloe would always have been a non-starter since she'd always been hanging around Troy whenever she'd been in Jamal's midst.

It was madness to be sitting in the park beside a rucksack containing nineteen thousand pounds and an MP5. Grinding his cigarette stump into the floor with his heel, he lit up another, and pulled out Chloe's card. His sorrowful brown eyes traced her low-achieving-girl handwriting: *the packi wich will set you free like she done me all you got to do is ask her.*

The Paki Witch wouldn't take out Gaz, though, would she?

As morning bloomed in Shriveton while Jamal sat chain-smoking on the swings beside his submachine-gun, drug-money and dead brother's wreaths, his thoughts meandered to Chloe's baby, Joel. It would have been nice if Troy had been the father, especially now the Paki Witch had got mother and child out of Shriveton. The kid might just grow up all right in a different environment. Whatever, Troy could not possibly be the father of Chloe's blonde-haired, fair-skinned, Caucasian son. Therefore all that Troy had left behind was his alcoholic Nan and a brother with no balls.

Powerless to halt the grief heaving within him, Jamal's head slumped to his lap and he buried his fist – which still clutched Chloe's card – in his froth of black hair. A giant tear wandered down his snub nose.

"You are out in the cold," came a gentle voice he recognised.

He jolted out of his tormented Rodin's *Thinker* position and saw none other than the Paki Witch, who was sitting still and smiling on the adjacent swing. For a moment he couldn't take in anything about her, except that she seemed as small as a primary school child. He felt he had always known her. Chloe's card suddenly felt impossibly hot in his hand. He shoved it into his jacket pocket and, pulling hard on his cigarette, mumbled, "Hi."

"Hi, back!"

He gave an embarrassed little half-laugh and said, "I've just finished work."

He felt it was necessary to explain his presence in the park, but immediately wondered why the hell he'd said it.

"I work," she replied.

"Oh."

"As a cleaner."

He looked at her closely now. She was bigger than he first thought, although very slightly built. Her features were unutterably perfect. Indeed, she was by far the most beautiful female he had ever seen or imagined. Beside her he felt unclean and ugly – to a degree that he wanted to hide himself in the shadows from her, like John Merrick in the film *Elephant Man*, which had made him cry when he was a kid.

"Oh."

He looked at her again and was afflicted by overwhelming desire which felt both sexual and spiritual and which launched a to-the-death battle of instincts within him. He wanted to skulk in the crevices and shadows of life's underground, hiding from her loveliness. At the same time he wanted to be forever in her, with her, on her, under her, of her.

He recalled her face looking up at him the previous night, from the Tallis car park. She'd been safer then, viewed from the threshold of his cocaine-factory home. Now she was close enough for him to reach out and *touch*.

What if she went, as quickly as she'd come? Could he maybe keep her there beside him for a few more moments? He seized on: "I saw you last night. In the car park."

"Good."

He was stumped by this obtuse response. But her smile encouraged him to persevere. "Erm... well, I've seen you around a couple of times."

"Good. I've seen you around, too."

"You have?" A tumour of emotion metastasized in his gullet: she had noticed *him*?

"Oh yes."

"What's your name. I mean, like, I don't think I ever heard your name."

Her smiling mouth was soft and full and pink in the weak morning sun. Her kiss would taste of strawberries and paradise milk. Henceforth his dreams would be bodily bursting with her.

"Well, that is not surprising since we only met just now," she said.

"Well, yeah. I know. But I seen you 'round, like. Just never got talkin', like."

"My name is Jessenia Rabia al-Rahoud."

"Oh."

Knowing he had not caught anything but the first syllable of this inchoate jumble of phonemes, he took another nervous pull on his cigarette, then realised he was still smoking and panicked. She might not like smoking, being a Muslim type.

"Is that Indian?" he asked.

He didn't know what to do with the cigarette. She might think badly of him if he added to the litter on the floor, so he kept it burning in his hand. When she looked away he'd drop it discreetly.

"No. I'm from Afghanistan."

"Oh. So, erm..."

He blanked, and had an urge to pick up his bag and run away forever. On the other hand, keeping the conversation going would mean that if he ever did get over his nerves he would have some sort of foothold for further acquaintance should they meet again. A neutral subject, which presumably Afghanistan could never be for her, was required, so he continued with, "Erm, so where do you work?"

"Everywhere."

She stood up from her swing and came near him, so her stomach and hips, swathed in folds of black material, were in line his upturned face. Later he would dream of kissing her belly and breathing in her intimate scents.

"Oh. Well, erm, like, who do you work for?"

"Love."

"Love?" he asked, baffled.

"Love, God, Allah. These are the same thing." She held out her hands to him, tiny and so pale next to the closely-fit black of her long sleeves. "Love is a good employer."

He quickly reached down towards his bag. It was an impromptu action to cover his refusal to take her still-proffered hands. It was too much. Too much. Anyway, she was some sort of religious nut. A Bible-thumper. A fanatic. A weirdo. He must not look at her and be swayed by her attractiveness.

"He gets a bad press, your Allah," he mumbled, still looking down. "Anyway, I don't believe in religion."

"But do you believe in love?" she said.

Disarmed, he hesitated. What was she trying to say? The tiny thought that she was coming on to him sprouted, like the disappointing sprout of light from a Roman candle firework. He didn't like it. He needed her to be a Catherine-wheel of purity, dazzlingly better than him and everyone around him. The choking feeling intensified and he couldn't speak.

"Because, Allah is just a word for love," she continued, seeming to know his turmoil. "In the realm of love, there is neither belief, nor unbelief."

Relieved that she had restated the metaphysical parameters, he spoke again. "Ask your Allah why he let me Mum and our Troy die."

"Love never dies, Jamal."

Jamal shook his head and said nothing.

"So! When do you start work?" she asked.

"I just finished my shift," he mumbled.

She was trying to convert him, to get him working for Allah. She was a religious fanatic, not the messiah the likes of Chloe believed in. Her English was accentless, with the natural speech rhythms of the indigenous speaker, and yet she described herself as an Afghani. Perhaps she was a jihadist recruiting new blood to spill in the name of her war-loving Allah. Whatever, if she were not a god but merely a woman, it was safe after all to allow his eyes to trace upwards, over the contours of her hips, waist and breasts.

"Start a new shift now," she said, demure as she intuited the intense desire mounting in him.

"Your employer fired me the day I was born, Je, erm, Ja – erm, sorry, what you say your name was, again?"

"Jessie Rout."

"Jessie Rout. Sounds familiar, dunno why, like. "

Her rose-petal palms were still reaching to him. He imagined them running along his bare back as he kissed her pink mouth, and felt his sex in hers. Even just to touch her would be to lose completely everything he was, had and knew.

"But most people here call me the Paki Witch," she said with a smile.

"Yeah, I know." He gave a small, apologetic laugh on behalf of the neighbourhood. "Bad, like."

She gave a light hearted shake of her head, and with her finger stroked to nothingness the tear-track still glistening on his cheek.

"Words come and go, like tears, Jamal. In love, nothing exists between heart and heart."

The contact with her living flesh reaffirmed her divinity, and seemed to fuse the good inside him with her immaculate self. His hand moved up to clutch hers, but stopped, to hover in the freezing morning air as he thought, *What would she say if she knew what he did for a living?*

By the end of next week all fifteen hundred bags of the garbage he had created last night would be in the North West sewage system in the excreta and vomit of regional users. He belonged in the gutter with all of that, not next to her.

"Love is so forgiving it is foolish, embarrassing even, Jamal!" she coaxed, her little hand cupping the perfect line of his jaw.

Suddenly resolute, he dug his heels in the floor to push the swing seat back and away, and stood up. From the instant of separation from her, his world was once more a wilderness of sorrow and pain.

The rucksack felt almost unbearably heavy as he lifted it.

"Gotta go," he mumbled, shivering with cold as he moved off.

"Jamal!" she called after him.

He turned round, and their eyes met across the space dividing them. She gave a curiously arch smile and announced, "I'll be thinking of you."

Then she walked away in the direction of the Shopping Parade, and, in moments, was out of sight.

St Theresa's Church, Shriveton

Father Kevin O'Connor stooped to pick up some the chip wrappers and drinks cartons in the doorway to his grill-windowed, gloomy mausoleum of a church, when a voice behind him called, "Excuse me, are you the priest around here?"

He turned round to see a red-haired, freckly young man holding out his hand. He was too healthy-looking and posh-sounding to be a local junkie wanting money, the usual state of anyone between the age of twelve and sixty who presented themselves.

"That's right." Shunting to one hand the large mass of rubbish, he freed his right hand to return the greeting. "I'm Father Kevin O'Connor. How can I help?"

"Ethan Greenberg. From the *Star*."

"Ah, Ethan Greenberg. "

"Yes. I was hoping I could talk to you about what happened in Lawdens Lane yesterday at Bob Reilly's house."

"Ah, Bob." A fresh-faced smile broke across the priest's pudgy, effeminate features. "He's a parishioner here, of course. And a happy man now. Well, I haven't got long. A funeral at ten, and Jewel is due any time soon. But come in. Could you hold these for me?"

He transferred the chip wrappers and other rubbish to Ethan, and then began a ritualistic opening up process, involving a huge bunch of keys, chains and variety of locks, plus alarm. Rubbish in hand so he couldn't make notes, Ethan maintained conversation and hoped he'd remember what was said.

"Troy Bannigan's funeral was here yesterday, wasn't it? By all accounts it was a big affair."

"Ah, Troy Bannigan. Well, today it's just a little old lady. There!"

The priest had concluded the complex entrance sequence by punching in a code on the key pad and throwing the light switch. The whine of the preliminary alarm stopped; ahead and illuminated was the altar, resplendent with bales of lilies, roses and other flowers Ethan didn't know the name of. Their perfume mixed deliciously with the waxen incense of the church interior.

"But at least Dorothy's funeral today puts the Incubo's flowers to use," said the priest, frowning.

"The gangs are big here?" asked Ethan. He looked around, impressed. "Hey this is nice. I've never been in a Catholic church."

The priest took the rubbish off him and walked briskly down the aisle with it, saying, "There's a bin in the sacristy. Gangs are big? Correct and incorrect. Yes, very big. But there is only one gang here. The Incubo's."

Ethan followed him, but couldn't resist dawdling to look at the fine stucco arches and pillars, each carrying a carved station of the cross, with a large roman numeral underneath. Would Shriveton people understand roman numerals, he wondered, running his hand over the flawless gloss of the orange wooden pews. Dipping a fingertip into the icy interior of a stoup of holy water, he read a notice about a trip to Lourdes next year.

The place reminded him of the *Titanic*'s Grand Staircase, built in a flush of optimism and can-do pride. Intact, and part of the sunk ship that was Shriveton, St Theresa's RC Church had the air of a forgotten tomb about it.

"So the Incubo gang runs –" Ethan's voice zipped up in pitch to a yelp as he tripped over a step and went crashing forward into the brass barricade separating altar and congregation.

"Mind the step there," said the priest, without looking round or stopping. "Yes the Incubo runs Shriveton. That corrupt Meyers you quoted in your article yesterday is a liar."

"So you read my article!" said Ethan, delighted, rubbing his knee and half-hopping after him into the sacristy, which he discovered was a chaotic offstage ante-chamber-cum-green room situated behind the altar.

"I did. It didn't say much."

"Well nobody would talk to me, so I was restricted. That's why I came here to–"

"Put the kettle on, would you?" The priest pointed at a cheap kettle on a surface cluttered with a disorder of religious artefacts and vestments. "Mind, because it doesn't switch itself off. Black no sugar for me. Hope you like it the same, because there's nothing but teabags."

The priest hunched down, huffing and puffing to himself, beside the small gas fire in the room, beneath a mantelpiece on which stood a small crucifix and a giant statue of a woman in Middle-Eastern dress, carrying beads and smiling beatifically at the grilled window opposite.

"Shit. It's out again! Teabags in the drawer. I'll try get this fire working. It's temperamental. Freaking thing!"

Meanwhile, his guest pulled some cheap teabags out of one of the shallow drawers of perfectly laundered vestments and altar linen, and asked, "Superintendent Meyers is corrupt, you say, Father?"

"Corrupt? Of course he's corrupt. He's been on the Incubo payroll for years. How else could a copper afford to live in Matherfield Park?"

"How do you know he's corrupt?"

Bottles and flasks of altar wine were lined up like sentries beside a Tupperware box bulging with communion wafers on the rotten window ledge. The boiling water made a fragrant sauna of sherry fumes. Overhead a solitary eco bulb dandled from the ceiling, absolutely losing the battle to the steam and fortified window, which admitted scarcely any daylight. It was a weird place. All the beautiful adornments were meticulously maintained, but the hardware was falling apart.

"Take a look around you," snapped the priest as he grappled with the fire. "Shriveton's run by the Incubo. The police here are as quiet in the face of evil as the Roman Catholic hierarchy are about paedophile priests, man."

"Wow, you sure aren't what I expected when I called."

"What did you expect, Ethan Greenberg? To be blamed for the killing of your fellow Jew, known as Jesus? Oh great!" There was an encouraging wheeze from the boiler. "It's coming on."

Soon the fire and pilot light were going, and they sat down on the care-home-type winged armchairs, each nursing a cup of tea.

"That's why I come in so early before Mass or a funeral, you see," the priest explained. "To get the central heating going. Don't want all my old ladies dying of hypothermia on me."

"Can't you get it fixed?"Ethan asked.

Father O'Connor guffawed, and said, "No money. This is a poor parish."

"Can't you get Lottery money or something?"

"We do get all of that. But I tend to use it for the poor. There's an unlimited supply of worthy recipients here."

Ethan thought for a moment, then said, "Here reminds me of that song, *All the Lonely People*."

Father O'Connor gave a sad smile, and said, "Ah, *Eleanor Rigby*. Genius."

Then, out of the blue, in surprisingly high, pure voice, a few lines of the song exploded from his lips.

Like a spirit of longing, risen from the vale of tears, the Beatles melody seemed to fill the great barn of a church, and hang with the incense, flowers, polish and altar wine fumes. Ethan stared at him, all at once shocked and embarrassed and, even, moved.

The priest stopped and took a noisy gulp of tea, smiling in satisfaction.

"That's me."

"It's – it's a lonely life."

"It is. Especially nowadays."

"Have you ever thought of leaving?"

"Oh, lots of times. But not lately. I'm enlightened now, you see. Enlightenment transcends all of that."

"All of what?"

"Oh, happiness, sadness, boredom, discontent."

"I thought enlightenment was for the Buddhists."

"There's no monopoly on it. This tea's awful."

"I'm sorry about the tea. But it's your tea. Would you mind if I asked you about the Paki Witch? That's what she's called round here isn't she?"

"Ah, the Paki Witch. My enlightenment was absolute and forever when I opened my eyes and saw *her*."

He stood up and spontaneously patted the huge statue on the mantelpiece.

Ethan looked, nonplussed, at the heavy-jowled lady adorned in a cement garland of flowers, sporting cream cape and brown pilot-like headwear. She certainly did not match the descriptions he had been given yesterday of the Paki Witch.

"So you saw *her*," he said, eyes on the statue, hoping his disappointment was not too obvious. "Who is she? The Virgin Mary, yeah?"

"Good grief, no, man." Kevin shook with laughter. "This is St Theresa."

"Oh."

"She cleaned floors in a French convent and wrote an autobiography."

"So, St Theresa appeared to you?"

"Well, you *could* look at it that way. But she doesn't look like that now, of course."

"OK. But what does she look like now?"

"Well hasn't anyone given you a description of her yet?"

"Well nobody's mentioned this Theresa at all, to be honest. I came to talk about the Paki Witch."

"Well that's who I am talking about."

Ethan paused, frustrated at the priest's obtuseness, but cautiously pleased that things were getting warmer. He scratched a few hasty notes in his pad, then said, "So unpicking our conversation just now, I am understanding that the person you saw when you opened your eyes was the Paki Witch."

"Correct. You are a clever young man."

"Well, when did you see her?"

"Yesterday. She wandered past shortly after I'd finished doing my Father McKenzie wiping of the hands act at the Bannigan funeral. I'd just got back from the Crematorium, and was feeling rather downcast and despondent, to tell you the truth. She was standing at my front door as I pulled up in my car. So I invited her in for a cup of tea. Anything to put off going to the wake" – he waved his hand vaguely in the direction of the parish social centre sited on the other side of the damp church wall – "with all those gangsters.

"Incidentally, she has a name, this Paki Witch. It's Jessie Rout."

"Rout? How are you spelling that?"

"Good grief, I don't know. Like trout or gout I suppose. I've only heard it. From her. Never seen it written."

"So," – Ethan was doing his very best to churn these unwieldy pieces of information before his audience with the priest ended – "you became enlightened yesterday as a result of having a cup of tea with the Paki – with Jessie Rout."

"Oh, good Lord, no," beamed the priest. "I opened my eyes to her a couple of months ago. And I have never looked back. She is everything to me now."

"Sounds like you, erm, may have fallen in love with her?"

"Oh, I have. Emphatically. But not in the sense you mean. And anyway, I am gay."

This admission was nearly as startling as the *Eleanor Rigby* refrain had been.

"Big Irish Catholic family like mine, there was no being gay," the priest went on, matter-of-factly. "People like me deny it, and come into the priesthood to hide from themselves and please their parents." He gave a heartfelt sigh. "Well, I no longer deny what I am. Moreover, my wonderful Jessie Rout has made me see that I *do* in fact have the vocation I'd always pretended to have."

A key turned in the door connecting the sacristy to outside, and now a young woman in a scruffy grey raincoat entered.

"Oh, sorry, Father," she yelped, downcast eyes, her fingers knitting and picking at each other.

"Jewel, Ethan, Ethan, Jewel – my lifesaver, aren't you Jewel?"

Jewel gave a prim smile and stood rooted to the spot, neurotic and silent.

"Now, listen, Ethan, I have to get on."

"You got to phone council 'bout Firework Night at the Community Centre," piped Jewel.

"Feck, yes! Thanks, Jewel. Nearly forgot."

Ethan felt panic rising. He mustn't lose this lead.

"You can come back another day and talk to me," assured the priest.

"Well, thanks, I will. One question before I go. Bob Reilly called the Paki Witch *The One*. Do you think she is the one?"

Jewel looked as if she were about to collapse with fright now as her dark eyes darted to and from priest to visitor. Her thumb fiddled with a poorly-fitting crown on her front tooth, and she looked like a little girl who might burst into tears at any moment.

The priest gave a little whelp of surprise, "Well of course!"

"But you're saying that this woman, a Muslim, is the messiah, and yet you are a Catholic priest."

"Father, careful," muttered Jewel, through her thumb.

Ever smiling and patient in the face of human doubt, Father O'Connor explained with a kindly smile, "Once you see the messiah, truly *see* the messiah, everything else – temple, shrine, mosque, church, street, brothel, prison, palace – is just," his arm made a flamboyant sweep of the sacristy gloom, "background."

"We have to sort out the Council, now," said Jewel, holding open the door through which she had just come. "Goodbye."

"Sorry, Jewel," said the priest, chastened into a complete return to the moment. Warmly shaking Ethan's hand he said, "Goodbye."

As Ethan walked out, the young woman's terror was like a pair of huge palms splayed on his back, shoving him away.

Shriveton Park

Flower Power

A respectful twenty-two hours after the funeral, Merseyside Police had arrived shortly before 8am to clear the bushels of flowers on the spot by the playground where Troy Bannigan had breathed his last. To avoid all contrariety, they had watched and waited in their van while the deceased's brother – clearly in view, and alone, with a full-looking rucksack at his feet – rocked to and fro on his swings, by turns sobbing and talking to himself.

New recruit PC Geraint "Taffy" Jones, who had been regarding the sorrowful scene with genuine compassion, muttered, "The kid's gone mad with grief. Tragic."

This incited the righteous ire of his superior, Superintendent Meyers. Events such as yesterday's gangland funeral, the absurd blind man miracle and the conversion of hardened crook Jimmy Benton, needed careful management. Hence Meyers' presence in the area this morning. From the perspective of his Incubo and Police Authority paymasters, it was vital that Meyers was seen to be doing the right thing.

Flicking his palm up and down in front of his own face – the code for *black* – he ranted, "They're all the same. Look at that bag by his foot there. What's in that, eh? Can't kid a kidder. Can't kid me. Trash they are. Just ask yourself why's he here at this time in the morning? *Usual* for them is lyin' in bed all day with their hoes, smoking ganja, while their rap shite deafens geriatrics in the next fuckin' post code. Meanwhile bleedin' heart tax-payers like you, Taffy, picks up the tab. You soft Welsh cunt.

"The only reason we can't pull that twat in right now is it will create a tidal wave round here. Feeling sorry for these people will get you fucked. Keep 'em down, under your boot. Trust me."

Outbursts of this sort were common from Meyers. Yet there was no arguing with the fact that he maintained order in the Shriveton area – no mean feat given the socio-economic complexion of the place. On paper Shriveton was virtually drug-free, a testament to the fact that Meyers was doing a good job, even though his troops on the ground saw a picture which was certainly not represented on said paper.

His officers were not paid to think, and Meyers counted on that. They did as bidden, clocking up the years until they could get out with the pension. A few years scrambling about, day and night, in humanity's most faecal annals, and the only up-side to the job was the thought of that pension.

So PC Jones nodded as if in agreement without saying anything, and once Jamal Bannigan had moved off, trailing his suspicious rucksack, he moved in. Flower-clearing was as much police action as the Super permitted in the area, and it seemed to work. In no time the mound of ribbon-wrapped wreaths and bouquets had been cleared, and visual neutrality restored.

The next job was to attempt to locate the Paki Witch.

"Well apparently she *does* exist," insisted Meyers.

PC Taffy Jones and colleagues had spent many fruitless man-hours at Meyers' behest in August, trawling benefits, immigration and housing records to find her. It was a wild goose chase which made the police look foolish.

"The woman is just a fairy story," said Taffy. "We haven't even got a name for her, boss. And she's not been involved in any crime. Nobody will speak to us about her. All we got last time is that she lives somewhere in Skylark, but she's not registered as living there."

"Well, they're my orders," was how Meyers concluded proceedings. He neglected to say that it was Zone Chief Tez who had given these orders.

He despatched Taffy on door-to-door enquiries in Skylark

Towers and surrounding residences. But who should Taffy say he was looking for? He could hardly ask after the *Paki Witch*, could he?

"Same as last time," said Meyers. "Describe her. Say she's *known as* the Paki Witch. Use your imagination!"

Meyers must be desperate if he was encouraging the deployment of imagination.

"If we can find Bin fuckin' Laden, we can find her," he added.

Tallis Tower

Dream of Home

Meeting Jessie Rout at the swings had made a hideous dream of everything except her. Jamal had dragged his weary body home, re-running in his mind their conversation. He wished he'd played it very differently, but her beauty and the sheer shock of her arrival had unbalanced him. She'd known his name, but he was virtually certain that he had not given it. Or had he? Perhaps he had.

The house was as quiet and cold as the grave when he got in, nineteen thousand pounds and a MP5 richer than when he'd left it. His Nan's snoring drifted through the odours of urine, sick and stale alcohol and tobacco. Still wearing her funeral clothes, she was splatted like a string-severed puppet on the bed, her wild dyed hair springing starkly from the off-white of pillow, which was smeared with make-up and sick.

When he was a little kid, big brother Troy had always urged that they must check their Nan's head and shoulders were upright if she crashed out. If she choked on her vomit like their idol Jimi Hendrix had done, he'd explained, they would have to go into care permanently.

Without thinking about it, Jamal propped her head up on the pillow and covered her with the duvet before retreating to his own room. He slumped, fully-clothed, on to the bed, wishing so much that he could pull Jessie Rout to him and bury his head in her swathe of blue-black hair. His eyes closed on a wonderland dream.

Jessie was dressed in skinny jeans and a string vest which showed off her little cleavage. Her limbs were long and brown, and her skin was soft beneath his touch. High heels meant she couldn't walk over the grass, so he lifted her in his arms and carried her over the Shriveton playing field. They took a bus and then a plane to her home, and she slept on his shoulder during the flight, the occidental bouquet of her hair and skin swarming his senses as he regarded cumulus heaven through the porthole window.

Her home was in a flat-topped town of paupers and soldiers, where carpenters rode on donkeys and wine came in bags. Outside was bonfire hot, but Jessie Rout's room was cool as cellar earthenware, and her gossamer bed linen, through which he could see her dark pubic triangle and nipples, smelt of lavender.

She was kind to him, and made him confident, despite his inexperience, because she knew what to do. And when he fingered the feminine delicacy of her collar bones, he wanted to weep because she was so divinely perfect and yet all his, forever. Her breasts were velvety under his tongue, and her kiss so giving; and he felt so wanted when she pushed his hand down so he could feel the wet warmth inside her.

She ignited an Olympic torch of desire within him, which no orgasm would discharge. All he wanted was to dissolve and dissolve in her, and keep dissolving until he was hers absolutely. But just as he penetrated her, and felt her mouth under his, and her happy eyes looking up to his as he moved in her, he woke up.

Thrust from her welcoming body and back into the horrible reality of his Tallis Tower bedroom with its drawer-top dusting of cocaine, he felt desperately cheated and would have given almost anything to carry on the dream. He thought of the addicts wandering in the wasteland beneath the flyovers leading to the Zone. And for the first time it made *total* sense: their shabby clothing hanging from wasted limbs, their rotten teeth and dirty nails, and their eyes fixed inwards on the opiate dream-screen running in the head they'd just paid the Incubo to get out of. The dream was so much better than the tinnitus of his Nan's snoring, the foul smells, and the paper chase of sympathy cards, and his heart's leaden weight of obligation to even for Troy.

Exhausted though he was, sleep, like a stripper who'd just bounced off his lap, beckoned and teased, but refused to come to back.

CHAPTER EIGHT

Tuesday 26th October 201-

The Marporley Arms, Marporley, Cheshire

From his window seat in the Marporley Arms, Callum Bowes-West had a prime view of the lush Cheshire landscape. Rolling, bright-green plains suddenly broke into a profusion of evergreen and deciduous orange forest with their carpets of fern, icy streams and wintry wildlife. Less than fifty miles away from Shriveton, Marporley felt as if it belonged to another continent and era. Its fine old sandstone, eponymous hostelry – with car park full of promising four-wheel drives and soft-tops – served excellent local ales, but never got the Champagne quite right. Still, it was a quiet and reassuringly expensive lunchtime refuge from the fussing of his housekeeper, Mrs Ingham, and her team of Marporley Hall domestic staff, who were clearing up after last night's function.

Yesterday's marathon – the Mayfair Ashok meeting, Claridge's hotel room clinch with Kachya, and then flight home to Marporley for the Health Authority dinner – would have been impossible without large quantities of cocaine. But he was paying the price now! A stinging belch pumped his own noxious stomach gases into the air he now inhaled: a warning to take stock. Instead he signalled to the bartender, a bustling, gossipy woman of around his own age. She brought along another glass almost immediately. For the sake of appearances, he ordered a chargrilled beef sandwich (knowing he would not eat it) and asked her to leave the bottle.

The Claridge's meeting with Ashok had secured a heroin deal with the Golden Crescent worth tens of millions. Moreover, the lavish dinner which had followed hours later in his Marporley country seat had firmly established his own saintliness in the minds of all guests, each an esteemed linchpin of his or her respective public and private sector organisation. Bowes-West should have felt buoyant beyond belief today, and yet nothing could be further from the truth.

His hand was shaking as he glugged back this second glass of bubbly. It had just turned noon. The rest of the bottle would be required to bring him down properly.

The fiasco in the Claridge's hotel room with Kachya – the idiotic Asian manservant and his trolley-pushing fat assistant in the corridor – was too bizarre to forget about. Too much cocaine and alcohol had compromised operations; he knew all about the pitfalls of kingpin drug-taking. The crazy Columbian cartel coke-heads he had dealt with over the years still served as a warning to him and anyone in the industry. But it wouldn't happen to him: the gear he used – his own, naturally (before it was cut to ribbons) – was almost a hundred per cent pure, which meant the come-down was significantly gentler than it was for the average Incubo end-user.

He gulped down a Lamprazole capsule and re-read the *Shriveton man claims miracle restored his sight* article phosphorescing among his pile of work papers spread out on the table. As well as depriving him of all appetite and all but a couple of hours of low-grade sleep, yesterday's cocaine was playing havoc with his ulcer. A spasm of fury spewed more stomach acid: the Shriveton miracle worker needed to go. He snatched up his phone.

"This blind man thing made last night's *Star*?" he said *sotto voce* to Zone Chief Tez, who believed he was speaking, as usual, with Zollo.

Excuses ensued: all of Tez's various attempts to locate the Paki Witch since the disappearance of Chloe Tudor had drawn a complete blank. She was supposed to live in Skylark Rise, but nobody knew which flat.

"Try harder."

But *all* avenues had been tried, protested Tez. Meyers had checked all Benefits Agency and Housing Association records, and drawn a blank. Tez had finally got him to agree to another single-manned door-to-door of the Skylark block, which would be happening imminently. No individual in the whole of Shriveton had any personal association with the woman. (Jimmy Benton, the robber supposedly redeemed by Shriveton's sorceress, had vanished.) So there was nobody to threaten or torture in the usual way. The *Star* article had only reported what Bob Reilly – a mad old loner by all accounts – had claimed. It wasn't as if the reporter had been able to identify the miracle woman. She remained insubstantial, a figment of everyone's imagination.

"I want – Inky tells me she's gotta be found," Bowes-West snarled.

He caught a glimpse of himself in the reflective surface of the phone screen as he hung up. His unshaven, sunken face hung cadaverously over the stiffness of his navy Barbour, giving him more the look of a Shriveton Zone customer than its kingpin. A closer inspection of himself on the phone's reverse camera confirmed that his face still bore orangey traces of yesterday's Paul Wilkins wide-boy tan.

Maintaining the Bowes-West character was a full-time job in itself. The country squire look was difficult when one has not been born to it. He always avoided the outer reaches of country-gent styles – plus-fours and *any* head gear, even caps – and had stuck religiously with Savile Row tailors.

Naturally, Callum Bowes-West would never stoop to the vulgarity of spray tans. To be out in the waxen oak and tapestry Bowes-West milieu with orangey streaks along his hair and jaw line was just another indicator that his game was slipping.

Rationalisation was required.

The Bangladesh deal would completely refinance the Incubo's legitimate central portfolios and might even enable him to withdraw completely from the drugs (and subsidiary sex-trafficking and arms) trade.

The American sub-prime crash and its spectral consequences, particularly the demise of Spain (where he had heavily invested in construction), had almost crippled the legitimate businesses underpinning this splendid country squire existence. Moreover, Incubo bailouts had become increasingly risk-fraught and costly in the post-recession era, as fiscal caution had reined in the free markets. Money laundering costs had rocketed, at times degrading Incubo gold to scrap iron. It was only the enormous income from the Shriveton Zone which had subverted bankruptcy so far.

Today he felt fragile and nervous – so far away from the cocaine cockiness of yesterday's idiocy with the Ukrainian maid. The *insanity* of booking into a hotel room with her! Depressingly enough, that episode was but a pale reflection of the preceding disastrous liaison with Chloe Tudor: dipping into that particular teenaged dirtbag had infected him with the Paki Witch virus.

To function long term in Incubo Land one must become immune to the feelings of others, because the time might come when you have to kill them. Whilst it was true to say that his principal regret was that he had *not* succeeded in killing Chloe Tudor, she continued to excite a multiplicity of strong, albeit negative, feelings of attachment in him.

The erotic aspects of their affair would spontaneously play in his head even now. Rapacious innocence wrapped in a teeny tart crust: she'd unintentionally ensnared him in the city centre night club where they met. Two weeks later he had persuaded her to accompany him as a friend on a business trip to Amsterdam. It had been the preliminary feeler-negotiation with Chowdhury's people.

Chloe – who had only been on two holidays in her life, both with her friend Ellen's family to a caravan in Towyn, North Wales – had been enraptured at the quality and cleanliness of the hotel.

"The last lot must of left their dressing gowns," she'd said, her false-nailed hand on the courtesy nightwear hanging behind the door. "Should we better tell 'em on reception? Where's my room?"

Oops, there had been an error in the booking. But not to worry. He'd sleep on the sofa by the window there.

She became immediately wary and tense, and had wanted to phone Ellen. Sadly, her mobile phone had disappeared en route.

To calm her he had bought her a large cocktail in the hotel bar. Once she'd finished that, he'd suggested she go to see Vincent Van Gogh's paintings with a couple of his security staff while he sorted out a bit of business. This idea met with blankness which swiftly turned to nose-wrinkling dismay when he explained who Van Gogh was.

"Don't want it turnin' into no fuckin' school trip," she'd grouched.

Later they had gone for a meal, and she'd ordered champagne. He'd noticed that she was drinking a lot to compensate for her unease. It was important she didn't pass out or vomit. Such a turn-off! So he organised a line of cocaine for her, which she seemed fairly pleased about, after he'd cajoled her a bit.

The cocaine did the trick. She became ever so affectionate after that, and was more than happy for him to take her back to the hotel room.

Taking Chloe Tudor's virginity was the best sexual experience of his life. He packed the blood-stained sheet in his suitcase the following morning, and kept it still among his most personal and treasured possessions in the Marporley Hall safe.

"You belong to me, now," he'd told her as soon as she opened her eyes the next morning. He was stroking her face, gravity and the foolishness of infatuation dragging all his features into a horrible portrait of corrupt middle-age.

"But I'm only fourteen," she'd said, tense and terrified and ill-looking.

"In Afghanistan, where a lot of my business is, most girls marry before they're sixteen."

But she'd curled up, and started to cry, and asked to phone Ellen. So he'd tried a different tack, and promised to take her out to the shops, where she could buy some nice things. Eventually, this, plus the assurance that they would be returning to Shriveton imminently, had cheered her, and she agreed to get up.

Everyone's eyes followed him and Chloe, which he attributed to her beauty rather than the disparity of their respective ages and attractiveness. At breakfast he'd been thrilled to hear an inexperienced waiter refer to her as *Madame*. She had the dependent innocence and breathtaking sexiness of a young Bardot or Monroe; and her walk and smile charmed and entranced everyone around her, provided she did not open her mouth. She couldn't help multiple *fuck* interpolations, and struggled to articulate even simple ideas such as ordering coffee. So he told her not to speak in public.

It was the sex which had hooked him into Chloe, and which continued to haunt him. Over a year on from their Amsterdam bliss, he felt a pang of loss whenever visited by memories of Chloe's tatty blond hair (plus extensions) on the pillow next to him, her firm neck and generally arousing puppy-fat person. She had been his porno dream girl: full and soft to touch, always wet and ready; she didn't talk, was perpetually entranced by what he considered cheap and ordinary. Most importantly, she had been exclusive to him.

Despite what he had regarded as a most auspicious start, Chloe had quickly become nothing more than an angry, junkie-hooker who despised him. Latterly, she'd realised that Zollo and Guy Turner, her record-producer-seducer, were one and the same person. And then she'd reasoned – reasoning never a strong point with Chloe, but nonetheless she'd managed it – that they might also be the Incubo.

It had pained him that her burgeoning addictions, intense dislike of him, and baby son had kept her fully occupied and remote. But as soon as she'd started making assumptions about his identity, there was no alternative: she had to go. Even as he prepared her two overdose vials, he feared it was too late, and that she had already said something to Troy Bannigan and that word might spread like nits in a nursery. She had always openly adored Troy with the intensity she despised Guy Turner.

This had stung. Unlike the other deadly sins, most of which were essential to the ongoing success of his empire, jealousy brought no user-benefit. Lust, gluttony, greed and pride paid dividends to supplier and user. Guy Turner's jealousy became an infestation. In his own mind it reduced to sawdust his wealth and status, without which he was nothing more than a nondescript middle-aged man. By contrast, the youthful and virile Troy could only scintillate.

Not another being had known he was going to kill his porno-dream girl that day. He had been Zollo, on one of his sporadic shifts in the Zone shop. That was nothing unusual. Periodically Zollo worked in the trading heart of the Zone as a sort of quality-control check. It kept the soldiers on their toes.

Nonetheless, the Paki Witch had come into the Zone that day to save daily customer Chloe Tudor from Zollo's poisoned chalice. There was no doubt about this in his mind, and it terrified him.

The fact was that Callum Bowes-West didn't just believe in the Paki Witch. He *knew* she was real.

"Chargrilled beef sandwich, Mr Bowes-West," announced the cheerful barmaid, struggling to fit his plate among the papers on the table.

"Splendid. Put it on my account."

"No problem, sir." She nudged the plate on to the table.

"Oooh, me Mum was telling me about that blind man thing in Shriveton in the paper, there," she said, reading the *Liverpool Star* on the table as she spoke.

All women were witches – all could at least multi-task, which was a form of low-level supernatural activity. Unfortunately, they were no good at killing to order or fighting, which was why his Zone staff were exclusively male. Only the sex workers were female. He wanted to put a gun to this woman's temple as she now emitted a friendly chuckle and brought her stubby finger on to the article, preventing its burial.

She continued, "Apparently he was totally cured by some sort of witch. My Mum's neighbour's husband went to school with him. The blind man, that is."

"Oh."

"Some sort of " – her tone lowered to a whisper – "Asian" – and rose again – "it was. She's well known in that area, 'pparently. Dunno if you know Shriveton."

"Not at all."

"It's all drugs and dole there, 'pparently. A slum. Full of dross, 'scuse my French! Not nice people like you, Mr B-W. Prob'ly why

95

you've never heard of it.

"Trouble is people won't work now will, they? Reference: places like Shriveton! Expect hand-outs nowadays, don't they?" She whispered again: "It's all the immigrants doin' the work now while our lot sit about. Between you and me, I think it's all wrong. But you can't say nothing, can you?

"Anyway, this" – whispering – "Asian" – and loud again – "woman has done quite a few miracles."

"Oh. Well, thank you," he said, his eyes fast on folds of beef bulging from the sandwich, willing her to go away.

She blabbered on, "Funny, really, 'cos me Mum's neighbour's husband says this miracle woman is going to be really big. Anyway," – much to his relief, at last she moved away – "must get on."

Shriveton Park

Snatch

Jamal's day had passed fretting, procrastinating and sorting. Cash money bulged from every orifice of his Tallis flat bedroom. Every cushion was stuffed with it, as was his mattress. More money was under the bathroom floor boards, along with the remainder of his cocaine, plus the paraphernalia of the drug dealer – scales, plastic sachets, blades, spoons and submachine-gun.

His position as lone kingpin felt untenable in the extreme, despite the MP5. It didn't feel enough. It *wasn't* enough. He'd get the Lidocaine from his university contact, Oz, on Thursday, and cut the remaining gear immediately thereafter. Selling it on to Krevvo would complete the first stage of his plan. The second stage was ... a blur. Panic swamped him at the mere contemplation of locating Troy's murderer, killing him or getting an assassin to do it, and absconding with all the money.

When he'd found Troy's booty of cocaine yesterday it had seemed much clearer – as well as possible, and natural. Now all he wanted was to see Jessie Rout again. Even just catching a glimpse would sustain him.

The strange thing was that he couldn't recall her face. Looking at her this morning had been like looking into the sun accidentally. Only the vaguest imprint of her form – expressionist blocks of colour on blood orange – had remained afterwards when he shut his eyes tight.

He wandered back up to Shriveton Park again. Night was

falling. Perched on the roundabout, he lit a cigarette and waited; his eyes, joyless and so very at odds with the levity of freckles on his nose, gazed longingly towards Skylark. But he couldn't see her. In a flush of despair, he flicked his foot to send the roundabout into slow rotation, hoping that somewhere in the slowly unfolding panoramic view he would see his Beloved.

The bizzies had cleared away the wreaths marking the spot where Troy had died to create a circus ring, distinct by its absence of vodka bottles, cans and spent lighters, spent cigarettes, Rizla and fast food packaging. In the distance, a young junkie-hooker and her middle-aged punter picked through the confetti of trash and entered the copse of orangey tree crowns on the other side of the field. Down in the estate, the twin towers of Tallis and Skylark cast chunky shadows that almost reached the Shopping Parade. The Zone would not close down with the wintry sun. Soon the first night shift would take over from the day boys, busily distributing their patriotic vials of gear by the Community Centre bins.

Please God, come again, he thought. Cleaners were surely either coming or going at teatime. All traffic, on foot or wheel, in and out of Shriveton had to pass the park. There was surely a chance he might see her now, here.

"Jammy!" came a shrill female voice from behind him.

He stopped turning and stood up to see Jodi Harris, a supposed half-sister of Chloe Tudor, plus her band of riotous girl mates, approaching him.

"Hey, Jam!" she shouted again, both of her hands plunging on a mini-swing seat as she passed by. It shot up and over its suspending bar, slumping down the other side to hang, contorted, like a crucifixion victim.

Jodi and her brigade advanced, their bobbing crowns of peroxide or jet black hair and spray-tanned skin giving them the appearance of Zulu warriors. Jamal groaned inwardly and outwardly at the sight of them. Closer to, they were more like Sesame Street toucans. Giggling, chattering and smoking, they stood before him, passing between themselves a two-litre bottle of cheap cider.

"Got any weed, Jam?" asked Jodi. Years of heavy smoking had made a Marshall guitar amp of her larynx, such that her voice sounded old.

She swaggered up directly in front of him, arching her back. An alluring toxicity of cigarettes, cider and sugary fragrance rose like trench gas from her expansive cleavage.

Jodi had always made a brazen beeline for the late Troy,

spurred by his attractiveness and supply of pot. Troy being gone, her desire to transact sexually and financially was now transferring to his very similar-looking brother.

"No, sorry, kid," said Jamal.

Noting that his eyes had come to momentary rest on her bosom, she grinned and opened trading with, "I'll suck your cock for a half-ounce of puff. Deal? Go on, Jammy, lovely lollipop 'ead."

Although only a year younger than he was, Jodi Harris was entirely alien to him. Somehow, despite her astonishing promiscuity, she inhabited still the land of childhood, from which recent events had closed him off forever. She was rumoured to be the half-sister of Chloe Tudor, although paternity of either girl was far from certain, and they had never shared any family life together. Since Chloe's disappearance in August, Jodi had occasionally claimed the kinship in order to get attention for herself from teachers and friends. Nonetheless, the fact was that Chloe and Jodi had never had much to do with each other beyond attending the same school, and the mutual hostility of their respective mothers.

"No can do, kid." Jamal crushed the urge to touch his black hair, which today was loose – a spongy halo above a red bandana, the Hendrix-style Troy always wore.

"Arrh, go on, Jammy," murmured Jodi into his neck, her little teeth nibbling his skin there. "It's me mate's birthday. We need some weed."

Alcohol fumes, explosive perfume and burger onions reeked from her small, trussed person, as her motionless bale of blonde hair bristled against his face. Without warning, her impudent little hand zoomed to his crotch and, before he could snatch it away, she'd unzipped his flies. With aplomb that only comes with plenty of practice, her plastic-nailed fingers had found his penis.

In the few seconds it had taken her to get achieve this, his beloved Jessie Rout had entered the park at the far corner by the oak trees. He took a sharp intake of breath and sprang to his feet, accidentally wrenching Jodi's wrist as he pulled away from her.

"Ouch!" she exclaimed.

So complete was his absorption in the other female that he had, for the moment, died to everything around him.

A gargantuan peevishness overtook Jodi. Annihilated and frustrated, she could only hate the rival who had scuppered her chance of scoring both fit older lad and weed. These feelings resonated with the viral hostility that ran in her family – the third generation in unemployment – towards job-stealing immigrants.

The same people held the view that the Paki Witch had kidnapped their Chloe (although this belief had never translated into any effort to find the missing girl, whose departure had been accepted without a whimper, much as her drug-taking and prostitution had been).

"You fuckin' pulled my wrist, twat!" Jodi bleated.

Jamal looked at her blankly for some moments, stupefied and compromised by her untimely undesirability.

"Sorry," he said. He took some steps away, adding, "I haven't got nothin' for yer, kid."

She called out to her friends: "Hey, he's fuckin' checkin' out the Paki Witch. That *is* the Paki Witch over there, innit?"

They responded variously:

"Think it is 'er, yeah."

"Dunno. Never seen the Paki Witch before."

"There's no Pakis except the Paki Witch in Shriveton, so it must be 'er."

"Yeah, it's definitely 'er. The one what kidnapped your Chloe!"

"She fuckin' did!" snarled Jodi, stung by the sudden recollection of her tribe's shallow grievance regarding their Chloe.

"Don't be soft," said Jamal, irritated, and not fully comprehending the malevolence building in her. "Look, I gotta get off, kid. See ya."

"Fuckin' Paki Witch kidnapped our Chloe!" shouted Jodi, following him, and snatching his hand. "Why have a fuckin' dirty Paki when you can have me, Jammy?!"

It frightened him that a dull, loud, rudimentary being like Jodi could pick up, as would the best of spies, the dreadful yearning within him. Now a chorus of inane sexual commentary sounded as her giggling, drunken school friends drew closer, certain that he was too gentle to strike out at them.

"You givin' 'er one, eh, Jammy?"

"You fuckin' gone all weird since your Troy."

"Yeah, now we know why yer mates are sayin' you gone fuckin' mental."

"You jibbed all yer mates 'cos you're shaggin the Paki Witch!"

"You gonna take 'er in the woods over there, eh, Jam?"

One of them even ran at him with the cider bottle, as if in a rugby tackle, screaming and wobbling with drunken glee, "'Ave some cider, Jammy, get yer in the mood."

A false nail pinged off as he wrenched free from Jodi's hand. She screamed and clawed his face, and was about to launch into a full-blown physical attack when a better idea occurred to her.

"Paki Witch!" she hollered and darted off towards the small, obscure figure in dark Muslim dress, who had now rounded the oak trees and was heading towards them.

Ribald glee bubbled from her troops, who followed, their variegated manes of sprayed and ironed hair bobbing and brash in the darkening scene.

In less than a minute the girls had reached their quarry.

"Suicide bomber!" shrieked Jodi as she crashed into the Paki Witch, who was surrounded and obscured by the gang.

Jodi looked back at Jamal, who was paralysed by the knowledge that defending his Beloved would cost him dear, and that right now exposure was the last thing he needed.

"Stop tormenting her!" he called, his words as faint as Jodi's perfume still on his skin and clothes.

"Paki Witch, do me a miracle," yelled Jodi, her gooey black-lined eyes glancing defiantly back at him as he started towards them.

"Yeah, get her a shag," shrieked her mate, "before it seals up!"

A bus pulled up ahead at the Park Road stop a few metres away on the other side of the perimeter wire fencing. With a groan and a hiss, the doors jerked open to release a waft of dust and diesel into the October air.

"Quick!" shrieked Jodi, ducking under the others who were jostling and crowding the Paki Witch.

With the speed and surgical dexterity she had just exhibited with regard to Jamal's crotch, Jodi unpicked the folds of black material wrapping her victim's head. Her friends yanked aside the Paki Witch's defending arms as Jodi wrestled clear the hijab from its underlying coil of shiny black hair, which now unrolled and was borne aloft in the wind, a sheet of satin, as the Paki Witch crashed to the floor.

"Fuckin' 'ell, she's got no ears!" screamed one of the girls.

For some moments everyone shrank back, aghast at the horrific mutilations to both sides of the cowering victim's head. To the right side of her face, beneath her sails of blue-black hair, was a rose-top of scarring, stark in her dark skin, around a pornographic epicentre of ear canal. To the other side of her head, more jagged scarring fluoresced beneath the ragged remnant of her right ear horn, the upper part of which was missing.

Jamal, who had only just reached them, froze. Time stopped. An anguish of hatred for whoever had mutilated her caught his breath and furrowed his face, and he sank his teeth into his own clenched fist. But following immediately was the terrible recognition of his own reluctance to assert himself in her defence right now.

"Give me back my scarf, please," his Beloved was pleading, in her small, accentless voice. Palms clamped flat against each side of her head, her fingers clawed her hair down and forward.

"Give it her back," he shouted, lunging forward to pull away some of the assailants, one of whom, a squealing, organic mantrap, responded by kicking him repeatedly in the shins. He shrank from volleying her away.

"Fuckin' no chance!" declared Jodi, triumphant and malign again, having recovered from the shock of beholding the Paki Witch's wounds.

Squealing with hysterical abandon, as if playing blind man's buff at a kids' party, she galloped away to the just-arrived bus on Park Road, trailing the black hijab like a windsock. The others flew after her, spewing insults as they went.

"Freak!"

"Bet you'd think twice about givin' 'er one now, Jammy, lad!"

"Thought she done miracles."

"Yeah, fuckin' fraud. Can't even fix her fuckin' self!"

Jamal sank to his haunches beside Jessie Rout. She wasn't crying. He would always remember that. It was as if being assaulted and reviled was nothing unusual.

She wanted to get up, but was afraid to take her hands away from her face. Jamal remembered from PE in school that only little kids can get up without using their hands. Adults can't. As he thought this, he untied the red bandana around his own forehead, making of it an oblong of material which now he passed under her hair, with a gentle, "This will cover you. Like a bandage."

"Thank you," she said.

Their eyes met, and he felt himself dissolving again, although confusion persisted, which simultaneously lessened and amplified his tidal wave of feeling. She was a woman, not a witch or miracle worker. Otherwise she would have healed her own wounds. The rumours about her were wrong. Surely this meant he might have a chance. The strange thing was that he loved her even more for her imperfection.

A dim thudding issued from the receding bus. Behind the mucky glass were pressed the clownish faces of Jodi and her friends. Jodi was smashing her hijab-draped fist against the roadside windows. Their age made the girls untouchable. Driven solely by their own will, they were crazed elephants plunging through the finer feelings and moral codes of everyone around them, until the legal age of responsibility, like a poacher's bullet in the brain, put an end to it all.

"Sorted it now," said Jamal, as, with big, trembling hands, he tied the bandana in a discreet knot to the side of Jessie Rout's face. Her skin smelled of lavender. How he longed to kiss her.

Helping her up, he forced himself to think about the orthopaedic factors involved – she might be bruised, or dizzy or both – to reduce the awe he felt at being so close. Her body was warm and solid and smooth beneath her black clothing. He wanted so much to maintain the physical contact, but he moved away from her as soon as she was steady and upright, because it felt wrong to touch her.

"Here, have my coat," he declared, wriggling out of it energetically, glad because the act of chivalry disguised his shaking.

"Oh, well, I –" she began, but stopped as he heaved his coat on to her shoulders.

Whereas it stopped by his navel, it must have reached to her knees – although he could not see her knees for the profusion of loose, floor-length black material enrobing her. Later he would recall feeling that, standing together, they were John and Yoko in the *Imagine* video.

"It's fine," he said, smiling and sincerely glad that, coatless, his trembling could be passed off as the effects of cold.

Suddenly she laughed. And he laughed, and he felt tears prick his eyes, but not from sadness, from sheer joy of being with her.

"You're freezing!" she giggled.

"No, I'm –"

And in the next instant his joy was snatched away as, from the corner of his eye, he observed a long-limbed, multicoloured figure lolloping in the direction of the Tallis Tower block.

Macca. He must have come on the bus which had ferried away Jodi and her pals.

Dread pushed a wash of sweat through Jamal's every pore. Even a half-hearted investigation of his bedroom might reveal his stash of cash. And, whereas all the cocaine and hardware was safely tucked in its original hiding place beneath the bath, the MP5 and ammunition was immediately visible behind the bath panel.

"I – I just gotta catch that fella over there," he stammered, looking from her to the dangerously quick Macca, who had turned off Park Road and was now out of view.

Her hand, cool and soothing, stole into his clammy palm.

"I understand, Jamal," she replied, applying a kindly squeeze to his hand, and smiling at him.

With Olympian speed, he sprinted to Macca, and managed to divert him with a lie about Tez being at their Tallis flat sorting out some business with Nanny Lilly. With an ominous, *Lookin' forward to a lickle talk, brother!* Macca changed course for the St Theresa's club, where Jamal promised to meet him shortly.

Lungs searing with intense exertion, Jamal raced back to the playground, only to find that she'd gone. She'd left his coat on the roundabout. With a sob, he slumped down beside it, the movement starting a slow rotation. Burying his face in the coat, he snorted its fabric womb in the hope of finding the ghost of his Beloved's body.

But only Jodi's sugary perfume came back to him.

CHAPTER NINE

Wednesday 27th October 201-

Shriveton

Moskowski

Like a broken spider, Moskowski scuttled across the flyover linking his maisonette flat, situated beside Skylark Tower, to the Shopping Parade. While in prison virtually every bone in his body had been fractured, and moving around was painful even ten years on. But it was necessary to do the newsagent-run every two or, ideally, three days. For the rest of the time he stayed indoors, away from the hating multitude.

Trips out must be confined to the hours when local school kids were ensconced in the classroom. He'd run out of tobacco the previous afternoon, but had endured the nicotine withdrawals rather than chance the post-funeral streets. But it was just after 10am now, and everywhere seemed pretty quiet.

Every time he went to the newsagent, he bought his *Vozlublennaya*[2] a sweetie, and left it outside Her front door on the way home. Visualising Her finding the sweetie, and picking it up, and smiling, suffused him with a joy that would sustain him between trips, and assuage the corrosive loneliness of his existence.

In the eyes of all but One of those around him, Moskowski was

---

2

Russian for *Beloved.*

vermin, the lowest of the low. Universally despised and abhorred, being out in daylight terrified him. Nonetheless, morning was the safest time for him, since the school kids were gone and everybody else was either asleep or back home. The cover of darkness also shielded the punitive actions of his legion of enemies. Morning was safer.

A deathly pallor – the consequence of no fresh air for over two decades, plus his homogenously junk food diet and heavy smoking – seemed to claim even his irises and self-cut hair, such that he had the appearance of a huge pumice stone, turned weirdly flaccid, as if extreme suffering and self-hatred had sucked out all rigidity.

The hating multitude: if *only* they could see that his heart and mind had been wholly cleansed by his *Vozlublennaya*.

Moskowski longed now for only one thing: to redeem himself.

A pair of supernaturally tall, thin teen girls passed by in an aura of sugary perfume, cigarettes and hairspray, hissing, "Fuckin' pervert."

He recoiled from them – to them he would be always a lardy, trembling, broken amalgam of his sins – and muttered his only prayer.

Moya Vozlublennaya, moya Spasitelnica, miloserdnaya tsarica Nebes, miloserdno smotrit na menya, greshnika.[3]

He'd never known any prayers because his childhood was spent in Communist Leningrad where religion was banned. So he had made up his *Vozlublennaya* prayer, which said all that he felt for Her. Over and over again he said it, spittle bubbling on his fat, moving lips, which never returned to shape because they had been split by various men's boots over the years, giving him a permanently clownish, grinning look. This facial default to apparent levity on his part alienated him absolutely from everyone around him.

Flabby and unshaven, with thinning and long, grotty hair, and sporting grubby clothes and filthy trainers, Moskowski cut a pitiable figure. Eyes closed fast against the brazen beauty of his teenage tormentors, his few remaining teeth airing as he mouthed his prayer, he shrank against the drainpipe separating Liu's Takeaway from Shriveton News.

A static energy of huge, unspent frustration hung like a thundercloud over Shriveton, and the outed spider Moskowski felt it keenly. If a group of young men met him now, inevitably he

---

3   My Beloved, my Saviour, merciful Queen of Heaven, look with mercy upon me, a sinner.

would be the weight to their pendulum of vigilante justice. The Troy Bannigan killing was really one big loose end. A corps of angry male youth in the area was itching to wrap it round the neck of a scapegoat. Organising and enacting the punishment would provide the illusion that they controlled their environment. Retribution's tyre swing would lift them from the collective wash of their own existential fury and ennui.

When he opened his eyes, the girls had gone, and the terrace overlooking the wider estate was quiet except for a pram-pushing woman and her little boy in the distance. Relief almost overwhelmed him to the extent that he felt a little faint. He'd expected them to be joined by boys. But, instead, a reprieve. The *Vozlublennaya* prayer had been answered. There was no time to lose: he must make his purchase and get back.

There was one customer inside the newsagents, a black youth with huge, sorrowful eyes and an explosive foam of black hair. Moskowski recognised him as Troy Bannigan's brother. Gentle, inward focusing and never aggressive, this boy represented the only young male in the district who had never been actively hostile towards Moskowski. Jamal passed out of the shop, clutching twenty cigarettes and a lighter, mumbling, "Sorry pal," as he accidentally brushed Moskowski's arm in the confined aisle.

Alone now in the shop, Moskowski could enjoy scanning the technicolour trove of confectionary – yellow gold *Crunchie*, onyx *Mars Bar*, amber *Fudge*, ruby *Bourneville*, sapphire *Boost* – in search of the blue pink diamond of a *Turkish Delight*. He always tried to get Her Turkish Delight. But Shriveton News often ran out of it, and they had today.

Chocolate Buttons, a large bag, were on offer, though. It would leave him slightly short, but he didn't care. He'd sit in with the lights and heater off more than usual if it meant getting his *Vozlublennaya* something special.

His *Vozlublennaya* was all the light and heat he needed.

He'd first heard about her a few months previously. She was supposed to have cured Mrs Liu, who'd been in a terrible state and wouldn't see a Western doctor.

Liu's Takeaway was, along with Shriveton News, the only place Moskowski dared visit. At Shriveton News, the silent contempt of staff was countered by the transactional necessity of his nicotine addiction. However, the Chinese people at Liu's treated him with neutrality when they served him. Provided Liu's was empty of customers, he would sometimes buy a hot meal from there. While there one time, he'd overheard the Chinese child who lived there

106

talking to his school friends, a boy and a little girl called Maisie, about how the Paki Witch had healed his Nan.

The Liu boy's story set up a huge conflict within him. He realised he'd tuned into it in the first place because it was the children, or more especially the girl called Maisie, who had drawn his attention, rather than the story itself. Epiphany had ensued: he could not delude himself any longer that he was all right. The multiple beatings – especially in jail – plus the endless tormenting, the hormonal and psychiatric treatment, and the complete social exclusion once he got out of prison had not truly changed him.

After awakening to this awful fact, he crept around in the shadows of the estate, not knowing what he was cruising for, only knowing that whatever came next would turn absolutely everything on its head.

And it did, three days later.

He'd been hurrying home from a tobacco run one afternoon in a panic. It was later than he'd thought – almost school let-out time. He oughtn't to be out at that time. He couldn't trust himself to be anywhere near children. Somewhere in his heart he recognised that subliminal urges had caused him to make this ill-timed expedition. A furnace of self-loathing, remorse and hopelessness raged within as he hobbled along the Skylark walkway, refusing to look down at the St Theresa's primary school yard to his left.

Then, for no reason, he stopped in his tracks and looked up from the concrete pathway and saw a tiny woman in Muslim dress standing less than a meter before him. She was definitely the Paki Witch the Chinese boy had been talking about in Liu's.

At first he tried to hide his face from her, drawing both his arms up, like a cornered boxer, shielding himself from her presence.

"Don't be afraid," she said, smiling a little at him. Small as a child, she was swaddled head-to-foot in black, like the old, bead-fingering, muttering women of his Soviet childhood.

"I am bad person," he replied, hands still up, peeking at her through the entrails of his ragged cardigan sleeves. She must be the *Diva Maria* to whom the old women of his childhood had appealed, in defiance of their Communist oppressors.

"Don't look at me," he pleaded.

"I have seen all I need to see." Her voice was soft and kind as a summer meadow, and her smile now unravelled him.

Like a collapsing bouncy castle, he sank ridiculously to the ground to assume a foetal crunch, head fast against his knees.

"I not worth your kindness," he blubbered tearfully, crazily hoping, as a toddler would, that because his eyes were shut tight he was invisible. "I bad person."

"You are forgiven." she told him.

Now he looked up at her, and she was as huge as the October Square statue of Lenin he'd saluted as a boy on annual loyalty-parades with his elementary school. Behind her, the Skylark tower loomed, and some goofy gulls soared in the vast space of Soviet-grey heaven above. Cowering, awestruck, he did not dare look directly at her face, so he ducked his head behind his knees again, rocking to and fro.

Suddenly, the dreadful machine driving him was stopped *dead*, and he felt himself outside of it, in the role of mystified observer of a suddenly defunct monster which had tyrannised him for years. It was rather like watching old film reels of tanks, and saluting Red Army soldiers filing past the Beaver-hatted oligarch on the Kremlin balcony. The old regime had fallen and could wreak no further havoc with the innocent. His imperious sex drive had truly gone.

He was forgiven. *Diva Maria* had forgiven him.

When he looked up again, she was gone, and he panicked. He hadn't even thanked her. Then, further along the flyover, he saw her turning into Skylark Tower, so he followed her, scrambling like a beached crab, hoping nobody would stop and hurt him as was usually the case if he stayed out too long.

Sweating, panting, more desperate to see her than he was fearful of being caught out in broad daylight, he made his way up the stairs of Skylark. He could see her small form ahead, above him, but he dared not call out to her in case he attracted attention to himself. Whereas the noise of his big boots reverberated from the interlocking parallelograms of the stairwell's hard surfaces, her divine feet made no sound. She was an angel, a goddess, ascending to her heavenly seat. He *must* thank her.

He lost sight of her on the way up, but finally, without knowing how, he came upon her room. The door was open. Inside was bare, except for a compass-embedded prayer mat on the floor, on which she sat like a child in a school assembly, looking up at him, smiling. Beside her was a small hardback book, in what looked like Arabic, open on a small wooden *rihal*.

She was even poorer than he was. Regarding her with adoration, he fell to his knees in the doorway. There was no trace of lust in his mind as he beheld her.

"Thank you," he stammered, and shook his head, looking down

at the floor. In the vicinity of her glorious person, he felt wretched, and could not keep his gaze on her. "People call me bad names. Beast. But you, you are kind. I –" he broke down, dissolving again.

"You have come to an altar where no walls or names exist," she said, standing up and crossing to him. He could feel her human warmth as she came near.

"You have saved me," he said, to the floor, trembling. "From myself."

He looked up at her. Her huge dark eyes were like those of the forbidden *Kristos* icons of his boyhood, to whom all the kneeling, terrified old women had prayed for their beloved husbands, sons, daughters, parents and friends snatched in the night during Stalin's purges, and never heard of again.

"I am not worthy to breathe same air as –"

She put her hand on his head. Any pain that followed couldn't be offset by the memory of her touch.

"You are redeemed," she told him. "Go in peace, and make your heart my altar, for I am always with you."

He stood up and, looking at Her one last time in adoration, left, purified. His *Vozlublennaya,* as he called her from that day forward, was all the light and heat he needed.

Now he emerged from the newsagents with tobacco, skins and Chocolate Buttons in hand, to find that the terrace was no longer empty. The thin teenage girls were back, with a group of boys. Three men were joining them, also: a fat, cruel one he recognised as Zone worker Billy, the boss with thinning dark hair who looked like a vulture, and an older one with dark-lens glasses who always wore a cap, and was an infrequent visitor to the estate.

The Shriveton News door shut and bolted fast behind him, leaving him no choice but to go forward, into the crowd. A couple of police officers had stepped on to the terrace, but when the vulture Zone boss crossed to them , they retreated with him from the scene, passing en route Troy Bannigan's brother, who had ducked behind a wall overlapping the stairs leading off the terrace.

"Fuckin' Choc'late Buttons in his 'and, the kiddie fiddlin' cunt," screamed one of the girls.

A chorus of abuse followed, centring round the sight of the Chocolate Buttons which Moskowski buried in his coat pocket. His whole body shook as a small band of hooded youths, modern day monks from Hell, encircled and started jostling him. One knocked off his spectacles which another crushed under foot.

"Look, I don't want trouble, boys," stuttered Moskowski, his unseeing eyes darting about the watercolour wash of his persecutors.

"Trouble is, you want boys," retorted one of his captors, to the hilarity of all except the hapless Moskowski, who, thanks to a knife being held to his back by one of the hooded teens, was prevented from escape.

"Who the Buttons for, Mozzy?"

To his left, the young mum he'd seen in the distance previously hissed, "Beast!"

Cigarette perpendicular to the handle of her pram and eyes fixed on Moskowski, she instructed the toddler beside her, "Don't fuckin' look, Jack!"

"Why have they got a knife in his back?" asked Jack, frightened.

Her cigarette fell to the floor as she slapped his head, whereupon the child in the pram started screaming.

"Look what you fuckin' made me do now, Jack, you little twat! And now Erin's kickin' off."

She dived for the cigarette, and jammed it in her mouth as she administered another slap to Jack. It sent him thudding against Liu's shop window as she hollered into the crowd: "Fuckin' twats like Mozzy shouldn't be nowhere near fuckin' kids!"

"But the Paki Witch cure me!" screamed Moskowski above the rousing and righteous refrain of similar abuse building noise around him. "She forgive me. I am sorry for my terrible things. Little boy, lady, listen, please. Every person, listen to me. The Paki –"

The crowd started prodding, pinching and pulling Moskowski's clothes and hair. The fact that two fairly senior Zone soldiers were presiding encouraged them no end. If the Zone approved, it was good.

"Evil perv!"

"Paedophile!"

"Fuckin' kiddie fiddler."

Moskowski's tearful objections somehow floated above the scramble of hatred: "My *Vozlublennaya* has saved me. I am cured."

"What the fuck are you talkin' about?" shrieked someone.

"The Paki Witch! She is my saviour. She cure me!"

"You're only saying it because you heard about Bob Reilly."

"Yeah, jumpin' on the fuckin' bandwagon," sneered Billy Stokes, who, along with his Zone co-worker, had remained silently approving and on the edge of the crowd until now. He moved in.

"Think we're all soft, ya cunt?" continued Billy. "How do we know you been cured?"

"Show him pictures of kids and see if he gets a hard on," screamed Jack's mum.

"Cunts like you should have their fuckin' dick cut off!" growled Billy Stokes.

And then the idea took hold. A few of the gang shrank from the horror of it, but were spurred by the enthusiasm of their peers, particularly Billy Stokes, who was now brandishing a black machete and seemed very keen to use it.

"It's no more than he deserves," piped Jack's mum. "After what he done to them girls."

More pleas bled from the victim's mouth: "Listen, twenty years ago I do very bad things. To the girls. But I am different now. The Paki Witch save me."

"Who the Buttons for, then, eh?"

"For *Vozlublennaya*. For Paki Witch. I buy her sweeties to say thank you for saving me. I bring her sweeties every time I buy my tobacco and papers. I bring Paki Witch sweetie."

The Zone man in the cap had come forward. There was a profound stillness to him, which somehow harnessed the energies of those around him such that, although he spoke softly, he was clearly audible above the jostling hubbub of Moskowski's persecutors.

"You know where the Paki Witch lives?"

Moskowski was silent. He had remembered the man's name. It was Zollo. He didn't know why he should recall this man's name, because he had had no special dealings with him over the years.

"Take me to the Paki Witch," said Zollo, coming up close to Moskowski.

The crowd were silent, and now Moskowski realised why he had remembered Zollo's name. Zollo was unlike everyone else around here. In the various skirmishes which Moskowski had had with the real law-enforcement in Shriveton – the Incubo's soldiers, the lowest ranks of which sometimes made sport of him as he shuffled near the Zone to buy his tobacco – Zollo had never regarded him with the slightest opprobrium. Zollo was entirely indifferent to him, and that was unique. Purged of his own dreadful proclivities, the doomed Russian could recognise in Zollo the antithesis of his *Vozlublennaya*.

"No. I will not take you."

Zollo thought for a few moments, and then gave a strange, high-sounding laugh of surprise.

"You should rethink that," he said calmly, signalling Billy, who, pushing aside the knife-wielding teen, wrapped his own sharp-nailed arm around his victim's neck and pushed his machete through Moskowski's jacket to pierce the flesh below. The crowd were delighted at this upping of the stakes.

Moskowski writhed and cried, as Billy tugged at his neck and nudged the blade into his back. But he refused to speak.

"All right, Billy," said Zollo, after a minute or two.

Billy stepped away as Zollo came in closer still to the trembling victim and guided him away to the Shriveton News front, just out of ear shot of the crowd. Moskowski had soiled himself, which invited raucous hostility from some among the spectators as he moved, trailing excreta.

"Look, I think you misunderstand me," said Zollo. "Have a smoke and calm yourself down."

Moskowski's fat hand dived into his pocket and pulled out his tobacco and skins, but he was too shaken to roll. So Zollo rolled him a fat cigarette with his pale, gentrified hands so at odds with the rest of his persona, saying, "I'm interested to meet the Paki Witch, that's all. My mother's been sick and I want the Paki Witch to take a look at her. It's very straightforward."

Moskowski was fast against the Shriveton News door, which was still tightly shut and bolted against the unfolding events. All CCTV cameras around the Parade were, of course, non-functioning, a special concession organised by the ever-obliging Superintendent Meyers.

Like a starving baby Moskowski suckled on the cigarette, knowing it would be his last. He thought only of inhaling, as deeply as possible, and savouring it. Smoking was his only vice now, and in any case, it was only harmful to himself. His *Vozlublennaya* had saved him. He repeated under his breath, eyes screwed shut,

"Moya Vozlublennaya, *moya Spasitelnica, miloserdnaya tsarica Nebes, miloserdno smotrit na menya, greshnika.*"

"You know where she lives, don't you?"

Moskowski was silent. His skin crawled as Zollo leaned over and whispered in his ear: "I can save you from all of this. I'll set you up in Mexico, give you a new identity. I have the power to do that. You know that. You'll live like a Tsar with a harem of soft-skinned, little girls years off their first period. They'll lie naked at your feet, calling your name."

Zollo stood back, a sincere and encouraging look upon his face. More than slightly smug at this coup (he'd expected it would be necessary to work *very* hard to locate the Paki Witch), he could afford a smile.

Of course, this wretched Russian would probably want proof of intention; the crowd would have to be dispersed, and a large sum of money handed over to him. Of course, as soon as the troublesome miracle worker had been located, Moskowski would be killed, and his body chopped up and fed to the gulls. Standard procedure. After all, no one would ever look for Moskowski.

Moskowski didn't answer. Every wisp of exhaled smoke was wrapped around the syllables of his home-made Russian prayer.

"Come on, now," coaxed Zollo. "Tonight you could be on a plane out of here. Away from that nasty crowd."

Still, the victim pulled on his cigarette, eyes closed, muttering his foreign little prayer. There was no begging for mercy, or bargaining. Zollo found this curious.

Then, decisively, Moskowski took his last drag, and cast the stub away from him. He stopped cringing and shaking and stared, defiant, at Zollo.

"No."

Zollo shook his head in genuine bewilderment. "Do you understand what I'm offering you?"

"I understand. I understand all of it. You think you give me what I want. But I don't want it, now. The Paki Witch has save me."

"But *I* can save you..." – Zollo indicated the crowd behind him, and the machete-brandishing, sadistic Billy in the foreground – "...from that!"

"Your price too high for me."

"All I want is to see the Paki Witch. To talk. So she can heal my old mum."

"You lie! You evil one, not Moskowski."

Angry now, Zollo grabbed him by the coat, snarling: "Either you do it my way, or Billy will get it out of you with his knife."

"No! I say NO."

With a powerful twist of his shoulders, Moskowski freed himself, and almost buckled over a stabbing pain in his upper body which made him gasp. A trickle of vomit fell from his mouth, and a tidal sweat soaked his whole person, beading on his brow. He felt dizzy again. Nonetheless, he remained upright staring out his adversary.

Zollo hoped that his own fear was not evident. Never in his experience had he encountered such tenacity in an opponent.

"You know what Billy will do to you, don't you? And there's not a single fucker in this whole place who'll stop him. And you'll squeal like a pig with no dick, but you'll have told us anyway. And it'll be worse for her that you didn't tell me. Understand? I'll make your *Votszu*-fuckin'-*Blennya* pay for you holding out."

With a gulp Moskowski collected phlegm and vomit and tears and tobacco strands in his mouth and spat it out – a huge, slimy bolus – directly in Zollo's face.

"I will *never* betray Paki Witch. She my saviour."

A few seconds, which seemed like an hour, went by, during which Zollo stood, dumbfounded as an ectoplasm of the convicted paedophile's spittle slithered from his nose and his glasses.

Onlookers could not fathom the defiant nobility of Moskowski, who appeared now to be almost indifferent to everything around him. His breathing was extremely laboured, and sweat streamed from his face, but he would not back down.

Zollo started wiping his face with improbably refined looking large silk handkerchief. With a terse, "Over to you, Billy – I'm off," he set in motion the inevitable.

Billy came over and grabbed Moskowski's arm, while Zollo made off towards the stairs leading down to the car park, only to stop abruptly and gasp, "Jesus... Troy?"

He stared in terrified disbelief at the spectre before him. From a wall beside the stairs leading off the terrace, a figure had stepped out. The dead were walking.

The terrace had fallen silent when they observed the radical change in Zollo's demeanour. It was as if Zollo instantly become someone else – smaller in status and stature, an awkward imposter. The man before them was uncomfortable, different, and scared in the way middle-class kids coming to Shriveton to score were scared.

The spectre spoke: "Erm, I'm Jamal."

"You OK, Zoll?" called Billy. He held the machete to Moskowski's neck.

"Yeah," said Zollo, ectoplasm still glistening on his face and glasses.

Briefly, Zollo and Jamal stared at each other, aware of the profound unease each created in the other. Jamal was seeing him not as a slightly lazy, ruthless Incubo capo who nobody ever crossed or got to know, but rather as a bank manager type in a gangland costume.

Nor could Jamal get one seemingly irrelevant thought out of his mind: why had Zollo not taken off his glasses and cleaned them? That would be the first thing you would do if anyone – especially a paedophile – spat in your face. But almost immediately this thought became engulfed by his eagerness to get away. He'd only called at the Parade to get cigarettes and had found himself watching another horror show. It frightened him how much he hated every single member of the noisy, salivating mob.

It was Zollo who looked away first as he mumbled, "Sorry, lad, you look like yer brother."

Self-anger suffused Zollo: blacks all look the same. Banquo's Ghost here had disarmed him, right on the Zone front line. He wanted to kill this kid with his own bare hands, but instead hastened away and down the stairs, shouting as he went, "Sort it, Billy."

With Zollo gone, Billy became the great white shark in the fish pond of teenager plankton.

"We're gonna do what shoulda been done a long time ago, Mozzy," he announced, relishing dominance and drawing a little blood with the machete blade from the dumpling grey of his victim's neck. "Unless you tell me where I can find the Paki Witch."

"I will never tell!" panted Moskowski. He fell back against the door of Liu's Takeaway, a look of immeasurable fatigue washing over him. Vomit bubbled from his mouth now, and his eyes were closing.

In a flash, insanity surged in Jamal, like frothing milk in a pan. He walked forward and shouted at Billy, "Look, just let him go!"

Billy looked at him in astonishment. "Are you 'avin a laugh?"

The two skinny teenage girls, realising the murderous intent of the ringleaders and perhaps swayed by their handsome and bereaved peer Jamal's call for mercy, became frightened and child-like. They peeled off to stand beside Jack and his mother and pram-strapped Erin outside Shriveton News.

"You're on the wrong side, Jammy, pal," said Billy.

With that Billy pushed Moskowski back into the blood-hungry mob. The hell monks started pushing him between themselves, as if he were a huge, soggy medicine ball. Moskowski staggered and gasped as he moved.

"Take him down Shrivie!" screamed Billy, to cheers of approval.

Everyone was hot with excitement and anticipation of ritualistic public punishment at Shriveton Park, and pulled in close around Billy, who once again had his long-nailed hand and machete blade on Moskowski's sweating, pallid flesh. The most base and primeval instincts of the many had been collectivised to form a single will which governed their organic whole. The mob-will *would* prevail, despite Jamal's continuing protestations. Blood *would* be let, and atonement made for the huge rip in the communal consciousness caused by Troy's being torn from them.

The crowd turned in the direction of Shriveton Park, but had processed no more than a couple of paces when, suddenly, Moskowski lunged forwards with a kangaroo vigour that sprang him from Billy's grip. In an instant he was a hideous caricature of a ballet soloist, frantically performing his swan song on the few flagstones of empty stage created as the crowd stepped back.

Charged into a chaotic last dance by a massive cardiac arrest, Moskowski's torso and limbs cleaved wildly the space around him. Just as his spirit finally parted from the lump of flesh which nobody anywhere had ever loved, he remembered Her touch.

And then She was standing before him, again, silhouetted against a sky white with dazzling stars, Her hand reaching out to him. *Vozlublennaya* had come again to take him home. With a beatific smile on his crooked lips, he collapsed, lifeless, to the ground, his open but unseeing eyes on the Soviet-grey sky above.

Instantly, the crowd dissolved. The Shriveton News door nudged open, and a cautious shop assistant looked out. Before she had the chance to close it again, Jack's mum pushed her way in, calling to her son, who was sobbing as he beheld the dead man on the terrace before him, "Jack, keep an eye on Erin while I grab me Lotto and ciggies."

CHAPTER TEN

<u>Thursday 28th October 201-</u>

BEAST OF BRIXTON DIES OF HEART ATTACK

Exclusive by Ethan Greenberg

Russian-born sex offender, Vladimir Moskowski (43), collapsed and died outside the Shriveton Shopping Parade yesterday. The cause of death is believed to be coronary heart failure, and police are not treating the death as suspicious.

Dubbed the Beast of Brixton, Moskowski was jailed in 1989 for kidnapping and assaulting two eight-year-old girls on their way home from their London primary school. After three days, he gave himself and them up to the Metropolitan Police.

Paroled in 1999, Moskowski moved to Liverpool. On several occasions he publicly apologised for his crimes.

<u>Liverpool</u>

<u>Jamal's Epiphany</u>

The appointment scheduled for 2pm with Lidocaine supplier, Oz, represented the final stage of preparations. After today, Jamal would *definitely* have the means to buy vengeance. But every time he thought about *how* vengeance would be achieved, he drew a blank, and instead started fantasising about Jessie Rout. Since yesterday's clash with Jodi Harris in Shriveton Park, these fantasies involved Californian plastic surgeons and beach houses, followed by a Las Vegas wedding, all bought with the proceeds of his drug dealing. The only way to escape from this *how-less* state, which thoughts of his Beloved triggered, was to return to the logistics of preparation for vengeance.

Much though he regretted it, it had become necessary to include Macca in his plans. Macca had wanted in – which was why he had come to Shriveton yesterday, to quiz his *lickle bro* about that bathroom mirror he'd glimpsed on top of the chest of drawers in Jammy's bedroom. Macca was only too willing to assist in return for a few ounces of puff. The real winner in all of this would be Liverpool University technician Oz, who sourced the perfectly legal Hong Kong-made Lidocaine at a tiny fraction of the price he charged Jamal.

The pick-up was at Blackwell's bookstore in the redbrick heart of the university. Jamal was using Macca's house in Toxteth, near town, to effect the transformation from estate youth to a university student, deploying a costume he had spent the previous day assembling from charity shops. From Macca's he would walk the short distance to Blackwell's, at the top of Brownlow Hill.

Once a fine house built, like so much of Liverpool's nineteenth-century architectural finery, with Slave Trade gains, Macca's Georgian Terrace bedsit was now rundown and litter-strewn. Even pressing the doorbell seemed to compromise the rotten wood on which it was fixed. Macca appeared, like a bizarre extra springing from the puppeteer's tent: all hat and hair; long, brightly clad limbs; and bleary red eyes. Usually so chilled – to the point of affectation – today he appeared mildly agitated.

"Housing threatening to cut me money," he explained, punching the dial pad of his iPhone to end the intense call he'd been having. "Anything for me, lickle bro?"

Jamal dropped him four golf balls of resin and passed into his bedsit with its filthy bedding, permanently closed curtains, mountainous ashtrays, and profusion of grubby, garish clothes.

"Royal Afghani, mmm!" drooled Macca.

Pocketing all but one, he peeled back the sepals of tinfoil wrapping, and sniffed. He disappeared down the hallway, announcing, "I'll skin up in the can while you get changed, lickle bro."

Jamal was glad that his own high levels of adrenalin thinned the choking smog of unwashed skin and clothes, overflowing bins and dirty plates in Macca's bedroom. Working quickly, not least to get back into the fresh air outside, he had almost effected the transformation into student, and was just about to put on his overcoat, when there was a furious banging from down the corridor.

118

A small female voice shouted through the letterbox, "I know you're in there Macca, yer fuckin' cheatin' TWAT!"

"Oh shit, it's Loraine!" yelped Macca, crashing into the bedroom, his conical spliff like a Harry Potter wand fast between his fingers. He threw himself in foetal position on the bed and put his tendrilled head in his hands.

"Jammy, go and tell 'er I not in."

Jamal froze, his every instinct threatened by the intrusion of Macca's lady friend Loraine, and the new scenario she introduced. Change was not good on a drop.

"Look, I don't want –"

"Jesus, man, get rid of 'er, please! She'll rip my fuckin' bollocks off."

From the variegated grimy wool of his jacket pocket Macca fished one of the cannabis golf balls.

"Tell 'er I gone to court. Give 'er this blow. It will shut 'er big scouse gob. I'm gonna shut me door till she's gone."

He sprang up, shooing Jamal ahead of him, and closed the bedroom door. With reluctance, Jamal approached the vibrating front door, which was still withstanding Loraine's battering. He peered through the peephole and saw Loraine, a whippet-thin woman, with hideous dyed black hair and black kohl eyes and brows stark against a peaky and lined white face. Jamal put the chain on and opened the door. Loath as he was to intervene, the fuss she was creating on the street outside had to be stopped.

"Macca's gone court," he said, chin above the chain bridging the aperture of the open door.

"Oh, yeah, think I was fuckin' born yesterday?" she sneered, and started screeching insults again, and punching the door. "TWAT!"

"He's left you an ounce," said Jamal in desperation, lifting into her view the silver golf ball of gear. "And he's goin' round yours straight after court."

She stopped screeching, eye on the cannabis.

"OK, then," she said, instantly appeased.

She raised her crocodile-claw hand up to the gap and snatched the tinfoil ball. With a tart, "You tell Macca to get his black ass round and see me," she turned and left.

"You done me a big favour there," breathed Macca once the click-clack of her high-heeled boots had receded from beyond the front door.

Suckling hard on his spliff (which, as was always the case, he never shared), he rocked to and fro on his single bed, babbling

119

anxiously.

"Look, Jammy, you gotta go. She'll be back. She's one crazy woman. *Tears fall from me eyes like rain, Loraine. A terrible pain in me brain, Loraine.* Linton Kwesi. That nigger is God, Jammy, you know that? People round your way only want the Paki Witch 'ho cos they never heard Linton Kwesi. You gotta go, now, though, Jammy. Fuck me brother, you gotta go now."

Staring at him now, Jamal experienced a surge of inexplicable hostility: Macca knew nothing worth knowing. His whole life had been spent as an extra in a ridiculous Rastafarian charade. Shifting and vapid as the smoke frothing from his spliff, he floated on the periphery of other people's culture, contributing only noxious smells.

"Don't call her a 'ho!" Jamal growled. He threw on his student overcoat and, picking up the rucksack, made his way to the front door

"Wha' you mean, nigger? She's a *mad* motherfuckin' 'ho, my Loraine."

"No, I mean the – the Paki Witch."

Macca hesitated, surprised. He shrugged, and said, with affected lightness, "Nigger, the Paki Witch is just a fuckin' fairy story. She never even made a record, man. Hey," – he stood up, ushering Jamal towards the front door – "this Afghani is fuckin' mind blowin'. Get your Nan some."

He shoved Jamal over the threshold, adding, "Get off, now, Jammy. Before Loraine come back with one of her sons. Bad motherfuckers, her sons, man. Hey!"

He cast an approving glance at Jamal's student disguise – black canvas bag slung over the shoulder, lace-up boots, cheap jeans, deep brown-rimmed spectacles, navy overcoat and fingerless gloves.

"You look the part, nigger!"

Without replying, Jamal walked off into the chill, sunny October afternoon. Loraine's pain had put him five minutes behind schedule. The overcoat was far too big for him, and felt more like Batman's cape. He half-ran all the way to Hope Street, past its Gotham City Philharmonic Hall, before checking the time again.

Five to two – he'd almost made the time up. Hastening on to Mount Pleasant, crowned by its Sphinx of creamy concrete parallelograms that made up the Roman Catholic Cathedral, got him back on schedule. He'd not been in this part of town since his primary school carol concerts had been held there. Passing the cathedral, he found himself recalling a carol concert in which he had done a reading because he was *sort of black* in the words (he'd overheard) of his teacher.

He entered Blackwell's bookshop and took his place at the Classic Literature section, a stitch searing his right side from the effort of running. Lines from his carol service speech were resonating in his mind: *The light shines in the darkness, but the darkness has not understood it.* His concentration felt weak. Time to get the focus necessary to complete the deal. Jamming the rucksack between his ankles, he plucked a random novel from the shelf and waited.

It was the simplest switch in the world. Oz would arrive and stand beside him. He would take a book and drop his identical rucksack (full of Lidocaine!) to the floor. They would remain there for some moments until Jamal, picking up Oz's bag, would wander over to the till to buy the book he was reading.

Without reading, Jamal's eyes ran over the words of *Heart of Darkness*. At least this was quite a short book. Most proper books went on forever, which was why only university students bothered with them.

"Hi there! Great to see you again. Ooh, like the specs. Need any help?" enquired a friendly sales assistant, angling her bespectacled head to see what he was reading. "Ooh, we did Conrad for A level. Your friend's just been in."

She gave a crooked toothed, dimpled smile that somehow seemed so redolent of book land, a world so far away from the one Jamal inhabited. Sweat sprouted on his neck like serum flooding a picked scab.

"Erm, erm, my friend?" stammered Jamal, wide eyed with terror. His hand started to shake.

"Yeah, the tall Australian you were with last time you came in. He was surprised I remembered him, too. Hey! You guys have the same bags, I remember. It's a wonder you didn't get them mixed –"

She was scrutinising him now as fear all but immobilised him. Somehow he managed a pretence that his phone had vibrated, and began speaking into it.

"All right, mate. Yeah, great. Cheers." He stooped for his bag, announcing to her, "Sorry got to go."

Then, still conducting an imaginary conversation, he went to the till and bought *Heart of Darkness* (he couldn't risk leaving it there with his prints on it).

Troy must have made the Lidocaine switch in this place last

time, and chatted her up while he waited. She was confusing him with his brother. Moreover, she'd blown the deal by recognising and talking to Oz today. Oz had been frightened off.

Still sweating profusely, he stuffed the Blackwell's book into his overcoat pocket and made off hastily along Brownlow Hill, his guts churning with the paranoiac feeling that a multiplicity of eyes and cameras were fixed on him.

After some minutes, a fizzing light-headedness came over him, forcing him to sink back against the Victoria Building wall. With trembling hand he lit a cigarette and regarded the sunny ordinariness of light traffic and campus activity all around him. Chattering and book-heavy clusters of student pedestrians wandered by, giving him no more of a glance than they did the inscription beside which he stood, *For the advancement of learning and ennoblement of life the Victoria Building was raised by the men of Liverpool in the year of Our Lord 1892.* He wondered how many of these passing students would be snorting his gear in the clubs this weekend on their journey towards graduate employment and respectability.

A gang of freshmen medical students passed him, volubly bemoaning an anatomy practical during which one of their number had fainted. They stopped and waited a few steps up the road as one of them retraced his steps.

"Hey mate, got any weed?" he asked Jamal, in posh and confidential tones.

The drug-dealing fraternity regarded medics, with their much vaunted work/play-hard ethos, as reliably good customers. *Heds to a man* Troy had once described them.

"No pal," Jamal mumbled, looking away from the student's open face, with its rude bloom of youth.

Nobody looked like that in Shriveton. This bright young thing probably had a name like Edward or Charles or Monty. A Hogwarts-like miniature of Edward/Charles/Monty's life formed in Jamal's mind. Mum wasn't a smackhead, but a plummy, fragrant creature who worried about things like son dropping a grade in Latin GCSE. She was married to debonair Dad, who wasn't serving a long-term jail sentence for drug dealing and assault. Rather, Dad varied cheering on Edward/Charles/Monty from the rugger sidelines with barked Blackberry instructions to his (licit) big business minions.

The Edward/Charles/Monty nucleus knew the difference between Brahms and Beethoven. They shopped at Waitrose. And when they went to Europe, it was not to organise shipments of cocaine or heroin, but rather to enjoy Mediterranean cuisine and practise their French.

In response to the Edward/Charles/Monty's question, Jamal had wanted to feign indignation with a horrified, *I'm not a dealer!* But a flash of insight had suddenly illuminated for him why this fresh-faced fellow knew he could score.

Jamal looked what he was. Although young, his skin was weathered by cyclonic cares and poverty. Tension lines shot perpendicularly from his brows, his lips, and his jaw line. The expensive brand of cigarettes in his hand, at odds with his slum demeanour, betrayed him. This was what Macca's *You look the part, nigger* really meant.

"Oh, sorry," mumbled the student, an embarrassed Gainsborough-girl portrait flush pinking up his cheeks. He smiled apologetically.

And then insanity gripped Jamal, for a wrinkle in time only, but enough for him to urge, "Don't throw it all away, mate."

In his ear, his own strong local accent clanged, like an empty kettle tied to the ankle of a tap dancer. It seemed lurid compared to the RP neutrality of Edward/Charles/Monty's puzzled, "I'm sorry?"

Jamal held him in his gaze and, with a small snort and shake of his head, heaved himself from the wall to walk away in the direction of town. But he had only progressed a few metres when a heavy grip on his shoulder immobilised him.

"Let's have a look in the bag, son," came a gruff voice from just behind his ear.

Instantly, Edward/Charles/Monty and the other medical students melted away from view, like farts in the air. Two uniformed men had come from nowhere and were either side of him.

As Jamal's insides liquefied, he could think only one thought: Jessie Rout would be disappointed in him.

"OK, open the bag, son."

At least it wasn't full of Lidocaine, he consoled himself as he opened the zip. A bag full of money was easier to explain. A police siren wail in the distance grew louder as it approached. One of the men was speaking into the walkie-talkie, obviously to the approaching squad car.

You look the part, nigger rang in his throbbing head.

One of the men was gutting the bag with his fat white hands. The other had an iron grip on Jamal's collar.

"I'm sorry, sir," said the uniformed man, eyeing the articles decanted on the pavement. He released Jamal, who turned to face their baffled expressions.

Then it clicked. And Jamal wanted to scream with relief. He wanted to leap and dance! Inside the rucksack, beneath the protective crust of old books and the legitimately purchased *Heart of Darkness*, was a stinking pile of old underwear.

"We made a mistake," confessed the same man, wafting the stench of the bag contents from his own nose as he spoke.

Immediately his colleague began talking into his radio again, with the consequence that the wailing siren ceased. In his blind panic, Jamal hadn't even clocked that they weren't even police, just uniformed security staff from Blackwell's, who had no doubt been alerted by the suspicious bespectacled sales assistant there.

Loraine's pain had all been a ruse to separate him from his rucksack full of cash, which Macca had replaced with his own fetid laundry. No wonder Macca had seemed agitated. Robbing cunt.

Jamal walked hastily away in the direction of the city centre. Neurotic projections danced like kids on Mcat in his mind. Macca had crossed him; Oz hadn't shown. Does each event spin the next link in the chain, or is the chain spun in advance by destiny? If the drop had gone ahead, and Oz had ended up with a bagful of unwashed underwear instead of three grand, what then?

Rounding the corner on to Lime Street brought him to the Adelphi Hotel. He could never see it without remembering one of the few good times of his childhood. His Nan, off the booze and in receipt of a huge win on Bingo, had treated him and Troy to afternoon tea in the chandelier-sparkling, springy-carpeted, creamy-corniced Adelphi, with its cheerful uniformed staff, and heaven-high scones with proper butter (with no toast crumbs in it), and real strawberries, as big as hearts.

Even given today's cash loss, he had enough money to *live* at the Adelphi for a month, or more.

Like Tez, and Inky, he was liquid, and therefore formless. He must slither and seep through the cracks of life, always moving, never standing tall, forever trickling and tending towards the lowest point. But, unlike them, Jamal had found a divine vessel into which his liquid life could flow and finally find form. If either the money or the Lidocaine had been found in that bag, a subsequent search of his Tallis flat would have convicted him there and then. He believed that Jessie Rout had intervened in some way today, and saved him.

The familiar cityscape was bursting into life. He could feel on his hollow cheek the wing-wind of pigeons and gulls springing away from his quick step on the pavements. Usually, he came into town on shoplifting expeditions with Troy (Jamal, being younger, was always the decoy). Not now. Not ever again.

Passing the vast glassy semicircle of Lime Street Station, he came to St George's Hall. He turned his back on its grandiose banks of stone steps and Corinthian columns to lean against one of the giant lion statues on the forecourt there. He and the lion gazed over at the brash *Blood Brothers* billboards of the Empire Theatre on the opposite side of the road. And, as if for the very first time, he tasted the Irish Sea salt and bus-diesel of the city air, and knew he had come home.

Evening; Matherfield Park

Promises

"I will *personally* guarantee your safety," Tez promised, hand cupped around the mouthpiece of his phone.

Flossie, his Staffordshire bull terrier, snarled as a young couple came into view of the bus shelter where he sat smoking, phone to his ear. Above, the light of Venus, brightest star of the sky, and a chalky full moon were failing to penetrate a milky vapour of gathering rainclouds. Quaint as a Christmas card, Matherfield General Stores threw a block of light across the glistening pavement on to which the young couple now stepped. Observing Matherfield Park embarrassment, cultural anomaly and deflator of local property prices, Tez, they halted abruptly.

"You got my word," Tez promised.

Eighteen-year-old Gaz was crying like a child down the phone. He had been holed up in Tower Hamlets for weeks, and still not been properly paid out. His terminally ill mother was calling for him from her deathbed in Liverpool Central Infirmary – lung cancer – and he needed to come back, urgently.

Not for the first time, the Zone Chief was glad he'd kept Gaz alive, rather than have him meet an unfortunate accident on the getaway from Shriveton Park. Jamal Bannigan was losing his mind: refusing to see visitors, and varying complete isolation at home with trips to the Shriveton park, where he'd been seen talking to himself near the site of his brother's murder. Granting Jamal's vengeance wish would hopefully prevent a complete breakdown.

Tez owed Jamal.

"Look, I'll sort it," promised Tez. "Get a train up tonight. I'll have Billy pick you up at Lime Street and take you straight to the LCI ... What time? ... OK ... Phone me back with the time, kid..."

The young couple opposite were now hurrying away. They would pay over a tenner for a taxi, or walk in the rain, rather than sit beside Tez at the stop where a bus would arrive imminently. Everyone in Matherfield Park avoided Tez.

Tez lit another cigarette from the end of his existing one, which he discarded. If *only* Jammy didn't look so much like his brother, then it would have been easier to get on with things. But they were so alike, although it was Troy whom Tez had loved. Obliviously heterosexual, foolish, soft-hearted and hard-bodied Troy had *almost* undone him.

Tez made a call to Meyers. "When I give you the nod, pick up Jamal Bannigan. Keep him until I say when."

Formby Beach Boy

If *only* Troy hadn't lifted that kee of cocaine from the Seaforth consignment, lamented Tez, suckling like a lamb on the nipple of his cigarette. Stealing from Inky was a capital offence. Troy had been a fool, with an inflated opinion of himself, probably created by the female attention paid constantly to his attractive looks and personality.

Zollo had been merciless in the face of incontrovertible evidence: he had *seen* Troy put that kee in his pocket. Game over. After dropping Troy off at Tallis Towers, Zollo and Tez had sat in Tez's old Vauxhall Corsa on Park Road, next to the Shriveton Park playground where in five days Troy would be gunned down.

Zollo's expensive aftershave had infused the small interior space, overtaking even the tobacco-rancid upholstery. Tez was always worried by the intense hatred he felt for Zollo: was it sufficiently disguised? For years, and daily, Tez had fantasised about killing him.

"Troy Bannigan's gotta pay," said Zollo, nonchalant.

Of course, Tez had tried to mitigate the death sentence, but the fact was that Zollo had always detested Troy – for no discernible reason – and remained adamant. It was as if the cocaine theft at Seaforth was just the excuse Zollo was looking for.

"But he's just a kid, and –" Tez protested.

"And what?" Zollo's soupy pale eyes, huge behind tinted spectacle lenses, fastened him. Tez hesitated, as Zollo repeated, "And what, Tez?"

"Nothin'," mumbled Tez, and then brightened as a defence

occurred to him. "It's just that Troy's pretty well liked round 'ere and it might draw attention, like. What with Chloe disappearing sudden, like. People might think he's behind it, and lose confidence, like, in the Zone. Just as we're tryin' to get back after we lost Southampton."

A slow smile of approval split Zollo's sallow face. "Nice to hear you thinking business, Tez, because for a moment there I thought you might be attached to his black ass. Speaking figuratively, of course."

"Fuckin' no chance!" said Tez, too quickly indignant and dismayed. "What yer fuckin' drivin' at, man? Am fuckin' married!"

"Take it easy," Zollo replied. Sitting back in his seat, his smile widened as he watched Tez's best efforts to feign barely-controlled outrage. "We need to remember that it *might* be Troy who organised Chloe's departure," he reminded.

Whenever Zollo talked about the disappearance of Chloe Tudor, his manner always became strained. A formality came into his voice, which seemed to belong to someone else. And his clean-nailed fingers twisted and flicked.

"Troy can barely skin up by 'imself, let alone organise a rescue mission for his fuckin' bird," said Tez. "He's a dreamer, not a schemer."

"Well he schemed his way to a whole kee of Inky's beak tonight."

"Yeah, but that's not the same as springin' Chloe Tudor from the middle of the Zone."

After a few pensive moments, Zollo enquired, a little self-conscious, "Chloe Tudor *wasn't* his bird was she?"

"Yer wha'?"

"Was she with 'im?"

"Chloe Tudor's shagged 'er way round the whole o' fuckin' Shrivie, mate. "

Zollo's whole person became suddenly charged, creating a prickling static between them which he broke by leaning over and snatching Tez's coat. A vicious mania surged Zollo's features, boggling his devil's eyes as he hissed, "I know that, but was she with *him*?"

Being physically connected with Zollo's smothering presence was instantaneously appalling. With uncoordinated urgency, Tez pushed himself free.

"No honest, definitely she weren't 'is bird," he bleated.

"But you just said –"

"Yeah, I never meant she was 'is bird. Was speakin', yer know –

"

"Figuratively."

"Yeah."

Tez shuddered, as he always did whenever he really *saw* Zollo, with his clean hands and choking perfumed skin. Little things betrayed him: the gentleman's hands, the weird dyed hair, the ease with which he summoned words like *figuratively*. Tez's wife Jewel called him the devil in a lorry driver costume.

"Anyway," he continued, intensely relieved that Zollo seemed to be calming down. "Don't worry about Troy, he's –"

"Inky wants him dead," cut in Zollo, fixing him with a demonic stare.

Tez couldn't even remember when he'd realised that Zollo was the Incubo, or why. It was something Tez had always kept to himself, although it had bothered him over the years, not least because there was something absurd, childish even, about Zollo's charade. Zollo's Zone was his own invented world where he came for thrills first and cash second, an ordering of priorities which was in itself questionable. Sometimes it felt like Zollo was laughing at everyone in this hell he had created. The only time he became fully part of that hell was whenever he spoke of Chloe Tudor.

"OK, I'll sort Troy," Tez mumbled, hating himself.

For all his Zone Chief status and wealth, Tez was in fact just Zollo's puppet. At least these days he could subcontract the dirty work. When he was just starting out as a new-recruit Continental runner, he had done the hits himself, three times.

The first two hits had been necessary to constrain rival gang activity. Thanks to his punitive steps, the Sons were well on side now, and had been for years. Tez used them for the low level work – warning beatings and threats/harrassment, security duties around the Zone perimeters, and the occasional hit.

The third and final murder which Tez had carried out personally – of a young foot soldier, Ben, suspected of being a police informant – had firmly established him as Zone Chief three years ago.

He'd dumped the body on Formby Beach, just as the sun rose over the plumes of marram grass that sprouted like magnified bristles from creamy sandhills. Transferring him with a thud from car boot to sandhillside, the victim's eyes had flickered open, a reflexive response to dawn light. Alive: the horror as Ben's plump face flesh – grey as a foetal scan – had moved around the word *Mum*. One last time, Ben's young eyes had rolled before being exploded into charred morsels on the beachgrass by another of

128

Tez's bullets, pumped in through the temple...

Tez's phone fizzed now in his pocket, bringing him back to the present: it was Gaz with the train times. Connecting the call, Tez fixed his eyes on the young couple who were clambering into a black cab outside Matherfield Stores.

"Billy will meet you at Lime Street," promised Tez, ending the call.

The young couple's taxi pulled away just as a town-bound bus arrived at the village green stop. The bus's illuminated cargo of ordinary commuters gave it the appearance of a visiting space ship from another, far better world. Alighting passengers quickened their pace as soon as they saw Tez, strange and still beside his growling dog. Now the muddy bus flank pulled away, returning the jolly Matherfield General Stores to view.

But all Tez could see was Formby Beach Ben's downy chin trembling around the word *Mum*.

11.43pm

Tallis Towers

"Jamal Bannigan, you're wanted in connection with car theft in the Matherfield Park area earlier this evening."

"B-b-but I've been 'ere all night."

"If you could come down to the station, please."

"But I can't even drive."

"Please come with us, sir."

Bewildered and still blinking the sleep from his eyes, Jamal followed the arresting officers to the waiting police car in the Tallis forecourt. His Nan cursed and babbled drunkenly after them from the top of the stairwell, and tried to get hold of Macca, whose phone had gone dead.

Outside, a pathetic and shivering Guantanamo was crouched beside the police car. At their approach, he stretched up a leprous-looking arm, and implored in a gravelly voice, "Got any spare change, Officer Taffy, mate?"

With a sigh, and notwithstanding the exasperated groan of his colleague, Taffy dropped some coins, plus the admonition, "You need to get to hospital with those arms, Guantanamo. Septicaemia, you got, man."

"I'm cleaning up tomorrow, Officer Taffy," promised Guantanamo, heaving his bag-of-bones, broken self up from the floor. Money clasped fast to his bony breast, he scampered away in the direction of the Zone.

"Don't believe you, Taff!" grumbled his colleague, bundling the passive and weary Jamal into the back of the police car.

As they pulled away from the Tallis forecourt, a small, black-robed figure came into view, by the roadside.

"Jessie!" screamed Jamal repeatedly, hammering like a madman on the window. Tears streamed from his eyes.

Taffy's alarm at this spasm of activity subsided the moment he looked out, too. Shaking his head, he said, "Come on now, buddy, there's nobody there."

CHAPTER ELEVEN

<u>**Friday 29th October 201-**</u>

<u>**Shriveton Custody Suite**</u>

The Shriveton custody suite reeked of disinfectant, sick and sweat, and was even less comfortable than home. To begin with, it had been a Mazda from Kirkby, but this changed to a Mini from Huyton, to an Audi from Croxteth, until it had become blatantly obvious that nobody in the entire police station knew why Jamal Bannigan had been taken into custody at all.

"Meyers wanted 'im in," the custody sergeant had eventually confessed to the WPC who booked in Jamal.

She'd shrugged and taken away Jamal's very few personal effects, then walked him to his cell, where he'd spent a wakeful night, hoping that Jessie Rout would appear to him, like the Virgin Mary had done to Bernadette in the French cave. But his beloved Jessie did not come, and, after a cup of horrible police station tea and a couple of broken crackers, he'd been released without charge just after seven a.m. the following day.

"Gary Skelton was found dead in the foundations of the LCI rebuild in the very early hours of this morning," confided the custody sergeant knowingly, as he handed a slack-jawed and wide-eyed Jamal his personal effects. "So that rules *you* out, son."

Jamal wandered back home in a daze. As he went up to the Parade to buy cigarettes, Incubo soldiers and one or two of the Sons made discreet Victory signs as they passed him, avoiding eye contact. He made his way down to the Shriveton Park playground and sat on the swings, smoking and hoping that Jessie Rout would come like she had before. But she didn't, and he started back home just as the pavements were filling with school-bound kids.

School boys saluted as they passed him.

Liverpool Central Infirmary

Brash notice boards outside the dirty grey, concrete angularity of the existing hospital proclaimed the goodness of benefactor Callum Bowes-West. On the pavements by the main entrance, suited and booted Ethan Greenberg paused beside a small cluster of hospital-gowned smokers, some attached via clear plastic tubing to drips-feeds like tall vacuum cleaners. Some were talking with misshapen, tattooed relatives, or into mobile phones, about the body of a gangster discovered in the foundations of the LCI rebuild site nearby. Police milled discreetly.

Ethan scoured in vain the paragraphs and pie charts – each vaunting the green, goodly, safe and healthy character of the rebuild work in progress – for a site map. Then, on the advice of a police sentry, he followed a stream of homeless types who had been moved out of the warmth of the hospital reception area by Security. They were going in the direction of the rebuild site.

Clutching their Special Brew and the cigarette stubs which they had scavenged from pavements and bins, the down-and-outs huddled around a burning stove the workmen had lit to the rear of the old hospital. Ethan picked his way through the tools, clay and gravel of the building site. He was trying to take consolation in the machine-washability of his M&S suit, given that his brand new work shoes were being devoured by the sticky mud all around. Muddy and hot from the trek, he finally reached the object of interest in the scene: a girl who was weeping hysterically by one of the partially erected steel supports, around which yellow scene-of-crime ribbon had been tied. Beside her, arm around her shoulder, was an old man.

Ethan gave a polite cough and said, "Excuse me," – he held out his boy-soft hand – "Ethan Greenberg, the *Star*. Sorry to disturb you, but did you know Gary Skelton at all?"

The girl was too upset to respond, but the man shook his hand, saying, "Me grandson. 'E was a good lad. At 'eart."

Ethan made encouraging and sympathetic noises, and hazarded, "Have you any idea what happened here?"

"Gangs," was the abrupt response. "Look, his girlfriend 'ere is too upset to speak, son, so –"

"Someone should speak," piped the girl, impassioned.

She impressed Ethan as a pretty girl, far more natural-looking than girls in this milieu, whom he found to be rather frightening on the whole.

Instantly, the grandad clamped her mouth shut with his hand, urging, "Don't say nothin', Leanne. We've 'ad enough!"

With a flick of his head, still physically gagging her, he indicated that Ethan should go.

"Look, she has a right to speak," said Ethan, staying put. His shoes were submerged in the clay of the building site, in any case.

"Words cost lives in our world, son. Think o' what 'appened to our Ben, girl."

He took his hand away from Leanne's mouth. She stayed mute, nodding in acknowledgement.

"Ben Skelton, son," the old man told Ethan. "You look up that and you'll understand. Come on, love."

He led her away, back to the cancer ward where his daughter, Gary Skelton's mother, lay in an oblivion of morphine.

BODY OF EIGHTEEN-YEAR-OLD IN NEW LCI FOUNDATIONS

Exclusive by Ethan Greenberg

The body of Shriveton man Gary Skelton, who turned eighteen last week, was discovered in the early hours of this morning on the Liverpool Central Infirmary Rebuild Project site. He had been shot in the head.

Mr. Skelton's terminally ill mother, Liz (45), a patient in the LCI, has not been informed of her son's death. Gary Skelton, reputed to be leader of a local teen gang, disappeared from the Shriveton area of the city following the gangland shooting of Troy Bannigan (18) earlier this month.

Police Superintendent Simon Meyers says, "As part of our on-going investigations, we had wanted to speak to Gary Skelton about recent events in Shriveton. We are treating his death as a murder investigation, and we would ask anyone with any information to come forward. We intend to apprehend his killer."

Gary's cousin, Ben Skelton (16), an alleged police informant and also associated with the Shriveton gang scene, was shot dead three years ago. His body was found on Formby Beach, to the north of the city. Although Ben's killer has yet to be identified, the family is hopeful that Gary's murder will result in an arrest and conviction.

"We will not stop until we achieve just that," said Superintendent Meyers.

St Theresa's Church

Sanctuary

"Afternoon, Father," said Jewel, handing him a clutch of post, avoiding eye contact, as she always did.

Jewel's hands always fidgeted and picked, and her gaze never fell on the few living souls in her midst. Swamped from chin to toe by loose-fitting, dull clothing, with her long, dark, dirty hair gathered in a ponytail by a grubby pink bobble, Jewel cowered in life's wings, a backstage shadow.

"Gonna sort the altar flowers now," she said. "They mainly dead from Monday."

Heavy in the air were the sickly-sweet fumes of dying-bloom bushels which still festooned the church from Troy Bannigan's funeral.

"Where would St Theresa's be without you, eh, Jew?" said Father O'Connor, taking from her the letters.

Pleasant associations of his Bray home in County Wicklow surged now as his eyes fell on his sister Caragh's conventual handwriting on one of the envelopes. When he'd been a boy, and the idyllic seaside town of Bray had been his home and entire universe, he'd wondered: what would happen if God got angry, and plucked away the ribbon of beach and stones dividing the town from the wild Irish sea?

To assuage the unpredictable and vengeful God who sent girls to Hell if they went to Liverpool to get abortions (like Caragh had done after falling pregnant by a married man), Kevin O'Connor had: become a priest; never had sexual relations – not even with the fellow seminarian he'd loved all those years ago; and given all his money away to the poor. In addition, he had remained in the hopeless parish of Shriveton – partly because the conservative Bishop didn't like him much, and partly because he knew he made a difference to people such as poor Jewel, the Zone Chief's wife, the lonely, hopelessly damaged woman who had cleaned his church for many years.

Still looking at the floor, Jewel responded to his appreciation of herself with a thrilled but prim smile. Then she hung her shabby,

134

grey rain coat with the broken belt– the same she'd worn forever – on the hook behind the sacristy door, and began seeking out her cleaning things from the cupboard beneath the sink in the sacristy.

Ten years ago, Father O'Connor had found a fat-lipped and bleeding Jewel crying in the stairwell that led from the St Theresa's car park down to the sacristy. Someone's boot had displaced her front tooth, and blood coursed over the swollen numbness of her chin. It streamed, also, from the bisected lobes of her ears, torn when her mother yanked out the hoop earrings there.

Without hesitation, Kevin had given her sanctuary. Social services couldn't let her stay with him, even though she wanted to, and had placed her in a kids' home in Bootle. Nonetheless, Jewel had kept resolutely in touch with St Theresa's, attending Mass there every week, and making herself indispensable as church cleaner and helper.

The horror of her childhood had atrophied her; Kevin saw her as the biblical character Lot's wife. The rituals of Catholicism were the pillars, joists, bricks and mortar Jewel had used to reconstruct her life. Indeed, so impregnable was her shield against reality that she believed her gangster boss husband was a carpet-fitter.

Or at least, that had always been Kevin's impression, until last August when the Paki Witch had turned up on St Theresa's Church doorstep along with Chloe and her baby.

Room at the Inn

Jewel had answered the door to them. Utterly devoid of social skills, Jewel usually scowled and mumbled at visitors, and closed the door on them while she fetched the priest. Often the visitors would have gone by the time he got there, believing themselves to have been turned away.

However, she brought in *these* visitors straight away, and ran ahead of them, calling, "Father O'Connor, come quick. Someone special has come."

For the first time *ever*, Jewel was as happy as a Disney child. Breathless with joy, eyes sparkling, she had almost fallen into the sacristy, where Kevin was sorting out jumble for the forthcoming August Bank Holiday car boot sale in the St Theresa's car park. Jewel proclaimed, "She's here!"

Jewel never touched anyone. But on that day in August she had pulled his arm, her joy turning to urgency in proportion to his bafflement.

"Who?" he said, allowing himself to be led into the main body of the church, in the aisle of which he saw a woman in black Islamic clothing.

Beside her was an impoverished-looking girl, whom Kevin recognised as Chloe Tudor. Chloe was pushing a ramshackle pram in which lay a baby in dirty clothes. Particulate light seemed to irradiate from them, and hang like a holy-family halo in the incense-scented air.

"The Paki Witch!" whispered Jewel, awe-struck.

Kevin approached the visitors, holding out his arms to them, knowing, but not understanding why, this was the defining moment in his life. The Muslim woman greeted him with a smile as Chloe said urgently, turning her head away as she spoke, "She's the Zone Chief's wife, though."

Then a doorbell peeled through the high-vaulted church, followed by thunderous banging on the front door. Simultaneously, Jewel's mobile phone went off.

"Tez," she said.

Chloe started shaking and crying.

"The Incubo will kill me now if he finds me," she sobbed.

The baby started screaming, so the Muslim woman picked him up, and held him close to her, calming him instantly.

Jewel looked at the nearly-hysterical Chloe for a moment, then connected the call, saying, "Hiya... On me way."

Then, with surprising agility, she pounced upon the very small stereo player beside the altar, and switched it on, flicking through tracks on the CD until Handel's *Halleluiah!* resounded, exuberant and brassy as a Moulin Rouge chorus line, in the sacred vastness all around.

"It's a dead loud track, and I've put it on repeat in case the babbee cries," Jewel announced, and made flickering eye contact with Kevin, who immediately nodded and began shepherding his visitors out of sight into the sacristy to the rear of the altar.

Above Handel's triumphant choir, distorting through the tiny speakers, Kevin and the visitors could just hear the exchange between Jewel and her husband at the back of the church.

"Why so long answerin' the fuckin' door?"

"Sortin' stuff for the car boot. You can't smoke in 'ere."

"Fuck that. Why all the noise? That music's terrible loud."

"Father's had confessions. So I always put on the CD so it's private, like."

"Is 'e 'ere?"

"Erm, no. 'E's out. Communion for 'ousebound."

"Listen, Jew, has the Paki Witch been 'ere?"

"Who?"

"The Paki Witch."

"Dunno. Don't know no Paki Witch. No one's been 'ere."

"Look, fuckin' four or five people seen 'er come in 'ere with Chloe Tudor and the babbee."

"Who?"

"Chloe Tudor."

"You wha'?"

"Look, never mind. Has anyone come in?"

"Don't be soft. It's all locked up. You'll 'ave to go now. Father'll go mad if 'e smells that ciggie when 'e comes back."

"Well, if a Paki woman comes here with a mum and babbee, you tell me, Jew. Yeah?"

"Fine."

"Them people out there was dead sure they seen her come in."

"Who?"

"The Paki fuckin' Witch. Jesus, woman, 'ow many times?"

"Well she's not 'ere."

"Oh. OK."

"OK. Well, terrah, then. I got Chicken Kiev for tea. Reduced."

"Nice one."

"And fat chips. Terrah."

"Look, Jew, you sure no one been 'ere? I better take a look."

"Don't you *dare* be walkin' all over me floor. Just polished it. You got eyes in yer 'ead, Terry?"

"Well –"

"Look, no one been 'ere. Dunno why you so uptight. Smokin' in the church! Anyway, thought you 'ad an 'all stairs and landin' in Huyton today."

"Yeah, summat else come up, and Zollo goin' mad 'bout the Paki Witch."

"Why?"

"She robbed summat from 'im."

"No Paki Witch come 'ere."

"Well, if you –"

"I *told* you, if I see 'er I'll be right on to you. What time you back tonight?"

"Dunno. Fuckin' massive kick-off 'ere."

"Just phone me an hour before, and I'll start tea."

"'K, love."

"Terrah."

Jewel shut and bolted the front door after him, and came into the sacristy. Kevin had pulled to the curtains there, reducing the room to semi-darkness, and yet somehow the Muslim woman, still holding the baby close, and Chloe were clearly visible. Both Jewel and the priest would recall this later – the strange luminosity of their visitors sitting in the sacristy gloom.

The Muslim woman crossed over to Jewel, and touched her arm, saying with a smile, "The jewel in the mine shaft wall does not change because you shine a light on it. It was *always* precious."

"You – you are the sunlight," stammered Jewel, eyes on her and the baby, blinking as if looking at the sun itself.

She tried to speak again, but instead dissolved into tears which did not subside even when Kevin gently guided her to sit in the fireside armchair. Now Chloe Tudor went over to crouch beside Jewel, saying, "Thank you."

Jewel shook her head and sobbed with renewed intensity, but did not pull away from Chloe's hand, which was on hers.

"I brought them to you," the Muslim woman told the priest, rocking the baby as she spoke, "because I have seen into your heart."

Kevin stared at her, lost for words. As governor of St Theresa's School he was, of course, familiar with Chloe Tudor's tragic decline. Baby Joel's father could be any one of scores of men. His wisps of white-blond hair and translucent palest-pink skin made a Rubens angel of him against the Rembrandt black of the Islamic woman's clothing. Her dark finger was delicately tracing his plump facial contours.

"My sister Caragh, in Ireland," he blurted, battling the urge to fall to his knees before the sight of this Muslim Madonna, who held the Kafir son of Everyman in her arms. "She'll take them in, if I ask her."

"Thank you," said the Muslim woman, smiling at him.

Then, briefly dipping her beautiful, dark face into the dandelion fluff of the baby's hair, she murmured, more to herself than anyone else, "I feast my eyes on your living face," and returned him to his mother.

Chloe clutched him close to her, and kissed his pretty face.

"Your hearts are now awake," said the Muslim woman very gently.

The baby started up with mild moaning and wriggling, which broke the moment and drew everyone's gaze.

"He's probably hungry by now," said Chloe. "I haven't got nothin' for him."

"I can see a bottle under the pram," said Jewel, crossing to the pram which had been wedged fast against the door through which, as a teenager, she had herself come for sanctuary many years ago.

A squat bottle, brimful with milk, peeked out from the changing bag she now brought over to mother and baby.

"There's three bottles, in 'ere," Jewel said, rummaging.

"He'll only have it warm –" began Chloe.

"It is warm," replied Jewel passing one across, to the perplexity of Chloe, who said, ashamed, "I never had nothin' in there for 'im, though," as she watched her son.

He was new, insistent life, determined to get through, and his tiny jaws chomped ravenously on the bottle teat.

Jewel rooted briefly in the bag again. "There's a red purse in 'ere, and clean clothes and nappies."

"I never had nothin' in there except that purse. I – I stole it from my best friend, Ellen, before."

Chloe became upset.

"I'll get the purse back to Ellen," said the priest, patting her head consolingly.

"No point," said Chloe, her palm kneading a flood of mascara-dark tears. "I emptied it to spend in the Zone."

He picked out the purse from the changing bag. It was fat with coins and a library of notes.

Then they realised, that the Muslim woman had gone.

Jewel ran out into the church. She returned, breathless, minutes later, in a heat of excitement, holding aloft her rattle of keys.

"I've checked everywhere. The Paki Witch 'as gone. But there's no way she could've gone out the front door, because I 'ave the keys!"

No one needed to observe that their illustrious visitor had gone out through the sacristy exit, blocked by the pram.

"And, eh, Father!" continued Jewel, "The plate at the back of the church is full, and I mean, overflowing with money. Notes and coins."

"Well that was empty all right," observed the priest, wryly. "And I doubt your Terry filled it up on his way out."

Baffled, awestruck, and empowered by the wonder of these happenings, Kevin and Jewel facilitated the safe passage to Ireland of Chloe Tudor and her child. Although they knew helping her was dangerous, none of them felt afraid – not even when Jewel had to run round to Chloe's house to fetch her passport, through the streets of Shriveton which were alive with rumour and activity surrounding the Paki Witch's appearance and intervention in the Zone earlier.

From the car boot jumble, Chloe threw on some baggy, nondescript clothing, and a hat to hide her hair. And when Jewel returned, with the passport retrieved from Chloe's empty house, Kevin drove them to the Passport Office in town to pick up one for Joel. By six o'clock that evening mother and child were on a plane flying out of John Lennon Airport. Caragh O'Connor met them at Dublin and gave them sanctuary in her modest little flat in Bray. The collection plate bounty had covered all costs.

Now, just two months later, Kevin opened his sister's latest letter.

"Joel's crawling," he said to Jewel. "Caragh's sent a photo of him."

Jewel dropped her cleaning things and darted beside him to drool.

"'E's so big now!" she declared, her whole face transformed by a smile as she looked at the picture.

They read Caragh's letter. Mother and child were contented and well. Chloe had enrolled at a local college, and Joel was in a nice nursery, part time. Chloe was settling in well, but she kept pining for someone called Jammy, whom she seemed to regard as being in danger somehow.

"She needs to forget about here," mused Kevin as they read the letter. "God knows, she took a chance coming back for Troy's funeral. Still, s'pose she was back with Caragh the same day."

"She needs to break all ties with 'ere," agreed Jewel, reading.

"We could say the same about you and me, Jew," groaned Kevin, handing her the letter, which he had finished reading before she was much beyond the first paragraph.

His mind transferred to other, pressing matters.

"I can't get anyone to listen to me about the Community Centre bonfire!" he grumbled, flicking on the kettle. "The kids keep loading up stuff. Have you seen it? They've even got a stuffed guy on the top. I wouldn't mind, but he looks a bit like me!"

"Yeah," murmured Jewel, still reading. "Ah, little Joelly's got loadsa teeth now."

"Well it's freakin' enormous, this mound of bonfire stuff and rubbish. I don't know where the police are."

"The bizzies don't care nothin' 'bout 'ere," said Jewel vaguely, still reading. "Your Caragh uses dead long words."

"I don't see what more we can do."

"Ah, Chloe's started an 'air and beauty course."

"But who *is* organising the bloody thing?"

"Dunno," shrugged Jewel, and made them each a cup of terrible church tea.

Shriveton Shopping Parade

Tribal anticipation and gunpowder hung in the air, which crackled and boomed periodically as the fireworks were detonated in crannies around the estate. Kids in Halloween masks on bikes, were prowling the perimeters of the Zone. Tez almost collided with one as he emerged from the top of the steps on to the Shopping Parade.

"Sorry, boss!" filtered through the fluorescent rubber mask. From under his arm, an old plywood bedside locker fell to the floor and split on the paving stones.

"What's that?" demanded Tez.

"It's for the bommy, boss. Takin' it while I was 'ere, anyway, like."

"I'm payin' you to watch the perimeter!" grouched Tez, administering a clip round the head. "Drop it on the bommy, and get back to work. Or I'll drop you" – Tez indicated the steps from which he had just come – "down there."

In a profusion of apologies, the kid picked up his firewood and shot off.

Tez strode across the paved apron of the Parade, his eyes everywhere. Strategically placed Incubo personnel made deferent nods from their sentry positions. He hailed over another kid on a bike, who zoomed across to him immediately, and stood to attention.

"Yeah, boss?" the kid said.

Tez reached across and snatched off his mask. The kid winced as the elastic pinged his ear, but did not raise a murmur of objection.

"It's not Halloween for a couple of days. Tell the others to get the masks off."

"Yeah, boss." Without picking up his mask, the kid started to pedal away, until Tez shouted out, "Get back 'ere."

The kid, in his early teens with downy, spotty skin, trembled before the Zone Chief who stared at him coldly.

"Pick it up," Tez said, pointing at the mask.

The kid threw down his bike and snatched up the mask from the floor, mumbling, "Sorry, boss."

It frightened Tez that he had so much power over this little life,

141

a life so unheeded it had already started work for the Incubo. His small nod of approval at the litter retrieval sent the terrified kid beetling away towards the other Incubo child-slaves. Within seconds they had all removed their Halloween masks.

Tez had come directly from a short meeting with Zollo regarding the urgent question of Meyers, who needed a bust or two in order to be *seen* to be doing something. Zollo contributed no ideas at all and kept checking his phone, and leaving the room to make calls, only to come back even more distracted than he'd gone out. Something was eating him, although Tez found it hard to believe that it was simply fury regarding Gary Skelton's body on the hospital-rebuild, or frustration that the Paki Witch had yet to be found.

Into view now came the familiar and pathetic Guantanamo. Fist fast around his purchases, Guantanamo stopped to lean against the wall that divided Liu's Chippy from Handy Bet.

What drugs hadn't done to him, the fists, boots, nails, blades and baseball bats of his creditors had. Guantanamo had hardly any teeth, and his arms, neck and legs were a minefield of punctures. Receptive only to the toxins which had turned him from a man to Satan's gimp, he was valuable to none save the Incubo, to whom he continued to give all of the little he had.

It was dark, and the shops were all shut and grilled, except for Liu's Chippy and Bargain Booze, which were drawing small but steady numbers of ordinary people. All looked discreetly and fearfully away as Guantanamo yanked back his orange sleeve to pinch and flick the flesh there; all except Tez, who demanded in hushed tones, "What you doing, twat?"

Guantanamo was jamming a needle tip into the crater of yellow- green pus on his forearm. His filthy-nailed thumb zoomed down the plunger, and his head went back, *bang*, against the bricks behind him, whereupon he smiled.

If hell existed, it was surely here, thought Tez, cracking him round the head as he issued an admonishing, "You can't shoot up 'ere!"

"Sorry, man," moaned Guantanamo, swaying forward.

Tez applied a vigorous push. Guantanamo's back felt horribly bent and bony under his palms, and for no reason, Tez found himself puzzling as to why the Paki Witch would put herself out for one of these specimens. Chloe Tudor, although younger and prettier than Guantanamo, had been no more nor less than he.

The displacement of the smallest clod of earth could cause an avalanche. It didn't do to ask even obvious questions, such as

What is the purpose of Guantanamo's continuing existence, since it is directed towards only pain, ignominy and oblivion? The only answer, Tez knew, was money. Guantanamo was good as long as he had cash to hand over. Tez's job was to collect it.

Money underscored the desperate paradox which defined and destroyed Tez's every waking moment. Lilly Bannigan, for example, regarded him as some sort of saviour because he'd paid for her grandson's whole lavish funeral, and (especially) because he kept her in alcohol day and night. And Tez had enjoyed all the compliments and awe his munificence earned; why, he had even allowed himself to feel he deserved this praise. Then he remembered that it was *he* who had had Troy shot. And then he remembered Troy himself – his kindly nature and physical perfection – whereupon a tumour-like sob, big as a boxing glove, would balloon in his chest.

A perennial migraine attended his overall responsibility, as Zone Chief, to monitor Shriveton's takings. Every single day, Incubo couriers took trains, planes and automobiles to meet with money-lenders, pawnbrokers, estate agents, stockbrokers, lawyers, bankers and foreign exchange merchants up and down the UK and further afield.

Consolation could not be found in his own personal ocean of money, which his eternally frigid and afraid wife Jewel refused to spend. It was in steel boxes under house and shed flooring, or within sofas, chairs and beds. While their slippered feet rested on the money grave he'd overlaid with marble tiles in the kitchen, Jewel fed him slum food – bangers and hotdogs from tins, canned spaghetti and beans, pastry-fat pies. She insisted on living in the kitchen, and watching TV in the bedroom, under the covers, to save on heat. All other rooms were closed from one month to the next. She boiled a kettle for a wash or the dishes, and told him to get showers at the gym to save money. If he ever attempted to challenge her, she became excessively nervous and started picking at the flesh of her arms and neck until it bled, like she used to do when he'd first met her.

His marriage to Jewel was also characterised by baffling paradox. They had met in the depths of their respective despair, in a kids' home, and until that moment had not only never been loved, but, for the main part, had known only cruelty and indifference. Within minutes of meeting, Jewel became his mother and his child. Sex being a thoroughly disturbing subject for each of them, they were perfectly matched. He understood that she never wanted any sort of sexual contact. And she understood that he

143

needed a wife who didn't want sexual contact.

Empathy bound them, far transcending the physical. They lived as fraternal flatmates, and never ever discussed feelings, or the past, or the future. Every day for all the years they had been together, they had looked after each other with the unconditional love of new parents. Yet they lived completely separate lives, with points of contact being meals, TV and household minutiae.

"Bill!" he said, nodding to Billy, who had just emerged from the alleyway connecting Zone shop to the Parade area.

Billy's hand dipped down to the buttock of a young female customer waiting by the alleyway. Tez recognised her as Chloe Tudor's relative, Jodi Harris. It was an act of defiance, feeling up the girl, rather than jumping to attention on seeing the Zone Chief. Billy took time to squeeze her bottom again, whispering something in her ear as he pushed his hand far under, between her legs, provoking a tarty but nervous giggle.

Then he walked over, his every non-urgent step irradiating grievance, to join Tez by the perimeter wall overlooking the Wasteland and wider estate. St Theresa's church was still lit up in the dell of the estate.

"Been tryin' to get in touch with you, Tez," he complained.

"Well you 'ave."

"Yeah, but job been done, like, and not 'eard off you."

"Job not to Inky's liking. He weren't happy you left the body at the LCI."

"Why?"

Genuine puzzlement bubbled through Billy's burgeoning rage. Tez had commissioned him to carry out this hit on the understanding that he would be made. "The job's been done, innit? I was gonna take 'im down the docks, like you said, but thought the bizzies was comin', so 'ad to leave 'im where 'e was."

Tez remembered what it was like to kill a man: downy chin, blue lips moving over the word *Mum*....creamy sand and marram grass...the extreme panic and fear when the best laid plans went wrong.

The truth was that Tez had no idea why the hospital Rebuild foundations as a final resting place for Gary Skelton was so problematic for Zollo. So he shrugged, and said, "I dunno. Maybe it's meant quicker discovery."

"But I 'eard a siren, like, and got windy, see. You know what it's like, Tez. Can't take no chances."

"I know, mate. I understand that."

"Well am I gonna be paid out or wha'?"

"Only a K, once you return the tool," he said. "Zollo's too mad."

"What? Fuckin' crazy. You promised. I done my part?"

"Look, like I said, Zollo's too mad right now. Leave it a few days. Where's the gun?"

Bitter, and furious, Billy stood still for a while, mastering himself. Tez knew Billy wanted to punch him and storm off. But to leave one's post at the trading heart of the Zone was a capital offence, and so, with a snort of disgust, Billy led him back to the alleyway. He didn't even grope Jodi Harris as they passed her en route to the Zone shop, by the bank of red bins at the end of the alleyway between the Community Centre and the empty library.

From one of the bins, Billy snatched a bin-liner-wrapped object, saying, "No prints."

Folding back the plastic to expose the nozzle, Tez nodded. He rewrapped it and buried it inside his coat, pulling out a brown paper package as he did so.

He passed it to Billy and said, "One K."

On the way back to his car, Tez passed the wood and combustible bonfire rubbish piled six feet high in the open space beyond the Community Centre. The boy soldier's plywood bedside cabinet was jammed on the slope which overlooked the Shriveton playground. Tez could make out the solitary form of Jamal Bannigan on one of the swings. His head slumped down, shoulders hunched, alone and inert, Jamal was the portrait of despair as he rocked to and fro.

The familiar sob ballooned in Tez's chest.

CHAPTER TWELVE

Friday 29th October 201-

Evening

Shriveton

Heart heavier than his boots, because he felt that his beloved Jessie had abandoned him, Jamal dragged himself up from the swing. As he started away, he saw the hulking silhouette of the Community Centre bonfire pile in the distance. A feeling of dread – incomprehensible but absolute – overwhelmed him, and an explosive dizziness forced him to resume his seat on the swing. It was as if the sum of the whole world's sorrows had gripped his core, stopping his breath. He had no idea whether the fit lasted for seconds or minutes, since time seemed to stop.

Afterwards, he was aware of being energised and yet physically spent, alone and yet watched over, and was mulling these paradoxes when suddenly he remembered that he hadn't eaten anything since the two crackers at the police station that morning. There had been nothing in to eat when he'd returned home from his depressing and absurd night in the Shriveton Custody Suite. His Nan was going through the worst drinking phase he had ever known in his whole sixteen years of life, and so the cupboard was bare, except for – predictably – the almost full bottle of Vitamin B tablets his brother had bought for her shortly before he died.

Troy's *Vitamin B stop 'em gettin' Korsakoff's* reverberating in his head, he resolved to buy some milk and fish and chips from Liu's. He would make a gruel with some of it for his Nan when he got back, and sneak in some ground Vitamin B pills.

On his way to Liu's he deliberately stopped at the foot of the huge pyre of combustible junk by the Community Centre. It made him shudder, especially the rotund Guy fastened to a stake at the top.

He took out Troy's mobile phone from his pocket, and fiddled to extract the SIM card then crushed the carcass underfoot. Using his lighter, he melted the tiny digital plectrum which stood proud on his thumb and forefinger: the only record of Troy's foray into drug dealing. When the heat nipped his flesh, he dropped it to the ground and crouched over it, re-applying his lighter flame until the SIM had curdled into a useless alloy of plastic and steel. He scooped it up with a shard of the shattered phone, and jammed the lot behind a broken bedside cabinet, pushing until it was the heart of the waiting bonfire.

"Hi, are you Troy Bannigan's brother?" came a posh voice from behind him.

Startled, he spun round to see a slight, red-haired fellow smiling at him, and holding out his hand.

"Ethan Greenberg, from the *Star*," he persevered. "I'm sorry, I didn't mean to startle you."

Spiked into reflexive defence, Jamal performed an instantaneous panoramic survey of the environs. Billy was rounding the corner of the defunct library and Zone. Black scarf pulled up just below his eyes, which were fixed on the interloper, and hood pulled low, Billy had his right hand inside the left lapel of his jacket, a sign that he was itching to use his firearm.

"You're in danger here," mumbled Jamal, without looking at Ethan Green. "'Ave you spoke to anyone else 'ere?"

"No. You're the first person I've spoken to."

"No one else?"

"No."

Feigning ordinariness as Billy arrived, Jamal said, "All right, Bill."

"What's this cunt doin' 'ere?" demanded Billy, poking Ethan, who matched him with a defiant glare. "This is Incubo Land, fire crotch. You got business 'ere?"

"He's me fuckin' social worker," groaned Jamal. "Me Nan's bad again and he come to find me."

"Oh," said Billy, stumped momentarily.

"Sorry, mate," said Jamal to Ethan. "Like I said, I'm pickin' up a chippy, and then I'll be right back."

"Great!" replied Ethan, who made the error of casting a sidelong sneer at the aggressive Billy, who sprang at him, and pulled him up by the scruff of his coat. Ethan spluttered and flailed.

"You fuckin' look at me, cunt, and I'll put a Kalashnikov up your ginger arse!" Billy shouted, the spittle from his bulbous lips firing all over Ethan's bloodless face.

"Leave 'im, Billy!" objected Jamal, applying a sharp shove to Billy's shoulder. "Or I'm gettin' Tez!"

With a snort of ire, Billy released his quarry. Everyone in the Zone knew that Tez was looking out for Jamal, and so to cross Jamal Bannigan was to cross the Zone Chief himself. Grunting and swearing, Billy stormed away to the entrance of the Zone's trading heart. He glowered and cursed and shook his head as Jamal, accompanied by Ethan, went into Liu's Chippy. Boy soldiers on bikes saluted as Jamal passed.

"Why are those kids making victory signs at you?" whispered Ethan, feeling his neck, which was still sore from being grabbed by the masked gangster.

Jamal shook his head, and refused to speak beyond completing his purchase with the Chinese woman behind the counter.

"Where you parked?" Jamal asked, as they emerged from Liu's. He offered Ethan a chip, then tucked in himself, ravenously.

Tallis and Skylark Towers in the distance were studded with lights, and the moon hung overhead like a huge disk of the same concrete from which most of Shriveton was made. The hot, delicious grease and starch of the takeaway revitalised Jamal. He looked for Jessie Rout along the Tallis walkway, but it was empty except for the crunched orange form of Guantanamo, slumped against the aperture it created in the Parade boundary wall.

"Lawdens Lane," said Ethan, munching a chip. "It's the only place I know here."

"Why've you come 'ere?"

"Because I think something big is happening here. This is the Zone, isn't it?"

Jamal said nothing.

"The Paki Witch, for instance," Ethan went on. Jamal did not speak. "She's a miracle worker right on the front line of, of all of this." He nodded towards the pathetic sight of Guantanamo, draped like a deflated bouncy castle, just metres from them.

Jamal replied, "I'll walk you back your car. Otherwise you'll end up in the boot."

They went down from the Parade and into the densely packed housing estate, Ethan firing, in a hushed voice, a multiplicity questions. What *had* happened to Troy Bannigan? And Gary Skelton? Was Shriveton a major drug distribution centre? Who was the Incubo? Who was that Bill they had seen just now? Did the police *ever* intervene? What drugs were sold, and where precisely on the Shopping Parade was the so-called Zone mentioned by his sources? But, to Ethan's increasing exasperation, his companion remained completely silent.

A short walk found Ethan safe again behind his steering wheel in Lawdens Lane. He leaned out of the driver-side window to ask one last question.

"Why did you help me?"

Jamal shrugged and said, "Because I could."

And, still eating his chippy food from its posy of papers, he ducked into a nearby passageway, and was absorbed by the labyrinthine estate all around.

Saturday 30th October 201-

Liverpool City Centre

Caught You

In the Far East, Zollo had observed ailing sex tourists hiring light-framed, nubile prostitutes to walk up and down their jammed spines in an effort to release an inter-vertebral trapped nerve.

Occasionally, Zollo's lower back went into spasm. This never coincided with his trips to the Far East. This time, it had gone on Wednesday when, at the Shriveton Shopping Parade, he had been confronted with the ghost of Troy Bannigan. His belief in the apparition had been intense and sufficiently long-lived to throw his spine out. The realisation that it was Troy's brother before him, and not the deceased, came too late; the disc had already slipped.

After a second night of agony, he'd come to Spider's parlour in the city centre, where he was due to meet with Miu Miu, a recent, six-stone import ideally fitted (being tiny) to the task of walking the tightened rope of Zollo's vertebrae.

Spider's latest batch of Chinese girls had arrived in a crate at Seaforth Docks, along with some Semtex, detonators, and hand grenades. Almost all of the girls he imported (in lorries or crates) believed they were coming into the UK for domestic service jobs, or the hospitality and catering trade. Their credulity and innocence when they first landed was quite charming. Several of the Incubo gangsters who broke the girls into their new occupation found their horror and reticence highly entertaining.

Zollo would, if he were in town, always enjoy his *droit de seigneur* with the pick of Spider's imported livestock. Seventeen-year-old Miu Miu, for example – who was now traversing his spine in Spider's premier city centre brothel which boasted kitsch red lights, a Welsh dresser full of sex toys, and an excellent relationship with the local constabulary – had been completely untouched when Spider had presented her to him several weeks ago.

Being a resourceful, practical and intelligent girl, she'd adapted to her new life (from which there was no escape, there being no passport) very quickly. Her English, for example, had come on faster than any of her contemporaries' who'd come in the same crate. She'd been able to capitalise on this by adopting a coy, precocious personality which pleased the men who used her.

"Off now, Miu Miu," he told her, slapping the leg of the bench on which he lay.

"Sir happy?" she said, alarmed, and jumping off. She disguised her significant fear with a ready smile, and ran her hands up and over her stomach and breast, grinding her hips, as she stood before him. Her little palms pulled and pressed her bright red string bikini in a manner she imagined would be titillating and distracting enough to avoid any retribution for not getting the spine-walking bit (entirely new to her) quite right.

"Help me up," said Zollo, heaving himself up from the bench.

Miu Miu was the human staff on which he now leaned – buckling her little body – in order to get from bench to standing position.

"Phone," he said, pointing at his jacket.

She laid his three mobile phones and his wallet on the massage bench. Smiling and pointing at the wallet, she sent her fondling hand into his underpants.

He pushed her off, and dialled on one of the phones.

The BSC ship had not sailed from Chittagong yesterday. Ashok had gone AWOL and was not answering any calls. This could be nothing – ships stayed in port for any number of reasons. But the fact that Ashok could not be contacted was ominous.

Angry, Zollo ended this latest attempt to make contact and started dressing. Shooting pains in his back every time he moved meant that Miu Miu had to help him get on his trousers, socks and shoes, for which he gave her – much to her squealing delight – a fifty pound note.

Now one of the other phones went off. He shooed Miu Miu out of the room as he answered it. Not that she would recognise the different voices he used, but more because each character deployed completely different physicality, none more so than Callum Bowes-West.

"Mrs Ingham?"

His housekeeper reported that the police had called at Marporley Hall wanting to speak with a Mr Wilkins.

The Claridge's scenario leapt to his mind: the garbled idiocy of the Asian porter; his flabby, lazy assistant slouched against the corridor, his hand on the cloth-covered trolley bearing Champagne and oysters; the lightning dash to the bathroom of the Ukrainian maid, who had no doubt transferred the digital footprint of avatar Paul Wilkins from his phone SIM before dropping it on the floor by his side of the bed as she dashed out of the room.

In concerned and confidential tones, his loyal housekeeper was telling him that a woman police officer had left her card. This officer had been most particular that her name, which Mrs Ingham now spelled out, was relayed to Mr Bowes-West whom she believed might be able to help with enquiries:

K-A-C-H-Y-A.

Shriveton

To forgive, divine.

Tez parked his old Corsa beside the other lowly vehicles in the Tallis Towers forecourt. Phone pressed to his ear, he walked across and into the Tallis building.

"Just got another appointment and then I'll be back...yeah...yeah. Not mash... yeah, chips...fat chips, better still."

Haggard and constantly on edge – the norm in gangland, no matter how rich and insulated from the frontline a soldier was – Tez looked more than ever like an underfed vulture, with his hooked nose, prematurely thinning dark hair, and narrow, hunched shoulders.

Somehow his wife, Jewel, who had just called regarding tonight's tea, believed he ran a carpet and floor tile business in Bootle, and was currently re-tiling someone's bathroom floor. He concluded his call to her now with, "Don't forget to record me wildlife programme. Terrah."

Beyond purchasing their Matherfield Park house, which he had (erroneously) believed Jewel would adore, Tez had always and without any sense of sacrifice eschewed the high life that came with his drug baronetcy. Looking and living like the Shriveton poor he served meant he was less likely to attract the attention of law-enforcement and Inland Revenue inquisitors.

Eleven years of service on the criminal frontline meant he was eternally quiet and alert, and staring with unblinking eyes into the abyss as he awaited the next horror. The Tallis Tower foyer now yielded that next horror, as he hailed the lift: a low-level one in the form of a noxious gust of urine and vomit as the lift doors partially opened. Retching, Tez crossed to the stairs, and nudged with his boot the orange form of Guantanamo, and likely source of the stench, who lay like an aborted foetus on the bottom step.

"Fuck off, man," the addict groaned, pulling in even closer his head and limbs.

A not-unfamiliar guilt gripped Tez. As Zone Chief it was his business to create and maintain addicts like this one at his feet. It was because of Tez that the whole horror show ran.

Yet again, he thought about killing Zollo.

If wishes were fishes, Zollo would have been sleeping with them long ago.

Incubo Land Initiation

Tez had started out, at fourteen years old, as an independent pot pusher. He'd sneak off daily from the North Liverpool kids' home, where he lived, to sell cannabis on Shriveton street corners. Shriveton was where his mother, a heroin addict, had ended up. He'd stopped seeing her a few years before he started dealing there. Tez had never known who his father was.

He'd chosen Shriveton simply because he'd known, through his mum, that it was easy to score there, and had mistakenly thought (being only fourteen years old) that he could set up in the heart of a community of like-minded merchants. Before long, Zone foot soldiers divested him of this illusion by administering a thrashing by the bins behind the Shopping Parade. They took his stock and his money and left him, bruised and bloody but still standing, whereupon Incubo-emissary Zollo approached.

Zollo was one of the few guys Tez would meet over the next eleven years who didn't wind up on the run, dead or in jail. Throughout those years, Zollo's appearance had never changed: nondescript, pudgy, with longish, mousey hair that hung limp and straight on either side of his incongruously gaunt face, he always wore a vintage leather cap, pulled down over steel-rimmed, tinted glasses that magnified his blinking and expressionless pale eyes. Supposedly, he ran a fleet of taxis in Everton Valley. Over the coming years, Tez would see him only sporadically in the Zone. In time, having become Zone Chief himself, Tez would answer only to Zollo.

"You're not a scallie, know what I mean?" said Zollo in his dense local accent, which seemed somehow to come and go. He had propped Tez against the bins and was dusting him down. "We've been watching you. You sell but you don't use. And you're intelligent. Inky likes that."

Tez was entirely silent, and concealing his terror very well.

"You heard of the Incubo, kid?"

Fourteen-year-old Tez kept silent, fighting the tears pricking his adolescent eyes. He wished there was something to fall back on, other than the stinking shopping parade bin. He wished his mum cared about him. He wished the kids' home where he'd ended up was like Hogwarts.

Zollo gave him a little prod with his finger: "Answer me."

"Yeah. I heard of the Incubo."

"Wanna work for him?"

Tez stalled, desperate: "I'm too young."

Zolllo's cod eyes stared coolly from the shadow cast by his leather cap. "That's a plus as far as we're concerned."

"I dunno," mumbled Tez.

"You'll get to go to Spain a lot, with a nice carer we'll sort for you."

"Foster care never worked for me," said Tez, suspicious and terrified of being placed with yet another awful family.

He wished he could be beamed back to the space ship, and just forget about this particular planet. He wished he had a dad who could arrive right now and twat this slob. He wished he was not just a muggle, but one of the magician elect who could go to Hogwarts for term time, and Ron Weasley's house for Christmas.

"You won't be in foster care. You'll be visiting your Aunty."

"I haven't got an Aunty."

"You have now."

"Oh."

"And going on holidays to Spain is better than going to Feltham for drug dealing, isn't it?" Zollo opened his leather-gloved hand to reveal the cling-wrapped pellets of pot which Tez's attackers had just confiscated.

153

Tez shuddered. One or two of the really crazy kids he'd met in care had been to Feltham youth prison. It was almost as if Zollo already knew this.

"No, I don't wanna go Feltham."

"Good. You done good getting into school most days, and keeping up your little weed business. Of course, that business needs to go now. So we'll be diverting your punters on to Sammy on Park Road."

And thus was Tez's fate decided. It never occurred to him that he could turn down the offer. At that time, he didn't much segregate action and intention into right and wrong. Survival was the name of his game.

Most of the adults in Terry Siddell's life had been either directly involved in, or on the fringes of, criminal activity. His mum had put in an order with local thieves for his first pushbike, which had duly been robbed from neighbouring, middle-class Matherfield Park (where Tez would later live with his wife).

He'd spent his early years strapped into to a pushchair in local boozers while drugs, contraband ciggies and other stolen goods zoomed about. His mum used to buy heroin with cash she got from hocking stuff she shoplifted, or from prostitution. He could still remember sitting outside her locked bedroom door and hearing the noisy, grunting men. Some of them were violent, but his mum never called the bizzies, not even when a punter beat up her and Tez really badly that time just before he got taken into care.

Tez's, "OK," completed his induction. He belonged to the Incubo.

Over a McDonald's, Zollo told fourteen-year-old Tez more about the role of information couriering for the Incubo. The days of communicating by conventional means were, of course, long gone. Drugs Squad had all their phones tapped. Crucial information must now be transferred in person.

"You do good, and you'll be rich," promised Zollo.

Tez's only thought was: get rich, get older and get out. He didn't like his life much. He'd like to live in a place like Hogwarts, where there was a library, like the one in town. He'd only taken up dealing weed to earn enough money to run away from the kids' home. Still, this Zollo had turned out OK, he consoled himself: he'd bought new-recruit Tez a Supersize meal *and* a McFlurry.

"OK," he answered, through a mouthful of Big Mac.

And so it came to pass that Tez and an Aunty Eileen from Croxteth – an invented and dear friend of his mum's – would fly from nearby John Lennon Airport to all sorts of European destinations, all paid for by the Incubo. While Aunty Eileen sunbathed by the pool, Tez would meet with Spain-based mobsters. To begin with, the information exchanged was innocuous and obscure, along the lines of *container Esciba VP left port* and *Fazakerley transfer achieved* and *hold back on Seaforth, await further instruction.*

There were times – especially around Christmas, which entailed more traffic and cargo coming through all major air and sea ports, meaning that containers and packages were less likely to be checked – when Tez and Aunty Ei would be going back and forth to Spain several times a week. To cover this, a Spanish waiter boyfriend for Eileen was appointed in Costa Del Sol.

An interesting few years ensued for Tez as the Incubo's Continental runner. Spain was nicer than Shriveton, and Tez was well regarded for his discretion and intelligence by all concerned. Once he had proved himself, the information he passed back and forward was richer. *SOCA have stopped all Iberian shipments, re-channel via Curaçao;* and *Sinaloa sorted transit through Bogota, main man waiting to receive Holland registered container in Seaforth next Tuesday.*

In this way, Tez learned about international cocaine smuggling, from its source in the Peruvian coca plantations, to the West African shipping routes which led to distribution in Europe, via Holland and the busy Liverpool ports. His mind was a map of maritime lines, contact names and numbers of nodal points on the cat's cradle of shipping routes.

As a teenaged Continental runner, Tez memorised every role, name and number of UK, continental and South American cocaine cartel personnel. Of course, things were made much easier because the Incubo ran everything from the peasant coca leaf farmer to the Shriveton foot soldiers selling wraps to UK junkies.

The Incubo had long ago established connections with Mexican drugs mafia Sinaloa and Los Zetas, with the result that dependence on middle men was greatly reduced, as was the number of people required to work from source to distribution. Mexico would always need the Incubo in the key port of Liverpool if they wanted to access the European markets. Tez's couriering of information was crucially important in maintaining working links between the Incubo and Mexico which, by the time Tez was appointed Zone Chief, had established world domination of the cocaine industry.

"The thing about you, kid, is you're totally fuckin' watertight,"

Zollo remarked on one of the infrequent occasions they met thereafter. "You'll get to the top, Inky reckons."

"The top?"

Tez had already been to the top. Once. It was a place he wanted to get back to, and about which the likes of Zollo knew nothing. He'd been there during a trip with the kids' home to Moel Famau in North Wales. Tez and the other unwanted and unmanageable kids went walking up a mountain to see the Jubilee Tower at the top. It was a hard climb because, like most of his fellow care home inmates, Tez spent most of his time inside watching TV and smoking.

The Moel Famau mountain air had been sweet with purple flowers. Later, he found out that this purple stuff was a plant called heather. Tez never forgot his own pained wonder at the glorious mountain scenery. Apparently, skylarks and black grouse lived on the gorse and grass green slopes, and Tez saw cruciform eagles floating like missiles on invisible wind currents.

When his hot, skinny body pressed against the Jubilee Tower ruin, he'd fallen mute with awe; it felt as if Nature, for all her magnificence, was sitting at his feet. Meanwhile the other kids complained that they'd climbed all this way to the top to find there was nothing there but a knackered old ruin and no shops.

"The top's where the Incubo is," answered Zollo.

"Will I see him?"

Zollo shrugged: "No one never sees him. Even I never seen the Incubo."

Although he got rich and older, Tez, like all of the Incubo's indentured apprentices, never did get out of Incubo Land. On the upside, he was never arrested or killed. When he hit the legally compromising age of sixteen, he was shunted on to Liverpool-based work which varied from running drugs and information between the Zone and clubs and brothels in town to meeting lorries and even containers with heroin consignments. His expertise in heroin increased in proportion to the amount of business the Incubo did with the Golden Crescent.

More than a decade on from that induction, Jamal Bannigan, a picture of dismay and unpreparedness, opened the door to him.

"Tez, erm, wasn't expectin' you."

"Thought I might 'ave 'eard from you by now," replied Tez, stepping in and shutting the door behind them.

"Jam, who's that?" came a wail from the front room.

"It's me, love. Tez," he said, going into the sitting-room,

156

followed by his host, who appeared most uncomfortable.

Lilly was lying on the couch, her fingers folded over the top of a dirty duvet, peeping over it like a little kid hoping for a bedtime story. Yellow and wasted of face, even the whites of her eyes were yellow as they rolled in the effort to focus on their visitor. The whole flat stank of urine. On the coffee table was a bowl with what looked like mashed up chips and peas in milk; sympathy cards as numerous as World War I gravestones; soggy, smelly flowers; a pint glass of water; and a jar of vitamin B tablets.

"The bizzies picked up our Jammy last night!" she bleated, thrashing her Muppet-limb arm out randomly. It knocked off the vitamin pills from the coffee table. "Fuckin' bizzies."

"I been back since yesterday mornin', Nan." Jamal shook his head.

"Oh. Has Tez brought you back, son?" Her head sank back against the cushion, and closed her eyes.

Jamal groaned. He sat beside her and lifted up her head, urging, "Get some water down you, Nan."

She shook her head, then buried it against the back of the sofa. In the next instant came the sound, like kitten claws in a pail of water, of her fingernails scrambling with the top of a vodka bottle nestling there. She took a deep swig, and confided to them and the sofa, "The Paki Witch come to see me, to tell me that me two picaninnies are stayin' with 'er."

"Nan, no more booze for now," said Jamal, reaching over her to take the bottle, and standing up. He switched on the TV."Watch a bit of *Emmerdale*, while I talk to Tez."

"We can go in the kitchen," he said to Tez, through her frail objections.

They went into the kitchen.

"You OK, kid?" asked Tez.

Jamal filled and put on the kettle, saying, "Gary Skelton's dead." He was edgy and partly hostile, partly defensive.

"I know. I thought – I thought you'd 'ave got in touch, Jam."

"Everyone thinks I done it!"

"Result."

Jamal looked defiantly at Tez. "It weren't me. I was in the fuckin' nick!"

Tez, looking away, fumbled with a fresh cigarette.

Jamal hesitated, scrutinising Tez, then said, "You did it?"

Careful to escape censure or praise, Tez gave an obtuse, "The score's been evened."

Their eyes met briefly.

"You've evened for your Troy in the eyes of everyone," Tez went on.

Jamal fiddled with mugs, teabags and UHT milk, his breathing fast and shallow. Tez went on in measured tones, "There's no scene of crime forensic evidence that'll ever convict you, because you weren't there. But people 'ere believe you done it. And they'll keep on believing it, just as they keep on believing in England winning the World Cup, or the Paki fuckin' Witch. They believe because they *want to believe.*"

"But listen, Tez, I –"

"Yeah, yeah, Jammy. Like I said at the club the other day, you're not cut out for this life. You're soft inside."

Jamal stammered, "Listen, I know I said I wanted him to answer for our Troy. But, somethi–"

"Now Gary Skelton *has* answered for your Troy. The matter is closed."

Existence for Tez was akin to an ache, a sigh that never finished. The sorrows and stains of humanity's gutter had permeated so much of him, but somewhere within him Jamal detected a residual, unsullied nobility as he went on, "Jammy, get this into your head: you are *free* to get out of here and start again. I'll help you."

"But, I –"

"You'll never cut it in Incubo Land, Jammy. Troy couldn't, neither. And," – he pulled very deeply on his cigarette – "this way you're clean, you're even and you're *free,* Jammy. If anyone had given me them things when I was young, well..." He bit his lip, frowned and sank his head on his chest, as if to stem the perennial grief from bubbling. "Well, I wouldn't be *'ere.*"

Jamal looked at him intently, still gripped by strong, tumbling emotions. "I was gonna –"

Tez held up his hand and gave a sardonic smile: "Yeah, you was gonna sort it. With your Paki Witch as an accomplice?"

Jamal scowled and moved forward, as if to square up to him.

"Whoah!" said Tez, holding up his hands defensively. "I only meant that you and her have been seen together, innit? Wannabe assassins don't generally seek her out, that's all."

"Leave her out of this."

The taut muscles of Tez's fleshless cheeks were latticed, the consequence of his perpetual and unconscious attempt to steel himself against the awful world he inhabited.

"Don't cross the Incubo, Jammy. He's a wicked cunt, lad. Remember that."

"You're gettin' *everything* all wrong, Tez," said Jamal, his lip trembling as he spoke. Now his eyes filled. "I didn't want to kill Gaz no more. I had *forgiven* him."

They stood in silence as the kettle finished boiling and Jamal made two drinks.

"Oh, fuck me!" was all that Tez could eventually say.

Handing him a dripping cup of milky tea, Jamal announced, "I got eighteen grand in used notes, an MP5, an 'alf kee of beak, and all the 'ardware in me room. Take it all, Tez. I'm gettin' out."

CHAPTER THIRTEEN

<u>Saturday 30th October 201-</u>

<u>Liverpool City Centre</u>

Everything was in place for his escape to Panama, where he had long ago set up a new life, via attorneys in Guatemala, who specialised in high-end disappearance. He'd moved millions, via anonymous corporations, funds transfers, diamond purchases and sales in various countries, into his Panama pot.

Every week, sometimes every day, for years, he had checked and amended his contingency exit plan, as necessary. Indeed, over the past eighteen months, he'd taken the precaution of creating a whole new identity – which included passport, driving licence, identity card and birth certificate – with name change certificate sealed in a Guatemalan judge's chamber. On the advice of one attorney there, he'd even undergone some dental restructuring lately, replacing fillings with crowns.

The Incubo would *never* serve a prison sentence.

"And a reel of Sellotape," he said, quietly, dropping a pile of clothes on the Oxfam counter. His hand reached to the searing pain in his lower back. He'd damaged it further in his panic following Mrs Ingham's baleful phone call.

A lump in his throat, big as a golf ball, was choking him. It was not panic but a proper and proportionate fear that he was a wanted man, who might be apprehended at any moment.

It was a consuming dread of his future as a low-profile retiree in Panama, a future without power.

The Incubo would spend the rest of his life hiding behind the impregnable attorney-client privilege of his privacy-orientated adopted Panama home. Most fugitives trying to disappear in this way had to undergo extensive and time-consuming plastic surgery en route. But because the Incubo was no more or less than a collection of avatars, each with its own unique disguise, all that was required was that he shed all of the disguises. His original self, Jude Atkinson, had been buried over twenty years ago, in the same plot as his alcoholic mother, in the middle-class Liverpool suburb of Childwall, where he grew up. All subsequent selves and years had changed him beyond recognition.

As he'd fled Spider's brothel, he'd been almost overcome by a strong and baffling urge to visit the grave. Recognising the insanity of this impulse reminded him that, to escape, he must utilise his two singular assets: his superior intelligence, and his ability to morph into different personas. Following his instincts would scupper him – as it had done most recently in the case of the luscious Kachya.

Beyond a few frantic pay-as-you-go phone calls and instant messaging to organise his escape, he must sever absolutely all contact with the outside world. Lying low, where he was, for twenty-four hours or so, would be wiser than trying to exit the UK immediately.

Nobody could be trusted. How long the police had been on to him was anyone's guess. The fact that glassy-green-eyed Kachya had arrived at Marporley Hall with a warrant for his arrest spoke for itself. The Incubo was finished, and a furnace of grief – worse by far than the agony caused by his horribly dislocated spine – was devouring him. For two decades he had been esteemed by the most estimable, feared by the most fearful. Now he was a fugitive.

"Can I interest you in becoming a regular Oxfam supporter?" asked the pierced and pleasant sales assistant as she bagged his pile of charity shop clothes. "Just five pounds a month can buy an African fam–"

He hurried out, and went directly into the Midland pub on Ranelagh Street to change in the gents. For the remainder of his time in Liverpool, he would be Eddie Kilbride. Tape-mended glasses, black beanie, shabby tartan hacking jacket, workman's boots, plus stained teeth, were Eddie's key notes. Scruffy and impoverished enough to discourage casual interaction, he had stopped short of the outright vagrancy which might attract attention from do-gooders or the police.

Eddie Kilbride holed up in a back-street bed and breakfast, just off Mount Pleasant. It was in the shadow of the Metropolitan Cathedral, a few streets away from the Liverpool Central Infirmary. From his window there, he watched as day turned to night, listening to the TV on the other side of the wall. From what he could make out, so far, there had been no headlines regarding himself.

At around 7.30pm, he crept out to take a longing last look at his first and last essay in philanthropy, the LCI rebuild. A multiplicity of healthy eating and how-to-quit-smoking posters had been splattered all over the information boards which once vaunted Callum Bowes-West as principal LCI Rebuild Sponsor.

That hurt. After all, money, like whores or rain or the scent of a rose, did not discriminate between good and bad as it bestowed its benefits. Losing Callum Bowes-West forever meant his core had been plundered. There was no substance to which he could attach this new character of Eddie, and the characters which must follow Eddie, as he made the transition to retired businessman in Panama.

Feeling as if a cruise missile had buried itself in his lower back, he broke his journey and leaned against the Victoria Building. He had come to the university quarter to try and score. A couple of jellies for his back, and some cocaine. He needed to stay alert.

Glad-ragged revellers and taxis streamed past him, bound for city-centre clubs. There, immaculately groomed girls like Chloe Tudor, with their plastic-nibbed fingers, and spray tanned, platform-heavy legs, would snort Incubo *I* beak off lavatory seats, behind their ironed curtains of hair.

His eyes filled up. Just hours previously, he had been establishment goody, public benefactor and country squire, Callum Bowes-West. Now he was cowering in the crevices of the glittering, brash, flash but also impoverished city which, only a few hours ago, he had owned. A black ink of rage washed his thinking.

Someone must pay.

Tallis Towers, Shriveton

"See this –"

Jamal opened his wobbly, single MDF house-of-cards wardrobe. Beside it was a Pisa tower of drawers of the same material on which lay, flat, a dusty bathroom mirror. Tez dipped his finger in the half-used slab of white powder which Jamal held out to him. Dabbing his tongue, he surveyed the MP5 gun, scales, plastic sachets, blades, spoons, and roll of white labels (embossed with the Incubo *I*), jammed on to a shelf between old school books, games consoles, shoes and other wardrobe junk.

"I don't want none of it, Tez."

"You out your mind, kid?" The tip of Tez's tongue numbed, and a glaze of sweat sprang on his tense, pinched face: "How long you been doing this?"

"Found it all on Monday, when I come in from the funeral. Under the bath. Our Troy had set it up, ready to go. I cut 'alf the beak with Lido, and was all set to pick up another kee of Lido when Macca fucked me over."

"Macca?"

"Macca said I could use his pad to change into me student outfit, when I were making the Lido switch by the University. But 'e took all me money. And anyway, me Lido contact never showed."

"Where's Macca now?"

"Gone AWOL. Me Nan says 'is phone gone dead."

Some agitated pacing and thinking prefaced Tez's response. "You're a fuckin' baby, Jammy. You know that? You don't know *nothing*. Cutting Incubo beak with Lido will *degrade* it. You'll recalibrate the local market. I –" – his voice became high pitched with fury, self-bafflement and shock – "I should *kill* you for this!"

Jamal hung his head, ashamed.

Tez slumped down on the single bed, and smoked ferociously for some moments, shaking his head, as if baffled at himself. Looking in despair around Jamal's bedroom-cum-cocaine factory, he thought out loud. "We can shift this gear on to Spider. He's a cunt, but he moves a lot of our beak in town."

"Haven't even counted the money prop'ly." Jamal patted a rucksack stuffed with money in his wardrobe. "Mad, innit?"

While Tez nosed into the rucksack of cash, Jamal shook some football boots out of a carrier bag. They thudded in a shower of dry mud on the floor.

"Tez, you know wha'?" He crammed in the incriminating paraphernalia – scales, blades, cling-film, mirrors, tiles, blades and plastic sachets. The bag hung off his hand like a deformed bunch of grapes.

"Wha'?"

"You're a good skin, Tez."

With a deep and exasperated sigh, and a cigarette wedged in his unsmiling mouth, Tez snatched the bag from him.

"Wipe the 'ardware – you need to get the prints off it. The money'll be OK, though."

Silent except for the scrambling blur of Nanny Lilly's *Emmerdale* in the adjacent room, they cleaned up all the hardware, re-packing it in a crumpled LFC Christmas sack which Jamal mined from the corner of the wardrobe. Tez polished, as if with love, every fold and curl of the MP5 himself, and wrapped it in a bin liner, while Jamal cocooned the cocaine in fresh Clingfilm on the drawer-top mirror.

"Mad, innit?" said Jamal, looking at the plastic sheathed gun, Christmas sack and rucksack full of money on his single bed.

"It *is* mad. But it's all there is round 'ere, Jammy. There ain't nothing else. And don't for–"

"But I *have* seen something else," said Jamal, gripping Tez's arm, his features suddenly lighting. "There is another way. I've seen it. Jessie Rout helped me see it."

"Who?"

"The Paki Witch!"

"Fuck that!" Tez snapped, shaking him off. "You got a death wish, Jammy? Look, kid, I might just about be able to spring you from this total fuckin' insanity. But you start messin' around with the Paki Witch, and Inky'll be on your case."

"The Paki Witch is stronger than the Incubo."

Now Tez grabbed Jamal's hand and held it, and looked into his eyes. His heart was wounded by a sudden, terrible recognition. The love that dared not speak its name had not only transferred from dead to living brother, but had intensified and somehow purified.

"The Incubo is going to annihilate your Paki Witch, Jammy, and all she stands for and all who stand with her. You hear me?"

"He won't succeed."

An urging compassion softened Tez's tone now. "There is no other way round here except Inky's way, Jammy. But *you* can leave. Even now, I think I can get you out. *I* can't. I'll never get out now – I'm too far in. But I can spring you. You've got no ties here now. I'll keep your Nan in ale, and she'll be fine.

"The money –" – Tez hesitated for a moment as temptation's cloud hovered briefly over the strange alliance of goodness he was forging with Jamal –"is yours."

Jammy shook his head.

Tez, to his own surprise, was adamant. "Take the money, Jammy. Fuckin' bury it somewhere. To get out and stay out, you'll need money. Money is power, lad. Money is all there is for fugitives from the Zone, kid. The Incubo don't know nothing about you yet. You can get out of this, Jammy. Get to college. You're smart. You're still *free*, Jammy."

"I know."

Jamal could think of no better alternative. Going to the police and confessing his new-found business and fortune was (of course) an absurd idea and would result in unthinkable reprisals from his gangland neighbours. He couldn't walk away and leave Nanny Lilly with the infrastructure, stock and takings of his cocaine workshop; at some point it would make her the target of gangland taxmen or police or both. And dumping everything on the embankment of the M62, or in the River Mersey, struck him as riskier than assimilating it, under the supervision of Tez, into Spider's existing business. So he did not argue with Tez about the money.

They transported the three bags of finger-print-free equipment out of the Tallis flat, leaving Lilly asleep on the couch, with the TV still on. On his way out, Jamal propped up her head on a couple of cushions. In an involuntary gesture of affection, he ran his finger over her jaundiced forehead.

"Fuckin' 'urry up!" growled Tez from the external landing.

Jamal sprinted after him down the hollow zigzag of stairs, and out into night air, so cold and peppery on his skin and lungs. Tez's key sent two pulses of light into the concrete, angular gloom of the Tallis forecourt; the boot yawned open.

Jamal could hardly believe he had become a drug dealer. Until his epiphany, when the bookshop security guards had stopped him on Brownlow Hill, he hadn't fully questioned what he was doing. Righteous vengeance had at once exonerated and driven him, and in a matter of days he had transmogrified from quiet, grief-stricken schoolboy, into a Class A dealing criminal. If he were caught now, he would go to jail.

Decanting the dead weight of the LFC Christmas sack into the hippo yawn of Tez's cluttered boot, he noticed a moving shadow on the periphery of his vision, and was paralysed by fear: *bizzies*. But looking up, to his delight, he saw his Beloved on the other side of the car park, visible despite the dark, as if illuminated from within. Her face, pale in the moonlight and framed by the harsh black hijab, broke into a smile once he had seen her.

Jamal's whole being went on hold with joy before his Beloved, the light bringer to his shadowy world. He wanted her so much that tears sprang in his eyes as he stared across, unable to move in case he lost sight of her.

"Don't stand there starin' into space," grouched Tez. He looked in the direction of Jamal's gaze, adding in agitation, "No one's there, lad. Keep focused. Nerves is contagious. Let's get off."

Jamal ducked into the car. When he looked across again, she wasn't there. Had he imagined it this time? Why was she always eluding him? The wave of petulant tears threatened to break. He wanted to run after her, to pull her into him, and bury his face in the molasses-gloss of her hair.

Kneading his eyes with his palms and clearing his throat, he forced back his anguish, and resolved that as soon as he had completed the business in hand, he would find Jessie Rout. He would go to the Skylark tower where she was supposed to live, and he'd visit every floor until he found her. Maybe a neighbour would be able to tell him which flat she lived in. The certainty that he *would* find her surprised him a little, and sustained him as they drove into town, to the Georgian quarter where the corrupt entity known as Spider lived, in the shadow of the huge Liverpool Anglican Cathedral.

Shriveton Zone

Fr Kevin O'Connor stared balefully at the mound of wood and combustible bric-a-brac tucked behind the Community Centre beside the defunct and lightless Shriveton library.

"Sorry," mumbled a Halloween-masked kid on a bike, who had wobbled into him after an emergency stop. The kid pulled a broken baseball bat from his coat and hoisted it upwards, almost toppling the rotund Guy pinned to a stake at the peak.

"Who's organising this bonfire?" Kevin asked as the kid launched his missile high on to the slope before them. "It's as high as the Community Centre, almost, and there's still a week to go!"

But, like a skate blade on ice, the kid zoomed away without answering.

Obloquy was the norm when it came to this infernal bonfire, Father O'Connor was finding. The local Council, Fire Service and Police had responded to his various questions and complaints by referring him to each other. He had done two loops of this circuit and was no further forward, for reasons never voiced by any of these agencies, but which everyone knew to be: chronic under-funding, and the fact that the police didn't move in Shriveton without the drug barons' consent.

Observation and discussions with some of his parishioners had confirmed that the bonfire was being built by Incubo boy foot soldiers. Since no responsible agency was organising, coordinating or admitting ownership of it, he had come this evening to the decommissioned library, knowing that its empty, dark shell formed a vital outer wall and barrier to the trading heart of Incubo Land. The real authority in Shriveton resided in that heart, located by the bins to the rear of the Shopping Parade. In the shadows of the library porch (breathing through his mouth to avoid the urine fumes there), he waited for a representative of this power.

Presently, one appeared: a young man he recognised as William Stokes exited the alleyway interface of the library and Community Centre. Fourteen-year-old Jodi Harris – whom Father O'Connor knew as a St Theresa's pupil with multiple problems, and the supposed half-sister of Chloe Tudor –crossed over from Liu's Chippy, where she had been standing alone on the otherwise empty terrace overlooking the wider estate.

"Got any, Billy?" she asked in her young, croaky voice, passing her arms around his large girth. She snuggled up to his belly.

"Maybe," he replied. He turned her round, bent her forward and started grinding his hips against her buttocks.

"William, can I have a word?" Kevin called out, moving forward and out of the shadows.

Garish as the painted masks of the milling child foot soldiers, his clerical collar seemed to fluoresce in the smoky night.

Instantly, Jodi ran away.

William cued the time when St Theresa's school governing body, with Father O'Connor as its newly appointed chair, had taken the decision to exclude fifteen-year-old Stokes for torturing an old woman's cat. Distinctly uncomfortable, and thrust back into the role of errant school boy, Billy shuffled over, casting glances all around him.

"Wha'?"

"That girl's fourteen years old."

Slow-witted Billy tried to feign shock and started mumbling, "She fuckin' told me she was eighteen. I mean –"

"Who's in charge of that bonfire round the corner?" said Kevin, cutting through his excuses. "Because it's a hazard to the public."

"The kids made it," said Billy, with a shrug. He made a small hand signal. "Nothin' to do with me."

Behind him, two young men appeared from the aperture between the Community Centre and the library. Only their eyes were visible in the purdah of hoody and scarf pulled over their lower faces.

"Look, you gotta go," warned Billy.

The hooded figures advanced menacingly towards the priest. Billy's potato form disappeared around the corner of the library.

"This bonfire's a danger to the public," Kevin persisted, standing his ground, and turning to them.

He would speak out! These hell monks were, after all, no more than unresolved case studies languishing in the St Theresa's Head Teacher's archives. How dare they hold a whole community to ransom in this way.

In the estate below, the diamante lights of the densely-packed poor – maisonettes, terraces, and towering Skylark and Tallis – twinkled, apologetic, in the Incubo dark. Cowed by the corruption, violence and poverty of their lives, ordinary people traipsed daily to Liu's Chippy, Handy Bet or Shriveton News. They were too terrified to object when girls in their midst like Jodi sold themselves for a few pounds, and primary schoolboys on bikes worked night shifts on the Zone.

It was wrong! Someone should stand up against it! But for all his righteous fury, Kevin's hands and legs were shaking, even as he added, "And so are thugs like you."

One of the hell-monks shoved him.

"I'm not going," declared Kevin, his voice no more than a girlish whimper since his larynx, like the rest of him, was fluttering fearfully.

One of them kneed him in the groin, sending him crashing to the floor, whereupon the other booted his head – once, twice, three times – and then volleyed his spine and kidneys. Hoisting him up – bleeding, unconscious – they dragged him across the Parade. One of his shoes came off as they bumped him down the steps; the hard, gnarled road grated the nails and skin of his exposed foot and legs, shredding his trousers.

They launched him like a stuffed, ragged bonfire guy, face down in the Wasteland mud, and ambled away, laughing behind their scarves.

CHAPTER FOURTEEN

Saturday 30th October 201-

Night

Georgian Quarter, Liverpool

Pimping, and pushing the Incubo's high-grade cocaine, had enabled Spider to spin for himself an extravagant, ostentatious lifestyle in the city centre. Tez had been as tolerant as he could within the boundaries of financial prudence (Spider shifted an *awful* lot of cocaine), but recently Spider had fallen behind on payments to the Zone.

"Inky sees him as a cunt who got it comin'," Tez mused as they pulled up in the alleyway bordering the small rear courtyard of Spider's fine Georgian town house. It was one of several prestige dwellings located alongside the adjacent and estimable city landmarks of Anglican Cathedral, Liverpool Institute of the Performing Arts and Philharmonic Hall. "These days he's snorting as much as he pushes through his brothels."

In the entry behind them now, two black cabs pulled up, spilling a horde of chattering, sparsely-clad and very young Oriental women on to the cobbles. All high heels, handbags and junk jewellery, they clacked in a gaggle past Tez's tired old car, into the yard, and up the steps to the back door.

Tez and Jamal followed, carrying two bags. Unobserved by Jamal, Tez dumped *two* bin-liner wrapped guns – Jamal's MP5 and the one with which Billy had shot Gary Skelton – in an aluminium tub containing a Japanese maple.

Billy Stokes opened the back door, ogling and fondling the girls as they streamed in.

"Oh!" he yelped, very nervously, spotting Tez and Jamal only latterly. "Spide! Spide, it's —"

"Let us in you soft twat," growled Tez. He pushed past Billy's flabby form. "You answer to me, not that cunt. Thought you was workin' tonight."

"Just come off shift, Tez," Billy simpered as Spider himself appeared ahead of them in the splendidly restored tiled hallway.

"Tez. Hey, great to see you man!" he said.

A bizarre multicoloured headband separated Spider's thick-browed face from a shock of unwashed hair. Dark, spindly and hirsute as his namesake, he inhabited the darkest crannies of humanity, as even the most cursory glance would establish. Affecting a noxious bonhomie, he now issued a friendly punch to Jamal's arm, declaring, "Hey, you're the spit of your Troy. Innit, Tez? You want a girl tonight, hey, brother of Troy? I got some. Chinese. *Young*. Come with me."

He came forward, tugging Jamal's arm, playing enthusiastic host.

"Inky needs this gear shifting," said Tez, handing him the Christmas sack.

"Christmas come early, my man, Tez!" said Spider, pulling aside the white fur border of the red sack. He grimaced, disappointed. "Only hardware?"

"Half a kee uncut beak in 'ere," Tez indicated Jamal's carrier bag . Wholly hostile and cold in contrast to Spider's effusiveness, he added menacingly. "You owe the Zone. Shift that beak. Am givin' it you on tick to kick-start you. Its owner had an unfortunate accident. And so will you if you don't square it with Inky."

Spider's arachnid features screwed as he scowled thunderously.

There was an unspoken standoff. and for no reason at all Spider softened, swaying and smiling. "Sure, Tez, mate. Hey, I owe a little bit. But that's because I've been screwed over. Fuckin' sweats on the take. Taxmen vermin had me, too. Screwed fuckin' over. But I'm on top, Tez."

"Good. Because Inky wants his money."

"Look, I *guarantee* the main man'll get that money, Tez. I'm a man of my word."

"Well, that makes all the difference, Spider," said Tez, mirthless.

"Relax!" crooned Spider. A heady, anticipant mania had come

on him, calming and detaching him from the scene. "Come on in. I'll show you, Tez. I'll show you I'm on top of me game, pal."

Spider showed them into the kitchen where the taxied arrivals – teen prostitutes painted and primped so that they resembled child versions of Madame Butterfly – were gathered. Some of them looked scared, but were trying to appear composed.

He gave a maniacal laugh, and shouted, "Hey girls, be nice to my guests here. Brother of Troy and Tez."

Like battery chickens when the light switch is thrown on, the girls became attentive, smiling and on cue. Spider started humming along to the chart music rattling softly in the background, to gee up the brashly perfumed, flute-voiced girls who wittered in the staccato monosyllables of Mandarin, obediently laughing.

Tez unpacked all the contents of the Christmas sack and carrier bag on to the kitchen surface behind them. He tapped on the half kilogram of plastic-wrapped white powder, warning: "Don't cut it."

Satisfaction traversed Spider's face as he tasted the contents. In party mood now, he pulled up two of the girls at the table, and called over to Jamal, who stood fast against the kitchen doorway, separate from the scene.

"Come on brother of Troy, join in!"

Spider was rocking to and fro to the music, with a girl in each arm. "Miu Miu, tell brother of Troy *dance*," he said to one of the still-seated girls, who seemed more self-assured than the others.

"Dance you like, Troy?" said Miu Miu, standing up, and putting her two swan-neck arms around his torso. She was as delicate as a buttercup, and unreal in a bright lemon Chinese-style silk dress. Her skin was very pale, and smooth and plump as a baby's, and her hair so shiny Jamal could almost see his face in it.

Jamal shook his head.

"But it's Spider's tea dance!"protested Spider, who flicked on the full and recently-boiled kettle on the surface beside him, and explained through the roar of its boil, "Dance with Miu Miu, brother of Troy! She's called Miu Miu because she has expensive taste. Just fallen out of a crate on to UK soil and already she's got designer bags. Isn't that right, Miu Miu?"

"Miu Miu!" she said, obviously not understanding what he was saying. She began swaying to the music, looking invitingly at Jamal and smiling.

Jamal separated himself from Miu Miu and went up to Spider. Calmly, as close to his face as he could bear to get, he hissed, "Listen, motherfucker, my name is Jamal, and I don't want to dance."

The kettle clicked off in the silence that had fallen. Miu Miu sat down again, mute and frightened, at the kitchen table.

"Message understood loud and clear," blurted Spider. With a robotic flick of his head, and bland as an answering machine, he looked at the young women and said, "Now girls, I got a bit of housekeeping to do here."

Tez eyed him with loathing: Spider's usefulness was outweighed by his unpredictability. In his heyday – which was perhaps as long ago as the late nineties – prostitution and cocaine had been staples in the Incubo's business. But certainly in the last five years, heroin had been coming in much more cheaply (and in greater quantities), reducing the emphasis on cocaine. Heroin sent the users to sleep, Zollo always said, whereas cocaine made them crazy. Dealing in heroin was better for that reason. Certainly Spider was not reliable enough anymore.

"You're a crazy cunt, Spider," he said, not looking up from the text he was writing to Meyers. The text would cue: *stand by for a police raid.* Jamal's stock, and the guns under the Japanese maple, would mean that Spider would take the fall. Meyers would get his major bust, Spider would be punished for not kicking up the pyramid, and all would be well.

Tez pressed *send*, and was about to leave with Jamal when Spider, ignoring his insult, announced, "And the lesson for today, girls, is that someone's been stealing from Spider, and that's wrong!"

Without any explanation or warning, Spider pulled the kettle from its cradle. Then, pinning her little form with his free arm as she attempted to bolt, he directed a steaming stream of boiling water on to the face and chest of Miu Miu. Shrieking, screaming, gasping in horror, the other girls scrambled to escape. Billy Stokes gulped and then gave a nervous grin, and stood against the kitchen door, blocking it with his bulk. Then, for some moments, nobody, except the agonised and screaming girl, moved, until Spider nodded to Billy and said, "My take, Billy. Put it on the table for Tez."

The empty kettle back clattered on the quarry-tiled floor as engulfing, impotent silence prevailed, despite Miu Miu's cries and the music still playing. Billy systematically emptied every girl's purse and aggregated the contents into a small pile in the centre of the table.

"Take this as a first instalment," said Spider, imparting to Tez a hideous smile of dirty, broken teeth.

"You crazy fuck!" Tez screamed, slamming his fist on the money-laden table.

Before the airborne cluster of pound coins had landed, he sprang at Spider, and pushed him against the wall-mounted cupboards.

Billy's hand twitched around his jacket. Nervously, he eyed Jamal who, with shaking hands, was soaking a towel with cold water, and wringing it out.

Jamal knelt beside Miu Miu and put the cold towel on her face. Vodka and perfume conspired with a strong smell of her own urine and steaming flesh. She flinched and rolled her eyes.

"She's fuckin on the take," snarled Spider as, smashing his dirty head once again against the cupboard, Tez released him.

Jamal was mumbling consolations to Miu Miu, knowing that she would not understand. He rocked to and fro on his haunches beside her, sure that if he engaged with her calamity on a practical level he would not capitulate to the horror, like he had done with Troy. With Troy he had been useless. He was going to focus on the fact that she was alive, and that perhaps the wet towel he was applying would forfend against scarring. She was young. Healing would be swift. There was hope, and he was with Tez. It wasn't like Troy.

Spider had scuttled away from Tez, rubbing the back of his neck and head. "Fuckin' sweat was on the take for herself. But Spider needs his eighty per cent."

"You're a crazy cunt," snarled Tez, watching with some anxiety Jamal's ministrations to the injured girl.

"You're goin' soft, Tez," said Spider.

He sat down and lit a cigarette. His hand was shaking, but he fixed Tez with the sort of bland gaze one directs at a crossword puzzle as he instructed, "Get the girls out to work, Bill. Time is money. Money is time. Unless you've changed your mind?" Grinning at Jamal, he waved an imperious hand across the line of trembling, distressed femininity backed against the walls of the room. "Do you want one of them, Florence fuckin' Nightingale?" He laughed again, rubbing his head.

"Cunt!" snarled Jamal.

With a grunt, Billy marshalled Miu Miu's compatriots, each carrying their moneyless handbag, into the waiting taxis which would take them to their next punters. They exited without a whimper, casting agonised backward glances at the fallen Miu Miu, whose bubbling, blistering flesh would not be sold for anyone's gain tonight or ever again.

Tez had fallen silent, and was watching Billy closely. He was weighing whether he should order Billy off the premises or leave him there for the police to pick up. Billy would have wiped the gun he'd used for the Skelton shooting, but ballistics would hopefully pin it to the murder, if not the perpetrator.

Billy returned now to the kitchen, his pudgy, stupid features alive with twisted exhilaration at tonight's cruelty.

"That fuckin' showed 'em Spidie," he said. He pointed at Miu Miu and asked, "What about 'er?"

"You answer to me, Billy, not that cunt," Tez reminded him, very calmly.

Glowering murderously at Spider, Jamal got up from beside Miu Miu and announced, "I'm going to get her to hospital."

"You little motherfucker, brother of Troy, you got balls!" whooped Spider. He gave a high-pitched, hysterical helium laugh, obscene against the macabre backdrop. It bounced off all the hard surfaces of the kitchen like a shower of razor blades. "Inky likes feisty, doesn't he, Tez?"

"He likes discretion more," snapped Tez. "Let's move, now, Jam."

In the next instant, Jamal sprang up, and threw a blood-drawing punch to Spider's jaw, following through so quickly with a smart head butt that the two movements appeared as one. Billy's gun in the small of his back halted him before he could segue into another combative move.

"Back off, Jam," said Billy. He looked over at Tez for approval, which was not forthcoming.

Manful because of the weapon pointing at his assailant, Spider hissed in Jamal's face, "You Paki screwing faggot! You never even squared for your Troy. Fuckin' Billy did."

"Billy, drop the tool," said Tez, pushing himself between them.

As Billy lowered the gun and backed away, Tez rounded on him, poking him viciously in the chest, warning, "You got a choice."

It was too dangerous leaving Billy on site for the imminent police raid. The police didn't do well with complexity. A simple bust was all Meyers needed. Tez poked him again. "Get back the Zone right now, and take over from Sammy on the night shift."

"I've just come off a fuckin' eight-hour shift!" Billy objected.

But he was cowed. The excitement had palled, leaving the stark truth that Tez was far more powerful than Spider.

"Do another," growled Tez.

With a sudden flick, Tez stung the back of Billy's hand with the burning cob of his cigarette, and followed through with a sharp

174

kick to his shin. Another firm shove propelled the whelping Billy through the door.

"Let's get her out of here, then," said Tez to Jamal.

Jamal's knuckles had split and his head throbbed, but all he was aware of was that Miu Miu's bodily defences had sent her into semi-consciousness, and her crying had ceased. Alarmed, he knelt beside her again, and saw the rise and fall of her chest, and she was shivering convulsively. He pulled off his overcoat and put it over her body.

"You're going soft, Tez," said Spider over the sound of Billy's receding footsteps and petulant back door slam. He gave one of his hysterical little laughs. "What's wrong with teaching the sweats a fuckin' lesson?"

"Broadmoor's full o' psychos like you," snarled Tez.

He nodded to Jamal, who lifted up Miu Miu, like a Crimean War soldier under his heavy overcoat.

"And *you're* a fuckin' faggot, Tez."

Spider flushed with the anger felt by the mentally ill when they are casually diagnosed by those in their midst.

"All this kick off over a beak sweat? She's just another fuckin' unit of production." He snatched up the small bag of white powder which burst in his fist, like Hammer Horror theatre dust on his dark clothing. The accident prompted not dismay, but just another crazy helium laugh as he continued, "There are a fuckin' thousand – ten thousand! – Chinese, Korean, Vietnamese sweats just waiting in the wings to fill her shoes. Gaggin' for the chance, they are. I can always sell them. I can always get them. Geisha dolls, fuckin' programmed to say *Hi, Hi, Hi*! They're expendable. And so are you, Tez, motherfucker. I don't need you or your fuckin' beak or your fuckin' Incubo. Yeah?"

Tez gave a casual shrug and took out his car keys, flicking out the barrel like a knife blade. Eyes on Spider, who was as white-dusted and still as a hideous extra in a zombie movie, he held open the kitchen door as Jamal carried Miu Miu over the threshold of safety, as if she were a bride in his arms. Tez kept his hand on his gun, and his eyes on Spider, who remained statue-still as he regarded their departure down the hallway and through the back yard. Safe on the other side of the yard wall, Tez connected a call to Meyers.

He noticed that there was a missed call from Sammy, but he didn't have time to deal with that right now. Meyers must have his raid – and what a jewel of a raid it would be. The Christmas sack of hardware would mean that Spider would be done for possession with intent to supply; the two guns in the Japanese maple would implicate him in the Skelton killing; and the two words Tez now spoke to Meyers sealed Spider's fate, "Job done."

Unfortunately for Tez, however, an extra job – sorting out the scalded girl – had been tagged on to his own shift this evening. He could barely believe that he was complicit in the rescue of an illegal immigrant prostitute whose existence was of no consequence to anyone. It felt as though destiny, and not his own mind, was leading him. If anyone had asked him why he was doing it, no answer could have been summoned. Driving her to the hospital in his own car was the most foolish scheme anyone in his position could embark upon. Nonetheless he was doing it, with the same hardened indifference that he displayed when engaging in drug or arms transactions on the Incubo's behalf.

Outside, the impartial moon was cold and intact against the blue-black sky, and a faint chorus of approaching sirens was penetrating the city traffic. Tez drove them away, Miu Miu lying on the back seat, shaking with terror and pain. Jamal's placating words and gestures were lost on her; she probably thought they were going to dump her on the roadside.

At the T-junction at the end of Spider's entry Tez indicated left, in the direction of the hospital.

"We need to get her back to Shrivie," said Jamal. He reached across and flicked off the indicator.

The truth dawned for Tez.

"Are you mad? Are you fuckin' 'aving a laugh?" There was no hospital in Shriveton; the LCI was less than a mile away from where they were. "You want to take her to the Paki Witch, don't you?"

Jamal nodded. "Then you'll see for yourself, Tez."

Tez slumped against the steering wheel, grinding his forehead on the back of his hands, and huffing and puffing.

"Tez?"

"Wha'?"

"Did Billy kill Gary Skelton?"

"Yeah."

"I thought you 'ad."

"No. Billy."

"I'm glad."

"Why?"

"It's like I *need* you to be good."

Tez's sharp intake of breath was the only external sign of the tsunami of grief which turned in him. With a defeated sigh he sat

176

back, threw the indicator downwards, and steered to the right.

Late Night

The Wasteland

Guantanamo waited in his lean-to home, made out of cardboard, rags and plastic bags, until the laughing of the hooded and masked pair of foot soldiers receded to nothing. Then he pulled aside the bin-liner curtain, and, peeking his louse-riddled head out, surveyed his Wasteland estate. The floor of milk crates elevated him from the mud in which, face down and twenty meters away, a victim lay.

Like a strange orange monkey, Guantanamo lolloped over and pulled the man's face up and sideways of the mud. The clerical collar and the sandy, balding pate were the only identifiers now that the victim's facial features were no more than a hash of mud and minced flesh.

Guantanamo began to shake and cry, partly because he was withdrawing horribly, and partly because this priest had always been kind to him, giving food and blankets and money; the priest had even collected milk crates for the floor of Guantanamo's Wasteland hovel.

"Is he alive?" came a girl's voice from behind him.

"Dunno," he answered, trembling.

Jodi came closer, and said, "I seen what they done to 'im."

She crouched down beside the victim. In her hand was a man's shoe.

"What shall we do?" said Guantanamo.

He was surprised at himself, because he had spent his entire life avoiding problems.

"I've called an ambulance," said Jodi, eyes on the priest.

She was surprised at herself. For some reason, all she could think of was the Paki Witch's hijab. It was stuffed in an old Primark handbag in Jodi's wardrobe, where it had lain like toxic waste, contaminating her serenity (such as it was) ever since.

Approaching sirens blossomed in the night.

"We might get accused if we stay," suggested Guantanamo. He was shivering convulsively.

"You go," said Jodi. "I'll wait with 'im."

Guantanamo scuttled away, only to return in the next instant with a milk crate, which he planted, inverted, beside the priest, and told Jodi, "Sit."

177

"Thanks," she said, sitting.

A peace, such as she had never known, and which was incomprehensible given the current circumstances, enveloped Jodi Harris.

His feet sinking into the mud, Guantanamo waited with her.

Skylark

"Somethin's not right," mumbled Tez as they turned into Boundary Lane. "Need to call Sam."

Across, over the Wasteland, inchoate beneath the walkway, the Shopping Parade was dark. Not even Liu's Chippy was open, although Jamal did not perceive this. Nor had he noticed the unmarked police cars: one on the edge of the Wasteland, at the base of the stairs that led up to the Parade; and another, grey and quiet as a woodlouse, parked outside St Theresa's.

Blue lights rolled like low-lying noxious gas on the edge of the Wasteland near the Parade.

"Can't see nothin'" said Jamal, looking around, perplexed.

Phone to his ear, Tez stopped the car beside the bank of red bins to the side of Skylark Tower. The area was cast in shadows, because the security lights and cameras had been vandalised so often that they were no longer replaced.

"Fuckin' twat. Sammy!" he fumed, panic rising in him because his phone call went unanswered.

He looked round in exasperation at the quiet, coat-cocooned form of Miu Miu on the back seat, and said to Jamal, "Stash her be'ind them bins and –" He dialled again on his phone. "Jew? You wha'?"

Horror – instant and absolute – atrophied Tez as he listened to his wife. So vehement was her stream of hatred that, despite the buffer of Tez's head, her audible but scrambled hostility seemed to fill the car interior. Then it ceased abruptly as she hung up on him.

Blanched and agitated, Tez signalled again to Jamal to get their passenger out, saying, "I gotta get off."

Baffled, and afraid – because of Tez's mood change, and because his own faith that he would find Jessie Rout was all he had to go with at that moment – Jamal coaxed Miu Miu up from the back seat and helped her out of the car. Tez drove away, the same way they had just come, in the direction of town.

In the gap between two of the bins, Jamal sat down with Miu Miu. Wrapped in his student coat, she lay like a sack of coal on his lap. Gently, he eased her on to the floor beside him. She started crying.

"Wait for me," he said, waving his arms in the direction he was about to take. "I come back here. I get help now."

Somehow, his semaphore of consolation and the word *wait*, which she understood, soothed her, and she nodded, her pained moaning subsiding into persistent gulps.

He ran around and into the Skylark Tower block, not even bothering to look around him to check whether he had been seen. His footsteps like rim shots in the silent hardness all around, he bounded up the Skylark staircases which folded and interlocked like an accordion belly. It hadn't even occurred to him to visit each landing on his way up. All he knew was that he must go on, and on, as if travelling into the heart of his faith in his Beloved.

And then he saw *her* – ahead of him, moving down the stairs towards him – and the world fell away. Immaculate, sculpted in ebony against the Magnolia emulsion of the Skylark stairwell, she was Good incarnate, and he stood trembling before her.

"Jessie, I –" he began, as she came close.

She was fragrant, but not like a perfume, more like the flowers that had bedecked Troy's coffin; and her eyes were so full of love. He wanted to collapse and kiss her feet, and sob and rub his face against even just the tiniest expanse of one of her toes.

She'd stopped a couple of steps above him, and seemed taller – huge, even – as now she put her arms on his shoulders, and pulled his head to her body, interrupting him with, "I know why you have come."

Even as he wrapped his arms around her, she patted him, and slid down and out of his grasp, like a child dismounting a playground ride.

He had to almost run to keep up with her as she went down the stairs. In what felt like just a few seconds, they were outside in the Skylark forecourt, their feet in a mulch of fallen leaves showing like pumpkin shards in the fluorescent tower block light.

Still ahead of him, for all his efforts to keep up, and knowing exactly where she was heading, his Beloved went directly to the injured prostitute.

Enveloped in Jamal's voluminous trench coat, Miu Miu's lemon-dressed form was stark as an evening primrose in peat. Jamal's eyes, still set for the bright interior lighting of the Skylark foyer and stairs, had not adjusted to the shadowy crevice in which she lay. Yet now he could see clearly Miu Miu's bubbling, cherry-red face and neck. Blue dye from her cheap, beaded necklace had run like varicose veins down her ruined decolletage. He could see

179

clearly the tears, bumping and glistening around the blister domes on the scarlet of her ruined face.

Jessie Rout was leaning over her, and talking to her, and all Jamal could think about was the light source. He couldn't see a wall light nearby; nor was Jessie carrying a torch. So how was it that he could see the pink of Jessie's palm and nails as now she drew her hand over Miu Miu's distorted flesh? And how could he see his Beloved's teeth and moist mouth, her smiling lips red against the brown of her skin?

Miu Miu spoke – a short series of separated, throaty syllables. Then, like an unfurling yellow flower bursting from the restrictive sepals of Jamal's trench coat, she stood up and walked forward, out of the shadows. Though inky clouds wisped across the rusk moon, there was light enough to distinguish her smiling face, plump and smooth as an apricot ripening on the branch.

CHAPTER FIFTEEN

Ten Years Earlier

Darley House NCH, Bootle

Twix

"Them pair don't know what they're doin'," she said, holding out a Twix bar.

Jewel had on the same dowdy grey coat she wore in and out of doors, and her dark hair hung like oilskin over her mild, brown eyes. Her front tooth was missing; and her bisected earlobes resembled shrivelled carrots.

She had entered his room and perched like a field mouse on his edge of the bed, where he lay curled up, crushed by life. Two of the long-term kids had spat on his lunch and stuck a fork in his leg. They'd done the same the previous day. And now he was starving. Sitting up, embarrassed, Tez ran his hands like over his teary, slum-dough face.

He took the Twix only when she gave it a little, insistent shake.

"Them lads what tease ya are just sawdust in 'ere." She tapped the side of her head. "All the glue sniffin' they done when they was small."

Like him, Jewel had no contact with any of her family, and was fending off another stint in foster care. Like him, nobody would adopt her now because in a year she could be released into the outside world and forgotten about.

Folding her arms about herself, Jewel rocked to and fro, eyes fastened on the floor. As he wolfed down her Twix bar, he regarded her with the profoundest gratitude.

And in the years that followed, he'd never cried again, because from that moment on, Terry Siddell and Jewel Moran became inseparable.

Liverpool City Infirmary

A blast of cold air flooded the entrance foyer of the hospital into which Tez now walked, his every step simultaneously hastened by absurd hope, and retarded by dread. Random images of his married life played in his mind as he went. As if she were a superimposed green-screen take, Jewel, in her cheap, drab clothes, featured in them all: registry office wedding with care home staff as witnesses; various awful bedsits, and then, finally, their Matherfield Park detached home.

His own gaunt, desperate self was reflected in the stainless steel doors of the hospital lift. But his mind's eye saw only a scene of home: a star-dotted sky frothing over the boundary walls and leylandii hedging of the cobbled, security-lit Matherfield courtyard; in the background, small and precious as a black diamond, was Jewel, silhouetted against the illuminated aperture of their open Matherfield front door.

In all the places, good and bad, rich and poor, where they had lived, Jewel had stood in the doorway, waiting for him to come home.

But now he'd lost her.

For the first time since those two kids had spat on his lunch in the kids' home, he started sobbing. The other people in the lift looked on sympathetically. An old lady even put her arm on his shoulder and said, *The darker the night, the brighter the stars* as she handed him a packet of paper tissues. But he was too chewed up to respond, and self-ejected at the next floor, staggering on through the labyrinth of corridors, somehow certain he would find her, even though he didn't know where he was heading.

In the wilderness of his life, Jewel had been the only grace. She'd given him a Twix, more than anyone had ever given him, ever. In return, he had given her everything. Her absolute sexual frigidity had always been an incredible bonus and relief to him. That her chastity had been stolen and her body soiled by her male relatives and their friends when she was fourteen did not hang like

182

sulphur in his imagination, choking his masculine instincts. He adored her, feeling none of the desire a man feels for a woman, loving her for her field mouse self alone. Reticent, plain – and so far away from the ridiculous name assigned to her by her abusive and inadequate parents – Jewel had been central to his well-being from the moment she had given him her Twix.

He was gangland overlord. She was priest's housekeeper. They were opposite poles between which the convection currents of their shared life ran, always back to her. A protective magnetosphere had sprung up around them from the Twix-gift start; it completely deflected all the horrors of the outside world.

Now the high and white corridor, like an empty set from the after-life, acquired stage furniture and extras – another drinks machine, and some languid, green-uniformed auxiliary staff pushing trolleys laden with supplies. Ahead, in a small seated area, he saw Jewel, in her grey raincoat, rocking to and fro, her eyes on the floor.

"Excuse me," came a voice from behind him, which, with a hasty jostle, transfigured into a dark-suited man in a clerical collar, running in the direction of Jewel.

Jewel leapt to her feet as the priest paused to press her hand consolingly, and said to her, "I came as quickly as I could!"

With unceremonious urgency, a cluster of medical personnel, like assorted mints in their green and white uniforms and masks, led him away through opaque-glazed double doors.

Only then did Jewel notice her husband, who had run the final few metres to her. For a few moments, it seemed as if time and motion were suspended, as Jewel, her eyes puffy as a boxer's, faced him. Then, with the dreadful abandon of a lunatic, she launched herself bodily at him, screaming, "I hate you!"

He tried and failed to grab her arms as she pounded his chest with her fists. A boiling, multi-directional spray of accusation issued from her bloodless lips.

"Your Zone men have killed Kevin!"

"Shush!" implored Tez, looking around desperately. "I don't know nothin' about this. What's 'appened to Kevin?"

"I know what you are, you fuckin' *gangsta*. I tried to shut it out, like I done with everythin' else. But I always knew. I always knew *you*!"

Tez finally caught her by the wrists, and she spat repeatedly in his face, wriggling so violently that he had to release her for fear of snapping her bones, so small in his hand. It destroyed him to see her this way.

A nearby nurse made to intervene, but held off in fear as Jewel ranted on: "Two of 'em beat 'im up cos 'e asked about the bonfire by the library."

"This is the first I've –"

She got free and started hitting him again, kicking his shins. An arriving male nurse clasped her shoulders and said, "You'll have to go out if –"

Tez opened and shut his mouth. His hands reached reflexively first to his gun pocket, and then to his cigarette pocket, then fell limply to his sides.

Jewel stopped, exhausted, defeated. She flopped into the nearest seat, arms tight around her belly, rocking to and fro again.

"I kept denyin' what you really was all the while," she said, *sotto voce*, wretched. She did not move as Tez sat beside her, but snapped free as he tried to put his arm around her.

"'Cos I knew you was trapped by that, that devil," extreme hostility and loathing made a gargoyle of her face as she choked on, "that Satan snake, that Zollo."

"Jew, I'll pack it all in," pleaded Tez, kneeling before her. "I'll go the bizzies. I never wanted it. It was Zollo. He got me when I was a kid."

"Yeah, and you done the same to all them kids that ride around *your* Zone."

"No. It's different."

"No it's not."

She looked at him directly. Pity crept into her gaze for a moment, only to be banished as she recalled, rocking with renewed agitation, "Kevin's face was like raw meat. I wouldn't've recognised him 'cept for the priest's collar."

"I never knew nothin' 'bout –"

She became very quiet and still for some moments – perhaps as much as a minute – before making the defiant declaration. "Me and Kevin helped the Paki Witch get Chloe Tudor and her baby away from you."

Tez opened and shut his mouth.

"That day you come into the church lookin' for Chloe Tudor and the Paki Witch. Remember?"

"Yeah."

"An' I 'ad that music on dead loud?"

"Yeah."

"Well, the Paki Witch was there in the back, with Kevin and Chloe fuckin' Tudor and 'er babbee."

Jewel picked up her bag, and stood up, looking down on him in scorn.

"An' you know wha'? I was glad to get 'em away from you, Terry. An' you know wha'? I knew on that day that I actually hated your guts. Yeah!" She snorted, and drew her sleeve under her running nose. "I can tell you now if it was you in there and not Kevin, I – I wouldn't be like –"

"Jew, tell me you don't mean that?" he whelped, scrambling to his feet.

"I shouldn't've stayed as long as I did. But we sort of fitted together, and it was easy." She chewed her lip, shaking her head, ashamed. "Well, just to let you know that we've mainly lived all these years on *my* wages. Ninety-four pound a week. I never wanted none of your fuckin' money 'cos I know 'ow you get it. An' I'm not goin' back to you or that fuckin' 'ouse after this. You 'ear me? I fuckin' hate that 'ouse, an' all them snotty Matherfield Park pricks who treat me like a fuckin' leper."

A theatre nurse, togged in mask and protective head scarf, emerged from the double doors, and told Jewel, "It's time to say goodbye now, Mrs Siddell. We've put him in a nice side room through here." The nurse held the door open for her. "He's very peaceful. Father Francis is with him."

With a sigh so loud and desperate it seemed to separate her from everything forever, Jewel staggered forward.

"Jewel, listen to me," pleaded Tez, following her. "I'll find who done this. And I'll make 'em pay, Jewel. But you gotta believe me when I say I never knew nothin' 'bout this till now."

She turned round, glowering, furious. "Make 'em pay, Terry?"

"Fuckin' too right, Jew –"

"But Terry, don't you see?" She was almost laughing. Contempt followed hard upon. "Don't you *see*? All o' that just leads to the same again, and again. You could've stopped it. You could've been a better man. But you kept choosin' it by makin' 'em pay. You kept *in* it!"

She moved to the door and the theatre nurse. Tez pulled her arm.

"Jew, you're my whole world. There's nothin' left without you. Everythin' I done was to keep you and me safe."

"Well you fuckin' failed!" she yelled. "And that makes me feel even worse! To think you done this for me, it... it fuckin' destroys me!"

Sobbing, cringing, bowing around her as he attempted to embrace her, he begged "I'll make it right, Jew. I'll show you."

He sank to the floor, his arms sliding down over her body,

which he had never known. Clasping her knees, he was crying her name into the cheap fabric of her loose-fitting trousers as she declared, clipped and cold as secateurs, "The only person who can make anythin' right is the Paki Witch." She moved free of him. "All my trust, all my hope, all my life – I give it to the Paki Witch. Not to you."

Flipping to inexplicable but real tenderness, with the tip of her finger she stroked his youth-dark, thinning hair. Then, resolute, she stepped away, out of his arms, and said, "I don't want you 'ere when I get out from –" She faltered and closed her eyes, releasing streams of tears which hung off the bony ledge of her jaw like little diamonds. "– sayin' bye to Kevin. I never want nothin' to do with you ever again."

Shriveton

Sanctuary

As they approached it, Jamal noticed that everything was changed at the Shopping Parade. There were no boys on bikes to salute him, or hooded soldiers lurking in the shadows, or shambling, clucking punters making their way to the defunct library.

Liu's Chippy was shuttered and dark, so Jamal, Miu Miu and his Beloved Jessie Rout had to walk, via the Boxing Gym and pile of bonfire material, to the rear entrance. They ascended the steps to the flats above the Parade. Below was the bank of bright red bins, quiet as the grave. Day and night this crucial perimeter would be patrolled by armed Incubo soldiers on foot and motorbikes. But now the only defence was the barricade of motor-auction rejects at the rear of the Parade, flanking the bins.

It took almost ten minutes of quiet knocking and pleading before Grandma Liu opened the door, standing beside her grandson, in pyjamas.

"It's the Paki Witch!" Liu squealed, awestruck.

His grandmother appeared behind him, fearful at the sight of Jamal, who betokened gangland trouble. But she softened immediately as the Paki Witch stepped forward and spoke briefly to her. Nodding and smiling, the old woman held open the door, and ushered in Miu Miu, who was still wrapped in Jamal's student coat.

Miu Miu smiled and cried at the same time, as she went in to safety. The old woman put a protective arm around her shoulder.

"We'll look after 'er, Paki Witch," chirped Liu. "Anythin' for you, me Nan says."

The Paki Witch smiled at the little boy, and then she and Jamal Bannigan walked away, like movie lovers under a star-studded sky.

She faltered briefly on the steps leading down from the flats, and he put a steadying arm around her. And when she stabilised he didn't take it away, but hugged her to him as they walked, glad that he'd lost the trench coat to Miu Miu because it meant that his Beloved's body was closer to his.

Her robe was satiny soft, like the set of cushions his Nan had robbed from George Henry Lee's when he and Troy were kids. Jessie Rout satiated his every sense and need, just by walking beside him, in companionable silence. It felt, about halfway along the Skylark Walkway, as if she leaned into him, and was resting the side of her head on his chest.

He had dimly computed police cars and people milling in the Wasteland below. Something big was going on, but all he knew was her presence beside him as they walked.

Liverpool City Centre

Twenty-two-year-old Ethan Greenberg's failure to make it financially and romantically prompted a weekly Shabbat phone call from his mother, who would furnish him with updates about his successful peers in the hope that the Lord would deliver him from provincial journalism into a respectable banking career. Tonight, Momma had treated him to a thorough account of cousin Solly's latest mercantile miracles at Charterhouse, and neighbour Moses' engagement to New York heiress Golda, who was not only a beauty, but a fine skier, with strong maternal instincts and nice parents.

On learning that for his Saturday evening meal her jewel and treasure had had *another* McDonald's, Momma was urging him to live comfortably with his Aunty Miriam in Childwall.

"Well this apartment's handy for work, Momma," mumbled Ethan, trying to make his keyboard taps as inaudible as possible. "How is Solly doing with the electric cigarettes?"

Momma suddenly remembered that Zayde had seen a nice financial journalism job for Ethan in the City. Ethan could live with Solly in Golders Green. Solly's mother kept house so well, and was bound to introduce Ethan to a suitable young lady. With considerable enthusiasm, Momma described the star-spangled life which would unfold were Ethan to take this job.

He could picture her now, aproned and bustling in her immaculate Solihull kitchen, force-feeding everyone in sight, and telling off Auschwitz-survivor grandfather about his untidiness. Other people found his Yiddish Momma endearingly funny. Unfortunately, Ethan found her suffocating. The thought of living with the more extreme version of Momma – such as Miriam, her Liverpool Childwall cousin, or (even worse again) her Golders Green sister and perfect nephew, financial wizard Solomon – truly appalled him. Nor did Ethan wish to find and be maritally smothered by a younger version of his mother – skiing and childbearing skills notwithstanding. Ever. He considered that he had left the Tribe forever after seeing YouTube footage about the Occupied Palestinian Territories when he was at university.

"I don't want that, Momma," he interrupted her.

Her whole spirit seemed to deflate. This always happened, and signalled to him that he must bring the Saturday evening phone call to an end with, "I need to get my journalism career going. I love you, Momma. I'll be home next holiday."

Usually after the Shabbat call, Ethan would go to the pub and wash away her reproofs with rather too many beers. Tonight, however, he stayed at his computer, working. For days, during every spare moment, he'd been trawling all the public housing, health, immigration and police data bases – the ones available to all *Star* journalists, and the ones his own computing cleverness enabled him to hack. But all he had to search with was: Paki Witch, Jessie Rout (all permutations of spellings, here), Shriveton, Liverpool and Muslim. There was no description or photograph of her, and he didn't even know how old she was. So far he had drawn a blank.

But the conversation with Momma just now had flicked a switch: he had prided himself on separating from his family and culture since his university awakening to the iniquity of Zionism. But, actually, he now realised, he hadn't his left the Tribe at all. He was in contact with Momma and Zayde at least once a week, and would be home next holiday, and the holiday after that. If he was in London, he usually met up with the abominably smug, secret cigarette-smoking Solly. During and since university he had never been more than ten miles away from a good Jewish *balabusta* [4]rel

---

4

ative whom he could call on or even stay with. Even eating smoky bacon crisps filled him with a traitor's angst.

Now it occurred to him that the so-called Paki Witch was *completely* dislocated from her culture, and had never been assimilated into the white community of Shriveton. On a hunch that the reason was connected with war, he spent the next few hours revisiting all the leads and articles he had saved so far about Muslim conflict hot spots such as Syria, Iran, Iraq, Lebanon, Palestine and Afghanistan.

It was almost midnight when he found a two-year-old report about an Afghan teenager called Jessenia Rabia al-Rahoud, which his previous investigations had thrown out, but which he had rejected. Tonight, however, the photograph of this mutilated Afghani girl claimed him absolutely. One of her ears had been cut off, and the other hung, spliced in the blood-wet of her hair. The blood streaming from sausage fat lips had coagulated in the delicate hollows at the base of her throat and collar bones. A British Army coat partially covered her naked, lacerated body.

There were particularly grievous wounds to the inside of her thighs, where the girl's husband savaged her with a knife, after his gang of Taliban militia friends had finished raping her. An unnamed British soldier had interrupted them, and they fled, leaving her naked body crawling with flies on the Hindu Kush mountainside. Covering her with his jacket, the unknown soldier had summoned help.

As Ethan devoured the article, and all army, hospital, Afghani and related news records, he kept flicking back to the image of her. The girl's eyes – dark, serene and infinitely kind despite *everything* else depicted in that Hindu Kush mountain photograph – seduced him into complete, unswerving belief that, impossible though it seemed, he had indeed found the Paki Witch.

And so Ethan Greenberg stopped searching, and, closing his own eyes, and seeing hers in his mind, he leaned back in his chair, suffused with joy. He didn't know what to do with this joy. The only person who would understand it would be the oddball Shriveton priest. But just as he was about to dial the St Theresa's Presbytery, there came an incoming call from his source at Merseyside Police: Fr Kevin O'Connor was on his deathbed in the LCI, following an unprovoked attack at the Shriveton Shopping

Good homemaker

189

Parade.

All Ethan could think of was his own, sudden longing to be home with Momma and Zayde.

Shriveton

Starry, Starry Night

His hand on the satin fullness of her waist, they walked away from the Shopping Parade. A cosmos of Tiffany stars, iridescent in the clearest winter sky, lit their path. Jamal felt as if all the blossoms of spring, all the honey of summer, and fruits of harvest had been gifted to him in the small, warm person of his Beloved, held close. His breath plumed the air, like the feather wrap of a Disneyland dancer. It would condense in a myriad of tiny opaque beads in his hair, which would eventually assume the appearance of snowy topiary. But he didn't care.

Every so often, he dug the nails into the flesh of his free hand, buried in his pocket, to make sure this wasn't a dream. It was real.

They walked out of the estate, along Boundary Lane, where, from his hearse in Troy's funeral cortège, he had seen her talking to Guantanamo outside his Wasteland lean-to home. At that time she had been on the periphery of his consciousness – the imagined saviour of the mad and the destitute – like a singer or actor he didn't follow. Now, her warm body next to his as they walked, he knew she was real, and he felt confident enough to finally ask, "Jessie, who are you?"

"Who do *you* say I am?"

"Well I think you're –" he paused, then pushed out the crazy idea that had been rolling around his mind like a cat on heat – " from somewhere else."

She laughed, "Well, I am."

"Where?"

She hesitated, and then sighed. "Well, I came from Afghanistan."

"Yes, well, that's not quite what I meant."

"Oh."

"So how come you're here, walking with me now, in...well 'ere in Britain, like? If you don't mind saying."

She thought for a moment.

"I can tell you. But it doesn't answer your question. Just remember that."

He laughed, muddled now as to what his question actually was.

"I was living in the village of Langar, to the North," she began. "It is a beautiful place, you know."

She seemed wistful and sad at the recollection.

"Tell me what it's like," he encouraged.

"Well, it is pretty – full of very simple, stone cottages, pale and squat – like little loaves on the vast green plains!" Excitement, even joy, was on her now. "Everywhere, there are goats and sheep, their neck bells clanking under a sheet of blue sky. And the people are sun-stained and wiry. The old ones have raisin faces. And their wise eyes are like black sea pearls in which you see the whole world – like exploding confetti, Jamal.

"There is no horizon, just the mountains – hulking. Like lovers. Sometimes purple, sometimes dusty brown depending on where the sun is. That is my home. I can smell coffee and *obi non* from my mother's little stove even now."

"I want to go there with you, Jessie," said Jamal, entranced to almost madness by the bucolic scene her words created. He stopped walking, and pulled her round to face him. "We can go together. We – we could get married."

She smiled, and lifted her hand up to his face. Covering it with his own, he stared into her eyes as she continued, "All is well, Jamal."

"I love you so much, Jessie. There's no words to tell you how much."

"And I love you, Jamal."

"Oh, my God, I –"

"Before the light of this night had even begun its battle to escape each star's molten core – *long* before your mother's womb wove your bones – I have loved you. Every star will burn away, but love never dies, Jamal."

"But – but until now I always thought that love does die. It dies and you never hear about it again. Troy. Me Mum. Me –" He couldn't bring himself to say *Dad*. It had just occurred to him that his father had been the most disappointing of all his inadequate relatives.

"What is your favourite song?" Jessie Rout interrupted him. Forcing a levity of mood, she grabbed both his hands, as if they were about to start a giddy reel.

He was stumped for a moment, but dutifully applied his mind to the question, as she rocked his hands slowly from side to side, smiling up at him.

"Well, I dunno," he mumbled, entranced by her, but stiff and unyielding to her movements. "*Tracks of My Tears*, maybe?

191

Smokey Robinson. Me an' Troy used to dance around the house, and do the Miracles dance. Like nutters."

"Run it now in your head."

"What d'you mean?"

"Hear it in your head, and dance with me. We will be nutters, like you and Troy."

"I –"

"Don't be boring!" she was laughing, teasing, cajoling, bewitching.

"But you can't hear it."

"As long as you can hear it, you can dance with me, silly. So?"

"So what?"

"So, Jamal, are you dancing?"

The levy burst, and with an embarrassed laugh which subsided into wonder, he pulled her close, and felt her breasts and belly against him, as he said, "Yes."

His palm was open on the small of her back. Her other hand, in his, was up near her shoulder, like on Fred and Ginger films he and Troy used to watch on YouTube. Now he saw, peeking from beneath the rim of her hijab, the red bandanna he had given her. It accentuated the bloom of her lips, and the melted chocolate of her laughing eyes.

Keeping her body on his, he swayed with her beneath the starry, starry night. In the estate below, diamante Monopoly houses twinkled like a myriad of homage-paying Zippo lighters. In the years that followed he would remember with joy his dance with Jessie Rout, which seemed at the time to last forever.

Finally, she lifted her head from his shoulder, and, looking into his eyes, said, "Love is the music which plays itself, though every instrument has been burned, and the tongue cut out of every singer."

Panic started consuming him as, gently, she extracted her hands from his.

"Stay with me, Jessie," he begged.

"I will see you tomorrow," she said, after a small pause in which it seemed she might cry.

"Where shall I meet you?"

"Don't worry, you will know where to come."

"Stay with me," he begged again. "At yours or –" he grimaced a little – "mine, only me Nan's a bit ill, like, so the place is, like, scruffy. I mean, I would sleep on the sofa."

She held him with her gaze. Until that moment, he had assumed, but avoided admitting it to himself, that the passion lay on his side, that he was just indulging what she perceived to be an adolescent crush. But now he felt enfolded in her love; it was a love so pure and strong and real that he could not doubt it.

"We have tomorrow, Jamal," she said, her eyes running with tears. And, fast as fire, she kissed him quickly on the lips, and was gone.

Billy

Billy had returned from Spider's lair to find that the whole Zone had vaporised. An overt police presence had been established on the Wasteland where paramedics had found Billy's troublesome priest shortly before 11pm, and taken the fatally wounded man directly to the LCI.

From the dark Shopping Parade stairwell, Billy had watched the forensic team combing the Wasteland crime scene as he took Sammy's call. It was just after midnight, and his shins were still stinging from the nasty kick administered by Tez. Staring into the pulverised blue of the police cars' lights, he listened as Sammy reported that Zone Chief Tez and Spider had been arrested, Zollo had gone to ground, and the Incubo was abroad already.

Too afraid to go home to his Dad's Tallis Row flat, in case an arresting officer was waiting there for him, and having no money on him, Billy had made his way from the abandoned Zone, creeping in the shadows of housing estate which bordered the Wasteland. He would spend the night in an empty house, which the local addicts didn't know about, on Boundary Lane. In the morning, he knew he would be able to get what he needed from his father's house, hopefully, and make a getaway.

The attack on the well-loved priest – plus Jodi and Guantanamo's astonishing defiance of Incubo Land law in staying with Kevin until the ambulance they had called arrived – had sparked a miniature rebellion in the estate, Billy discovered. Dozens of parishioners were gathered outside St Theresa's, wrapped in blankets, their hands cupped around tea, candles, torches, and a little stove someone had made of some of the combustible rubbish piled high on the Community Centre bonfire. Whereas only hours ago, with a mere flick of his head, Billy could command the destruction of their spiritual leader, now he must cleave to the shadows as he passed Kevin's faithful.

Before turning on to Boundary Lane, Billy looked back, for no reason, towards the Tallis and Skylark towers. The forecourt, which was perhaps a hundred yards away, looked like a well-lit stage between the two tower blocks straddling it. Beneath the moon and stars, which had suddenly seemed brilliant as a thousand miniature suns in the royal blue sky, he thought he could see the Paki Witch dancing with someone, a young man. Billy had stared in disbelief and considerable fear, for the last time he had seen the Paki Witch had been at very close quarters in the dark Zone alleyway, when his sharp, fat fingers were still moist and fishy from feeling up Chloe Tudor's desolated sex. Billy squinted and stared at the dancers, and a new terror gripped him: she was dancing with the dead Troy Bannigan.

Trembling at the apparition, Billy ran the rest of the way to the Boundary Lane squat. As soon as he was cut off from the outside world – he didn't dare use his phone after speaking to Sammy last night – the Paki Witch and ghostly Troy filled his mind.

Only the certainty of the yellow tin, where his Dad had money set aside for bills, waiting for him on the Tallis Row living room mantelpiece, consoled him. Billy had siphoned off all of his Dad's building society savings a long time ago. Now, in this dark hour of need, he regretted this prematurity: his Dad's life savings would have been so useful now. As things stood, the yellow tin cash would just about fund the coach fare to London, where Billy had decided to head, with a view to pursuing, as Sammy was doing, the Albanian *fare* contacts in Soho.

All night long, every creak and shadow appalled him.

CHAPTER SIXTEEN

Sunday 31st October

Morning

Matherfield Park

Awakenings

Tez had hung around in the hospital waiting room after Jewel went in to see her beloved priest. But she'd refused absolutely to come out again until he had gone; and when hospital security escorted him away, he finally Woke Up. Every veil, every buffer, fell away. All that was left was himself, his own true nature, and all that he had done and failed to do.

By the LCI entrance he'd leaned against one of the freshly papered healthy-eating and quit-smoking posters – still wet with glue – as a call came in from an unrecognised number. It was Zollo, issuing the final command to close the Zone immediately, and evacuate all resources and personnel, "Mayday, mayday, mayday. Troops out."

In his last act of duty towards his men, Tez relayed the *Mayday* instruction to Sammy. He didn't even think of escape, or killing the Incubo, but instead came back to Matherfield Park, fed Flossie, his dog, and pulled a note-pad and a biro from a kitchen drawer. He'd spent most of the night writing, his right fist around the pen, his left around his handgun; his ears pricked, listening, listening.

But the only sound had been the night birds. Still and upright in the gloom, with tens of thousands of cash beneath the floorboards on which his chair stood, he had varied writing with careful consideration of the birdsong. He'd identified blackbirds, thrushes and robins.

The standard procedure for gangsters facing the triple *Mayday* message was to flee. He should be on a plane, with Jewel, plus the under-floor cash, put by for this eventuality. But instead, he was home with his dog, and now it was just after seven a.m. and the sun had risen on a new day. Tez had three handwritten letters in envelopes. He switched off the kitchen light, and listened some more to the birds singing in the blue-milk light of dawn.

"Jew, I can't do nothin' without you," he mumbled then, as he searched cupboards he had never opened because Jewel had always managed the kitchen.

With a muscular shrug, his dozy Staffordshire bull terrier waddled up to him from her basket and nuzzled his calf. Flossie was the only being in the world who gave him affection.

"No dog food, girl," he told her, crouching down and cuddling her, kneading her firm, warm flank with his forehead. He wished he could hold on to her warm, loving, silly form forever. "I'll make yer some toast."

He opened the fridge, remembering to catch the door, which always lunged out due to a broken hinge, and pulled out a lonely tub of margarine. It looked and smelt like the wax polish Jewel used for the St Theresa's church pews. All these years he had assumed his wife didn't like butter, or rolls, or meat, or good, strong tea, or fancy biscuits; that she hadn't known or wanted any better than the two slices of brilliant white sponge he was plunging into the toaster.

Now he knew why everything was cheap and broken; he knew that, all along, she'd hated this house as surely as he hated the Zone. His eyes welled up: she'd come to hate him, too.

Awareness, like an atom bomb, was mushrooming and the result was too terrible to contemplate. How he envied the Teflon conscience of psychos like Billy and Spider. How good it was to sleep as they did, every moment of their lives.

By contrast, Tez was an insomniac strapped to a chair watching the horror show he had produced. Featured were the groaning wounded: bag-of-bones addicts and underlings whom he had slashed, poisoned, knee-capped and tortured on his way up. His dead victims stared goggle-eyed from the mud of this No Man's Land, too. They were all so young. He could see Ben Skelton's plump face flesh – grey as a foetal scan – moving around the word

Mum, his young eyes rolling.

Tez couldn't remember ever choosing *any of this.*

Now Troy's lovely image floated into his mind. Tez could recall – that sad diversity of misery and joy – choosing fifteen-year-old Troy in the Community Centre boxing gym. Dancing, ducking, diving masculine perfection: black-skinned Troy had been stronger and faster than the other fighters in there. The boy's musculature – taut, shiny, luxurious – kindled the unspeakable nature which Tez had always battled within himself, and which he had denied even as he called the boy over after the sparring. Instead, Tez persuaded himself that it was right to reward Troy, who had minded a smoking gun for him a couple of weeks earlier, asking no questions.

Embarrassed, deferent and hastily towelling the sweat from his loins, Troy had come, and dissolved with rapture when the illustrious Zone Chief offered him an Incubo foot soldier job. Tez had even taken the eager new recruit to the Liverpool game to consolidate the agreement. It was the only time they ever went together. Troy had swayed and bayed with the impassioned crowd, staring with adolescent intensity at every play of the ball.

Football, like women, did not stir the slightest passion in Tez. But the goals and the favourable referee decisions meant hugs with Troy. On the way home from Anfield, throughout Troy's deluded, partisan commentary of every pass of the game, Tez relived those freely given hugs.

He relived them now, and smiled for a moment through his tears.

Troy's ashes were nourishing the Anfield turf which his quick, brown eyes had watched so keenly that day.

It was time to go.

Ah, but the birdsong – that spiky, keyless scat on the theme of a new day begun – broke his old, old heart. He sat just a little longer, listening attentive as a composer at the premier of his dearest work, while Flossie gobbled up her bleached bread and pew-wax toast. Then he fastened her lead, and, stuffing his gun and cigarettes, the letters and an empty envelope into his pocket, Tez went out.

Liverpool City Centre

Morning

The Incubo had known he was destined for greatness since, still

197

nothing but a dinosaur-obsessed schoolboy, his teacher had informed him that Loch Ness had three metres of eels on its bed, and that the largest of these was probably what people mistook for the monster.

"And did you know, Jude," the teacher had added, "that Liverpool comes from the word *Elverpool?*[5] And *elver* is just another word for eel."

"No. I thought Nessie was a plesiosaur," Jude had mumbled, crestfallen.

The teacher looked at him with the kindly patience she reserved for the kids she didn't really take to, like Jude, who, although from a nice address in Childwall, was strange and dirty because his mother was a drinker. Handing him a tissue for his snotty tears, she'd said, "Nessie is an ordinary eel, just like any other, except bigger. But she's got the whole world fooled! Now write an essay about how the *pool of life* got its name."

"The pool of life?"

"Our home town, Liverpool. Carl Jung described it as the *pool of life.*"

"Does 'e play for Everton, Miss?"

Who would have guessed that Jude Atkinson would go on to become the biggest eel in the Pool, fooling the whole world for years?

Now, suddenly, outrageously, the Incubo's pool of life had been drained, beaching the fruits of his genius in the baking heat of law and order. While the staff of Marporley Hall and the Zone flapped in desperation on legitimacy's hostile shores, their mighty leader was marooned in a back-street B&B.

From his hotel window he could see, uplighted in the still-dark morning and looming as imperiously fantastical as a Star Trek vessel, the Roman Catholic cathedral. His mum used to drag him

---

5

The earliest recorded form of the name, dating from 1194, is Leuerpul (the letter v was commonly written as a u in medieval documents). The first element is derived from Old English lifrig, meaning 'coagulated, clotted, livered'. A more accurate translation of the place-name is therefore the one given by Eilert Ekwall in The Concise Oxford Dictionary of Place-Names: 'pool with thick water'.

there to light candles. Once she'd been so pissed she'd accidentally set her hair on fire. He'd stood and watched, impassive, until a priest intervened.

He could smell her burning hair, now.

He *must* stay awake. From the paper litany of hotel tea, coffee, sugar and powdered milk sachets, he plucked an unspent wrap of *I* cocaine, and lined it up on the wobbly dressing table. Standards had slipped in the Zone, whence all *I* gear came: this batch was cut with a placebo – such as Lidocaine – he could tell.

But now that didn't matter. What mattered was that he could access his accounts abroad, and that the passage to Panama was organised. There was no doubt that he would survive.

Bitter anguish devoured him at the thought of his future, yawning into a pointless, low-profile infinity in the Panamanian sun.

Someone must pay!

From in-between the Gideon Bible and economy bulb bedside light, he plucked his spectacles and beanie hat. Yet again, he checked his boarding pass, new passport, driving licence and credit cards, flight ticket, and Euros, and keys to Zollo's secret lock-up, one of the unused garages to the rear of the Shriveton Shopping Parade. Stuffing them all into his pockets, he went out, to the red-brick, gothic heart of the University on Brownlow Hill, where he'd scored last night.

The sun had risen, and gulls were shrieking through out-of-sync church bells tolling the half-hour across the city. He went into an internet café flanking Blackwell's bookshop, and ordered a mug of tea. On his way to the obscurest seat, a screen caught his eye, and he stopped to read over the shoulder of a uniformed council street-cleaner, who was reading.

Exclusive by Ethan Greenberg

Serious Organised Crime Agency (SOCA) have intercepted a Rotterdam-bound vessel in Chittagong, with a sizeable cargo of heroin believed to be headed for Liverpool. Said one SOCA source, "The Chittagong find reveals that the drug traders' net is cast more widely than we believed, extending beyond the Golden Crescent [Pakistan, Afghanistan and Iran] to Bangladesh."

An undercover police operation in an exclusive Mayfair hotel revealed a link to millionaire Cheshire businessman and benefactor of the Liverpool Central Infirmary Rebuild Project, Callum Bowes-West. Using a different identity, Bowes-West brokered the Chittagong heroin deal over a lunchtime meeting with an alleged associate of the Bangladeshi government.

Bowes-West, who is believed to have fled the country, is thought to number members of the British aristocracy, celebrity A-list and business elite among his contacts. One of his multiple identities is The Incubo, head of the so-called UK Zones, these being sink housing estates which have been effectively taken over by drug barons.

Speaking of the largest and most lucrative of these, Liverpool's Shriveton Zone, one SOCA source stated: "Shriveton is an impossible nut to crack. It bears a frightening similarity to the mafia-run Scampia housing estate in Naples. You have a potentially incendiary situation [in Shriveton], with vast sums of money and huge quantities of narcotics changing hands every minute of every day and night."

The same source went on to describe the suspension yesterday evening of Shriveton Police Superintendent Simon Meyers as, "Significant."

The recent shootings of Liverpool teenagers Troy Bannigan and Gary Skelton are thought to be the result of internal disputes within UK gangs vying for supremacy in a ruthless international narcotics market. Both youths were allegedly involved in the notorious Incubo Zone which operates out of Shriveton

Breaking News: Priest who opposed Liverpool gangs beaten to death outside Shriveton chip shop

Outspoken critic of the Shriveton gang culture, Fr Kevin O'Connor, was the victim of an unprovoked and brutal attack outside Liu's Chippy in Shriveton yesterday evening. Two hooded attackers dumped their victim on an area of undeveloped land, known locally as the Wasteland, near the Shriveton shopping parade.

Father O'Connor, who served as parish priest at St Theresa's church in Shriveton for over ten years, was later taken to the Liverpool Central Infirmary, where he died in the early hours of this morning. Shriveton residents began a candlelit vigil outside St Theresa's Church last night. One of them, who did not wish to be identified, said, "He was killed because he spoke out against the gangs at Troy Bannigan's funeral."

A deliberate cough came from behind, startling the Incubo. He turned round to face a generically pierced and tattooed young waitress. Looking with barely concealed disdain at his dirty tartan fleece and tape-mended spectacles, she admonished, "Look, if you wanna use the computers, you have to pay."

Midday

Dream Wedding

Afterwards, he met her in the grassland. Troupes of gnats and cabbage butterflies danced in the sweet summer breeze which lifted her wedding veil and liquorice hair. She'd enticed him away from the wedding guests, with a whispered, "Jamal, I need to show you the yellow flower," as her lips brushed his ear lobe.

Dressed in his finest clothes, he'd followed her eagerly through the wild garden of purple thistles and cow parsley, until she stopped to cup the head of an earthbound flower in her brown hand.

"It will bloom before your eyes, my Beloved," she told him.

Seeing not the flower, but only the liquid sunlight of her wedding band, he kissed her strawberry mouth, begging her to lie down on a nuptial bed of yellow flowers all around. Only when she pulled away, smiling, did he look at the flower again.

"These green fists" – she stroked the sepals clenching the folds of lemon silk – "will loosen, and release the bloom."

And exactly as she said, the tight fragrant whorl of lemony petals unravelled to reveal a cave of powdery, genetic treasure.

"It's a miracle," he said, and kissed her neck, and breathed in her body scent.

From nowhere, a busy, buzzing bee nosed into the flower.

"Shoo!" said Jamal, embarrassed at his own inadequacy as, ignoring him, the lustful, spoiling insect penetrated and fertilised the flower womb.

"The flower will be dead tomorrow," said his Beloved, as he lay her on the floor. Mouth on hers, his hands pulled clear her gossamer white wedding gown.

But each kiss, every stroke of her naked, glorious body increased his hunger for her, until the pain of wanting was unbearable.

Tallis Tower

A loud thud woke him up to his wintry and unappealing bedroom. It was midday. He could hardly believe he'd slept so

201

long. He ran in the direction of the noise which had awakened him, to his Nan's room, where he found her convulsing on the floor. Foaming, spluttering and eyes rolling, she was like an agonised horse in fire.

She'd had fits before. The first time, he and Troy had poured all the booze away as they waited for the doctor, only to be told that if it happened again, they should give her some alcohol. Now Jamal trickled some vodka into the bottle lid, and crouched beside her, waiting for her shuddering to stop.

"Nan, 'ave this his, an' I'll phone the doctor," he said when she was quiet, cradling her as he managed to pour a little of it into her mouth.

Her lips had a horrible blue tinge, which, against the yellow of her skin, gave her face the appearance of one big bruise. In past fits, pouring in a few drops of alcohol had brought her round. But this time, her dark brown irises rolled back in her head, and all he could see was the venous mustard-yellow of the eye balls. Incontinent and paralytic in his arms, she repulsed and terrified him so much that he wanted to cast her away and leave her to die. All his life she'd seemed to want not her *little piccaninnies*, as she'd always (so embarrassingly) referred to himself and Troy, but rather oblivion.

Her eyes closing, she managed to gargle through the vodka, blood, sick and frothy sputum, "Not the doctor. I want –"

It had always been what *she* wanted, thought Jamal bitterly. If she'd looked after her *piccaninnies* properly, Troy wouldn't have ended up in the Zone. If tea had been on the table, instead of in her cirrhotic liver, Troy wouldn't have been shot eating chips in the park.

"– the Paki Witch."

Shriveton

2pm

The afternoon sun cast short shadows from the twin towers of Skylark and Tallis over the uniform streets and houses. Now and then, in the blue screen of sky, a seagull's scream broke the pervading quiet. Banger cars and the odd battered transit van hulked against the kerb of the roads threading identical lines of terraced dwellings.

The time had come, and the agitated orange shell-suited addict, waiting beside the public phone box on the Skylark forecourt, was jolted from his pathological self-preoccupation: a singular troupe of people was marching by. Leading, with a purposeful stride, was the Paki Witch, followed by two single mums with prams, social worker Morwenna Griffiths, Bob Reilly with Maisie and Tom, and an elderly man on a rusty Raleigh Shopper.

"Where you goin'?" asked Guantanamo, reaching out to one of the pram-pushing mums. His skin and clothes were dirty and his teeth rotten.

"Dunno," said the single mum, shrinking from him. "But you should come, too."

She looked down at the flesh of his lower arm, exposed as he'd reached out to her. Gouged in the bony paleness were raw and pus-filled injection sites.

"The Paki Witch will save you like she done Chloe Tudor," said the single mum, failing to conceal her horror at the state of his arm.

He hesitated, and looked back at the phone box, then, turning his back on all that he knew, he joined them.

They walked briskly through the estate, following the Paki Witch without knowing where she was heading, and their number swelled as schoolchildren and other passers-by joined, some with phones to their ears, exhorting others to come.

News of the priest's death had spread, and since the small hours more than twenty parishioners, people who would normally shrink far away from gang violence, had held a defiant vigil outside St Theresa's. But when they saw the Paki Witch, they left their post to follow her.

A rush of hope energised the low voices of the people moving, like a bubbling stream, to the lowest point in Shriveton. By the time they had turned into the Wasteland, perhaps a hundred people made up the crowd, and one or two were holding their phone cameras aloft. More were joining every moment. Two police sentries by the yellow-taped scene-of-crime area near the Parade made tentative enquiries of the crowd, then worried into walkie-talkies.

The Paki Witch stopped by a halfway-point concrete pillar anchoring the belly of Skylark Walkway overhead. Everyone drew close, regarding her with expectation, hoping that she would speak first, but she didn't. So, eventually, the Raleigh Shopper cyclist, called out, "Paki Witch, who are you?"

"I am your true love," she replied, and smiled at him.

"I love you, Paki Witch," the old man said, biting his lower lip, and looking at her with devotion.

She lowered her eyes, demure, pleased, then looked up and smiled at the silent crowd again as she beckoned Guantanamo to come over.

"Me?" he croaked, shaking.

"Hello, old friend. What is your name?"

He was trembling violently as he said, "I – I am my demons."

Those near him looked at him with sympathy, but none dared touch him since he appeared to be having some sort of fit, which launched him sideways and down, into the muddy, weedy floor of the Wasteland.

The Paki Witch crossed to him and crouched beside his writhing form. She placed her pink-palmed hand on his butting head, meanwhile muttering quiet words, which nobody could interpret. Immediately he calmed, and opened his eyes, blinking at a flush of gulls which now swooped so low that the crowd had to duck. The gulls veered up again into the air and then, as if piloted by something other than themselves, they smashed, every one of them, into the Shopping Parade barrier to the left, and slid, down and dead, into the mud below, beyond the furthest reach of the ever swelling crowd.

Astonished gasps, and wildfire reporting to those out of view, rose from the crowd. It was some moments before anyone looked back to Guantanamo, who was standing up and surveying with curiosity his own muddy self.

"What's your name?" asked the Paki Witch again.

"My name's Todd," he said, staring at her, but not daring to approach her. "My name's Todd, Todd Dean."

Awe overtook him, as he scrutinised her face and proclaimed, "Oh, my God, I've just realised who you are!"

As if he had just landed from another world and found himself in the body of an indigenous alien, he looked down without recognition at his orange-clad and filthy person again. The single mum, whom he'd talked to by the phone box before, came over to him with him some wet wipes from her pram tray. Her eyes, questioning and hopeful, were on his lower arm. Obligingly, he pulled back his orange sleeve.

All the injection wounds were gone.

"His arm!" she screamed, turning around to the others. "Oh my fuckin' God! His arm. Before he 'ad track lines all over it. Now it's clear."

But Todd became afraid as the crowd moved in around him, and dropped the wet wipes, pleading with the Paki Witch, "What shall I do?"

And she said, holding out her hand, in a gesture at once regal and fraternal, "Go home to your friends, and tell them about me."

He clutched her hand to his teary, dirty cheek, and released, from the depth of his being, the words, "I will tell all the world about you."

He disappeared into the sea of people.

An exponential increase in numbers meant that now the whole Wasteland was half full, and more were arriving with each passing second. Now somebody shouted, "Look, above, at the flyover."

Everyone's gaze followed the instruction and came to rest on a small person, her blanket-wrapped body in a cat's cradle of ropes and tied sheets, who was being lowered from the walkway overhead by four people, one of whom was calling, "Jessie!"

The Paki Witch lifted up receiving arms. Others did the same. A forest of arms caught the swaying bundle and brought it safely down to the floor. It was an old woman, with dyed black hair and skin the colour of a buttercup. In the marionette lines around her chin, sick and sputum had collected, and her blue lips were dry.

"Think it's Lilly Bannigan, from Tallis," someone said, then shouted up, "We got her!"

Four people on the walkway, a black youth, and three Chinese people – an old woman, a beautiful girl in a yellow dress, and a small boy – peered over. Satisfied their cargo was safely delivered, they allowed the cabling to fall from their hands to earth after her, and stayed watching.

Lilly Bannigan's eyes opened on a sky-blocking dome of onlookers, who were regarding her with concern. On seeing among them the Paki Witch, she gave tiny cry which pierced the cloistered silence. Then she whispered, "I need to tell you."

Exerting supreme effort now, she raised her head, and reached out her hand to the Paki Witch. It was yellow, broken-nailed, shaking and bony as a cricket's leg against the young, brown fingers which now enfolded it.

"My piccaninnies is dead 'cos I never looked after 'em," gasped Lilly.

She shook her head, and her face crumpled with despairing self-hatred. She slumped back, desolate, into the folds of blanket, her eyes rolling back to unseeing blank yellow.

The Paki Witch stood up, applying a gentle tug to the tormented woman's hand, and said, simply, "You are forgiven."

The crowd moved back, and the blue sky showed, big and bright.

Lilly's eyes opened, wide and white with dark irises. The

yellowness from her skin had gone. She jerked herself to sitting position with her free arm, and lifted her face to the sky, like a rapt little bird, just hatched from its egg.

"I am forgiven?" she said, incredulous. "But –"

As if it were a bowl of the sweetest wine, the Paki Witch cupped Lilly's upturned face with her tiny brown hand, saying, with the broadest, most indulgent smile, "Yes! Take your things and go home."

Lilly stood up, straight and strong as a young girl, to the astonishment of all around her.

"Thank you!" she said, her face full of joy. "You – you are the light of the world."

After one last look at the face of her redeemer, she gathered up her blankets and ropes. Lithe as a Peter Pan Darling child in her nightdress and slippers, she darted away into the crowd.

Renewed excitement panned across the masses, obscuring the approaching police sirens.

You'll Never Walk Alone chanting began and, like a flame on petrol, word spread that the Paki Witch was the Messiah who had come to save Shriveton from the gangs.

A child foot soldier, his Halloween mask pushed back from his face and his hood down around his shoulders, showing the plump contours of his face and neck, not long out of babyhood, spoke up. "Paki Witch, who are you?"

"Who do you say I am?"

"I think you're Jesus in a Paki costume."

The Rodgers & Hammerstein song had mutated to *Mess-i-ah walk us home.* Using the two prams of the single mums as barriers, Morwenna and Bob were managing to preserve a tiny court of space around the Paki Witch. Three pitiable addicts pushed forward into it. Sunken and filthy of face, in ragged clothes, they threw themselves on the floor before her. She touched each one, and, as they stood up, bright eyed and rejoicing, she announced in a small voice, which seemed nonetheless to carry over the rabble, "I have come to light a fire in Paradise and pour water on hell."

Everyone went quiet. A young man with red hair and a note-pad had pushed to the front.

Ethan Greenberg had been in the area since long before daybreak, as soon as he'd heard about the death of Shriveton priest, Father O'Connor. He had not seen any of the miracles the crowd were chattering ecstatically about, because it was only now that he had managed to get close to the Shriveton Messiah.

Ethan's shock and sadness at the despicable killing of the kindly, odd priest, were forgotten as, mouth agape, he stared at the Muslim woman. She was the most beautiful being he had ever seen or dreamed of. A strong feeling of reverence came upon him, and his head started exploding with memories of a family trip to Jerusalem, in his Bar Mitzvah year. Ethan recalled the acute emotion Zayde had displayed as they stood before the Western Wall. The inky blur of the Auschwitz serial number showing just below the knobble of his elbow, Zayde had stretched out to stuff a prayer message in one of the grooves, and then shuffled away as fast as his tortured old body could go.

At the time, his great-grandfather's profound reverence and loud tears of gratitude, and the fact that Ethan had been forced to wear a Kippur in public, had been embarrassing. But under the infinitely kind gaze of the Muslim woman before him here in this slum, Ethan understood his grandfather's reverence and tears. He understood why Zayde had stuffed his note in the Western Wall crack while nobody was looking, and crept away, before the light of divine goodness bore down on the deep, dark crevices of his own flawed self.

"But why did you come *here?*" Ethan asked her.

"To see you."

"Me?" Ethan Greenberg was taken aback.

"Yes."

Her gaze, so deep and loving it made him want to weep, would stay with him for the rest of his life. She went on, "To tell you about love."

"Are you a preacher?"

He was so overwhelmed that he wasn't even writing down what she was saying, but continued to stare at her, adoring as a schoolboy with a crush.

"I am the message."

"So... erm... erm, what religion are you?"

"My religion is love."

The *Messiah* chant started again, *sotto voce.*

"How do we know you're not a TV magician or something, though?" said Ethan quickly, before the song built and enveloped them.

"Taste, Ethan," she said, smiling. Her voice was clear despite the blooming sound of the crowd. "The one who tastes knows."

That she knew his name shocked and stumped him. All he could think was that all Father O'Connor had said about her was true.

"This is a police message," crackled an amplified voice over the crowd. Helicopters were chugging overhead. "Please clear the area. Please clear the area."

Riot police had walled off some of the perimeters with a series of gladiatorial plastic shields. The dreadful spectre of Hillsborough passed telepathically through older members of the crowd, and there were the beginnings of panic, as hot bodies squeezed and jostled.

With the help of Morwenna and Bob, the Paki Witch climbed on to one of the prams.

"Do not be afraid!" she told the people. They fell silent and still. "For I have redeemed you."

CHAPTER SEVENTEEN

Sunday 31st October 201-

Mid-Afternoon

The Wasteland

At the Shriveton Shopping Parade, the Incubo joined a small crowd looking out towards the Wasteland. It was the same place he'd come to in the early '90s with a suitcase full of heroin from his Edgware Road scam. In those days the drug lords had consisted of a few nine-stone slow-witted local lads who were periodically tortured out of their ill-gotten gains by a Rolls-Royce-owning underworld taxman called the Eel. Incubo bought them all off. Then he'd personally decapitated the Eel, and (after scrubbing up – decapitation being a messy affair) he'd stuck the head on the Silver Lady of the Rolls Royce, and parked it outside Shriveton Police Station. The Zone was born, transforming the Shriveton slum into the most profitable outlet in the country, and making him the supreme ruler in Hell.

Now the Incubo's Shriveton goldmine was overrun by a plague of freed slaves: benefit-scrounging, new-millennium oddities and obesities, with their empty Epsilon[6] heads and big Scouse gobs,

---

6

and rickety teeth and celebrity religion. The Paki Witch had turned them, in a matter of moments, from useful units of Incubo Land production towards her light.

"Look at them birds!" shrieked a woman beside him. Half her head was in rollers. Like so many of those present, she had dropped everything and come into the Shriveton streets to see it all for herself.

Everyone on the Parade terrace stopped dead: a flock of seagulls was swooping up, like a foamy wave, from the heaving mass of humanity below. Next, a giant intake of breath from the Wasteland hordes seemed to suck to almost nothing the atmospheric pressure as every one of the birds smashed into the concrete barrier of the Shopping Parade, the dull staccato of their arrow-head beaks on concrete like a percussion of war.

The Incubo and the others ran to the barricade. On the ground below, lifeless grey and white gulls were strung like discarded trainers. In the middle distance, by one of the concrete Tallis flyover pillars, a clearing had formed around a small woman wearing a dressing-gown and slippers.

"That's Lilly Bannigan!" shouted the roller-wearer.

Others at the barricade commented, "Last time I seen 'er she was all yellow."

"Alco'olic she is."

"An' 'er daughter died young. Smack'ead she was."

Bundle under her arm, strong and upright, Lilly Bannigan merged into the crowd.

"We gotta get down there. It's fillin' up so fast we'll never get to see the Paki Witch!" declared the roller woman.

Everyone, including the Incubo, followed along. Arriving at the Wasteland periphery, they met with droves of police at the cordoned-off scene-of-crime where the dying priest had been found last night.

A bizarre, energetic character in bright orange ducked under one of the yellow ribbon barriers, beside the Incubo, and crossed to a shack which lay within the crime scene.

"The Paki Witch has cured me. She *is* the Messiah!" proclaimed Guantanamo, tall and proud on the milk-crate doorstep of his erstwhile abode, and waving his bared forearms in frantic jubilation. A jumble of hypodermic needles, like defunct Christmas

---

The lowest social stratum in Aldous Huxley's *Brave New World*.

tree lights, littered the threshold of the hovel.

"Come on now, Guantanamo," said an approaching policeman, smiling nervously. "We've got to keep this scene of crime sterile, see."

"Officer Taffy, see for yourself," persisted the orange-suited man, pulling back further his sleeves.

Close to, now, the policeman looked at Guantanamo's arms and blanched. His mouth opened and closed like a fish, but no words came.

"When I was in a bad way you used to point to my arms," went on Guantanamo. "Septicaemia you used to say, didn't you, Officer Taffy?"

Officer Taffy stared mutely at the fellow's forearms, nodding his head.

"And tell me to get to hospital?"

Taffy nodded again.

Leaving his colleagues, Taffy wandered away into the crowd by himself.

"What the Paki Witch do, mate?" the Incubo asked Guantanamo.

From the mud slop ground, Guantanamo picked up a cluster of syringes, each plastic barrel part full clay-earth water, and declared, "She got me out of the jaws of hell!" He punched the air with his fistfuls of barbs, then with a flick of his fingers, scattered the syringes like spores.

"How she do it, mate?" The Incubo's eyes fixed on Guantanamo's unblemished arm flesh.

"She put her hand on my head," said Guantanamo, his eyes truly alive, searching the face of each person who regarded him. Now he put his hands on his head, as if doing some drunken move on a nightclub dance floor. "And she said –"

"What she say, mate?"

"She said, *Go home to your friends, and tell them about me.*"

Like a deranged orang-utan, Guantanamo turned to his shack, and started dismantling it aggressively, throwing the component parts up and away as he shouted, "The Paki Witch freed me from this prison!"

As his erstwhile home collapsed, flat on its milk crate floor, he looked in triumph again at his onlookers, and was about to speak when his gaze fell once more upon the Incubo. A frown of revulsion crossed his face.

"Hey, aren't you Zollo?"

But the Incubo melted into the whirling Epsilon sea; in earnest he began pushing his way towards its illustrious epicentre. The Paki Witch's miracles had stunned some of the obstructing bodies into silence. Others babbled joyously to a willing audience of police and crowd members who had not been close enough to see at first hand.

With each passing moment, phones on heaven-stretching arms infected the internet with more footage of the Paki Witch and her miracles. Occasionally, a muted strain of *Messiah, walk us home* erupted from the crowd. The stench of their pauper bodies and homes – tobacco, food grease, sweat, excreta and the sebum from their unwashed skin and hair – suffused the Incubo with murderous and generic loathing. He had never felt more keenly his own superiority, nor the supreme irony of being a fugitive, an outcast in the very Land he had tilled and furrowed for over two decades.

Then, the Messiah of the Slums came in his sight. Somehow elevated above the crowd, she was no more than a black-bandaged doll in the distance. But he was now close enough to see the features of her face, and feel the inexorable pull her goodness seemed to exert on all the human matter around her. Every part of him must strive to resist her. It was as much as he could do to stand, dumb and still and staring, among the chattering paupers.

"You 'ear about the priest?"

"That's why the Paki Witch come – to save Shriveton from the gangs."

"Everyone's sayin' so."

"They killed Father Kevin cos 'e was against the Incubo gang."

"We should've all stuck up for 'im more."

"I know. If they killed 'im, there's no 'ope 'ere."

"There is – the Paki Witch. Open your fuckin' eyes."

"Yeah, the Paki Witch is the Messiah, like they all sayin'."

"God 'elp 'er, then. 'Cos if the Incubo can kill the priest, 'e can kill the Paki Witch."

The Welsh policeman, clutching a loudspeaker to his mouth, was advancing through the crowd towards the pillar of universal focus. The people created a corridor for him as he went. Into Taffy's wake the Incubo now stepped , surreptitiously skirting the wall of people, his eyes resolutely on the ground as he moved.

"It's a scene-of-crime area, see," Taffy was explaining through the speaker, in apologetic tones. When Taffy saw properly the Paki Witch ahead of him, he stopped dead, dropping the loudspeaker in the mud beside an abandoned, upturned sofa.

Her singular presence overwhelmed him with a sense of what

he would later describe as *the divine*.

"She – she is real!" he spluttered, staring, as his mind jolted out of its long-held view that Islamic women existed on the end of prams, or in submissive huddles, trailing men.

And now the Incubo's eyes swivelled furiously behind the dirty lenses of his broken glasses, as he rode every bump and fall of the Paki Witch's body. How awful was her beauty: it made him want to collapse amongst the Epsilon shoes sinking in the red clay earth below. But instead of bawling with loser's grief, he imagined his fingers bumping over the rib grate which guarded her human heart, and then going to her neck, and squeezing until the last atom of air had gone from her.

And as he imagined this, her eyes found the Incubo.

It was as if a line were drawn around the tiny patch of space he occupied in the weedy, junk-strewn Wasteland. And even as he stood alone, and entirely separate from the wealth of spirit infusing the scene, he realised that he, not she, had drawn the line, and that any time he could reach out to her and be forgiven for his heinous and innumerable crimes.

Looking away from him, the Messiah of the Slums opened her arms to the people. As if lifted by its own purity, her voice – clear, high and pure as celestial music – rang out.

"Do not be afraid! For I have redeemed you."

All went silent and still except for the police messages to disperse, shooting like laser beams from ground and prowling helicopters. Camera crews had arrived, and were attempting to wade through the crowd.

 Scared, the Incubo reabsorbed himself into the body of the crowd. He watched the Paki Witch step down to earth, helped by a protective old man and plump middle-aged woman. Her valiant, triumphant tone had inflamed him. There was no doubt in his sick, heaving mind anymore: s*he* would pay for reducing him to a fugitive vagrant in the Hell he had once ruled.

And suddenly he felt afraid, and truly alone in this sea of goodness all around. The Welsh policeman nearby was babbling about her being an angel, tears streaming down his face. Everywhere people were embracing each other in a delirium of ecstasy such as the best of the Incubo's drugs, new and old, could not deliver.

Even as he seethed, and schemed her destruction, the Incubo knew that he could allow himself to be assimilated by the universal adoration, that even now, She would save him.

There was no longer a Hell to rule, but the Incubo would never serve in heaven. And his defiance resolved him to finish it.

Gerry Stokes

The MS nurse had rung to say she would be late since couldn't get through the crowds that stretched as far back as Boundary Lane. It was just after 3pm, and she still hadn't come, and Gerry's son, Billy, hadn't come home last night.

Trenchant depression normally inured Gerry to frustrations such as being left alone and unchanged in bed in the curtained and grotty front room of his Tallis Row maisonette home. On balance, in the twenty-six years since being diagnosed with MS, the mental consequences had been more disabling than the disease itself, which had sent Billy's mother off to another town with another man. Now the doctors were thinking his depression might be a side-effect of the Interferon he took to prevent MS relapses. With a dismissive, "These doctors only see the case notes. I see the reality!" his MS nurse clearly thought the perpetual disappointment of son Billy was to blame, and said so, often. Gerry wondered whether his son was intrinsically bad, or whether being abandoned by his mother, to poverty, sorrow and chronic sickness, was to blame. As the boy had grown, school had fed home unwelcome reports of cruelty to animals and a pornographic attitude towards girls, and nefarious activities with the Shriveton Sons, from which he'd graduated to working for the Incubo. Fast in his wheelchair, dependent on his son for day-to-day care, Gerry's impotence in the face of it all had destroyed whatever was left of him. Bringing no consolation, but only shame, the subject of his son enticed suicidal thoughts, those teasing and pleasing lap dancers, close enough to smell, but always beyond his cripple's reach.

Even as he struggled into the wheelchair beside his bed and wheeled it across to the window, he didn't know why he sought the light of day when all he wanted was to extinguish the damp and spluttering match flame of his life. He had endured so much, for so little and yet *something* had kept him going all these years, despite the evaporation of all hope that his son would turn good. He pulled aside the curtain and looked out to see the crowds, like a caviar carpet on the Wasteland. Helicopters were circling overhead, and he thought he could see a BBC van in the distance.

Hastily, he pulled an anorak on over his night clothes, shoved his unsocked feet into the old tartan slippers, which had never borne the weight of his failed body, and wheeled himself out of the house, on to the forecourt in front of his flat and the Tallis and Skylark Towers. He didn't have a clue what was happening. The smothering blackness of his depression always shut the world out, and because his son hadn't come back, there had been no TV or radio news on in the house.

But now, as he shivered violently in the cold outdoors – Billy always kept the heating full on in the flat, even in summer, which meant that Gerry had no resistance to the cold – Gerry knew that the *something* had come at last.

"The Paki Witch – she done loads of miracles. Loads of birds crashed into the Parade wall," garbled a distracted girl on the terrace when he asked her what was happening.

He recognised her as Jodi from a neighbouring flat on Tallis Row, the pathetic kid who, for reasons unfathomable to Gerry, hung around his Billy. Pawnshop gold coils, ropes and buckles circumscribed her pasty-skinned neck, ear lobes, nostrils and every finger. Reticent, hopeful and anxious, she was staring intently at the Wasteland masses.

"And Guantanamo is 'ealed. 'E's, like, preachin' down where his 'ouse used to be on the Wasteland."

"Who's Guantanamo?"

"You must've seen Guannie. Everyone knows 'im. 'E used to be in the Army, but then 'e become a total bag'ead, an' –"

"Please, take me to this Paki Witch, love," he interrupted. "Me arms isn't strong enough to wheel me over there."

Jodi's eyes, still on the crowds, and gooey with black make-up in her doughy face, suddenly filled with tears. "Thing is, I was mean to the Paki Witch, one time," she mumbled. "I can't –"

"Please, take me to the Paki Witch, love," he begged again.

"Well, I dunno," said the girl, suddenly taking hold of the wheelchair handles and moving him swiftly away.

She pushed Gerry to the periphery of people on the Wasteland. Songs and hysteria bubbled, and the heat of bodies shimmered in the sunny cold air above the countless heads.

"I can't get you no further 'cos of the grass," she announced. Then, prodding one of the men in front of them, she shouted, "Eh, mate, can you 'elp this cripple get to the Paki Witch?"

Two men hoisted Gerry up, calling out, "This fella can't walk. Help him through!"

Gerry was passed forward and through the crowd, each of his carriers calling out to the next. In minutes he was in the middle of the multitudes. Soon, small as a doll, but seeming nonetheless to dwarf everything around her, the Messiah of the Slums came into view ahead of him. Flanked by an old man and a plump middle-aged woman, who had protective arms around her little back, two single mums with prams, and the old man with the Raleigh Shopper bike, she was moving through the jostling density of people, who were pressing against her.

Kept upright in the grip of men and women he didn't know, Gerry stared at the glorious being before him, a sob of ecstasy and fulfilment breaking in his heart. All he could think was that this Muslim woman was what *immaculate* meant. Everything he had endured was for the moment which now followed. With a twist of his shoulders, he lunged free of the kindly strangers holding him up and, with his good arm, touched the Paki Witch's robe.

"Who touched me?"

Her voice, small as a goat bell, stilled the crowd. As she turned, a space cleared around her, revealing the supplicant Gerry, who was standing, unaided, before her, a short distance away. His legs were steady and strong in the trampled mud which was devouring his never-walked-in tartan slippers; mouth, agape like a caught fish, he tried to speak.

Holding out her hand to him, the Paki Witch smiled. Gerry's feet, pale and soft as virginal Play Doh, moved many paces across the Wasteland to reach her. A hush spread outwards from the epicentre of his new wholeness as Gerry took her hand and brought it to his lips.

She smiled at him again and gave him a blessing, then moved away, back into the hub of the hoard, while Gerry danced for joy and proclaimed her divinity.

Billy

His raw agitation unsoothed because he had hardly slept, Billy stepped outside to find that the streets were filling with people, all mumbling about the Paki Witch, who had just passed by. Billy joined them, thinking that his Dad's MS nurse might still be in the house anyway, so it was better to wait as long as possible before getting out what he needed. Ridiculous hope that perhaps some of his old comrades had reconvened (they had not, of course), plus acute hunger, drew him to the Shopping Parade, where he managed to filch a packet of biscuits from an old lady's shopping bag as she stood, slack-mouthed and oblivious, by the barrier which was being pounded by seabirds. He was so hungry that he gobbled the Value Shortcake all up, missing the mass suicide of the birds – which was a shame, because he liked stuff like that.

Fear of arrest left him. Everything was so chaotic that there was no way he would be noticed in the crowd, especially with his hood pulled low over his face, and so Billy focused on pick-pocketing as much as he could while the going was good.

Women's purses being like bricks, it was not long before the need to decant his wares was greater than the magnificent opportunity for further thieving afforded by the Paki Witch distraction, especially now that everyone was chanting and cheering about miracles. Billy had to make a detour to the only hiding place he could think of – the barricade of defunct vehicles to the rear of the Parade. He had a key to an old Toyota Carina there, which he used occasionally to stash stolen goods while on shift in the Zone. He emptied the wallets and purses in the car, stuffing their shells in the bank of bins on his way back to the Parade.

If he made enough, he might not even need to go back to his Dad's at all. The tide was turning in his favour. Billy made his way through the estate, towards the Boundary Lane artery where he attached himself to the droves arriving on the strength of social network hysteria about the extraordinary events unfolding.

In the thick of the crowd again, he was about to resume his thieving when, halfway along Boundary Lane, he espied Frankie Moran, the taxi-driver who owed him money.

"Hey, you, robbin' cunt!" Snatching Moran's coat sleeve, Billy spun him round and hissed in his ear, "You still owe a ton for them Thai sweats. Giz it now."

Looking with recognition into the tunnel of hood leading to Billy's pudgy, mean-eyed face, all Frankie Moran could manage was a weak, "Billy, 'ave you seen your Dad, mate?"

Billy was perplexed. Moran should have been quaking with fear, and lame excuses for *not* paying his prostitute debts to Spider should have been tumbling from his foul-breathed mouth. Instead he seemed completely disconnected from the exigency of being in the clutches of his violent creditor.

"Your Dad's been cured by the Paki Witch," insisted Moran. "I seen it with me own eyes. 'E's walking about in the crowd."

Releasing him, Billy shrank back into the shadows of the nearest building, afraid. Driven now by the singular imperative that he *must* get back home before his Dad did, he shoved and barged and scuttled his way to Tallis Row to find his Dad's empty wheelchair in the porch. Billy opened the peeling door and called for his Dad. No reply. Just as he stepped inside, a scruffy, middle-aged man in a tartan hacking jacket, dirty cap and wearing thick-rimmed spectacles, came forward.

"Billy!" said the Incubo, holding up a defensive pair of palms, for Billy had lunged towards him, glowering murderously. "It's me, Zollo. Been following you since the back of the Parade."

"Zoll –" spluttered Billy. He peered and added a contrite, "Didn't fuckin' recognise ya, man."

Pushing him aside, the Incubo went through the open door into Billy's flat. Billy scampered after him, bleating apologies and worries about the collapse of the world they shared. The Incubo ignored him and put his head round the door of every room, checking they were alone.

"Hot in here, and it stinks of weed," said the Incubo, flatly, looking askance at Billy, who was trailing him, and still twittering about their misfortunes, and insisting they were alone.

"Me Dad's MS. Means he gotta be kept war-"

"This one's locked." The Incubo applied a hard kick to the closed door, from the base of which hot white light spilled into the smelly gloom of the narrow hall way. "Open it."

As Billy fumbled with keys, padlock and Yale lock to the bedroom door, desperate ratiocination racked his slow mind until he came up with, "Yeah, me Dad's MS means he smokes weed. It's like a cure for MS, Zoll."

A block of heated, herby air expanded as Billy opened the door on his fluorescent cannabis hothouse. Crammed inside were trestles bearing countless trays of plants, each a little green fountain of chemicals and money.

"So I growed this for 'im, like. Weren't sellin' it, like," Billy blurted, as the man he believed to be Incubo intermediary Zollo rubbed and sniffed the leaves, and pronounced, "This is good shit."

"Like I said," gabbled Billy, sweat gushing down the composite of flesh Teletubby domes which made up his face, "I weren't like doin' it on the side."

"Goodness, no," cooed the Incubo, a ridiculing smile twitching but not manifesting. "And anyway, Inky likes initiative. Which is why I've come here to find you."

"Me?" Billy's thick, sweaty lips hung open in bafflement.

"Yes, you. Inky was extremely impressed with the way you handled Gary Skelton."

"But – but Tez said I wasn't gonna be made, 'cos Inky went mad 'bout it 'app'nin' in the LCI, like."

"Ah, Tez!" the Incubo gave a long, tired sigh. "Why do you think everything has collapsed?"

"'Cos of the priest, like?"

"No. No one cares about *that*. The Zone has collapsed because Tez is a police informant."

Incredulity washed Billy's entire being as he pondered this fact for some moments. "Tez 'as gone the bizzies?" he said presently.

"Tez has been a rat for years. He will pay the price. I've got some people on that."

Billy shook his dull head and stared vacantly at the weed he'd come back to harvest before his newly-mobile Dad put the clampers on the whole operation. "I thought you an' the Incubo might've disapproved, like, of me growing a bit o' weed," he mumbled, vaguely, pressing his thumb into the dark soil of the nearest plant to check for moisture.

"Oh, no. Inky likes enterprise, Billy. He's not interested in minnows –" On seeing Billy's non-comprehension of the word *minnow* he replaced it with, "little people like Tez and Sammy. He's looking for..." – the Incubo tapped his temple and smiled villainously at Billy, who was completely taken in –"natural intelligence!"

"Well, I never done good at school, but I'm not soft, Zoll."

"We know that. That's why he wants to set you up over in Spain."

"Spain? Fuck me. That'd be *great*."

"In Spain, we can get our hands on the actual gear before it's distributed, see. Which means there's a little take for us, see?"

"Count me in."

"I've got your ticket." The Incubo pulled out his own boarding card, and flashed it briefly in front of Billy, who did not have a chance to look at it properly. "Hope you don't mind, but I assumed you'd say yes."

"Wow, Zollo, man, you're a life-saver!"

Billy felt relief salve him like water on a leathern tongue. He would not, after all, have to hope for crumbs from the Albanian mafia's human trafficking table in London. He would be no more than an expendable, albeit UK indigenous, foot soldier to them, useful only for getting the crates of women through English ports and on to London brothels. There was no security in that line of work, because the Albanians looked after their own people, never outsiders. Nor was it remunerative; and, as Spider always said, once you'd had one *sweat* you'd had them all, so the access to the cargo soon ceased to be a bonus.

"A man of your quality can't be left in the sinking ship," the Incubo went on. "They were my instructions from Inky. Now first of all, we gotta make a point here, that Inky is not to be fucked over. So I need a bit of help."

"Anythin', Zoll, mate. You name it."

"Good. Oh, by the way, what's your take on today's events in the Wasteland?"

"Fuckin' proper thrown me, man. Me Dad's 'pparently walkin', lad. Been a proper cripple for as long as I can remember, like."

"So what's happened then? In your opinion."

"Fuckin' dunno. But the Paki Witch must've done a miracle on 'im."

"She needs takin' out."

Billy gulped and stammered, wordless and blinking.

"But, you needn't worry about that," reassured the Incubo, with an avuncular chuckle. He patted Billy's pork fat back, and reflected privately that when he killed Billy, it would be like binning an old shoe, or squeezing a large, oily blackhead.

Billy sagged with sheer relief again, and snorted laughingly, "For a fuckin' minute then, Zoll, thought you wanted me to take her out, like. 'Cos that's a fuckin' –" Without finishing his sentence, Billy subsided into a perplexed sigh, and kept shaking his head.

The Incubo patted him on the shoulder and, exiting, said, "No. I just need you to help me find her. It won't take long. And then you'll be in sunny Spain. Now, let's bag up all this gear, and get off."

Doubt, like rats on offal, chewed Billy's psyche as he harvested his green gold, stuffed it into two Tesco bags, and then followed the Incubo out.

CHAPTER EIGHTEEN

Sunday October 31st 201-

Morning

Shriveton/Moel Famau

The last day of Terry Siddell's short life had begun. Flossie's breath hung, opaque, in the morning chill as he tied her up outside Matherfield General Stores, beside bowls of water and dog biscuits set out on the pavement.

Inside, shopkeeper Mad Maggie, so-called because of her animal rights activism, was sorting out the Sunday papers.

"You got a pen, love?" he asked her. Tez was her only customer.

Mad Maggie considered her radical self to be at odds with the posh and carnivorous Matherfield Park set; except, that is, whenever Tez or his wife came into the shop, whereupon she would align herself absolutely with whichever customer was in at the time. Glancing at the consoling security camera above the counter, she slid over a biro, and continued sorting a packet of Sunday papers.

Tez stuffed his empty envelope so full of money that it could not be sealed shut, while, safe behind her till, Mad Maggie cast suspicious glances over her cube of *Sunday Telegraphs*. Ignoring her *Don't you be movin' them!* he swept aside the animal charity collection boxes, lined up like skittles on the counter, and wrote on the envelope:

Please look after my Flossie. She is a good dog. She diserves a beter ownor than me. Tell her I am sorry but it for the best. T.

Then he bought a book of first class stamps and forty cigarettes. When Maggie held out his change, he shook his head, pushed the fat envelope into her knobbly hand, and went out into the bright morning air.

On the pavement outside, Tez fumbled with his stamps and the three remaining envelopes as tears streamed down his crumpled face. Maggie's shrill, "Hey, I can't take this money!" and Flossie's bereft yelping resounded in the Sunday morning village emptiness.

She arrived at his side, humped and furious in shop overalls and loose slippers, and planted her rheumatoid hand, like a ginger root, on his arm.

"I'll look after your dog, son, but this 'ere's blood money."

Stepping away from of her, he stuffed his three handwritten letters, respectively addressed to the Chief Constable of the Merseyside, Metropolitan and Cheshire police forces, into the post box. His eyes, sunken and tragic, met hers as he made his oblique response.

"You are everything I could never be, until today."

She paused, shocked by her own recognition of his humanity. Before she could reply, he had ducked into his old Vauxhall, askew on the double-yellow-lined kerb outside the shop.

In his wing mirror, as he drove away, he could see her – eternally individual, principled and feisty – fussing his Flossie. Guttural sobs exploded in him: giving up Flossie severed his final tie to life. Now he must complete the last stage of his plan, fifty miles away from Shriveton's Incubo Land.

And so it was that he drove to Moel Famau in North Wales, by far the most beautiful place he had ever known or conceived of. Throughout the journey, the same old horror show of his own crimes ran in his mind. Mumbled curses fell like Rosary prayers from the ice-blue lips of his youthful dead – Troy, Ben and Gary Skelton, and all the nameless junkies.

Only a bullet in his own brain would silence them.

But the moment he stepped out into the car park at the base of the Famau mountain, a sunny day, full of sweet, milky Welsh air, infused his ruined lungs. It flushed out the accusing spectres from his ruined psyche. It bore away the dreadful sorrow that had weighed him for all of his short, old life.

Wonder washed his soul, as, motionless in the car park, he

beheld the vast, rolling, folding vales, and their flotsam of villages, and dinky, creamy sheep, and the wind-warped, lonely trees – which always reminded him of himself – poking up like oil-slick seabirds from wintry patches of gauze and heather. Being at Moel Famau, the grandest mountain in the Clywdian Range, filled to the brim his empty heart with a plangent, savouring joy.

This would be his last day on earth (he would not see the scented purple bloom of heather next summer). Gun bumping against his bone-bubbled, wheezing chest, he began the ascent along the trail, which wound through and up the valley to the Jubilee Tower ruin on the Famau mountain-top. A cluster of passing ramblers – grey-haired, fleece-wearing, thick-socked and impossibly happy – hailed him cheerfully, but Tez did not respond. Moel Famau would always belong to those airy, happy beings; never to his kind, whom the dust of life had weighed down and choked in the gutter, before the first steps of childhood could be attempted.

Mid-Afternoon

Shriveton

Shriveton Sons

Like iron filings on a huge magnet of their own fear, the Shriveton Sons had gathered together as the strange events unfolded on the Wasteland. The terror of peer retribution had outweighed each Son's curiosity in the Paki Witch parade. Eager to demonstrate loyalty to the group, they'd assembled mid afternoon behind the Community Centre, tucked out of sight by the bonfire mound which had cost Fr Kevin his life. Embarrassed yet exultant about their defiant separation from the majority, they waited to see how the land would lie.

Masculine strength, and the double SS helix badge on their hoodies, was all they had to defend and define themselves from the disgust they excited in nearly everyone. Beside a solitary litre-bottle of cheap cider, a ghetto-blaster provided tinny and inchoate accompaniment to their suspended state. These unloved and unintelligent rejects would elicit a smile from nobody except the Incubo, who, smiling, approached them now, entirely confident that this collective of young male failures was exactly what he needed. All eyes, each pair above a wall of obscuring scarf, fixed fearfully on him, betraying the feigned nonchalance of their skinny bodies, supine and draped over push-bike handles. Only their chief squared up to meet the supplicant stranger.

"You in charge?" asked the Incubo. "I got business for you."

"Wha' business?" the boy replied, his voice shaking a little. Behind him, his comrades shuffled, nervous.

"Business that'll make you money."

"'Ow we know you norra bizzie?"

In a matter of hours, the Sons' place in the order of things had radically changed. For years now, thanks to Tez's micro management, they had been no more than auxiliaries of the Incubo, whose sudden departure had cut off their power supply. A consequent and strong sense of being out of charge diminished the pleasure of being in sole charge (now the Zone was gone) of local badness. The Incubo capitalised on their apprehension with,

"Inky sent me. He wants to re-establish a new crew here."

He opened a holdall in which were three guns, some grenades and two bulging Tesco bags, tied at the handles. "Interested?"

The boy's eyes goggled at the contents.

"Yeah. Well. Maybe."

"This is just a start," coaxed the Incubo, pulling out one of the carrier bags. Loosening the handles, with a quick thrust he shoved it up into the boy's face.

The boy stepped back, startled. His fellows drew near, but did not act. Inexperienced and conscious that the whole area was saturated with police, they did not know how to respond to this strange interloper.

"Quality skunk – worth hundreds," soothed the Incubo.

The boy sniffed, cautious, nodded at his comrades, and asked, "Wha' you want?"

"Not much, honestly. This Paki Witch thing is very bad for business. Once we can reopen the Zone, everyone will be happy."

"I thought the Incubo and all of 'em 'ad gone, like," said the boy, still afraid.

"No, Inky's just withdrawn until this is cleared up. Once it's all sorted, it'll be your crew that runs things here."

The boy paused, then said, "How do we know you're for real?"

"Well," said the Incubo, shoving the carrier bag of skunk into the boy's chicken chest. The boy's thin fingers, white and smooth and delicate as a Pre-Raphaelite girl's, snapped over it greedily. "There's a down payment. You won't need all these 'nades, today, so there'll be some left for your own personal use. Plus you can keep the MAC-10s."

The Incubo sighed inwardly at the inflationary prices he was having to pay for these morons. Ten years ago he'd got Tez, the best worker he'd ever had, for a Big Mac and ice cream.

The boy was stalling, and gesturing at his peers.

"We'll 'ave to –"

The Incubo frowned, affecting solicitous concern as he added, "You knew that, though?"

"Eh?"

"You *did* recognise that they are MAC-10s?"

"MAC-10s? Course I fuckin' did, man!"

"And the grenades there. You know how to use them?"

"Yeah. But what are you after, like, man?"

"It's easy. Nothing heavy. That's a promise. Then it's a grand for each of you. And *you*" – he fingered the boy's downy cheekbone above the scarf – "get your own crew on the Zone."

The others were nodding.

"OK," said the boy, unconsciously scrubbing off the Incubo's touch with his scarf and nails.

The Incubo pulled out and unwrapped a brand new pack of expensive cigarettes, adding, "Let's sit down and have a smoke and talk about the job I got in mind."

The boy instructed the other Sons to pull some of the wooden crates and boxes down from the adjacent combustible mountain. In the shadows of the unlit bonfire, the newly-formed Incubo war cabinet discussed tactics over real cigarettes and the remains of their cheap cider.

Panis Angelicus

After her miraculous healing, Lilly Bannigan, still in her night clothes, had stayed in the Wasteland, giving animated testimony to anyone who would listen. But when a film crew, complete with airborne spongy microphone and airbrushed presenter (whose high heels were sinking into the Wasteland mud), appeared for an interview, she panicked.

"I don't wanna be on TV in me nightie, Jammy!" she whispered, ducking behind him, out of fame's view.

Her wild delirium of gratitude had passed, and all she wanted was to be quiet and alone. So Jamal took her home. At Tallis Row, they passed Jodi Harris, who was pushing a man in a wheelchair towards the Wasteland.

"Please, take me to the Paki Witch, love," Gerry Stokes was begging her.

Zapped by a lightning stick of shame, Jodi averted her eyes as soon as they fell on Jamal. Snatching the wheelchair handles, she moved quickly out of view.

Poor Jodi, thought Jamal. The Shriveton rumour machine was churning out tales of her heroism in staying beside the dying priest last night. Now she was helping Gerry Stokes. If she hadn't moved away so fast, Jamal would have said something comforting to her.

He and his Nan continued home. When she stepped across their Tallis flat threshold, Lilly wrinkled her nose in disgust.

"Oh my God, it stinks in here!" she declared, looking around the living-room, without recognition. Their acute domestic squalor registered in her conscious mind for the first time *ever*, ironing flat her elation. "This is how we've lived, Jammy?"

"I done me best, Nan," mumbled Jamal.

A familiar fear, that a glimpse of reality might send her back on the bottle, knotted in his stomach. The paper chase of sympathy cards covering every surface was drawing on her unspoken grief, now. Tears tumbled down her newly-pink cheeks. Cast in the role of carer, nurse, cook, cleaner and alcohol counsellor since he was a toddler, Jamal's fortunes and feelings naturally ebbed and flowed with hers; but, just as the latest miraculous cause for believing in his Nan threatened to be false after all, she wiped her eyes with a resolute fist, and announced, "You 'ave, son. Now, I'm going to look after *you*, Jammy-picaninny."

Immediately, she became a centrifuge of purposeful activity, wholly engaged in a clean-up operation such as he had never witnessed or believed possible. Refusing his offers of help (which he was glad about, because he wanted so much to go back out, to find his Beloved Jessie), she marshalled him with the whirring vacuum cleaner, out of her way.

Looking out of the living-room window, it seemed like years ago since he'd seen his Beloved standing on the Tallis forecourt, gazing up at him while freeloading Macca had smoked Lilly's puff. So much had changed since then.

It was late afternoon now, but still light enough for him to see the swathes of people folding and falling around a focal point in the middle of the Wasteland, where She must be. Anxiety was flushing him. His Beloved was alone and tiny in the multitudes, and he needed to be at her side.

"Nan, I got to go back out," he said, through the roar of the vacuum cleaner. "In case anything happens."

He pecked her on the cheek, and passed out of the living-room.

In case anything happens. A terrible prescience, like an indissoluble gobstopper in his throat, had been choking him all day. The joy which was exploding in the hearts of so many had failed to dislodge it; this nameless, indigestible dread had persisted even as, with his own eyes, he had seen his Nan and Guantanamo healed of their deep afflictions. He busied himself with the idea that his Beloved would be tired, and thirsty – drained by the endless petitions and wanting of everyone around her. Refreshments were needed!

He went into the kitchen, knowing the cupboards would be bare, but thinking that if he could bring a bottle of tap water, it would make all the difference; and that there might even be a packet of biscuits in the bread bin. There was no way he would get through the crowd to the Shopping Parade to buy anything. Anyway, the Parade would be shut because everyone in the world had left their post to see the Paki Witch.

A wholly unexpected sight on the kitchen worktop stopped him dead in his tracks. Next to the bread bin and kettle were five bottles of water and a small mound of crusty bread rolls. The kitchen had never, at any point, housed anything nearly as appetising as those cobs looked. They couldn't have been there earlier, or he would have seen them. Wouldn't he? Doubt suffused him. Earlier was a blur, up to the point when his Nan had got up from the Wasteland floor, whole again.

Anyway, there wasn't time to think about the hows and whys of these things. He stuffed the lot into a plastic carrier bag and left, with an unfamiliar bouquet of bleach and polish fumes, from his Nan's homemaking efforts, lingering pleasantly in his nostrils.

Things were getting better. The gobstopper dread was just *himself* being pessimistic, the consequence of being brought up by a crazy, unpredictable alcoholic. If only he'd stayed on at school and carried on with his A Level Psychology, he would have understood more about how the mind plays tricks like this dread was doing. Today was a great day, and the Wasteland felt like Woodstock would have done had the Beatles *and* Jimi Hendrix played there on the same afternoon. He would just keep *trying* to abandon himself to the intense euphoria of the moment.

After much ducking, pushing and squeezing, which almost suffocated him, he found his Beloved, the world's most illustrious act, better than the Beatles or Jimi Hendrix. When she turned and smiled at him, Jamal's heart almost burst with joy, and all his gloom was entirely forgotten. His eyes filled, his stomach churned and knotted, and he hardly knew how he managed to say, "Jessie, I brought you something to eat. And some water."

"You are so wonderful, Jamal!" she said, looking inside the bag with excitement. Delight spread across her features.

"It's not much," he mumbled, as he passed her one of the cobs, embarrassed that his gift felt so small.

"It is not," she replied, and after a teasing pause, added, "Since you have already given me the best gift of all. Your heart."

A smile, which would forever blanch every other into obscurity, lit her beautiful face. For all the hot, noisy multitudes surrounding them, it felt to Jamal as if it was just him and her, alone and together, Somewhere Else.

Later, his mind would reinvent an elaborate homecoming scene... He had brought home food for her to prepare in their own white, flat-roofed house... His Beloved was the best wife... She kept their home cool despite the Middle-Eastern sun... When she cooked at her simple stove, he would steal behind her... Clumsy as a cart-horse, he would nudge aside the ebony fall of her scented hair... And, as he nuzzled her neck, his arms would reach round the mound of her belly, and feel the kick of his child in there...

"I would like to rest for a while," she said, leaning against an adjacent upturned sofa. "Could you share out the food and water to everyone who wants it, Jamal?"

"B-but there's not enough, Jessie!" he said.

"Only believe!" she chided.

She bit into her cob, then giggled, because a chunk of crust had lodged in the fold of her hijab. Chivalry seized Jamal, and he stepped forward to assist. Amused and pleased, she kept flicking her eyes demurely to and from his own as he attempted to dislodge, gently, the crumbs from the material folds below her chin. When the task was accomplished, and the crust fell to the muddy floor, he didn't notice, because all he could see was the softness of her brown skin, and her lustrous eyes – an organic gloss of brilliant white, barley sugar and treacle – and her smiling, pink lips, with crumbs stuck in the human moisture there.

"Thank you, my beloved," she said. She held his gaze with her own.

"Beloved – that's what I call you, in me 'ead, like," he stammered, still and staring.

"I know, Jamal. And I love you."

With a little jump, she hoisted herself up on the upturned sofa, and dandled her small feet against the back, saying, "Now give the people something to eat and drink!"

At best, there was only enough food and water for a handful, so his embarrassed and deliberately understated sales pitch – "Got some cobs and a drink, if you want 'em," – did not carry beyond the first tier of people.

To begin with, only a few presented themselves, and Jamal began distributing the fare, expecting to run out almost immediately. But the more he gave out, the heavier his bag became, until he had to decant armfuls of cobs and water bottles into the arms of Bob Reilly, and Morwenna the social worker, as well as the single mums' empty pushchairs.

Word whipped around about how the Paki Witch's cobs tasted heavenly. More and more people came forward. Even those who were not hungry and thirsty presented themselves, eager to get a closer glimpse of the Paki Witch as she sat on the wreck of a sofa, laughing and chatting easily with anyone who came to her.

By the time everyone had eaten and drunk all they wanted, the sun had begun to set. The troughs in the muddy Wasteland floor were full of bread crumbs, like dumplings in mince. And helpers collected seven bin-bags full of empty water bottles.

Moel Famau

Eventually, wiry grass gave way to a shale stretch directly before the crowning Famau monument. Tez had just stopped (once again) to catch his breath, this time at the base of the stone steps leading to the monument itself, when a smiling sheepdog flashed over the shale, her body almost flat on the floor as she ran, typical of that breed. She glued herself to his side, sniffing and nudging his legs with her liquorice nose.

Sinking down on his haunches, Tez cuddled her lolloping, affectionate form, looking around all the while for her owner. There was nobody about. The walkers who had greeted him were long gone. It was as if the dog, with her shiny, benign eyes and winsome grin, had come from nowhere. The fact that she was tame and – he judged by her luscious, glossy coat – well cared for, meant she was a domestic and not a farm dog. Her owner must be having a sit down in the fort ahead, reasoned Tez.

Still wheezing, a glaze of sweat on his unshaven, dirty face, Tez reached the Jubilee Tower, to find a woman and child standing on the far turret, gazing out across the patchwork terrain, to the Irish Sea in the distance.

"Is this your dog?" he called to them.

They turned round, and, after a puzzled pause, the woman said, "Sorry?"

"Is this your dog?" Tez stooped to pat the dog's head, silky and warm under his hand. He smiled and shook his head, adding,

"She's beautiful, isn't she?"

But the woman looked very alarmed, and, pulling her child close to her, hastened away down the steps. He could hear her shushes as the child insisted, "Mum, there was no dog there!"

Well, Tez had *never* understood women, and it was too late now. With a shrug and a click of his tongue, he moved towards the parapet, where he sat, arm around the dog perched on the stone sill beside him. In the far distance, beyond the snaking sheen of Mersey and Dee waterways icing the low-lying table of green plains, his home city was as tiny as a pre-school lunch.

Here was faraway. Here was safe. Here was heaven.

For over an hour he sat beside the dog, gazing on the intersecting Wales, Cheshire and Merseyside landscape, his mind empty of cares. Only the pang of hunger brought him back to the moment; and it had no sooner come than the dog darted to a far part of the hillfort ruin and retrieved from a gap in the slate-chunk wall a package, which she carried back to him. Inside were cheese sandwiches, a Twix bar, and a bottle of water. Enough for him. The frightened woman and child must have left it behind, he thought.

On the springy bank below the fort, Tez sat on a rock and ate his lunch, as the dog snoozed, her kindly head on his foot. The sandwiches were made using real butter, and the cheese was strong and good. No meal had ever given him the satisfaction this one did.

Afterwards, he varied throwing sticks for the dog with marvelling at the teeming life all around. Insects tumbled on every pole and blade of grass, and on leaves and winter-emptied sepals; overhead buzzards, redwings, wood pigeons, and even gulls floated. Every so often hikers passed, and Tez returned their greetings. The suicidal imperative which had brought him to Moel Famau was entirely banished by his own, profound reverence of Nature's majesty.

It was only as he followed the dog, as she ran intently down the slope towards the car park, that he realised the sun had almost set on this day, and that, far from being dead by his own hand at the top of the mountain, he was overflowing with life and back in the car park. She was waiting beside his solitary car, and the late amber sun was low in the inky gloom.

Now he noticed that the dog had a collar, and he wondered about this, because he hadn't spotted it before, and thought that very strange, because usually the first thing to do when you find a dog is to look at the collar. In the tiny light of his phone, Tez turned the little bronze name disk between his thick thumb and finger, knowing what he would find. Energy – a bolt of whitest light – surged through him as he read the name. Crouching down beside her, he put his arms around her, and leaned his head against her fluffy, strong neck.

An anguish gripped him as he stood up. Now it really *was* time to go, and he unlocked and pulled open the car door. When he looked back again, his companion had gone. He called and searched, knowing he would not find her. But as he drove back to Shriveton, consolation strengthened his whole being. *Jessie.* So Jammy's Paki Witch had come to him, after all.

CHAPTER NINETEEN

October 31st 201-

Early Evening

The Wasteland

Billy and the Kid

"Hey, kid, wanna iPad?"said Billy to the little boy on the edge of the crowd.

"Wha'?"

From inside his jacket pocket, Billy produced the iPad he had lifted from a woman's tote bag earlier. His index finger stump, its long nail-crest ingrained with dirt, ran over the glossy screen which blossomed now into light and colour.

"See?" he said, loading one of the apps, "Loadsa games."

"Wow!" said Jack, wiping the snot from his nose with his sleeve.

"You can 'ave it, mate," said Billy. "But take it up to the Parade, away from yer Ma, like."

Billy was one of the bleary-eyed boyfriends Jack bumped into in the kitchen some mornings.

"Why?" said the child, taking the iPad with his kiddie hands, and loading his favourite game.

"Cos yer Ma and me 'ave fell out."

"Oh."

Without lifting his eyes from the screen, or seeking permission from his uninterested mother nearby (who had not seen this exchange because she was on tiptoes, intently looking over the crowd for evidence of the Paki Witch's magic), Jack took Billy's hand.

"See all them birds," said Billy as they passed the gull corpses strewn in the mud at the foot of the Parade wall. But the child did not even look up from his screen, and Billy led him up the stairs to the terrace above.

"Sit outside the bettin' shop, kid," Billy told him, as he texted the Incubo with his long-nailed thumb.

"OK."

"I'll gerrus a chippy after, kid," said Billy, almost believing himself. "Liu's is openin' up in a bit from the looks of it."

The Incubo and Jack's Mum

"Hey, love, I seen your boy go over there with one of the Zone fellas," said the dishevelled man in a tartan fleece. He wore opaque, askew spectacles, with a scab of tape on one of the arm joints.

She shrugged, uninterested. Several of the Zone soldiers were frequent visitors to her home. In return for their skunk and cocaine, she gave them sex if she was out of cash.

"Wha' one?" she said, eyes scanning him from top to toe, and looking away with distaste.

"Dunno."

"Oh, 'e's always wandrin' off," she replied, without moving. "Giz a ciggie, Rach," she asked her friend beside her, who obliged reluctantly.

"Think 'e was sort of led off, though," persisted the Incubo, astonished at the lack of concern.

"Where?"

"Down the alleyway by the library."

"It'll be fine," she said, vague.

Embellishment was required. "'E was cryin' love, and callin' out for you, like. It's dark now."

She stayed still, although a modicum of concern was stirring, which the Incubo stoked now with, "So I would go get him, or the social will be on to you, and you'll lose your money."

"Fuckin' 'ell!" moaned the woman, at last turning around to look up towards the Parade. "I wanted to see the Paki Witch do one of 'er tricks." She groaned at the thought of exerting herself to climb the steps, and shoved the pram beside her over to her friend, saying, "Rach, mind Erin while I geddar Jack."

King-size cigarette wand in hand, like a Disney wicked stepmother she strode in the direction of her lost son.

The Alleyway

"Is me mum dead?" said the boy, trembling. It was horrible in the dark alleyway between the defunct library and Community Centre, and he wished Billy hadn't brought him here.

Jack's mum was still and crumpled on the floor. Her face, normally pinched and mean, was soft and very young in the light of the iPad Billy held over her.

"Hey, man, she's not –" hissed Billy urgently into the Incubo's ear.

"Just a few diazzies," replied the Incubo, then addressed the child. "Only the Paki Witch will wake her up for you, Jack."

"But is she dead?" asked the child.

"Well, it's like Sleeping Beauty," said the Incubo. "You know Sleeping Beauty?"

"No. Me mum has sleeping *pills* sometimes."

"Well, we need the Paki Witch to wake your Mum up, anyway," groaned the Incubo. The Epsilon spawn knew *nothing* of cultural import. "So Billy'll take you to get her."

"OK, but is me mum dead?" The boy was starting to sob as he beheld the lifeless form of his mother in the iPad beam. "There's blood at the back of 'er 'ead."

"The Paki Witch is the only one who can cure her. You go and tell her to come by herself. Not with the crowd. If she comes with the crowd, your mum will die of shock."

"Oh."

"Go on. Remember, whatever happens, you gotta get the Paki Witch to your mum, or she'll die."

The Incubo had thought and thought about this, and explored every permutation of fate – a failure in communication, hardware, or timing; or the boy refusing to go through with it; or the crowd following the Paki Witch. But his bets were hedged. All that was required was to get the Paki Witch from the centre towards the Parade edge of the crowd. The rest was easy.

"Come on, Jack," said Billy, hesitant. In the iPad glow he thought he could see marks around the woman's neck. And she was so still, slumped exactly where Chloe had been that afternoon that the Paki Witch had appeared and rescued her.

An involuntary shiver convulsed Billy now. He wanted to confirm with Zollo that the supine woman was alive, but could not summon the courage.

As if reading his doubt, the Incubo now whispered in his ear, "You'll just sit with beautiful birds guzzling cocktails on your yacht, Billy, while your Costa del Sol crew make your money. Trust me. You do trust me, don't you?"

"Course, Zoll."

The Incubo pressed a half bottle of vodka into his hand, and advised, "Have a good drink. Dutch courage, lad."

Obedient, but still shivering, Billy took the vodka, and then the weeping child's hand, and led him out of the spooky alleyway.

The Paki Witch and Jack

"Paki Witch, can you come an' 'elp me Mum? She's dead."

"I think it's an overdose, love," said Billy, looking down at the floor as he spoke to the woman hailed as the Messiah of the Slums. He took another slug from the half-litre of vodka, emptying it. "She's up on the Parade," he added. "The kid wants you to go there."

Jamal felt his Beloved stiffen beneath his arm, which was slung gently around her back. An intense sorrow washed her countenance as she moved away from him, towards the boy.

"A man told me only the Paki Witch could fix me Mum," pleaded the boy. "She's dead."

With a sob, he sank to the breadcrumb and mud floor, exhausted.

The Paki Witch picked him up and kissed his tear- and food-smeared cheek.

"All will be well, little one," she said in a soft voice, holding him close.

"She's over by the Parade, by the libr'ry, like," said Billy.

The boy's arms slid around her shoulders, and his face nestled into the nape of her neck. In all the world he hadn't a care, it seemed, for instantly he fell sound asleep in her arms.

"Lie 'im in 'ere, love," suggested the old man with the Raleigh Shopper bike; he had been with the Paki Witch from the start.

He patted the big basket on the handlebars of his bike. It was just big enough to accommodate the sleeping boy. The Messiah of the Slums laid him in, and, with great tenderness, ran her finger around the cherubic contours of his face. With a wistful smile, she turned and walked towards Incubo Land's heart of darkness, followed by her friends.

On the way a woman called Jewel pulled the hand of the

Messiah of the Slums, who stopped to listen to her.

"Please, please 'elp Kevin," stammered Jewel, casting wary glances at Jamal, who was staying close to his Beloved. "'E was such a good man, and, and – I know I am nothing, and I am so ashamed to be even near you, but I know that if you said the word, 'e would be, be brought to life."

Jewel kissed the Messiah's hand, and washed it with her tears.

"Jewel," said the Messiah of the Slums, her voice kind and gentle. Jewel looked up, delighted and afraid to have been remembered. "Do not weep, for all is well."

Jewel, whose crying became more intense, tried to speak, but subsided into more kneading of the Messiah's hand against her own face.

The Messiah embraced her, and held her for a while, then pulled back to say, "And please –" her hand clutched Jewel's now, and their eyes met – " forgive him."

"Who? Kevin?"

"No."

"Terry?"

"Yes. Love is ever-forgiving, all-forbearing."

Jewel nodded, defeated and victorious all at once, and then left, almost running, towards the car park behind the Parade, which provided the only clear exit out of Shriveton due to the crowds.

The Messiah of the Slums and her party continued in the same direction, towards the Parade. Merging into the heaving frogspawn of people, Billy trailed them at a distance, his hood low, and his scarf high, Zone-style. Unobserved, youths in Halloween masks and hoodies closed in near their Paki Witch target, waiting for their signal.

Dies Irae

Whether it was the first explosion, or the adolescent male cries, of, "Terrorist attack!" which induced panic in the crowd would be forever disputed. To begin with, the rapid succession of staccato explosions around the Wasteland perimeter were recognised as grenades only by those close by. To the majority around the Wasteland crowd perimeters, they were initially mistaken for wildcat fireworks. After the fourth blast, a zombie-masked teen in a hoody squeezed himself between Jamal and the Messiah of the Slums, and hollered, "The Paki Witch is a suicide bomber!"

Someone behind them fired a rifle into the air. Screaming panic ensued as people scrambled over each other to get away. Another hooded teen, wearing a vampire mask, materialised, and dropped a grenade into the clearing around himself and the Zombie. Jamal was knocked to the ground by the stampede of people, fleeing for their lives. As he rolled free from the oncoming masses, he saw Billy Stokes grab Jessie Rout and disappear with her into the Brownian motion of madness all around. Jamal stumbled to his feet, and had begun pushing through the oncoming droves in the direction of his Beloved, when a voice sounded in his ear.

"Hey, Bannie!"

He swung round to see the Zombie, just as the inky night air split with a gigantic crack. The Shopping Parade shuddered, as a huge explosion took out the Handy Bet shop front, spewing forth a vast screed of smoke and fire, like dirty orange fibre glass. The flat above Liu's Chippy sank like a kneeling pilgrim into the shop beneath.

Meltdown.

In the nightmare of smoke, brick dust, sirens and screaming, police were attempting to funnel the people away via St Theresa's Church, and on, via Boundary Lane, and the nearby motorway banks of open space.

As if Jamal's every brain receptor was laid out, like a carpet, each detail of events unfolding simultaneously imprinted themselves: the attack on the Shopping Parade, the abduction of his Beloved, and the machete-wielding Zombie before him. But, in the single moment of these multiple impressions, there was insufficient space to act.

An ice cold spike somewhere inside Jamal buckled his knees. The Zombie snarled in his half-broken voice, "That's for Gary Skelton!" and disappeared into the chaos.

Morwenna, the social worker, knelt beside Jamal, and stroked his forehead.

"Get the ambulance!" she was calling to passers-by.

Her touch felt very warm. He wanted to move his hand up to hers, but he feared he had urinated in his clothes, for his hand was soaking wet, with warm fluid somehow oozing from his belly.

"Call an ambulance!" Mo was screaming. "This kid's haemorrhaging here!"

"Jessie," he whispered.

"It's a set-up!" Mo was crying out as people ran on by. "They're trying to turn us against the Paki Witch! And reinstate the Zone! The gangs have stabbed this kid! Get an ambulance or he'll die."

He wanted to weep, because he'd failed to protect his Beloved, but his tears were solid, and he was realising that his whole face had become solid fat over a skeletal mesh, like his Nan's old chip pan. The machete wound was firing now like a raging blow torch, bubbling his cold, living flesh. He could hear his name being called by various faraway voices, and was trying to respond to the one that sounded like Troy's.

Fuzzy uniformed goblins loomed over him, growling, "Could be coeliac artery."

"Looks like it's gone through the pancreas."

"May have even ruptured the spine."

"Christ, he's finished."

A snowstorm buried the goblins. Wintry unconsciousness delivered him from the pain.

Redemption

Little Liu was screaming and thrashing about in the arms of a policewoman.

"Me Nan and Miu Miu are still in there!" he shrieked

Tez came close. Recognising him as the notorious Zone Chief, the policewoman's eyes widened, and she held Liu tighter.

"Whereabouts?" Tez asked.

"In the shop," said Liu. "A, like, beam 'as fell down and blocked 'em in one of the back rooms!"

Tez looked up at the inferno raging on the terrace of the Shopping Parade. Liu's Chippy shop unit ceiling had collapsed, and smoke was belching from the gaping wounds to the infrastructure, which was otherwise weirdly dark. Power must have been lost in the explosion.

"Get off the terrace!" hollered Tez to the small crowd gathered alongside him. "The 'ole thing might collapse."

The vestige of his kingpin authority weighed the onlookers, who began to move, chaperoned by the arriving police, away from the scene. Despite the policewoman's cajoling, the hysterical Liu refused to go. Now fire crews rushed in, clumsy angel- atronauts in lurid protective clothing, bearing auxiliary life-saving equipment. Tez heard one of them fret about the weight of water on the damaged infrastructure where at least two people were trapped.

"It's Semtex," announced Tez, interrupting him. "Zollo – the Incubo – kept it in one of the garages round the back. And he had detonators. The lot. He must've laid it all around the back of the shops. Them other explosions was prob'ly grenades. 'E 'ad loads of 'em stashed."

From the stairwell in the far corner of the terrace, Jewel came running towards them, crying out, "I seen who done it. It was Billy Stokes. 'E 'ad like a phone thing in 'is 'and. I seen 'im press it, round the back by that line of cars be'ind the bins. And then this 'appened."

She walked up to her husband, panting with exertion, her field-mouse features animated with the adrenalin of the moment. Reaching out, with one finger, she touched his gaunt, desolate face, and gave a little smile. In the glassy reflection of their eyes, locked on each other, blue emergency and fire lights danced. The world was in chaos, but they were one. Just like the old times. The ghost of a smile turned his lips for a moment, and then, fast as a greyhound, he darted towards the blaze.

Like a soft-boned monkey he grabbed hold of the drainpipe at the far end of the Shopping Parade. Using the drainpipe and sills, brick holes and the burglar alarm case as purchase for his feet, light as a dragonfly's, he swung himself on to the concrete hood which ran perpendicular to and over all Parade shop fronts, beneath the upper lying flats.

On his belly, he snaked beneath the flames and smoke billowing from the exploded first window of the flat above Liu's Chippy. The next unit on must have been the bombsite, for Handy Bet was no more than a flaming empty shell. The impact must have destabilised the whole structure, for just as he reached Liu's, the whole parapet began to subside beneath him. With a sharp kick, the second window, the same since Shriveton was built just after the Second World War, pulverised, and he tumbled in to the Lius' flat.

Ringing in his ears, and reaching him through the wild noises of fear, machines, and sirens, were the warnings hollered up to him through speakers from the rescue teams assembling on the terrace below.

"The back of the Parade is collapsing – don't go in!"

From the terrace below, the emergency services directed a fat beam of light. They were calling up to him, cautioning him to stop, shouting warnings that the back of the Lius' was about to go.

Inside, through a huge crater at the site of the lower staircase, Tez could see into the shop below. Scrambling across the dusty shale of rubble, a moonscape in the spotlight, he came to the perimeter of the hole, splayed his body on the floor to distribute his weight, and looked into the pit below.

"Can you 'ear me?" he called out into the smoky pit below

Faint cries – *jiùyuán[7], jiùyuán, jiùyuán* – floated from what looked like a cupboard below. A fallen joist lay across the door. From the window where he had just entered, Tez could hear the fire fighters, and he called out to them, "They're down 'ere," as he jumped into the pit, and landed, like a cat, on the joist. The door before him was partly ajar, and through the crack he could see the beautiful Chinese girl in the yellow dress from Spider's lair last night. Her skin was healed, he noticed, and she was babbling in her foreign tones, and gesturing towards an old woman, lying trapped under what looked like a collapsed set of shelves.

As Tez shifted the barring joist, the wall and upper flooring above began to give way.

"Get out!" he implored the girl, but she shook her head, refusing to leave the old woman.

"I will get her out," said Tez, pointing with stagey hands, like tentacles, at his own heart and at the old woman.

He hauled the reluctant girl over the joist, and passed her up to the outstretched hands of a fireman now at the perimeter of the crater above.

"The wall's going to go in that side of the building, mate. Get out!" one of the fire crew roared at him. A rope was lowering towards him. "The whole joist and supporting wall's gone, lad. You got seconds. Grab the rope. It's safe. We've attached it to one of the outer walls."

Tez grabbed the rope. It had a clip on the end of it. Their desperate instructions did not register as he went into the darkness, where the old woman lay, bleeding and broken in a rubble of bricks, shelves, and Chinese cooking ingredients. He could see her eyes follow him as he hauled off the detritus and fastened his own belt twice around her tiny midriff. It felt as if the whole earth was trembling as he clipped the rope end to the belt.

"Hero," she croaked as, with all his might, he slid her little body through the acute angle of the floor tiles and fallen joist.

As he watched her being hoisted up and away to safety, the ceiling above shuddered and buckled. The firemen had lowered the rope again, and were imploring him to grab it, but he simply stared at them with unseeing eyes. Only as the ceiling and whole

---

7

Help (Mandarin)

rear wall of the building crashed down did Tez fall. As he lay dying among the tons of rubble, he was unaware of much that would have consoled him. For Jamal and Lilly Bannigan, he would always be the family saviour and hero; they would never learn that it was he, and not Gary Skelton, who had commissioned Troy's execution. Jewel would find out that it was Billy, not Tez, who had ordered Fr Kevin's beating; she had already forgiven him for all the bad things he did. Jewel, and indeed the police, would ensure that posterity regarded him as the tragic, indentured boy soldier who went on to become a genuine penitent whose written confessions to three police forces were instrumental in dismantling the Incubo's international crime syndicate.

All Tez knew was that he was sorry in his heart for all the wicked things he'd done, and that his own preventative actions meant that Jammy's soul had not been stained by Incubo Land.

CHAPTER TWENTY

31st October 201-

One Dark Night

The Wasteland

Seeing Jamal and his Nan on the Tallis forecourt had flushed Jodi with shame. It brought into even sharper focus her recent madness, when, peevish at Jamal's lack of interest in her, she'd knocked her rival to the floor and stolen the hijab. Remorse had been eating away at Jodi ever since, and everyone was saying how withdrawn and distracted she seemed.

For the first time ever, the knowledge that she had done an innocent person wrong was undoing Jodi's mind. She knew she must make restoration, and the best way was to return the hijab. So, after helping Gerry Stokes on to the Wasteland, she had taken his wheelchair back to his Tallis Row maisonette and left it in the porch. Then she went home and fetched the hijab she had hidden in one of her old handbags.

When she returned to the Wasteland, everyone was rejoicing that the Paki Witch had made Gerry Stokes walk again. Jodi was pleased that her faith had been justified: it had been right to return the wheelchair to Gerry's porch in the belief that he would never need it again. She made her way to the centre of the crowd, and stayed near, although out of sight of, the Paki Witch. As if glued, Jamal was at the side his beloved; he looked afraid, despite the joy underpinning the scene.

After everyone had eaten the bread rolls, Jodi was one of the helpers who went with a bin-liner around the Wasteland, collecting empty water bottles. Still she kept out of the way of Jamal, performing her assistant duties anonymously by passing her bin-liner to one of the other helpers once it was full.

When the explosions started, Jodi stayed close to the Paki Witch, even when the Zombie and Vampire appeared with their grenades and knives. She witnessed the stabbing of Jamal, and the abduction, by Billy Stokes, of the Paki Witch. For some minutes she was so shocked that she'd just stood rigid by the paramedics as they crouched around Jamal, dipping into their bags for medicine and supplies. It was only when one of them made the doomful *Christ, he's finished* remark that she stepped forward.

Like a magician, she drew the long, torn hijab from her bomber jacket pocket, and dropped it on Jamal's blood-flooded open wound. Then she fell down beside him, planting her hand on the scarf.

Jamal opened his eyes and sat up, blinking. The paramedics were utterly lost for words when he stood, his hand clasping the scarf, and demanded, "Where's my Jessie?"

His clothes were cut, but his flesh entirely unmarked.

A Horror to be Veiled[8]

"Tom, the Paki Witch is burning!" screamed Maisie, her eyes goggling at flames licking the sugary stars.

In the cross-currents of panicking humanity, Maisie and Tom had become separated from their grandad, and had fled to the rear of the Shopping Parade to get away from the bombs and knives. They were cowering by the bins, their feet on a straw of discarded hypodermics and empty Incubo vials, when a bright light, accompanied by a low whoosh, of fresh flames, displaced the wild and noisy atmosphere. Instantly, the bonfire, tucked out of sight behind the Community Centre, became a huge torch in the night, pumping black smoke along with blue-orange flames, and a

---

[8]

'The crucifixion should never be depicted. It is a horror to be veiled.'
William Golding.

noxious smell of burning oil.

Tom stepped forward to join his sister and get a clearer view of the savage fire claiming the heap of bric-à-brac, wood, and clothes. The deposed Guy, a ragged rotundity, lay fat and free on the fiery slope. In his place, at the peak, a black-robed human figure was discernible in the blaze.

Writhing. Alive.

"Oh my God!" yelped Tom. "We gotta get the firemen over here."

Maisie remembered her Nan's funeral, when she had run her kiddie-plump fingers through the candles at the feet of a statue of Mary holding the baby Jesus. The heart of the flame was cool, although a black sooty trace, which wiped off as easy as eye shadow, was left on the skin.

"Please God, make the fire cold for the Paki Witch," she prayed aloud.

Part of the rear wall of the Parade collapsed further along from where they were standing. This caused a furore amongst the emergency teams, who were all on foot because the fire engines and ambulances hadn't yet penetrated the barricade of banger cars at the rear of the Parade. Tom, dragging Maisie behind him, ran towards the firemen.

His desperate panoramic plea – "Fire at the back of the Community Centre, help! The Paki Witch is in the fire!" – was heard by one of them, whereupon Tom and Maisie ran back and up to the bonfire, ignoring the injunctions of the fire crews to come back.

"Paki Witch, do a miracle on yerself!" screamed Tom when they reached her pyre.

Large numbers of people were arriving at the scene, flouting police instructions to flee the Wasteland. Horror showed on every face as the stench – later, with a shudder, they would recognise it to be burning flesh and petrol – swamped their olfactory senses. An orchestra of sirens joined the chorus of shouting and wailing, and another fire engine rumbled up via Shriveton Park, only to be halted by the embankment of defunct cars. Hoses were being fed from behind the barricade, and men from the crowd were running over to try to shift some of the old car hulks,

"I can 'ear 'er screaming," cried Maisie into Bob Reilly's coat, for he had just arrived, and embraced her and Tom.

"I thought I'd lost you," Bob kept repeating, over and over to both children, now in his arms. He pressed their faces into his torso to prevent them seeing any more.

Frenetic comments fired from the crowd.

"...I can see 'er tears dead clear..."

"... It's the Paki Witch, definitely..."

"...She's alive..."

"...I can 'ear 'er screaming..."

"...Get the kids back...they can't see this."

"...Oh, God can't we get 'er out..."

"...It's too hot even to go near..."

"...It's petrol or oil..."

Bob suddenly passed the children to Morwenna, who had appeared beside him. He tore off his jacket and flapped it at the flames in a pathetic attempt to quell the furnace. Sharp-toothed fire, like a school of piranhas, devoured the fabric until it was no more than tiny black kites of ash dancing in the heat. He fell back, into the arms of a policeman.

"I can see you, love," he screamed at the Messiah, trying to shield his face from the intense heat as it singed his long white eyebrows. "I know who you are. Love. I know that's what you are."

Hysteria escalated now. Those closest to the grim spectacle were thrown back as explosions at the base of the pile threw out blazing spikes beyond the boundaries of stacked wood and junk.

"Molotov cocktails in the fire!"

Black plumes of smoke-burning oil climbed into the sky, suffocating the stars but extending not the same obfuscating mercy to the writhing figure at the heart of the bonfire below. The victim's familiar black hijab finally ignited. For a few seconds her head shook and shook, only to free her hair, bound by a red scarf, which also caught fire. Yet more explosions at the base intensified the fire feeding on her flesh.

The horror.

In the few moments since their discovery of her and her death, the crowd's shock and incredulity gave way to a burgeoning sense of impotence, and then a terrible grief. People were clinging on to each other, and sobbing distractedly. Their sorrow was so great as to obliterate not only their own fear of further explosion, but also the stench, the stars and the smoke.

From nowhere, a crazed young man with torn clothes and a black puff of Afro hair, rushed to the bonfire perimeters. Abject horror stretched his facial features around the cavernous hole of his lips, as he yelled, "No-o-o-o-o!"

As the searing, gurgling, endless negative still sounded in his throat, Jamal lunged towards the inferno, only to be pulled back sharply by the gloved hand of a fireman, whose colleagues now variously pumped dousing liquid and foam into the dreadful furnace.

A purdah of smoke shielded the victim's last agonies from view.

Afterwards

"Oh God, they're taking her down," gulped Jamal, tears streaming from his huge dark eyes fixed on the charred bonfire remains.

Bob Reilly yanked him by the hair, forcing him to look away. By the time Bob released him, a medical team was leaning over her body, shaking their heads. A forensic doctor arrived, and knelt beside her, exchanging gloomy remarks with the paramedics and police as he examined the charred remains. Then he, too, shook his head, which signalled a redoubling of efforts in the police personnel all around in their efforts to sterilise the scene. Yellow crime-scene ribbons were rolled out.

Splodges of rain began to fall, conjuring damp soil in the charred air as Jamal pushed forward to view her body. Her face was still recognisable, but most of her flesh was like melted bin-liners, and her limbs misshapen liquorice. A ghastly and unforgettable scent – a macabre blend of grease and carbon – was cleaving to every follicle of his untouched skin. Why was he whole, and she like *this*?

Her glorious body, the body he had dreamed about, and loved with such tenderness and respect, had been burned alive. But it was the simple thought that Her sleeping eyes would never again open that made him demented. He staggered away from Her body to the library, and started bashing his head against the wall, drawing blood. Bob Reilly followed him. Planting his weak hands on Jamal's shoulders, he heaved the boy round to face him, urging, "Courage, lad!"

"What's the use of courage, or hope, or love, if she's gone?" sobbed Jamal, swaying. Blood was running down the side of his face, thinning in his tears. "She was pure and good. She was truth. She was love. And nothing is left. Nothing!"

"We're left!" piped Maisie, tugging at Jamal's coat.

"You gotta carry the torch, don't you see?" insisted Bob, shaking him a little. "You gotta light the path for the others. That what she done, lad."

"There must be something you can do," Jamal yelled to the medical team. "Revive her. Please God, I will go mad!"

The doctor looked away, shaking his head again, wordless in

246

the face of such impassioned and hopeless exhortation. Two police officers restrained him as he returned to her bier and tried to embrace the body. In a high, pained tone, Jamal shrieked through their sympathetic comments, "Tell me she's not dead, though. Just tell me that."

But nobody could tell him this, of course, and so he returned to the library wall, and sank down against it, sobbing into his knees, mumbling to himself, "Why didn't you save yourself instead of me? Why have you killed my heart and revived my body? What good is my long life without you, my Beloved? My immortal Beloved."

The press arrived, creating another furore, as the police battled to move them and the onlooking crowd away. In the shadows nearby, the Incubo watched the little red haired journalist – who was himself sorely upset – dart around trying to get people to tell him what had happened.

Lilac, velvet ribbons of expensive cigarette smoke oozed from the Incubo's thin lips. His life had been directed to this tawdry victory. Beyond it was a void.

If only he had had a little more time. He'd always seen himself rather like a physicist, seeking a unification theory which would rationalise his licit and illicit activities, and create a permanent niche for himself in society, alongside the great and the good – Sugar, Branson and Gates (to start with – the PM and British royalty thereafter). These men were almost as clever as he was. Instead, he must grow into an elderly émigré in Panama, where his great genius would be as much in the shade as sun-factored skin beneath an old-man's brimmed hat. Why, it was so outrageous he could almost weep!

But he must not dwell on the paucity of his lot. The corpse of Billy Stokes nearby in the shadows of the alleyway raised a faint smile. As expected, Billy had been reluctant to assist with the final stage of the plan. But after much cajoling in the shape of Costa del Sol high-life fantasies, and a caterpillar thick line of cocaine, vodka-numb Billy had hoisted up and tied to the stake their illustrious victim while the Incubo kept watch, glad that his own, agonised back had been spared this lifting job. After which, Billy served no further purpose (obviously). Firing a bullet into Billy's trusting, meaty head *had* been almost as satisfying as expected. However, this reflection did not lift the Incubo's heaviness of spirit now, as he took leave of the wreck of his former kingdom for the last time.

Inky clouds obscured the moon and stars. Brightly clad emergency personnel continued their rescue efforts, scrambling like flightless parrots over the smouldering Parade. Under falling rain and blue rotating lights, the Messiah of the Slums was zipped into a body bag, then shunted into an ambulance.

A horde of believers watched in deathly silence.

Liverpool Airport

The Incubo's skin felt cool and taut from the shower in the airport hotel, but the stench of grease and charcoal lingered in his nose, despite the Chanel aftershave he'd applied liberally to his person. From the airport lounge window, in the distance, he fancied he could see Shriveton, still burning, in the rainy night.

This cheered him. It was proof that he had triumphed. And he had triumphed because he was a member of the intellectual and moral elect who knew that, behind the meat curtain of life's rawness, there lurked no kindly creator waiting to welcome everyone home. In his perpetual quest for food, shelter and safety in the wilderness, Man fought and flew, hunted and gathered, killed and was killed; all the while hearkening back to his Eden bliss, when, curled up on womb's hearth, with a placental parachute of nutrients on tap, all his troubles seemed so far away.

The Incubo knew this.

The Paki Witch, and the fools who had followed her, were deceived by the terrible beauty of Creation: morning dew beads in the perfumed crevices of the evening primrose, which had unfolded before your very eyes the night before; or nosy moles burrowing the black earth, safe from the eagle owl's orange glassy eye; or the tomcat's yawn – white triangle teeth, plastic pile tongue, and his cathedral-perfect collagen mouth-roof arches.

But the Incubo was not fooled. He knew that earthly joy was a tutu-trussed elephant on a knife edge between numbness and disaster. He recognised that lust alone forced old life to buy into new; and that the new so very quickly became the old, with all the same problems. He knew that, desperate for a solution, people stuffed a big fat zero, *O*, into their gods, to make *goods* which they dedicated their whole lives to acquiring. Goods, made before their very eyes here on earth, were a safer bet than gods, which were made up. People crammed their goods into stomachs, cupboards, lofts, outhouse, garages, holiday homes, barns, warehouses, rivers and oceans – only to pass back, dead from the effort of acquiring and defending their goods, as empty-handed as they'd come, mewling and puking through the meat curtain.

Nothing, going to nothing.

The Incubo knew everything about this nothing.

The Incubo knew that scientists were the luckiest humans because they smothered the terrible beauty in facts and theory. Their answers to everyone's *whys*, could so easily be passed off as an end in themselves: *Why is love?* Love is the means for the genes to pass to the next generation; altruism is self-interest in disguise.

The Incubo knew that the artists were the unluckiest humans, since through their plays, poems, songs, films, symphonies, pictures and novels, they not only lived the terrible beauty, but immortalised it.

The Incubo knew that the religious were the most dangerous humans. The religions, with their sundry lies of eternal bliss, made ordinary, tawdry life bearable, and enabled people to leave the terrible beauty behind.

It was almost time to check in. He had only hand luggage, so there was time to pick up a newspaper from the stand. To his surprise, he found a *Liverpool Star*. It was the first time the paper had printed on a Sunday since Hillsborough in 1989, so the kiosk attendant told him.

Returning to his seat by the window, he looked out again, and realised that it wasn't Shriveton fires he could see out in the distance, but the runway traffic control lights.

GIRL DEAD IN HALLOWEEN FIRE

Exclusive by Ethan Greenberg

Police and fire services have sealed off the entire Shriveton Shopping Parade area as a scene of crime.

The victim of tonight's fatal fire has been named as Jessenia Rabia al-Rahoud, from the the Shriveton area of Liverpool.

Ms al-Rahoud lived in the Skylark Tower block close to where she died.

None of the articles, except the lead by Ethan Greenberg, contained anything he hadn't seen himself. The whole paper was packed with overtly sentimental first-hand accounts, from Shriveton Epsilon attention-seekers, of the violence. Only numbskull comments from the police, to the effect that the drug barons had lost, provided any sort of relief from the emotive

249

drivel. "We will root out and destroy the Incubo," the new police superintendent vaunted in one article entitled *The Incubo's Reign of Terror Ends*.

Every page contained grainy mobile phone pictures of the Messiah of the Slums, and the recipients of her miracle making, none of whom seemed to have anything tangible to say about their experience beyond, "The Paki Witch saved me!" Fools! The Paki Witch hadn't even saved herself.

Very little is known yet about the victim. Originally from Afghanistan, she was flown to the UK for surgery following a grievous assault by a gang of Taliban militia two years ago. An unidentified British soldier had heroically interrupted them on the Hindu Kush mountainside, and they fled.

Police are investigating the possibility of an honour killing.

The Incubo stood up, rolled up the newspaper into a telescope, and looked around for a bin. As he did so, he felt his stomach somersault. Approaching, with a pram carrying a bonny blond baby, and a suitcase precariously balanced on the hood, was Chloe Tudor. Her hair, still fair, but more natural-looking than he recalled, tumbled down and around her full, pretty face. The madness for her took over him, sudden as fire on petrol. Men passing by were looking at her covetously, and the Incubo had to stem the urge to rush at them and scratch out their eyes, and bundle his living doll away, and lock her up in a trunk to which only he had the key.

And then she saw him watching her, and she flicked her eyes to and from him a few times, then suddenly grabbed the arm of a security man, and, pointing, screamed out, "That man in the pale suit is the Incubo. 'E drugged and abused me. 'E's the Kingpin of Shriveton."

Whereupon the Incubo made his second terrible mistake (his first was to look for a bin in an airport, of course): he ran. And, as he ran, his mind was infested with visions of Chloe Tudor's bewitching huge green eyes, and dolly mouth, and gummy small teeth, and yummy puppy-fat body.

"Can you come with us, please, sir?" said a British Transport policeman, who intersected his path near the airport lounge exit.

The Incubo ducked and dived and ran, until a host of security and police descended on him, inches from the check-out, pinning him down and handcuffing him. When he twisted his head on the cold slip of the marble floor, he saw Chloe Tudor standing there, staring at him grimly, as she babbled to the policewoman beside her, "I've come back from Ireland 'cos 'is men killed the priest what saved me..."

The Incubo turned his head away, grimacing as a chastising police heel in his painful spine was accompanied by a growled, *Don't move!* He slumped where he was, like an eel pinned to the loch bed, and rested his head on the cold sheen of the floor. Resigned and desolate, he sighed long and hard. The ignominy of it: for all his genius, he had been brought down by nothing more than a dull-witted slum prostitute.

1st Nov 201-

Dawn

Shriveton Park

Early morning mists mingled like ostrich fluff with the smouldering remains of the Shopping Parade, beneath the seeping reds and oranges of the rising sun. On the Wasteland, gulls and pigeons swooped down for the breadcrumbs lingering from yesterday. Everywhere was coated in a slippery dew. Jamal had spent the night sleeping, as close as he could, beside the bonfire site. The police had taken pity on him and let him stay by the yellow scene-of-crime boundary. Throughout the night they'd given him cups of soup and tea. A policewoman had given him her copy of the *Star* and a coffee in the morning. He thought it was the same bizzie who'd looked after him when Troy died. Fearful of bursting into tears in front of her, he moved away, down to the swings.

He'd just finished the lead article when a young, red-haired man arrived beside him. It was the reporter, Ethan, offering sympathies and solicitations, which Jamal deflected with, "I read your report in 'ere."

"It's not the real story," said Ethan, settling himself on the adjacent swing. His hair was luridly vibrant against the grim landscape, which the Incubo's bombs had corroded like acid on tooth enamel. "But I'm leaving everyone else to find out. If I'd written the truth, my editor wouldn't have printed it."

"So what is the truth?" Even as he said it, Jamal was engulfed by desolation's smog. What did truth matter, anymore? All that was left was rubble and charcoal. Then, fools' gold hope lit the darkness within, as he pleaded:

"Tell me she wasn't gang raped by the Taliban in Afghanistan. Tell me that bit wasn't true."

Ethan looked quickly away, embarrassed almost by the spasm of tragedy this fact provoked in Jamal's lonely heart.

"That bit is true."

Jamal slumped forward, his face in his hands.

"But a British soldier interrupted them, and they fled," said Ethan. "He stopped it. They must have presumed he was with his battalion or something, but he wasn't. He was out alone. He summoned help, and the army flew her to the UK for surgery from Kabul the following day."

He paused.

"Good," was all Jamal could muster, through the muff his palms made over his lips.

"But she died on the way into the operating theatre at the Queen Elizabeth Hospital in Birmingham."

"Died?" Jamal's moribund torpor fell away. He sat up, staring at Ethan. "Well – well, our Jessie Rout must be someone else, then."

Ethan shook his head. "All the photographs of this woman found on the Hindu Kush mountains match the Paki Witch of Shriveton. I have studied every photograph myself. And I have seen her with my own eyes, yesterday, remember."

Ethan had expected his news would provoke bafflement, objection or even anger. Instead, Jamal sat still, deep in thought.

"It took me ages to get my head round it," continued Ethan. "She came to Shriveton to find Todd Dean, the soldier who'd risked his life to save her."

"Todd Dean – never 'eard of 'im."

"Guantanamo?"

"What? She came back for... Guantanamo?"

Incredulity washed Jamal's features.

"Todd Dean picked up a heroin habit while serving in Afghanistan," explained Ethan. "I reckon he was probably out by himself trying to score when he came upon the Taliban men and your Jessie. He intervened. But he was never credited as a hero, because days afterwards, his drug addiction meant that he was discharged from the Army and sent home. He settled in Shriveton, where heroin is on tap.

"I think she came to Shriveton to save him, and everyone else, from the Incubo."

Jamal put his head in his hands, and mumbled, "So are you telling me she's some sort of ghost?"

Ethan pondered a moment. "Some sort of holy ghost, I guess, maybe."

"I – I dunno where that leaves everything," said Jamal, chewing his lip, and strangely accepting.

He felt sick and dizzy, and leaned forward again with his head in his knees.

Ethan patted his back, and said, ruefully, "That's exactly what I thought as I was writing it up. So I decided I'd just present the facts and leave people to find out for themselves. They already *are* finding out. I heard just before coming here now that, when the ambulance carrying her body from the fire reached the LCI last night, she wasn't in it."

"What?" Jamal jerked up, and felt his head spin in a kaleidoscope of lights.

"Apparently she wasn't in the ambulance. The straps and zip of the body bag had been opened. All that were left were a few burned bits of clothing, but no body."

"My God!"

"It's true. They're investigating it now, but I am almost certain they'll find nothing. No DNA in the ambulance, or where she died. I'm telling you, she died two years ago."

"B-but she was real. I have – I have held her in my arms. Thousands of people saw her yesterday. They were filming her on their phones."

"They were. Loads of footage has come into our office now. And that's why she'll be given some sort of public send-off. But I'm telling you."

Ethan pulled out a printout of Jessenia Rabia al-Rahoud's passport picture. It showed the wounds to the side of her head, which Jamal had himself seen.

"This person died two years ago." Ethan tapped the image with his thin, white finger.

Jamal looked hard at the picture for a while, then stood up and went to the edge of the playground, looking out towards Park Road, and the Tallis and Skylark flats.

"I will always love her," he said, "whatever she is or isn't."

With the toe of his shoe, he traced a heart in the black soil below.

"Look, I prob'ly best get off," said Ethan, walking up beside him. "I just wanted to tell you first, before it all came out."

"Thanks. I appreciate it."

Ethan hovered for a while, and even started to leave. Then, on a whim, he turned round and suggested, "Hey, it'd be great to keep in touch. Any plans?"

Jamal shrugged, his eyes stayed on his heart outline in the soil.

"Dunno," he said, adding, with a degree of nervous hesitation, "Did you go to university?"

"Yeah, I went to one in London."

"I always wanted to go. Knew I never would, like."

"You could go."

"Don't know 'ow to now. Left school. I was OK at school."

"I'll help you get started. I can show you how to go about it."

"You could?"

"Yeah."

"Well. Well... Maybe in a couple weeks."

"Couple weeks is fine."

After another long pause, Ethan ventured, "Hey, Jammy. She chose *you*, you know. You know that don't you?"

Jamal gulped back a sob. "She broke me. That's all I know."

Patting his shoulder once more, Ethan left.

Alone, Jamal squeezed his eyes shut, as tightly as he could, to keep the day out. He wanted to dream of her hand in his, her body close, as they danced beneath a canopy of diamante stars. But all he could see were black and orangey dots, like a furnace.

A sudden waft of lavender on a warm breeze drew him back to the present, and he opened his eyes to see a plump, shiny strawberry resting in the centre of the heart his foot had just etched in the earth. There was nobody in sight. He picked it up. Luscious and full of the promise of English summertime, it sat, big as a heart, in his hand, shining in the morning sun. After pinching himself to verify he was not dreaming, he bit into its succulent, rosy flesh. A plenitude of sticky juice exploded on his taste buds, energising him with the sugar of life, running down his chin and throat like the sweetest, best wine.

And then he saw his Beloved, clothed in bride-white, waiting for him by the old oak tree at the edge of the little wood, on the opposite side of the park. Her arms were opened to him, and her black hair spilled around the red bandana he had wrapped around her wounds a lifetime ago. All other trees were bare, but her oak was crowned with green, and the burgeoning sun threw its summery shadow on the empty playing field.

Jamal ran to her, knowing that, although she would not be here for long, this time she had come back for him alone. He fell into her arms, and felt her mouth, sweeter than strawberries, on his. His hands ran over the gossamer of her gown, then caressed gently her face, which was healed and whole. Ineffable joy suffused his whole being, satisfying and completing him.

"My Beloved," he whispered.

Pulling her close, he breathed in the scents of her warm skin and veil of glossy hair. Their eyes combined, and the purest love irradiated from her immaculate being.

"I'll wait for you, Jamal," she told him, her human hands cradling his face. "We'll dance again, and see what summer brings."

I abandoned and forgot myself, laying my face on my Beloved; all things ceased; I went out from myself, leaving my cares, forgotten among the lilies.

(St John of the Cross)

Afterword

If you ask the question, 'What would "redemption" look like today as a genuinely challenging, genuinely miraculous transaction?' you have to recognise that simply repeating what has always been said won't do. What the gospel stories relate is a set of events in which people suffering from acute and terrible suffering, slavery to powers beyond their imagination, let alone control, are allowed to be human once more. And this happens because of the presence and action of a figure who is in no way at all part of the accepted religious machinery, and who prompts the most violent reaction possible from those who hold the reins of power. Whether we like it or not, repeating the original story only gets us so far. We can insist that we have lost the radical edge of that story and try to explain what all this initially must have sounded like. But mere explanation is never going to be enough: we need to be shown; we need to be shocked into a new understanding.

Charlotte has taken enormous risks with this story, deliberately confronting some of the most neuralgic of religious and political prejudices we know in our present context. The saviour figure here is female and Muslim; as if only by facing what we assume about women (if we are a certain kind of Christian) and Muslims (if we are a certain kind of Christian *and* a certain kind of anxious nationalist) can we understand the kind of shock that would have been involved in proclaiming the crucified labourer from the North as anointed redeemer in first century Israel. The result is memorable: a raw and unconsoling story, but one in which real liberation is described – and real, tragic damnation too, people locked up so firmly in their own self-hatred and self-destruction that we cannot imagine whether or how love will ever reach them. Part of the force of the book is Charlotte's ability to create characters who are painfully credible, characters about whom the reader cares. She illustrates St Augustine's insight that more sins than we think are committed by people 'weeping and groaning', people who can't get free of inner and outer compulsions. There is no mistaking the trace of first-hand knowledge of such lives in this book, and it is the author's manifest compassion that prompts the reader's horrified engagement and pity and helpless grief for these spirits in prison. They are not patronised, idealised or condemned; they are allowed to be three-dimensional – and because this is so, the book will and should stir anger and amazement that our society should be silently accepting the scale of human waste depicted here. Why don't the records of these desolate places in our cities shock us into more intelligent and compassionate action?

But this is more than a call to better social provision. Charlotte does not shrink from the central gospel affirmation that redemption comes not by welfare alone but by love and by miracle. The liberation that matters is more than benevolent support and improved education, however much we long to see these. At the end of the day, it is about limitlessly powerful love accepting all the consequences of human life in the middle of unspeakable violence and despair, and that is undeniably a matter of something more than the sum total of human goodness. We are faced with a vivid evocation of what miraculous love might feel like in such a setting; and what levels of hatred it might also provoke.

Not a comfortable book, not a pious one, not a neat allegory of doctrine; this is a story of credible human beings – and of credible divine love. It takes all kinds of risks, imaginative, stylistic, imaginative; and so it should. The basic stories of Christian faith are not exactly risk-averse, and so long as we speak as if they were, we shall not be able to convey how and why the narrative of Jesus made the difference it did and does. That's why this is such a significant and moving book, and I am very grateful to have read it.

- *Dr Rowan Williams*
Theologian, Poet, Master of Magdalene College Cambridge,
former Archbishop of Canterbury.

ABOUT THE AUTHOR

Charlotte Pickering's fiction and non-fiction is concerned with human nature, social justice issues and the expressive arts. A graduate of St Andrews, Liverpool and Open universities, and the London College of Music, the author also works as a music producer, arranger, director and educator. Creating the Messiah of the Slums novel and trailer films inspired the author to found Off Script Project, a community venture offering support for people experiencing stress or distress relating to their work or personal circumstances. Charlotte lives in the North West of England with her three children and various pianos

www.ingramcontent.com/pod-product-compliance
Lightning Source LLC
Chambersburg PA
CBHW060535260626
47161CB00003B/909